UNTIMELY DEATHS

Chris Stevens

WARRINGTON
PUBLISHING

Danbury, Connecticut

Untimely Deaths
Copyright © 2026 by Chris Stevens
Warrington Publishing

Printed in the United States of America
First Edition

ISBN: 978-1-969359-19-4 (paperback)
       978-1-969359-18-7 (ebook)
       978-1-969359-20-0 (hardcover)

Book cover designed by JD&J
Edited by Mike Watiz of

For Liz and Wyatt

Prologue

Dan Parker got out of his car and stood for a moment, looking up at the Harrington House Museum—a sprawling, turn-of-the-century Tudor mansion complete with manicured lawns, ivy-covered brick walls, and the inescapable feeling that coming here was like literally stepping back in time.

A little routine work on the foundations of the old place late last night had turned up a room that'd been blocked off for who only knew how long, complete with a large cache of old file boxes. And when Paul Mitchell, the museum curator, had called earlier this morning to ask for help sorting through it, Dan had already started grabbing for his shoes before ending the call.

"I really appreciate you helping us out like this on such short notice," Paul had said. "I hope this isn't an imposition on your weekend."

"No, not at all," Dan had said, and it hadn't just been him being polite.

Since he and Carly had broken up some months back, his Saturdays consisted of grading papers while parked in front of the TV, catching up on the things burning a hole in his Netflix queue. Not bad in itself, but it did get boring after a while. Even if it hadn't, there'd have been no way in the world he'd have missed a chance like this.

So here he was, running a hand across the back pocket of his beat-up jeans, making sure that he'd actually grabbed his wallet, walking toward the front doors where Paul stood waiting for him.

"When I called the historical society, they recommended you straight away. Is it true you've been volunteering there since high school?" Paul said as they took seats in the small, but cozy curator's office.

"Yep. And here too for a couple of summers back in the day."

"I guess that makes you doubly qualified. You have an appreciation for both the history of New Chapel and Harrington House itself."

"All that and a history teacher too. Guess I'm a guy who just can't help living in the past."

"There are far worse things in this day and age," Paul said. "Now, as I mentioned over the phone, there's construction going on down in the basements…shoring up the old foundations of the place mainly, and when the contractors walked through this latest part of the project doing their inspections, they found the boarded-over doorway behind an old bookcase and the room beyond. They're off for the next couple of days until the items inside the room have been catalogued and cleared out—that's where I'd like your help."

"And you said it's mainly boxes of papers, right?"

"Appears to be, yes," Paul said and cleared his throat. "There are no surviving members of the Harrington family. The woman who ran this place as a women's boarding house from the 1930s to the 1950s, Ruth Harrington, was the last and childless. She left the house in a trust, that it would be preserved as part of the town's history."

Dan knew about the last boarding house days of the place, and the grander times before. Also, that Ruth Harrington was hardly the last; there were several illegitimate Harrington descendants all over the place, including a few in town still, but Dan only nodded.

"All that is to say, everything in here belongs to the Harrington House Museum Trust. And if there's nothing significant worth putting on display here, then I'd really like those things to be donated to the historical society, for posterity."

"I'm more than happy to help."

After a little more conversation, Dan accepted an offered pair of vinyl gloves, an N95 mask, a clipboard, and apologies about having to do some of the initial review work at an active construction site. Everything in hand, he followed Paul down the grand staircase, out the front door, and around the back of the house, where a set of cellar doors stood open to the cavernous basement. Paul led him down the stairs around the stacks of loose bricks and boards and to the newly uncovered room.

"This is where I'll have to leave you for a while, I'm afraid," Paul said. "Most of our big business these days is from renting out the ground floor and ballroom for events like weddings and meetings – that sort of thing. There's a dinner for some investing firm later tonight, and I have a meeting with their event organizer to make sure the rules are clear about what is and isn't off limits. If you need me, I'll have my cell on. Just shoot me a text. If not, I'll be back in a few hours."

Dan watched the man disappear back up the steps before turning to the doorway he'd been left by.

The formerly hidden room was dank and dusty, and the air inside was stale. He wondered if this was what it felt like breaking into a tomb that'd been sealed up for a few centuries. Probably not, but it had to at least be in the ballpark. But thanks to someone helpfully putting up several of those painters' work lights all around, at least it was brightly lit.

Up against the far wall, there was a diseased-looking four-poster bed that looked to be somehow both dusty and moldy, a busted-up dresser next to it, and not much else. It wasn't too hard to think of *why* there was a bed and dresser in a hidden room with no windows; rumors about bastard kids were far from the only ones he and a lot of other people in town knew about the family who'd built this place.

Turning away, Dan instead focused his attention on a line of moldering old cardboard boxes lined up against the opposite wall. Slipping on his glove and mask, Dan squatted down next to the first box and began flipping through its contents.

There was mold and mildew on a lot of this stuff, and he was happy not to have to touch it with his bare hands; getting some nasty infection or something was too high a price to pay for a little historical exploration.

Minutes passed as he thumbed through stacks of receipts, bills of lading, letters, newspaper clippings, journals…most of it faded, eaten up by mold or both. After a while, Dan thought that maybe the museum would've been better off calling one of the old timers he volunteered with; one of them might know better than him what to do with documents that were in this sort of condition. Still, he continued looking, fascinated by what little he *could* read.

The big find was a red leather journal, dated 1904 and belonging to Edward Harrington, the guy who built this mansion. Out of everything in this room, Dan thought this was bound to be the big prize. Edward Harrington had been one of those turn-of-the-twentieth-century wealthy eccentrics. Back in the day, there'd been lavish parties, seances, guests of every kind from politicians and scientists to low-life thugs. Demonstrations of electrical oddities. Upstairs, there were displays from Harrington's journeys across the world hunting for rare things, foreign game…

"Foreign women too, probably," Dan said, cracking the journal open, excited at what sort of secrets he might learn from the man himself. But the feeling didn't last long. A wave of disappointment hit him almost at once as he realized that only the first page or so of the journal was readable…something about preparations for a Christmas party. The rest of the pages appeared black and stuck together, and he didn't dare try pulling the pages apart for fear of destroying them.

Setting the Harrington journal aside, Dan stood and stretched some life back into his legs. He walked out the door and back up the stairs leading outside, desperate for fresh air. No sooner had he pulled off his gloves, the N95, and lay down in the cool grass, than his phone started to buzz. Reaching into his pocket, Dan pulled it out, looked at the screen, and sighed before accepting the call.

"Hi Carly"

"You still have my credit card."

"Huh?"

"You…still…have…my…credit…card. What part of that didn't you get?"

Dan rubbed at his eyes, making himself breathe and think before he spoke. There was so much he didn't get to say…and didn't feel like getting into now…before she'd ended things. Very publicly ended things—in Harrington House, as a matter of fact.

Paul told him that one of the ways that the museum stayed financially solvent was by event hosting, and Dan knew that all too well. He and Carly had been at a friend's wedding reception here when spending what'd apparently been a few minutes too long for a celebratory cigar with the groomsman spiraled out hard into something else, and everything that'd been unsaid for so long came bubbling to the surface.

"I can't do this," Dan had said when he'd been able to get in a word edgewise, both of them standing in front of the grand staircase, Carly with her arms crossed over her chest, looking like she either wanted to cry or scratch his eyes out.

"Can't do what? Can't own up and just apologize without finding some way to turn this around on me and make yourself look good?"

"You could've gotten up and mingled tonight," he'd said, keeping to a low whisper so as not to attract any more eyes than they already were."Hell, you knew exactly where I was. You could've come and hung out with the rest of us if we were taking too long, and we all would've been happy to have you. Maybe part of that's on me for not thinking to just bring you along anyway, but…this isn't healthy, Carly. Not for either of us. We can't keep going with you so attached and dependent on me."

Dan had stopped, not knowing exactly what he'd meant to say after that, but knowing somehow that if he'd kept going, he'd venture into seriously hurting her feelings, which was the last thing he'd ever wanted to do, especially not about this. She had issues. Well, everyone has issues, but hers were on another level to him. A dad who peaced out for the coast before she was ten, a neglectful mom, eventually resulting in an endless stream of foster homes, where the situation couldn't be said to have been much better. It left scars.

But Carly wouldn't talk to anyone about it; she had never *really* talked to anyone about it before him. It'd done her good to let those things out after so long, and Dan had only been too happy to listen. But it seemed that after a while, something in their relationship shifted. Sweet, but somehow passive-aggressive comments when he'd apparently gone too long without responding to a text after seeing it had been read. Wanting to know the names of the other teachers at the high school so she could look them up online and "put faces to the name". Or whenever they'd be driving somewhere or just chilling out at home, and he'd go quiet just for the sake of enjoying a little quiet, it was about a seventy-thirty chance in favor that she'd start asking if she'd done something wrong to upset him.

And he'd stood there by that staircase, thinking about her unwillingness and even hostility when he even gently tried bringing up the idea of her talking to a counselor or something, had been the first in a series of red flags. And his not being insistent about it anyway, instead letting himself become her de facto therapist, had been his mistake. It was only then that he'd realized how much that'd been wearing him down. Carly had stepped forward then, her voice surprisingly soft.

"You say attached like it's a bad thing. Isn't that what a relationship is supposed to be? A good one, anyway? You're tight and close about everything. We're here for each other in everything, in every way. And you check in to make sure that everything is all right, and if it isn't, you step up and help or say something. If I didn't love you so much, I wouldn't give a shit. Can't you see that?"

Yes, he'd seen it. Clearly, and for the first time. Dan had taken a deep breath.

"What I see is someone who needs help...*real* help, and has for a long time. Help that I can't give you. Carly, I love you, really. But you've steadily clung onto me more and more in a way that's not good for anyone. I think part of me has known that for a while, and that's on me for not pushing the issue out of love and just wanting to pretend that everything's okay. Well, I'm pushing it now."

"Pushing what?"

"I want you to talk to someone. Someone qualified to listen and help you process things in a way that I just can't. I'll help you, babe, honestly. I'll be there to support you every step of the way. I can only imagine how heavy everything you've been through hangs, but I really think things can be better if."

But Dan didn't get to finish that thought. Instead of tears or nails, Carly reached out and shoved him back, causing him to trip over the first step and land on his ass. She'd stood over him then, her pretty face now a mask of bitter hate.

"How dare you?! I trusted you! I told you everything! And what do you do with it? Use it against me because I called you out, and now…now, you're giving me this jacked-up ultimatum? With all this fake, loving boyfriend shit? You just wanna abandon me like everyone else has! I'm done with Carly, guess it's time to pass her along."

"Carly, that's not—"

She'd raised one black high-heeled show and Dan had flinched, wondering where the spike of the heel would come down. When nothing came, he opened his eyes and looked around. People were stopped in the foyer, staring; no one was even pretending that they weren't looking. Carly was aware of it too and lowered her foot. Hate had still been on her face, but so were tears now. Dan cleared his throat, his voice so low he almost couldn't hear himself.

"We should."

Carly brought her foot back and swung it forward, the sharp point of her shoe connecting with his ribs, knocking the air out of him.

"Go to hell," she'd said, then turned and made for the front door.

Dan held the phone to his ear, only vaguely aware that he'd started to rub the spot where she'd kicked him and the bruise had lingered for about a month.

"I need my card, Dan," Carly said. "And if I check my statement and find out you've been using it—"

"I haven't been using it. Honestly, I'd forgotten it was there until you called and asked about it. You'd had me hold onto it when we went to the reception so you wouldn't have to carry a clutch, and it's been there ever since."

"It better be. Where are you?"

"Harrington House. Doing a little volunteer work. If you can swing by, I'm at the back of the house. There's an open set of cellar doors where I'm working in the basement and—"

"Fine. My car's acting up, but I guess I'll come all the way over there and get it myself."

"Listen, I can…"

The line went dead in Dan's ear, and shaking his head, he slipped the phone back into his pocket. He lay on the grass for a while, not doing much besides watching the clouds go by. He thought about texting Carly, saying he'd bring it over, but thought better of it. If she'd been pissed enough to call instead of texting him in the first place, then she was likely already nearly to the mansion by now.

But as the minutes began to creep by and she didn't put in an appearance, Dan thought that, Carly or not, he should probably be getting back to the boxes. Standing and doing his best to shake the call and the memories, mentally preparing himself to face her in person soon, Dan put his earbuds in, turned on some music, and headed back down into the basement.

Despite the work lights, it somehow seemed darker than it had before, leaving the room feeling that much more ominous. When he stepped back inside, Dan looked around the room again, his eyes once again falling on the bed and the dresser, and hoping that it'd just been set up for some consensual extramarital sneaking around back in the day and not something much more sinister like the hairs on the back of his neck seemed to think it was.

Bending down, Dan continued to look through boxes. More moldy papers—basements really are the worst place to keep things like this. Though as he went through, cracking the top on those boxes Paul and his staff hadn't gotten around to yet, he ran across some drier specimens and found himself digging around the receipts and things, hoping for another one of those Harrington journals.

There didn't seem to be any more of those, but still, it was hard not to get wrapped up in even mundane things like bakery orders and toilet paper deliveries, and time started to slip away. At some point, Dan's legs reported that he'd been squatting on them too long. He sat cross-legged on the dusty stone floor and continued looking.

After a while, his back started in on the fun, little jolts of pain telling him that he'd been in the hunched position he'd been in, and so he leaned back, stretching. As he did, feeling the stiffness ease, something caught Dan's attention.

Underneath that bed was another box, not pulled out and lined up with all the others. Ignoring the stiffness in his back and the tingling still in his legs, Dan got on his hands and knees, pulled out his phone, and used the flashlight on it, raising the ruffle running along the bottom of the bed to get a better look.

It was covered in what looked like an old, canvas tarp thick with dust and appearing to reflect a purplish light from somewhere else in the room. Dan wondered how long it'd been down here.

Maybe this is where the rest of the journals are, he thought, then stretching, reached underneath the old, rotting bed and pulled out the box. Wincing slightly against the dust he stirred up, Dan sat cross-legged again and brought the box to him. He ran his flashlight over the canvas, deciding that the phone's flashlight wasn't enough to do the trick, and moved so that he could be near the work lights, his back to the open door.

Carrying it over, it felt strange. Not heavy, not exactly, but there was something about whatever this was that felt weird in his hands. Settling himself back onto the floor, grateful for the N95, he worked to undo the canvas, which just seemed to pull away like rotting flesh. Dan's stomach lurched a little, though he wasn't sure why.

Letting the rotting canvas fall away, Dan took in a sharp breath, wincing against the purple light…not reflected, but clearly emanating from what looked to be a brass box. Rivets ran along its corners and sides, and brass dials ran across the top. Squinting to get a better look, Dan felt his brow furrow…the dials were showing today's date.

"What the hell?" he asked, then began running his hands along the surface.

It was old and beautifully made. And through the little glass window in front, Dan saw what looked to be a massive shard of some precious stone, the source of the purple light. He thought it looked like a giant chunk of quartz or something like that, but whatever it was, it seemed to be the power source for this strange clock.

And an impressive thing that was, because assuming that the thing had been left here and forgotten in the neighborhood of a century ago, it was still keeping perfect time…down to the minute. The only dial Dan couldn't place was one with numbers zero through one hundred listed, but no units. The needle stood at "nine," and he wondered if it was the charge level or something like that.

"What the hell?"

Dan continued running his fingers all along the thing, his hand eventually finding a small lever on the side. He looked at it for a moment, wondering. And without really guessing what the lever might do, he pulled the lever toward him.

Nausea hit him in an instant. Not bad enough for him to give up his breakfast…not yet, but more than enough for him to shut his eyes.

Idiot! This is probably radioactive! People used to have X-ray machines in shoe stores to check the fit and had shit like this in toys before they knew how dangerous it was!

The idea that he might've just given himself a massive dose of some unknown radiation forced his eyes open again, and he grabbed the lever, moving it forward to where it'd been, shutting the damper on whatever he'd just opened on himself, and looked around. Then, focusing hard, looked again.

All the boxes he'd been looking through were where they'd been before, but all the lids were back on. The papers and the journal he'd set aside were nowhere to be seen. The work lights were gone. Instead, the room was lit with the purple glow coming from the brass box. Dan got to his feet and turned around…the doorway was gone.

Or rather, it was still there, but the loose bricks and boards that'd been removed sometime late yesterday were in place and looked like they had been for a long time.

He ran to the wall, the music blaring in his ears all but forgotten, but found he could do little more than breathe fast and gently touch the old, solidly stacked stones with shaking hands, the purple light coming from behind causing him to cast shadows as he did so.

Dan turned and fell back to the stone floor on his knees in front of the strange clock, staring unbelievingly at the date now on its spun brass dials: July 17th, 1947.

"No…way," he said, then grinned as he reached for the lever once more.

Chapter One

Dan jerked awake on the couch, one arm flailing and sending his forgotten plate of toast to the floor, and the newspaper he'd fallen asleep with right along with it. He sat up, trying to find the toast before the butter soaked into the rug. Setting everything to rights again, Dan rubbed the sleep out of his eyes, picked up the newspaper, and fluttered it out a bit, trying to remember where he'd left off reading before drifting off.

He scanned through the usual run of things, trying to find his place…classified, gossip columns, ads for everything from Folgers to Fords, and coverage of just about everything worth covering in a smallish rural town like New Chapel, Ohio.

Finding his place again…an article by one Penny Prescott about an upcoming fundraiser to put an extension on the high school library, Dan finished up, making a mental note to stop by and make a donation at some point in the next few days. As he folded the paper up and set it on the coffee table, the date caught his eye: September 17, 1947.

"How time flies," he said, leaning back onto the couch, slipping his phone out of his pocket.

Looking at its blank screen, he thought about the dream, about Carly calling him on it, asking about her credit card, then never showing up. Just over two years ago now—for him anyway. That day was still about eighty years ahead for the rest of the world. Holding the side button, Dan powered it on for what he thought had to be the first time in at least a month.

Part of him wondered why he'd bothered bringing this, the Kindle, or the laptop along for the trip in the first place. Okay, well, there was a reason for the laptop, but the rest of it? Ashamed as he was to admit it, though, he knew. At the time, he thought he'd go absolutely crazy without screens, internet-connected or not, and so, he'd brought them along. But it turns out that the joke had been on him…the laptop and Kindle were sitting in a small box under his bed, untouched for even longer than the phone.

If I plan on hanging out any longer, I'll just take them back.

Probably a good idea and something he should've done a while ago. Especially since his *real* wallet was in there too—Dan having slipped the thing in his back pocket out of long-established habit before making the trip here. Or maybe he'd just leave all that shit up there in the box. It's not like it was hurting anything.

He watched the phone power on, then flash a Low Battery message on the screen. The charger was down here somewhere, either shoved into the bookcase or the record cabinet, the last time he'd had surprise company. He ought to check for that soon, but for the moment, he didn't feel much like looking for it. Whatever brief urge had compelled him to look at his phone was already gone, so he turned it off again and slipped it back into his pocket.

Grabbing his plate with the now floor-dusty toast, Dan thought more about the memory posing as a dream from earlier. Particularly about after and how sitting on the ground with the strange clock in front of him that day, back where he'd come from with the wall open and the work lights blaring once more, Carly and her decision not to show up after all had been the furthest thing from his mind. So many strange and wonderful things had become possible that day.

Like earlier this year, me being in two places at the same time just for a minute…one walled up behind a forgotten room in Harrington House, while I went about what's become life as usual.

Dan bent down, wiped up a little bit of butter with a tea towel, then stood, plate in hand. He'd gone as far as the archway leading out of the living room when his phone rang…the one on a small table in a corner that actually had service these days. Taking a few steps back, Dan picked up the receiver.

"Hello?"

"Well, if it ain't Dan Parker, big as life and twice as ugly."

"Still makes me better lookin' than you," Dan said, grinning, and the voice on the other end started to laugh.

Jack Lawrence had him beat in the looks department by a mile, and Dan couldn't even pretend to kid himself about it.

Not long after he'd set up here, Dan found himself heading over to Sullivan's Hardware & Repairs pretty often to get stuff for the house. A box of fuses, basic household tools…heavy-duty padlocks…

Jack had been the clerk who'd sold him most of those things and more. Plenty of time to strike up a conversation and get to know one another if the circumstances are right, and they had been. In a matter of a week or two, he'd gone from Mr. Parker to Dan. After that, it was invites for beers down at the Broken Wheel. And after that, invites to hang out with Jack and his girlfriend Lucy, both of whom he now considered close friends.

The first time he'd met Lucy was during a cookout that Dan knew he'd never forget. On the other side of town, both ends of Brighton Street had been closed off and lined the whole way with tables and chairs, and despite rationing still going on, the neighborhood had put out one hell of a spread…it was V-E Day.

He'd seen plenty of pictures of parties like that one, people reveling in the good news that some of their boys would finally be coming home. He'd even included video clips of those parties in his classes when the unit on World War 2 came to a close. But it was another thing entirely to be in the midst of that energy…not just an observer, but a part of it. That wanting to know what it'd be like to be so much more than a researcher looking back had been one of the driving factors for doing this crazy thing once he'd fully understood the possibilities now open to him.

Jack laughed so hard that he started coughing into the other end of the receiver, bringing Dan back to the present.

"That's good," he said, "I'm stealin' that. Hey, listen, I'm just wantin' to let you know that Lucy, I guess, picked up a shift over at the diner. Asked if we could come meet her after we're off work later on, then head to the fair from there."

Dan tilted the arm holding the plate, checking his watch.

"That'll be fine, I could probably stand to grab a slice of pie or somethin'. Listen, Jack, speaking of work, I gotta get movin', or I'll hear about it from Ollie the rest of the day."

"Say no more. You're off at 4:00 today, same as me, right?"

"4:30."

"Ah, well, I'll head over around 4:00 and browse for a while then. We'll talk later."

"Bye now."

Dan hung up the phone, still not quite over the giddy relief of not being reachable by anyone and everyone 24/7, and headed into the kitchen. He set his plate in the sink, grabbed his house keys, and headed out the back door.

Chapter Two

Around the beginning of 1946, the start-up nest egg Dan had put together for this little extended work-study program had started to run dry.

After realizing what he'd happened upon was a real thing and not some sort of fever dream brought on by mold exposure or something, he'd done the only prudent thing he could think of: get hold of clothes that would at least pass as period-correct, head to that antiques warehouse not far away that sold just about everything to grab some vintage cash, then head back to 1939 to buy as many copies of Action Comics #1 he could get his hands on.

They weren't hard to sell when he got back. All seven comic books were original and pristine. And why wouldn't they be? They were brand new. And when he'd dropped the cover story of just happening to find them tucked away and forgotten in an attic trunk at some relative's house, Dan thought he could see one of the auctioneers with drool starting to run down his lip.

Once the comics sold at auction, Dan walked away with money to buy a new house, a new car, freedom from student loans, and the ability to quit teaching and live comfortably off the interest in his bank account alone if he wanted. But the bigger idea had started to take shape right after that first trip, and a few months later, he found himself back at the antiques warehouse, grabbing more things…period cash, a watch, jewelry to hock for more period cash, and even some clothes.

But between the house…the one he'd bought in '45, and living expenses, the nest egg had gotten pretty small.

He'd thought about heading back to replenish his funds, or maybe just calling the experience quits then and there, when he'd been walking toward the corner grocery store downtown in January of '46. Thinking about the coffee he wanted…Folgers or Maxwell House, Dan saw a Help Wanted sign in the window of Walker's Fine Books. He'd walked inside, just wanting to get out of the cold and take a look around, but instead he'd walked out half an hour later with a job.

And now, just over a year and a half later, standing behind the counter, minding a mostly empty store, Dan thought he'd made the right call. Besides, hadn't part of the point of this…experiment…been to immerse himself and learn? What could be better for that than getting a job?

It was a peaceful gig. Keeping the shelves neat, cashing people out, sweeping the floors occasionally throughout the day, and making sure that the kids who wandered in were behaving themselves. Not to mention plenty of downtime to get some reading in. Then there was the guy who owned the place, Ollie Walker.

Ollie was a retired English professor from Ohio State who grew bored with retirement after about six weeks and decided to open a bookstore. He was as scholarly as he was no-bullshit, and Dan liked him.

Not long after he started, Dan remembered grabbing a copy of The Hobbit off the shelf, wondering just how much he could get for a nearly pristine first edition on eBay or something, when Ollie came out of his office, looking like—

Rap-rap-rap!

Forced out of his thoughts, Dan jumped at the sound and looked around. Through the window on his right stood a well-built younger guy, a cigarette tucked behind his ear, and the late afternoon sunlight gleaming off his jet black, Brylcreemed hair and gold-rimmed glasses. Grinning, he disappeared from view, then stepped through the propped-open door.

"Funny stuff, Jack," Dan said, but he was grinning too.

"It's what I do," Jack said, coming up to the counter and leaning against it. "Busy day?"

Dan lifted his hand, showing Jack a book roughly the thickness of a large brick with his finger stuck in just past the halfway point.

"I started this right after lunch."

"Really? I could've finished that by now, the way business ended up bein' for us."

"The way you talk, I doubt it," Dan said, grinning. "You gonna pick up another one of those Westerns you love so much while you wait?"

"No, I've got enough of those I ain't gotten around to yet without addin' to the pile. But I am gonna have a look around."

"Say what you want, but I bet you'll walk outta here with two books at least," Dan said. "Hey, with business being slow, you didn't happen to put a good edge on my straight razor, did you? I'm starting to feel like sandpaper."

Jack, already with a book in hand, hung his head briefly, then looked up.

"Ah, hell, I'm sorry. It's still in my car; I forgot all about it. I'll get to it tomorrow."

Dan said that was fine, and they chatted, killing the last fifteen minutes or so of his shift while Jack roamed the shelves. After a while, he looked at the clock mounted over a shelf behind him. Close enough. Excusing himself, Dan stepped out from behind the counter and headed toward the back of the store.

"Hey Ollie," Dan said, stepping just inside the door to the small back office and giving a sharp tap-tap on the door with one knuckle. "Just letting you know I'm headin' out."

Ollie, who was sitting kicked back in his chair with the ledgers in his lap and a dazed expression on his face, looked up.

"That time already?"

"Yessir."

"That new girl, Elise Crawford…she's gonna be in tomorrow bright and early. You leave her some notes like I asked?"

"I did. They're under the cash drawer if Elise needs them, but she's bright enough that I think she'll be just fine."

"Well," he said, setting the ledgers down with audible relief, "you go enjoy yourself then." He leaned past Dan, looking back out into the shop, and called out. "Hey, Lawrence!"

Jack appeared at the doorway a moment later, not with Westerns but with a few Agatha Christie books in hand, looking between the two of them.

"What's up, doc?"

"Make sure this fool," Ollie said, nodding at Dan, "gets into a little trouble tonight, huh? Preferably with a good-lookin' dame on his arm?"

Jack put on the look of a long-suffering spouse, and despite the feeling of flushed embarrassment creeping up his neck at the moment, Dan still wanted to punch him.

"I'll do what I can, but you know how he is. He'll grab glances at the prettier ones, so I know he's not queer, but I still think he's gotta be trainin' to be one of those monks you hear about, spending their days in thought and readin' their books."

You'd maybe think twice if you were in my position, too.

On the heels of that, Dan wondered…not for the first time, just why he'd chosen his own hometown for this? Why not some place further away, where he might not have to be as careful if he wanted to, well, take his immersion experience a bit further.

The answer, maybe not a good one, but the one he kept circling back to was: familiar would probably be better. His family hadn't moved to New Chapel until the mid-nineties, so he thought the chances were good he wouldn't screw with his family history. Also, he'd been a volunteer at the Kent County Historical Society for years; he knew their wish list. That'd been one of the reasons he'd been keeping a good chunk of his newspapers for the past couple of years, stashing them away in the closet under the stairs.

"Fun as it is listening to you two critique my personal life," Dan said, snapping back to reality, but Jack clapped him on the shoulder, cutting him off.

"Relax, we're lookin' out for ya is all. C'mon."

"You boys have fun," Ollie said, getting up out of his chair and following them out into the store.

Dan ended up cashing Jack out, writing out the receipt and signing his name at the bottom before sticking it into a copy of *The Mysterious Affair at Styles*, then following Jack out the front door.

Chapter Three

New Chapel, Ohio. A mid-sized Midwestern town, sitting like an oasis in a seemingly endless sea of corn, bean, and wheat fields spreading out in all directions. Neighborhoods, quiet and cozy for the most part, were a sort of barrier between the fields, farms, and the town proper: a crossing of two main roads with smaller ones branching off, all packed full of open shops with people coming and going. Farmers to bankers and everyone in between, rubbing shoulders. And thanks to a city council with its act more or less together, it hadn't been much of an adjustment for Dan. Even in the days of Walmart, Amazon, and two-day shipping, you could still walk downtown, get a haircut, pick up a prescription, buy a book, and grab something to eat.

Walking the few short blocks between the bookstore and Bill's Diner, Dan felt like, if he concentrated, he could see both versions of New Chapel. The hipster coffee place he liked was overlaying the dress shop. A great Chinese place sitting on top of the electronics store where radios and this new thing called a television sat in the display window. The barbershop, and well, the barbershop…that actually hadn't changed much. But the exercise did start to strain after a minute or two, and Dan rubbed at his temples, trying to will away the beginnings of a headache.

"You all right?" Jack said, as they walked, books tucked under his arm.

"Oh yeah, I'm fine."

They continued down the next couple of blocks, chatting about everything and nothing, when Bill's Diner finally came into view. It was an old steel railcar-looking place. Red neon lights spelling out

"Bill's" and "Open", and a chalkboard sign in the window telling passersby what flavor pies were waiting inside.

Dan thought the place looked like Pop's Diner from the old Archie comics. He'd made the comment to Jack once, Archie being one of the few current pop culture references Dan knew enough to talk about, and Jack had started looking around, saying he was keeping an eye out for Betty and Veronica.

As they left the sidewalk, their steps now crunching on Bill's gravel parking lot, Dan's gaze fell on one of the few parked cars; Jack's ride...a 1932 Ford Victoria, or just "the Vic". A gorgeous thing. Bright steel blue, whitewall tires with red rims, and an engine big enough to throw you back in the seat in the blink of an eye if you really floored it. Which Dan had done once and ended up with a crick in his neck for the better part of a week. Still, it beat the hell out of his '29 Model A, which felt like it went zero to forty-five in roughly two days.

"Talk about dead," Dan said, letting a hand slide across the Vic's front fender. Jack laughed and tossed his books inside.

"You bet. Half the town, not to mention half of every other town in the county, is down there at the fairgrounds. Plenty of chances to get you into some trouble like the professor said."

"I'll do my best."

"I hope you do a little better than that," Jack said, then put a hand on his shoulder, bringing them both to a stop. He looked at Dan for a long moment before speaking again. "All joking aside, you've seemed sorta wound tight these last few months, I'm not sure why, and you don't have to say nothin' if you don't want to, but I think you could do with a little fun, is all."

Jack wasn't entirely off; Dan had to give him that. He'd sorta been in his head the last few months about going home. After all, it'd been two years. But despite that, and despite what sort of fabulous things were waiting for him now that working had become a choice instead of a necessity, Dan still didn't feel in any great hurry to say goodbye to his life here. There were societal problems he struggled with morally, and there were tons of things he missed, but on the whole, his life had taken a major turn toward peace and quiet, and it'd only gotten harder to walk away.

The worst part was that there was no one he could talk to about it. Not unless he tweaked the details, making it about going back to where he *told* people he was from as part of his cover story. He supposed he could journal just to get the thoughts off his chest, then turn around and torch the pages, but it wasn't the same.

Still, it was nice to be seen. And not for the first time, Dan thought about how it'd taken coming all this way to find the sort of caring, receptive friends that he'd always wanted but never really had, then clapped Jack on the shoulder.

"I'll try to have some fun, honest. Now come on, I'm starving."

Chapter Four

A bell tinkled overhead as he and Jack stepped into Bill's. As if the near-barren parking lot wasn't enough evidence that business wasn't usual, Dan saw a grand total of three other diners in the place: two teenagers in a corner booth sharing a plate of fries and whispering to each other, and an old man at the far side of the counter…a newspaper in one hand and a coffee in the other. Fans mounted in the corners of the place swung slowly back and forth, while something jazzy played from the kitchen.

"Hey there, boys!"

Dan, who'd been headed to the jukebox, turned and saw Lucy come through a swinging door behind the counter.

Lucy was on the taller side, with wavy dark brown hair that touched her shoulders, striking blue eyes, and the sort of smile that always made her look excited. Her white apron was splattered brownish in several places, and the yellow dress she wore hung off her in that slightly jacked-up way that only company-issued clothing can.

He and Jack walked up to the counter, grabbing their usual spots.

"Looks like it'll be another twenty minutes til I'm free to go, you guys hungry?"

They said that they were, and Lucy pulled a pencil and paper from an apron pocket, leaning against the counter and giving her pencil a "well, come on" twirl. Jack gave his order first, and Dan followed. Sighing but still smiling, Lucy scribbled on her pad and tore off the top sheet of paper.

"Cheeseburger, fries, and a Coke for you," she said, playfully jabbing her pencil at Jack. "A club sandwich and baked beans for you." This time, the pencil came Dan's way, and grinning, he pretended to dodge it.

"I swear, I don't know why I bother asking you two anymore, I don't think either one of you has ordered anything different in six months."

Lucy turned, stuck the slip of paper…with their admittedly unoriginal orders, onto the pass-through's spike and rang a bell. A large, meaty hand grabbed the slip of paper and pulled it back.

Elmer, the fry cook on duty most times, was a big guy; three hundred fifty pounds at least, if he was there at all. There wasn't a lot of room back in that kitchen for a guy of Elmer's size to move, judging by what you could see from the counter, but magic happened back there all the same. Hand on heart, some of the best meals Dan had ever had in his life had come through that little window…the man was a culinary force of nature.

"Well," Jack said, when Lucy turned to face them again, "if it ain't broke don't fix it, right?"

"Uh-huh," she said, looking unimpressed but amused, then turning to Dan, "and what's your excuse?"

"The way you read out my order just sounds so lovely, like reading poetry while listening to Mozart."

"Now is that because you like your club sandwiches that much or because you think I have a pretty voice?"

Her smile was coy, and Dan felt a red flush creeping up his neck. Still, before he could do more than clear his throat, Lucy had already turned, grabbed a pot of coffee from behind the counter, and set off toward the older man with the mug and the newspaper.

"A top off, honey?"

Her voice is pretty, he thought, then shook it away.

He turned to Jack, expecting to either meet with a disapproving stare or a quick pop across the jaw for that little exchange, which, while totally messing around, still could've been taken the wrong way. But if Jack had heard, he didn't give any indication. He'd taken up one of the abandoned newspapers, totally engrossed in the police blotter…a fun little offering from the cops reporting what sorts of jackassery had been going on lately; in New Chapel, there was never too much.

"They finally busted that Rollins kid," Dan said, after studying the page for a few minutes.

"Yeah," Jack said, "but I'd heard about that one before. Bill Crawford came in the other day, tellin' me about how that snot-nose little shit had been racing down between his farm and the Sherbrooke place, and get this, his wife—"

"Alright," Lucy said, stopping in front of them, coffee pot in hand. "Either of you need anything?"

"Order up!" a deep, growling voice called from the pass-through window.

"My food would be a great start," Jack said, laughing and shaking the newspaper a little.

Dan gave a sort of weak, half-grin, but that little joke…if it'd been intended as a joke, wasn't funny. Jack might've been laughing, but his tone sounded unnecessarily mean-spirited.

Or you could be reading too much into it.

Lucy set down the coffee, grabbed the plates, then put down first his food, then Jack's.

"Eat up," she said, her smile looking strained.

Okay, maybe not.

Jack set the paper aside and went for his food at once. Not sloppily or anything, but with real gusto. Someone who was on the border of starving, but with proper table manners hardwired into them.

"Thanks, Lucy," Dan said, then, with a sweep of his foot under the counter, gave Jack a nice, hard whack on the shin.

Jack jumped, looking confused as a little runner of mustard ran down his chin.

"Oh, yeah, sorry…thanks, doll."

Lucy smiled again and nodded. Turning, she headed through the swinging door leading to the kitchen.

"The hell's wrong with you?" Dan said before he realized he was going to open his mouth at all, making sure to pitch his voice low.

"Huh?" Jack said, grabbing a napkin to wipe away the mustard.

"You're being a little, I don't know, rude, don't you think?"

"The bringing me my food thing? C'mon, that was just a joke, and she knows that, so just relax, okay?"

Dan didn't say anything for a long moment. Jack's tone was as calm as ever, but there was something in that clap-back not exactly like him. Snippy comments and forgetting his manners with Lucy weren't like him either. Dan thought about rebutting the point, saying that not all jokes are funny, and he didn't believe it was a joke in the first place. But when he opened his mouth, thinking about what Jack had said to him in the parking lot about seeming wound tight, he went in a different direction.

"Are you all right?"

He braced himself for pushback and deflection but got none of it. Instead, Jack's face fell, and he set his burger down, reaching for what had to be the second...or maybe it was the third, Lucky Strike cigarette since they'd gotten here.

"I'm just tired. They've had me out on a lot of those house call repairs just lately, and I don't know, maybe I haven't been restin' enough in between. I'll mind myself, I promise."

And now that he was paying more attention, Dan thought Jack's face did look a little more tired and worn lately. The bags under the eyes, the cheekbones more pronounced...he wondered how he'd missed it.

"If you need to talk..." Dan said, letting the words trail off, trusting that he didn't need to say more.

Jack appeared to get the message, then after several long moments, nodded, lit the cancer stick, and gave something close to his normal smile. They started to eat, Jack with less gusto and Dan with less interest, while listening to the soothing sounds of Elmer's radio. Soon Lucy reappeared through the door, wiping at the bottom of her eye with a side towel. Dan watched her check on the teenagers in the corner before coming back to him and Jack.

The three of them chatted for a while longer about this and that. Book recommendations went all around, as did stories about everyone's workday, starting off with how slow business had been and branching off from there. By the time she'd gotten around to sharing some updates about the six or seven other girls who roomed with her at Harrington House, Lucy's smiles had turned easy again. Jack had started laughing and joking in his good-natured way again, too, but Dan noticed the cigarettes still disappearing with scary speed.

Before long, the little bell above the door tinkled again, and another woman wearing an identical yellow dress to Lucy's stepped in, looking half-asleep and like she wanted to be anywhere else but here. She disappeared behind the swinging door, and Dan heard the click-thunk of a time clock.

"I'll just cash you boys out real quick, then I'll go change," Lucy said.

"Here," Jack said, reaching a hand into his pocket.

"Save it,' Dan said. "You got lunch at Sal's last time; I still owe you."

Jack shrugged, letting his arm fall, and began folding up the newspaper he'd been looking at earlier. Dan handed over the cash and watched Lucy walk over to the ornate register to make his change.

"Hey, pal, I'll be right back," Jack said, sliding down off the stool and giving him a tap on the shoulder.

"Everything alright?" Dan said, watching Lucy for a second longer before turning.

"Fine," Jack said, putting out whatever number cigarette this was now, then running a hand through his hair. "Just remembered that I had to make a telephone call. Work things. Won't be a minute."

A little confused, seeing as how they'd all just been talking about how dead things had been in town since the fair started up, Dan watched as Jack headed toward the other end of the counter, hung a left, stepped into the small phone booth, and shut the door behind him.

Chapter Five

"Yes, I heard," Jack said, looking out the booth window at Lucy and Dan standing by the diner's front door, waiting for him. "That sink backing up on Mrs. Morris again, right. Uh-huh, well, I'm thinkin' I won't be available tonight is the thing."

"Oh no," the voice said, sounding sultry and sweet, "but nobody fixes my pipes like you do, sweetie."

Jack hated that voice. Hated that despite everything, it was still giving him an erection. He should've known this telephone call wouldn't go his way. The plan had been to duck out after things wound down at the fair, then head over to her place and sleep over. Why couldn't he have just not shown up and dealt with it in the morning? Just what in the hell had he been thinking?

You've not been thinkin' at all, you damn fool.

Boy, wasn't that the truth? A few minor squabbles with Lucy, where he'd come away looking like the jerk, had set him on edge, just waiting for a chance to get back at her. Then, going out to fix an electrical box in that damn house, that damn floozy had taken a run at him, and he'd let her. Then a few weeks later, he'd gone and done it again, and the guilt had been eating him alive ever since.

Didn't stop you from making plans with her again, though, did it? Dan noticed somethin' hasn't been right. Lucy probably has too. How long can you possibly keep this up and still face yourself in the mirror, pretending you're a good man?

The realization that he couldn't…wouldn't pretend anymore had been enough to get him off the stool, wanting to do something about this mess here and now. Preferably leaving no one the wiser, so there'd be at least a chance of enjoying this night and the nights to come; how wrong he was.

"I understand it's puttin' ya in a bind, but I can't. Not tomorrow either."

Silence hung over the line just long enough for Jack to pull out a cigarette, then light it with shaking hands. Finally, she spoke.

"You sure about that, sweetie? 'Cus, Dick doesn't like getting bad news. Why, in high school, a sweet boy named Jimmy once tried to kiss me when I didn't wanna kiss him. Dick heard, and he didn't like it. Poor Jimmy, it took a whole month for the swelling in his face to go down. And he never did walk right after that."

"What're you…"

At first, her story didn't make a lick of sense, then it did. He glanced over his shoulder, making sure Lucy and Dan were still chatting away before turning back, dropping his voice…and the ruse.

"You bitch," he said, feeling his jaws clench, molars scraping off one another. A laugh came from the other end of the line that made him want to grab the phonebook in front of him, drive over there, and beat her senseless with it.

"Aww, you should be flattered," she said. "I like you, that's all. But if you're so sore about it, how about this? You come tonight, one last little fling while Dick's out of town, then we're done. You go back to your girl, and I'll never say a word."

Jack turned, looking through the booth window again at Lucy. She caught his eye and waved. Smiling, he waved back, feeling a pang of guilt and longing and deep, deep shame. Clearing his throat, he readjusted the receiver. *Do I have a choice?* was the first thing he'd thought about asking, but that was easy enough to answer on his own. Of course, he had a choice, plenty of them…all bad ones.

"You'll keep your word?"

"Why, of course I will!" she said. Maybe too quickly, maybe not.

Relying on the word of a cheatin' hussy, Jack thought, before realizing he wasn't too far removed from that himself, and the shame welled up again.

"Fine," Jack said, then remembering his cover, poor as it was, added, "I'll grab a few tools and be there as soon as I can, gotta be quick though."

"We'll see."

Jack's hand tightened hard, and he slammed the receiver back in its cradle before that woman got in another word.

Chapter Six

"Oh, Jack, you can't be serious."

Dan had been waiting with Lucy by the front door for what felt like a while, talking. Gone was the unflattering yellow dress, and in its place was a red silk blouse and a grey skirt that stopped just below her knees. All of it nice and hugging in a way that was hard not to keep noticing. Luckily, there'd been plenty in the way of good conversation to keep his attention where he knew it ought to be.

What in the hell is wrong with me today? He'd had the thought, but before his brain gave up much in the way of an answer, the phone booth door opened, and Jack stepped out looking red in the face.

"Oh, that's not good," Dan had said, and he'd been right.

The three of them had moved out into the parking lot when Jack broke the news that he'd have to meet them at the fairgrounds later on.

"I know," Jack said, scratching his eyebrow with the back of his thumb after Lucy had gotten the first word. "But they're sendin' me out to Mrs. Morris again."

"Again?" Dan said. "Last time she'd called for some help with a few light switches, and you ended up looking at a leaky basement. She'd probably be better off selling the place and starting over."

"Yeah, I wish I'd never called in if I'm bein' honest," Jack said, with a laugh that didn't quite reach his eyes.

"Well," Lucy said, slipping on her sunglasses. "We can, I mean, I don't mind keepin' you company if…"

"No, you'd both best stay here. Sounds like a bad pipe fitting under the kitchen sink. God willing, it shouldn't take long."

"I hate when you get these calls," Lucy said, crossing her arms. "I don't know what it is these past few months. Or why you thought now would be a good time to call in the first place."

"I know, but—"

Dan turned and took a good few steps away, pretending to be interested in a particularly jagged rock near the rear tire of one of the parked cars, then at the sign tied to two lampposts spanning Main Street, reading:

Kent Co. Fair
Sept 10th – 17th, 1947
Gates open at 11 a.m.!
Come one, come all!

He stared at the sign, red letters against ivory canvas, wondering just how he'd found himself here—pretending not to listen to two post-war greatest generation twenty somethings having a squabble in a parking lot where he knew one day the diner behind them would be gone. And in its place, there'd be a small strip mall with a tanning place, a Boost Mobile, and a Chipotle.

But, of course, he knew how.

Today had hardly been the first time he'd dreamed about what'd happened that afternoon. And everything was still so clear it felt like it'd all happened two days ago, not two years ago. Walking down into the vast, cavernous space underneath Harrington House…bright light spilling on the line of boxes in that forgotten room…the purple glow coming from that strange clock…feeling like reality had just split open with possibilities once he'd realized—

"Danny?"

Dan turned and blinked, the memory of the room printed on his eyes, almost like an afterimage. When it cleared, he saw Lucy standing in front of him, Jack bringing up the rear.

"Everything okay?" he said.

"I'm fine," Lucy said, though not sounding half as fine as she'd probably been aiming for. "Sorry about all this."

"Don't worry about it."

He watched as Jack finished off the last of his latest cigarette, then pitched the butt into the rocks before stamping it out and walking over to join them. Lucy popped up on her toes to give Jack a short hug…but no kiss. When they broke, Dan took a step forward and clapped him on the back.

"Get lost, then get back here," Dan said, trying for a falsely cheery tone he didn't feel, but hoped might help to rebound from whatever had just happened. "You've done a lot of runnin' your mouth about how you're practically Annie Oakley at the shooting gallery. I say you're full of shit."

"Boy, these eyeglasses aren't just for making my face look pretty," Jack said, pushing his glasses back up on his nose with his middle finger.

Dan smiled and watched as Jack turned, then headed toward the Vic.

Chapter Seven

"Just a reminder, folks, that fair time is now 6:45. Quilt judging is starting over at the Crafts building here in fifteen minutes, so be sure to stop on by! And once again, thanks for joining us here at the Kent County Fair!"

Penny Prescott looked up at the loudspeaker mounted on a nearby pole, scooting away from it on the bench, the announcer's voice still ringing in her ear. Once it'd passed, she looked back down at the notebook in her lap where her coverage of the pie bake-off sat among the pages as hurried scribbles.

All around her, she could hear folks carrying on and having a good time. Music played over loudspeakers as well as the occasional announcement. Bright neon lights flashed, and savory smells like popcorn and hot dogs mixed with sweeter smells like cotton candy and funnel cake.

Work first, she told herself, forcing her attention away from the nearby kettle corn stand and back to her notebook, flicking her pen along its edge. She turned to a fresh sheet of paper, then, going back and forth, started to recopy the scribbles into something legible while she could still make out what it was she'd been meaning to write. But no sooner had she started when a gust of wind took her press badge out from between the pages, sending it to the ground.

"Oh no, you don't," she said, managing to get the heel of her shoe on the thing before it went much further.

Once she'd stowed the press badge safely back in her handbag, Penny looked at the new page again at the dozen or so now readable words. Her pen was poised over the page, ready to start again, but all at once the sights and sounds, not to mention the smells, hit her fresh, and the urgency for this little bit of housekeeping disappeared like water when you pull the drain plug. Recapping the pen, Penny slipped both it and the small notebook back into her handbag.

It'll be alright, she thought, watching a group of boys give her an approving look before moving along. *You don't need to turn in that first draft til day after tomorrow anyway.*

Besides, copying her notes over would be the only hard part of her assignment tonight. As with most of what she wrote for the New Chapel Gazette, the pie bake-off coverage was fluff. She enjoyed writing, loved being out talking to folks and learning things, and was determined to turn in her best work every time…but that didn't change the fact that it was all still fluff.

Standing, Penny made in the direction of the kettle corn and stepped in line. It was plenty long, and there was time, too much of it, to reflect on how this was the first year she'd come to the fair alone. Sighing, she stood there, trying not to think about Eddie and all the fun times they'd had here. What they'd done, they'd done for the best, she knew, but it was still lonely sometimes.

Isn't it time we finally turned the page on that old news? Tonight's supposed to be fun. If you're so desperate for a gab while you're here that isn't about pie, why not look around and see if you can't find someone you know?

Moving forward, the smells of kettle corn getting stronger, Penny did just that.

But with this little shindig being for the entire county and having a big turnout at that, there weren't many people she recognized just now. The only one she could say for sure was her dentist, and he'd raise all hell if he saw her standing here, ready to subject her teeth to such a treatment as kettle corn.

Penny moved forward in line and, turning her head the other direction, saw someone else she thought she knew. Derek or Daniel…at the moment, she couldn't remember which, but she did know he was the fella who worked at the bookstore in town. And he looked pretty cozy with a gal Penny thought she could just about place, too. She'd almost had the name when they disappeared through the doors to the Merchants building, where they had all those sales booths, and the spell broke.

"'Scuse me, miss, you're next."

Turning back toward the line, Penny saw that she was standing several paces back from a wide-open booth, a tired-looking man, and a large kettle behind it.

"Oh yes, thank you!" Penny said and moved forward.

Chapter Eight

Jack pulled the Vic over to the side of Eastbridge Road, a house down from Dan's place. He put it in park, the engine still running, then leaned his head against the steering wheel.

Just what in the hell are you doing?

Talk about a question that had too damn many answers.

Up until a moment ago, he'd been driving like a madman to get this mess over with, counting on Sheriff Buck's habit of being too in his cups to do his job. His boys are likely too busy keeping an eye on things at the fairgrounds and over at the Broken Wheel Tavern to be out and about, ready to grab speeders like him. Before that, he'd been standing in a parking lot, lying to his pal and his girl about having to work. Then, trying not to look at them in the rear-view mirror as he pulled away and set about trying to get himself out of this jam.

Part of him…a big part of him, hoped one of them would get suspicious and telephone the store to ask about his "assignment". Roger would tell them he hadn't sent him out anywhere, and from there the whole thing would likely come unraveled pretty quick. He couldn't start the ruination on his own, but he damn sure wouldn't try to deny it if it got out, and he'd take whatever came like a man: Lucy dumping him like yesterday's garbage…big, built-like-a-brick-shithouse Dick Sherbrooke using him for boxing practice, all of it.

Someone come find me quick before I do this crazy thing.

But no one was coming, and Jack knew it. He knew that if he looked up and squinted his eyes, he could see Sherbrooke Dairy off in the distance, and in a few minutes, he knew that's just exactly where he'd be. At this point, knocking boots with that woman up there one last time and hoping she'd keep her word was about all the hope he had left of making it out of this mess and saving his skin in the process.

Kuh-rash!

Jack sat ramrod straight, looking out the Vic's front windshield. Just up ahead, three younger boys stood in the middle of the road, one letting his bat go slack in his hand while his buddies backed away, slow at first, then starting to turn tail and run. And after a moment, Jack saw the house they were running from.

"Hey!"

He got out of the car, killing the engine and forgetting about his own troubles for the moment, and made toward the center of the road. The two cowards were all the way down the other end of the block, and bat-boy, who'd only seemed to just realize what'd happened, started to move along with his friends when Jack caught him by the arm.

"Lemme go, I didn't do nothin'!"

"Nice try, kid, that's my pal's window you just broke."

"Listen, mister, I'm sorry, I—"

"Don't say it to me, kid. You get your behind back here tomorrow morning and tell my buddy face-to-face like a man, understand? He's a fair enough sort of guy."

That last part seemed to ease the kid. The struggling stopped, and Jack let go.

"But," he said, not wanting the kid to be too easy about it, "if you don't show, believe me, I'll find out. You look sorta familiar, and I think I could place your daddy if I had a mind to try, and if I'm right, he don't strike me as fair-minded…do I need to spell the rest out for you?"

"No, sir."

"Good. Now go get your ball and beat it."

Jack followed the kid a few paces behind, watched him pick up his ball, then run back down the driveway and down the street in the direction his snot-nose friends had taken off. He turned to face the house.

It took him a minute to see just where the damage was, and he thought Danny Boy had gotten off lucky that fly ball had smashed one of those little basement windows instead of that nice big one in his sitting room. But as he moved closer, broken glass crunching under his feet, something didn't seem quite right. After squatting down to get a closer look, hearing more glass crunch under his feet, it came to him.

He'd knocked his share of baseballs through windows in his day. And while, yes, sometimes you'd have to walk through a little broken glass to get your ball back, first off, it was never this much. And second, you'd always have to go inside somewhere to get it back…it was never just sitting outside…

Jack looked up at the newly busted window, the darkness beyond those jagged shards of glass looking like teeth in a monster's mouth. Reaching out, he meant to try and put his hand through, but at the last moment made a fist and knocked instead.

"What gives?"

From what he could see, this window, and a few others, had been nailed over with blackboards. Just why he couldn't say, but that's what'd been done all right. How had he never noticed it before? He thought about trying to take a peek inside to see what the deal was, but stood, shaking the thought away.

Alright, Monsieur Poirot, enough investigation…let's get this done and over with.

This little diversion had been interesting, but it was time to get moving. He was in a hell of a fix, and Lucy was waiting for him at the other end of it. There'd be plenty of time to ask Dan about the basement later tonight or maybe tomorrow, especially seeing as he'd likely be drafted to help fix it.

Jack turned and walked back down the driveway. He slid in behind the Vic's wheel, started her up, and headed off again.

Chapter Nine

"What'd you find, Danny?"

Danny turned, and Lucy saw what he'd been looking at. A straight razor with a chromed steel blade and what had to be a cherry wood handle. He handed it over to her.

"Jack absconded with my razor, and I need a shave."

"I'll say, you're startin' to look a little rough there, silly."

Before she realized what she was doing, Lucy reached up and let her thumb run across the little scruff on the cleft of his chin. Blushing, she took her hand back.

Despite how the evening had begun and the fact that they hadn't done much else besides walk and talk, Lucy was enjoying herself quite a bit. After Jack had taken off, they'd decided to head to the fairgrounds on foot, the nice weather being all the reason either of them seemed to need. She supposed they could've taken her car, it'd only been sitting behind the diner, but…

But you liked the idea of taking more time with him just on your own. And let's skip the part where you try lying to yourself and say it ain't so, shall we?

Oh, that was true, and no, she wouldn't lie about it. Not anymore than she'd lie about what she'd originally intended this night to be: something fun to see if she and Jack couldn't come back together a bit. Over the past few months, there'd been some growing distance. Slow at first, but then one day, the fella she'd been holding hands with felt like a stranger. She didn't know how it happened, only that it had.

Before, it'd felt like she ought to at least try and do something about it, but after the little squabbles since…after today, his carrying on in that parking lot about how he was sorry and how this would be the last of it, he swears. He was going to give his boss a talking to once he got back, before taking off anyway, instead of calling that man back and demanding he send someone else? Well, doing something about all that distance she felt didn't seem so important anymore…if it ever really had in the first place.

"So, what've you found so far?" Danny said, smiling.

"Oh, a few things, but this one…" she said, turning to the display of jewelry in front of her.

Ever since they'd walked into the Merchant's building, weaving in and out between lookie-loos and dodging some of the more ambitious salesmen, seeing everything from handmade kitchen tea towels to farm equipment, she'd been hoping to find this particular jewelry stand again. It'd been here the year before, but she hadn't bought anything then. But now, running her fingers over the delicate displays, Lucy found what she'd just been looking at and thought this year she'd treat herself.

"Ah, now, what do you think of this?" she said, holding the necklace out toward Danny.

It was a fine thing. Delicate silver chain with a purple stone that seemed to catch the light and hold it deep down inside in a way that felt…different than all the other necklaces she'd ever owned or even looked at before. The way the light reflected off the facets made it look like there was an electrical storm caught just inside.

"It's gorgeous," he said, and it felt like he was looking more at her than the necklace. She flushed but smiled big all the same.

Lucy took a small step forward, the necklace still in her hand. The thought occurred to her that she'd like help trying it on…maybe hold her hair along one shoulder while Danny slipped it gently around her neck and—

Would you please mind yourself, Lucy, dear? What would happen if someone you knew walked by and saw a thing like that?

"Well," Lucy said, clearing her throat and closing her hand over the necklace, "how about we pay, then find somethin' else to spend our hard-earned cash on?"

"Deal."

As it turned out, there weren't many places either of them felt like spending their wages on, but it was a fine time just the same. Seemed like every business worth its salt from Springdale, Harlan Heights, and New Chapel had a booth set up here, and there was more than plenty to look at. And as they continued to walk, now peeking at the center rows, they seemed to start running into folks they knew one right after another.

By the way Danny was chatting, he didn't seem much bothered by it, but Lucy found herself a little nervous. It was common enough knowledge that she was with Jack…at least for the time being, and coming to a thing like this without him? Well, people in town have a nasty long nose for other people's business…

Not nervous enough to say goodnight, though, are you? No, not enough, she thought, continuing to smile and even nestling her hand a little more in the crook of Danny's arm in spite of herself as they stood outside the Merchants building talking to Deputy Eddie Prescott, who'd caught up with them right near the exit and followed them out. Lucy saw him a couple of times a week at Bill's and liked him. She found him to be a calm, down to earth sorta of fella.

"So, how've things been keeping watch over all the fun tonight, Eddie?" Lucy said.

"Slow, mostly," Eddie said. "Marv Roberts and Pete Townsend got into it about fair resale prices on cattle, and Marv threw a punch. But one of the 4-H girls came and got me before things got much past that. Other than that, though, can't say I've been doin' much more than walkin' around, sorta making my presence known and trying to keep myself away from the sweets."

"No chasing around roaming packs of delinquent high school kids?" Danny said, laughing, but Eddie only grinned and shook his head.

"Where're you from, Dan?"

"Fairvale, Indiana. It's a bigger city, but still not much worth being there for, that's why I moved," he said, almost in a single breath, and Lucy wanted to laugh because it sounded so funny.

"Alright, consider Fairvale off my travel list," Eddie said, and Lucy felt the muscles in Danny's arm relax. "But here, unlike the bigger places, our kids pretty well mind themselves and everyone else. Cuttin' up is kept to a bare minimum, and I thank God for that."

"It's a nice place," Lucy said, patting Danny's arm, and Eddie agreed.

"So, is Jack around? Been meaning to stop into Sullivan's for a chat. He said somethin' a little bit ago about how he could redo some of the bad wiring in the station on the cheap, and me and Sheriff Buck have a few questions."

Lucy felt herself tense just a bit. Out of everyone they'd run into, Eddie had been the first to wonder…out loud at least, where Jack was. And though there wasn't anything too funny about the situation, it still felt a little like she'd been caught doing something wrong.

"He got pulled out on a service call," Danny said, and Lucy relaxed. "Out to Harlan Heights, if I remember right. I'd thought he'd be done by now, but you know how he gets sometimes…probably stuck talkin' some poor sap's ear off as we speak."

Eddie laughed, nodding in agreement. But as the laughter died away, she watched him do a once-over. Not the kind of look fellas sometimes give when you're made up particularly fine that day, but a long, appraising look between the two of them…first her, then Danny, then back to her.

"Well, he'll turn up sooner or later. A mess down the front of his shirt from whatever he's been up to and an apology bouquet of cotton candy in hand, Lucy, don't you worry."

She smiled, but thought that if Jack meant to make a gesture of apology that stood even the slimmest chance with her at this point, he'd have to do a lot better than cotton candy…

They stood there talking for a few minutes longer before Eddie checked his watch, then excused himself, saying he needed to do a few more rounds before heading back into the police station. Touching the brim of his hat, he wished them goodnight, then walked down the short flight of steps, disappearing around the far corner of the building.

"So," Danny said, looking over at her. "Where're we off to now? Cotton candy stand, or are you wanting to hold off for that apology bouquet?"

Lucy laughed, shaking her head and giving him a playful jab in the ribs, but said nothing. Just where did she want to go? Certainly not back to her rented room at Harrington House…in her night things and reading before the sun went down, just waiting to fall asleep. But something about the way Eddie had stared left her feeling a little uneasy about hanging around too much longer. Despite that feeling, though, somehow, she wasn't ready to call it a night just yet.

She looked over to see Danny checking his watch.

"It does feel like Jack should've been back by now," he said, looking over toward the front gate where they were supposed to meet.

"Well," Lucy said, "do you maybe wanna finish our stroll around the place, grab a hotdog, and if he still isn't waiting close to the front gate when we get back, and no one calls our names over the announcements saying there's a telephone call, we leave?"

He appeared to consider this for a moment before nodding.

"Be a shame not to enjoy this for at least a little longer," he said, offering his arm again, and Lucy took it.

"Lead the way, mister."

Chapter Ten

Jack slowly descended the stairs of the old Sherbrooke family farmhouse, feeling like his brain had just gone three rounds with a cake mixer.

There'd been no last-minute salvation, and he'd found his was here just like he knew he would. He pulled into the small shed, ditching the Vic where he had the last couple of times, and got out to find her standing at the back door to meet him, naked as the day she was born except for a short, thin silk robe and high-heeled shoes. And why not? Nobody was around to see.

He'd been hard then, but at the same time, he hated her. Hated her for what she was making him do. Hating himself that he wasn't man enough to do the right thing, telling her off, and just accepting whatever consequences surely were heading his way, no matter how it all shook out tonight.

"Well, if it ain't the repair man, come at last," she'd said, her voice breathy and soft as he crossed the distance between them in a few quick strides.

Jack didn't answer. Couldn't answer. Instead, he pulled her roughly…maybe too roughly, into his arms. Her mouth was on his in an instant, feeling delicious and horrible all at once. And the rougher he was, pushing her back through the open kitchen door and slamming it behind him, only to grab her again, the more excited she seemed to get, letting the robe fall to the floor before going to work on his shirt.

For a moment, he considered just putting her up against the kitchen table and having her then and there, and heading right back out to the Vic. To hell with the cover story to make the timing of this mess somewhat believable. Fast and hard, then his dealings with this horrible woman could be done, and he could put her behind him for good…hopefully.

But he couldn't make it go quick. In spite of loving Lucy – and whatever was left of his better judgement, they'd gone upstairs and he'd taken his time…taken all he wanted from her before the bad feelings showed their faces again.

But he'd expected all that. It was no different than any other time they'd snuck around…just some more guilt he'd have to carry. No, what really left him feeling stunned and confused had happened once playtime was over, both of them with their ashes hauled, and he'd started to gather himself.

He'd slid his jeans back on, then sat on the corner of the bed to light a cigarette, staring at the boards between his bare feet when she spoke up.

"I'm sorry."

Dorothy Sherbrooke sat, looking like a Hollywood starlet after some big-shot director had called cut at the end of a long day; gorgeous, but tired and worn down. Unlike past times when they'd finished, she'd gone on laughing, smoking, and teasing some to see if he had another round in him. She now sat with her legs drawn up to her chin, dark red hair hanging down in limp waves, covering her face.

"Dorothy?"

"I'm sorry," she said again, still hidden by that hair. "Dick isn't around much, and when he is, he doesn't look twice at me anymore. He's always going to those trade shows, and I just know he's out, and…"

She raised her head to look at him, tears running down her face. Not the few crocodile tears some women can manage, but the real thing.

"It's not an excuse, and everything I said earlier I meant. I won't tell, I…I'm just so sorry."

Jack thought about everything he'd been through, everything she'd put him through, wanting to scream in her face that she'd damn well better be sorry, but found he couldn't. So far as he could tell, that apology was real and deadly serious. And like other times in his life when someone said sorry and was genuine about it, his anger just faded away.

"Thank you."

He wanted to put a hand on her back, something to show a little comfort, but stopped, wondering if it'd send the wrong message. After a moment, he decided to risk it anyway.

They sat there talking for some time. About Dick, about her life since she'd moved here…far away from everything she'd known, about how between that and Dick, she'd never felt so lonely in her entire life. The Ladies Baptist Circle is leaving her out of everything these days, almost like they knew what she'd been up to and saw fit to judge her for it instead of leaving it to God and treating her with kindness…all that talk about loving the sinner being just that, talk.

When they finally finished pulling their clothes on again, Dorothy talked about getting away. Just waiting for the next trade show, filling a suitcase, and leaving. Maybe with a note, or maybe let the empty bed and dresser do all the talking for her.

"Don't wait," Jack said, slipping his smokes back into his pocket and walking over to her. "Do it now while you've got your courage up. If you don't, you'll keep findin' excuses not to, then you'll be stuck."

Dorothy reached for him, pulling him into a tight hug. And after a long while, she pulled away, smiling…the first genuine one he thought he'd ever seen from her.

"Go on," she said, waving her hand at him. "Take a walk before my husband gets home."

Long overdue, he thought, coming to the end of the stairs, hanging a left toward the kitchen, and heading out the back door.

Footsteps crunching in the gravel, Jack walked toward the small shed where he'd stashed the Vic. Up above, the sky had already gone into dark oranges and purples, a sure sign that summer was just about done. Off to the right, he saw the vague shapes of cows moving in their fields, making their rustlings and deep moos.

Jack went to the front of the shed and stood for a moment, staring into the dark opening. Light from one of the nearby poles clicked on, and from inside he could see a bright, silvery swatch of the Vic's front bumper staring back at him. A shiver ran down his spine at the sight of it, though he couldn't say just why. He reached a shaking hand into the front pocket of his jeans before stepping inside.

He'd never admitted it to anyone before, but dark, shadowy places like this gave him the deep-down creeps. So, before he could think too much about it, Jack opened the Vic's door, threw himself in, and for the first time in a long while, locked both doors.

Gripping the steering wheel, a little peace started to slip back, and his heart…a thing he hadn't realized til now had been racing, began to settle down.

"Idiot," he said, managing a half-grin and looking over at the passenger seat. "Too many of those damn Agatha Christie books, that's what I think."

His hand jittered a bit, reaching toward the dashboard, but he managed to find the ignition and slip the key in. But just as he was about to turn it, he heard something…a small rustle and a gasp, coming from the backseat.

Jack felt his breath stop dead in his chest.

"Who- "

Wham!

Something connected with the back of his head, forcing it forward into the steering wheel. The impact lit up his vision with bursts of light like Fourth of July fireworks. He felt a sting and a snap from the bridge of his nose, then his eyeglasses slid down, now hanging on either side of his head.

Jack cried out, bringing his violently shaking hands to his cheeks and feeling warm blood. Moving his hands up, something sharp jabbed him in the finger, and he tried to open his eyes. But as he did, the stinging in his face turned to bright bolts of pain, and he screamed again.

"Can't! Can't open…"

Speaking it out loud broke the confusion, and he understood what'd happened. Breathing in short bursts, Jack pinched one of the shards of his broken lenses between two fingers and began to pull it out of his eye. The pain was nothing short of agony, and it felt like he'd faint dead away, but he had to see, had to…

A cry came from the backseat, but before he'd gotten the chance to do more than turn, meaning to raise his arm and reach back, he felt something hard flash across his throat, quick as lightning, and he began to cough, all of a sudden not able to get enough air. Hot blood began to force its way up his throat like a backed drain, and it was like he was drowning.

Blind, he felt around on the dashboard with fingers that'd already started to grow cold. Still, they knew what they were looking for, and the Vic's engine roared into life. Fumbling one hand onto the wheel and the other onto the gear shift, Jack dropped the transmission into something he dearly hoped was a forward gear and hit the gas. Only, he popped the clutch and the engine stalled before it'd gone more than six feet, its nose sticking out of the shed.

No, he thought, his newly blurred vision beginning to go dark, his body shivering with a deep cold as warm blood ran in buckets down the front of his shirt.

A moment later, the darkness was complete, and Jack knew no more.

Chapter Eleven

Carly Wells managed to work the passenger side door open and nearly fell out of the blue Ford, a shaking, bloody hand pressed to her lips to stop the puke threatening to come up. Getting shakily to her feet, she staggered back, seeing the car half sticking out of the garage or barn or whatever it was, then turning to face a spot just a few yards ahead.

He could've driven right into that pole and killed me.

The thought brought a tear-choked bark of laughter, and that was enough for her to lose her hold. Carly bent forward, emptying her stomach into the nearby grass.

You killed him.

It hadn't been the plan, but yes, she had.

The Ford had driven past only an hour or so before, and she'd recognized it at once. Had seen it the other day when…whoever this was, parked and Dan walked out to meet him. She'd been on the other side of the street, but there was no mistaking him, not for a second.

Carly had about run out to Dan then and there. Just bolting across the street, dodging traffic, calling for him that she was here, that there'd been an accident or a mistake or something. She'd go up to him, pull him around, and…that's when something had pinged in the back of her mind…a memory from before…

She'd gone to *him* that day…however many months ago it was at this point. But instead of meeting her at the door, she'd had to go looking, and when she'd found him…the flash…had he known? It didn't seem possible, but she'd been wrong about him before.

Instead of running, Carly had stayed right where she was across the street, watching Dan laugh and carry on.

For her, the past months had been lonely, confusing, and terrifying. How she'd kept her shit together enough to survive was anyone's guess; sheer force of will and luck probably. Every day she woke up was like a weird, almost-nightmare where just getting out of the bed she'd managed to rent was a sheer act of defiance…and here he was, smiling, joking around with friends…happy, seemingly without a care in the world…

Blood had begun to rush in her ears, blocking out the sound of life going on all around her. She'd clenched her fists and started to walk.

But she'd no more than taken a step in that direction when Dan and the other guy slipped into the blue Ford, backed up, and just as she'd decided she'd make a run for it…took off, disappearing around the corner. Carly could only stand there with her resentment and her building rage, wondering how long it'd be til she got her next opportunity to make him explain and answer for every single thing he'd done to her. She'd thought that might be some time…until today, that was.

Deciding to give the fair a pass…more happy, smiling faces than she thought she could take at the moment, she'd decided to go out for a stroll past her family's farm before work. Even though no one there would have the slightest idea who she was if she'd introduced herself, there was a weird sort of comfort to the act, and she was grateful for that much.

While walking on the side of the road away from the farm, she'd seen that same blue Ford again. Dan wasn't in the car this time, but it was enough that she'd recognized this guy. Carly watched from a little way away as he pulled into the dairy and disappeared. With only the slimmest idea of what she'd meant to say, she found herself hurrying to follow.

"You've got a friend, a guy named Dan Parker," Carly had whispered under her breath as she'd followed the gravel lane up, "you tell him I need to talk to him right now. Better yet, you bring me to him."

It sounded okay…a place to start anyway, but as soon as she'd gotten up the hill toward the house, sounds came to her from one of the open windows, and she knew she might have to wait a while. Carly had considered just knocking on the door anyway to interrupt the screw fest going on inside, but instead sat on a nearby bench. And once the giggles and moans became too much, she decided to walk toward the small shed and have a closer look at the Ford.

She'd tried one of the doors, and it'd opened at once, because why not? One of the things she'd learned since being stranded here was that people rarely locked anything. Looking around to make sure that no one was looking, thinking that this might be a better place to wait away from the noise, she slid inside.

Carly had sat there in the passenger seat for a long time, thinking about opening the books just to have something to do while she waited, but decided against it. Light was fading for one thing, and for another, she was rarely, if ever, a reader. And on the rare occasion she did pick up a book, murder mysteries were never her first choice.

But she did stare for a long time at the name on the receipt. Just seeing his signature caused the anger still burning hot inside her from yesterday to grow even more.

"He's got a nice, cozy little job. What's next? A house and a wife with a stupid little dog out back?"

It didn't seem possible. They had to have been blasted back here at the same time, but who knows? Maybe he'd been here a lot longer than her. Enough to find a happy little job and some happy little friends…

Carly had taken out her phone, remembered that it didn't really do much anymore, and slipped it back into the pocket of her dress. Instead, she started looking around inside the Ford, not that there was much to look at. Inside the glove box, she found something interesting…a razor that looked like something straight out of Sweeney Todd with "D.M.P." etched into the handle.

She stared at it for a long time in the dying light, first at the initials, then flipping it open, at the blade itself.

Happy little job, happy little friends…happy little life…you shouldn't get to be happy after everything you've done…

A single thought began to kindle somewhere deep down inside her. Slow and dull at first, then it began to burn hotter and more intensely with each passing second, scaring her. Carly tried to push the thought away, but found she couldn't.

It was crazy, and it was wrong. And under normal circumstances where things weren't so desperately hopeless, Carly wouldn't have dared think about it…immorality aside, her entire career cried out against it.

But these weren't normal circumstances…and thanks to him, that bastard, she would never see normal circumstances again…this is what he deserves…

Carly stood, wiping her mouth on her shoulder, breathing in air both sour and fresh. She could feel the warm blood on her fingers, only just beginning to go cold. Her heart whammed in her chest, and she felt it absolutely everywhere, like the runner's high of runners' highs.

There was guilt, yes. Part of her wanted to get down on her knees and weep for what she'd done. But there was this other feeling too. And for everything he'd done to her, Carly felt in some way she owed Dan at least a small thank you. Because if normal life had gone on, she'd have never known this feeling now creeping its way across her entire being.

Looking through the Ford's front window, seeing the driver slumped over, Carly noticed something…there was a little less remorse than had been there even a minute or so ago. But she still had it, plenty of it, she wasn't a monster…she wasn't a monster…

Carly looked down at the razor still clutched in her bloody hand, and her grip tightened around it as she walked back toward the car.

There were no forensics these days, she was pretty sure…not like, CSI stuff anyway, but she knew well enough that fingerprints were still a thing. And so, she wiped the handle against the bottom of her dress, then tossed the razor back on the pile of books, sending everything skidding to the floor. She hiked up the hem of her dress, wiping everywhere she might've touched.

As she worked, Carly also brought out her phone, recording herself as she worked. Because later on, when this high abandoned her as they all eventually do, she'd for sure begin to panic and would need some way to reassure herself that she'd gotten everything.

In the light coming through the windshield, courtesy of the pole that could've been her death warrant, she looked up to see the head now leaning back against the seat. Her gaze flicked down to what little white there was left on the shirt, the wide-open mouth running underneath his jaw, the eyes pinned closed from broken glass.

Without a conscious reason why, Carly moved her phone up from the glove box and onto the man. She panned around, getting the now lifeless hands before slowly making her way up. Doing this made her want to cry or throw up again, but still she continued, feeling helpless to stop. Carly got out, moving around the driver's side, the camera never leaving him.

Why are you doing this? You're going to get caught.

Maybe it was all her senses alive and firing, maybe it was the sickening thrill she was starting to feel underneath all the guilt and horror at what she'd done, but Carly thought that considering the initials on the razor and the name on the book receipt, the cops might be more interested in someone else…

This is wrong! You know this is wrong! My God, can you even think right now? What if he could help you, what if—

The voice was right…maybe. But this, this was right too. Leaving Dan helpless, clueless, and mourning at the loss of a friend would certainly put a dent in his happy little life. But even better, if he was suspected, well, that'd ruin a lot more…his reputation, any other relationships he had these days probably because in the back of their minds, they'd always be wondering…all those dominos toppling with a single flick… that'd wipe the smile off his face for good and maybe then they'd be even.

A door opened, spilling out light from inside the house, and Carly jerked up, shoving her phone in her pocket. The lonely housewife that this guy had been screwing senseless not long ago stood in the doorway.

"Jack? Jack, are you still…oh, oh dear sweet Jesus!"

Over the years of being a nurse, Carly found there was a sort of calm reserve she could draw on when things got stressful, and she tapped into it.

Putting on her best, most professional "everything's under control" voice, Carly began to speak, deciding to throw in one real kicker at the last minute, just to really help things along.

When she was done, Carly braced for a scream, and that's exactly what she got…shrill and piercing. She made a move forward, meaning to try to calm her down, when the woman fainted and collapsed in the doorway.

Carly walked over to where she'd dropped, bent down, and putting her clean hand to the woman's neck, looked at her watch, checking the pulse. The heartbeat was slow, but steady. She hadn't heard anything hit on the way down, and she didn't see any blood.

Looking up into the kitchen, Carly saw a phone, made to go call the cops, but stopped herself. First reason, 911 wasn't a thing yet, and she didn't know the right number to call for help. Second, there'd be questions, and she most certainly had no interest in answering questions.

What if she comes to and spills her guts to the cops?

That seemed possible, even likely, but somehow, she didn't think that's how this would work out.

It was dark for one thing. And for another, the woman would most likely be sort of vague and fuzzy for a while when she finally came around again…Carly thought the chances might be good that she herself would end up being not much more than a dream or maybe written off as a hallucination in the woman's mind.

No, what was going to happen was in an hour or two, this woman would probably come around with a nasty headache, run for the phone, and then call the cops herself. No one would ever know that she, Carly, was here at all. Anyone even half paying attention would think of someone else before they thought of her…and he deserves it…

And if you're wrong? If someone else is in that house watching and waiting til you leave to call the cops, or if that woman remembers a lot more than you think she's going to? What then?

Carly thought for a moment, not liking the answer that came, but accepting it all the same. If men were waiting at her place, or at the hospital where she used to work once upon a time and where she'd managed to bullshit her way into some steady work nowadays, she'd get hold of a scalpel and slash her wrists before anyone could get cuffs over them…game over.

You're insane.

With that, Carly stepped over the unconscious woman in the doorway, washed her hands in the kitchen sink, careful to then wipe down anything she'd touched before heading back out into the night. She made the long walk back down the lane, turned left onto the road, and continued her walk, looking up at the bright, twinkling stars that'd just started to come out.

Chapter Twelve

After finishing the lap around the fairgrounds, checking out the booths and the games, looking in at the show barns, and sitting down near the entrance with what were some unfortunately mediocre hotdogs…Jack still not having shown, Lucy suggested they pull the pin on the whole thing, and Dan agreed. Whatever had Jack held up, he wouldn't be making it tonight.

During the short walk back into town, still chatting away like they'd only been together a few minutes at this point instead of a few hours, Dan thought about how the night had gone from him being a willing third wheel to Lucy's…well, date.

It should've made him uncomfortable; best friend's girl and all that, and it did. But it was still hard to be anything other than sort of glad at the way the night had turned out. Being with her just felt…nice. Though, to his credit, he'd been doing his best to keep thoughts like that shoved way back in his mind. The new plan was that they'd head to Bill's, where Lucy's car still sat parked out back, and grab a quick dessert. He'd catch a ride home if it were offered, then she'd go home, and that would be the end of it.

Seeing the place now, though, Dan wasn't so sure about dessert. The parking lot, which had been nearly abandoned earlier, was now so full that people were street parking at least a block down, then swarming on Bill's like a horde of zombies.

"My goodness," Lucy said, as they came to a stop just before the gravel, letting clumps of people walk around them.

"No kidding."

The line to get in had made it all the way down the steps, and more than halfway into the parking lot, the front door was propped open with a large rock.

"Do we chance it?" Dan said, turning to Lucy, who stood arms crossed, looking straight ahead.

"I think we'd get sat in about an hour…maybe. Well, you would anyhow. They'd haul me in the back, pull a yellow dress over my head, and shove me back into the crowd to take orders."

Between the growing line and the people, he could see through the window packed in like sardines; he thought that was probably just about right.

"We should back away slowly," Dan said, grinning. "Before someone spots you out the window."

"What about my car?' she said, turning toward him, those blue eyes fixed on his.

"We could walk," Dan said. "My place and Harrington House aren't terribly far away, so it shouldn't be too bad."

"Speak for yourself, mister. I've had just about all the walking a girl can take in these shoes."

"Okay, fair. After you, then."

They started to move, but only managed a few steps before Lucy stopped. He'd turned, meaning to ask what was up, but she spared him the trouble.

"Wait…I bet you anything Elmer has that kitchen door propped open tonight, and I'm parked right next to it. Oh, shoot…"

He continued to watch the swarm of diners, both current and hopeful, when Lucy started giggling and digging around in her purse. She pulled out a small key ring and held it out to him.

"Feel like being sneaky for me?"

Dan looked at the keys, grinning, and took them.

"Meet you out on the corner of Clay and Main," she said, tipping him a wink, hurrying away back down the sidewalk.

Jingling the keys in his hand, he started to move toward the left of the diner, slipping past the chattering, excited people who seemed too busy to notice he wasn't joining the line. Which was fine by him, because in his mind, the world had just gone widescreen…

He wore sunglasses and an expensive suit, constantly checking that he'd shaken whoever had been tailing him since that swanky nightclub a few blocks back. The keys in his hand were for a top-of-the-line Porsche, with a few…special additions. Submachine guns under the hood, bulletproof body panels, a jet engine turbo booster…

Relax O-O-Dumbass.

Dan shook the fantasy from his mind, still smiling in spite of it, and found himself already around the back of the diner and staring at the front of a gorgeous machine, shining in what little light was left in the sky. A 1940 Buick Special. Burgundy red with whitewall tires, a massive steel grill, and suicide doors. Like something a guy named 'Jimmy the Rat' would burst out of, his Tommy gun spewing hot lead.

Off to the right, Dan saw an orange square of light on the ground from the open door. He heard the sizzle of the grill, the moving of cookware, and a deep rumble of collective voices from the place. He thought the noise might be enough to cover him creeping around, but he took it slow anyway.

Dan moved along the passenger side of the Buick, around the rear, and back up toward the driver's side door. The smells of short-order fried goodness hit him hard, and he wondered half-joking if his grumbling stomach might give him away. Dan pulled the door open, hopped inside, and closed it as quietly as he could with a dull clunk.

He slipped the key into the ignition, and the V8 under the hood roared into life. He reached for the seatbelt, remembered that there wasn't one, and instead grabbed the gearshift and dropped the thing into Reverse, hoping that the engine wouldn't make too much noise if he just idled and let the thing roll back.

But he'd no sooner hit the brake, cranked down the window, and slipped the Buick into first when he heard a loud, bellowing yell.

"Parker!"

It was Elmer, his massive frame blocking most of the light coming from the back door. Dan froze, his foot still resting on the brake, more caught off guard by the fact that Elmer knew his name more than anything else.

"Yessir?" he said, leaning his head out the window.

"She in there?" Elmer said, pointing a meaty finger at the Buick.

"No, sir," he said, then added, "she's gone home early, something about her feet hurting. I'm picking this up as a sort of favor."

"Great, it's the end of days in here, and she's cozy with her feet up and – "

Over the still steady rumble of the crowd came a clash that sounded like something heavy falling in the kitchen. Elmer turned away. Not wanting to get caught in this conversation any longer than he had already, Dan let off the brake, then floored it out of the back lot.

The Buick bounced on its radial tires as it went from gravel to pavement, and Dan made a hard right, not wanting to risk looking back. He felt a wide grin that felt like it'd just split his face from ear to ear. This was fun, doing something stupid for a girl…it made him feel like he was seventeen again.

Another turn, then he saw Lucy standing under a streetlight, hands on her hips. He slowed and pulled up to the curb.

"Did I just hear…"

"Oh yeah," Dan said, laughing. "And he's pissed."

Reaching across the seat, he popped the passenger door open, and Lucy slid in.

"Well, g-go!" she said, pushing him on the shoulder, now starting to laugh herself.

Grinning so hard now that it'd started to hurt, Dan got them rolling, deciding at the last minute to really put the pedal down, then hanging a hard left onto Main Street. Tires squealed, and Lucy half-screamed, half-laughed, as she began to slide toward the middle of the seat.

"Stop," she said between giggles, "before you get the cops after us!"

"You mean you're not up for a car chase?" Dan said, laughing, dropping the beast back down to the speed limit. "We never did get that dessert."

"No, no, we didn't."

That's a shame, he thought, then forced that thought back where all its buddies had been hanging out most of the night.

What made that feeling all the worse was that he and Lucy had been vibing off each other all night, and he liked it, shitty as it made him feel.

Dan thought about Jack saying earlier about how he'd help him get into some trouble with a beautiful dame tonight, and the irony wasn't lost on him that Jack might've done the job after all…just a little differently than he'd probably meant to.

All the more reason to call it a night.

Chapter Thirteen

Martha Burke sat behind her desk, feet propped up, and a Life magazine in her hand that she was only barely interested in. She could just kick herself for not bringing a good book or four, and good ol' Duke Ellington on the radio wasn't helping much either. The tune was good, but slow, and she was fighting with her eyelids to stay awake.

She flipped idly through the pages for what had to be at least the third time, not really seeing them anymore, then closed it. It might be time to get up and wander around, see if there was anything decent in the place to read, though, with these boys, she doubted that "decent" would—

The sound of squealing tires split the stillness, and Martha looked up. Through the glass door leading out onto the street, reading "Kent Co. Sheriff's Office', Martha saw a car whiz by. Quick as she could, she tossed the magazine on her desk, hurried over to the door, and opened it, peeking out.

Down the street, she saw a reddish Buick, or maybe it was a Lincoln, headed down Main. And just as fast as it'd come, it'd disappeared into the darkness where the streetlights ended.

"What the hell was that?"

Eddie was standing just behind her, coffee cup in hand, and looking like he'd just been freshly turned out of bed, which he probably had been. About an hour ago, he said he'd be in the file room, "reviewing records", which was just these boys' code for taking a nap in that old, worn-out armchair that'd been shoved into a corner next to a few rusty filing cabinets.

"One of the Amish put a big Cadillac engine in a buggy…sure was something to see. Enjoy your rest?'

"I…did you get a plate number?"

"Do you see a badge pinned to my blouse?"

Martha shut the door and walked back to her desk, picking up Life again out of habit before letting it fall back where it'd been. Eddie joined her, leaning on the edge of her desk, sipping his coffee. The song changed to something with a little more spring in its step.

"Did your little walk around the fairgrounds wear you out so bad?"

"No, not too bad. Just been sleepin' a little rough is all. I swear, those cell bunks are comfier than that bed in my new place."

"Better get that fixed before you, you know, have yourself some company," Martha said, giving him a gentle knock with her shoe.

"Yeah," he said, with a laugh and a reddening of the cheeks.

Honestly, she really liked Eddie. He was funny, not bad to look at, and kind. The boys all loved him and had taken to calling him Sheriff whenever Buck wasn't around. But he went a little strange a few months ago, and that's when she'd noticed a thin, pale line where a gold wedding band had been.

He wouldn't say much about it to her, or to anyone else, she supposed. She could find out more if she wanted to. Momma and Aunt Sally cut the hair of just about every woman in town, and it'd only take a word for them to start putting their feelers out. That is, if one or both of them didn't know already. But it'd be a no-good, dirty thing to do to such a nice man who seemed to be doing his best to move on, even if he was still carrying a torch for Penny.

The music filling the empty station changed to something a bit more snappy. Eddie reached for the radio dial, then hesitated, looking at her.

"You mind if I turn this up? I'm a big Benny Goodman fan."

"You're the boss," she said, smiling, as the sound of clarinets filled the room.

They sat that way for a spell, Eddie drinking his coffee, both of them listening to the music. One song gave way to another, and Martha had an idea.

"About your place," she said, 'if you can't do much about the bed right now, you may wanna- "

Brrrinnngg!

Martha turned away from him at once, and off to her right, moving the radio microphone out of the way, and grabbing up the handset to the telephone.

"Kent County Sheriff's Office, this is Martha. How can I help you?"

No one spoke at first, and for a long moment, there was only the sound of screams. She'd been about to repeat herself and ask if things were all right when the screams faded away, and a clear voice came on the line.

"This is Bill Crawford, ma'am, out at Field Spring Road, the farm next to Sherbrooke Dairy."

"What can I do for you, Mr. Crawford?' she said, reaching for a pen and paper as Eddie moved close behind her.

"Well, ma'am, I can't say. About, well, ten minutes or so ago, I guess, there was a banging at my door. I opened it, and my neighbor, a Mrs. Sherbrooke, burst right in screaming and carryin' on."

"I see," she said, writing as fast and clear as she could. "Is she hurt? Is there anythin' she's said, or—"

"No ma'am, I don't think so, and no, can't get two straight words out of her. Bottom of her skirt is caked in mud, same as her bare feet, and I'm guessin' she ran the whole way here through the fields. Damned if I know what happened out at her place to get her out like this."

Martha scribbled out a few more words, then put the pen down.

"Thank you, sir. We'll send someone out to the dairy, and someone with an ambulance will be along to collect Mrs. Sherbrooke and take her to Price Memorial. Are y'all safe in the house?"

"Yes, ma'am, got a loaded scatter gun in my hand right now."

"Very good, Mr. Crawford, someone will be out soon."

She put the receiver down and turned to Eddie, all traces of sleepiness in his face gone.

"Remind me who's all out tonight," he said, and Martha checked her notes.

"Will and Bart are still at the fairgrounds. Let's see…Colin and Glenn headed out to the Broken Wheel about an hour ago. That leaves…"

"Perry and Alan,' he said, sighing and running a hand through his hair. "Call 'em both up and tell them to meet me out at Sherbrooke's place. Pull Will and Bart…maybe just Bart…and send him to the Crawfords."

"What about the Sheriff?"

"Wait till we find out what's goin' on first. I don't wanna catch hell waking him up if it turns out to be nothin'."

Martha turned back toward her desk, adjusted the radio controls, and got to work.

Chapter Fourteen

Dan drove. First out of downtown, then into the residential area among the colonials, craftsman bungalows, Depression-era tract housing, and everything in between. He took odd ways and backroads, windows rolled down, just enjoying the night.

You're only making it worse.

He knew it was true. Sooner or later, the date…*day*, would have to end. Time to quit playing pretend that it wouldn't.

They'd ended up doing a wide loop around the outskirts, driving along the hard-pack dirt roads in the rural parts of town. It took Dan a minute to get his bearings again, and once he had, he started heading back.

Lucy, who'd been in the middle of telling him about the new job she'd be starting at the New Chapel High School library in a few weeks, stopped mid-sentence.

"Everything all right?"

"Oh, yeah," he said, not realizing he'd been spacing out, yet not at all surprised. Seemed like he'd been doing that all freaking day. "Sorry, woolgathering."

"It is starting to get late," she said, checking her watch in the dim light of the dashboard. "Are you getting too tired to find your way home, or were you just bein' sweet so I could finish my story?"

He'd been about to open his mouth to tell her it was a little of both when red flashing lights caught his eye in the rear-view mirror, and he stopped. They seemed to get closer, and as they did, Dan started to pick up on the faint but growing sound of whirring sirens.

"What in the world?" Lucy said, turning to look directly out behind them.

The sirens continued to grow louder, the flashing red lights looking bigger by the second. Dan pulled the Buick to the side of the road just in time for a big, white Cadillac ambulance to flash past them. Then, as soon as it'd come, it'd started to disappear. Taillights fading into the distance, the wail of the siren growing faint.

"Wonder what that's all about," Dan said.

"Whoever's hurt, I hope they'll be all right," Lucy said.

Dan agreed and got them moving again. A few turns and a few minutes later, they'd left the farmland behind and were turning onto Eastbridge Road, then, finally, bringing the Buick to a stop in the driveway of his house. A two-story Sears kit home from the twenties, painted a shade of yellow he still couldn't decide if he liked or not.

"Here we are," he said, killing the engine and handing the keys over to Lucy.

Looking at her, a stream of post-date cliches ran through his mind… *"I had a really great time with you tonight,"* and *"We should really do this again. When are you free?"* were among some of the gems, and he shook them out of his mind.

"Tonight was really nice," he said, then mentally facepalmed.

"It was," she said, smiling, tucking a loose strand of hair behind her ear. "Nicer than I thought it was gonna be."

Dan smiled back, shifting a little in his seat.

Neither of them spoke for a long moment, and he gradually became aware that they were closer on the bench seat than they'd been when he'd pulled in the driveway—pretty sure anyway. But whether he'd moved or she had, Dan didn't know. Alarm bells were beginning to sound in the back of his mind, letting him know he was dangerously close to getting in real trouble.

"I should probably go," Lucy said, her voice soft, turning the car key over in her hand. "It's getting late and, well…I should be getting back."

"That's probably a good idea," Dan said, clearing his throat a little. "I'm sure one of us will be hearing from Jack soon. Hate to keep him waiting."

"Sure," Lucy said, then gave a small laugh that didn't quite reach her eyes. "I wonder what his excuse will be this time. You know it's not exactly the first time he's pulled a disappearing act like this."

"I'm sure he just got caught up talking or found a few other things to fix. He's probably at Harrington House right now with a bunch of flowers he grabbed out of someone's garden, just waiting to apologize. You know how he is."

"Yes," Lucy said, sighing, "yes, I really do, but…Danny? Can I…can I tell you something?"

He had a pretty decent idea of what this might be and knew that the thing to do now was pull back. Say that, yes, she could tell him something, but that it'd have to be quick because he was beat and wanted to go to bed. It'd hurt her at a time when she was clearly already hurting…probably more so than he'd thought earlier at Bill's, but still, his hands were tied.

"Of course," he said. "You know you can tell me anything."

Lucy nodded and smiled again, her eyes shining—tears sitting on the edge, but not falling.

"Today, with you…this has been the best time that I've had in longer than I can remember. And it's made me realize things…clarified some things for me, I guess you'd say. Things I've thought about for some time now, but…"

Her voice cracked a little, and she looked at him full in the face, her blue eyes fixed firmly on his.

Dan wanted to speak, but didn't know exactly what to say. It felt like anything he said now could only ruin the moment. And as the alarm bells in his head began to fade, replaced instead with the thoughts and feelings about her he'd been shoving into the back of his head all night…and longer if he was being honest, Dan realized with both unease and peace that the last thing he wanted to do was ruin the moment.

"I know I shouldn't be saying any of this…especially not here, of all places, when we're alone. But there are things that I can't…that I don't *want* to keep to myself anymore: Danny, I like you. Being around you feels safe, like nothing I've ever known before. You're funny, you make me feel like I matter and that I can be myself, and that's such a rare thing. And Jack, he…,"

Lucy shook her head and sighed. "That doesn't matter. I know that this doesn't make things simple, and if you're upset with me for saying something, I understand. I just, I couldn't stand biting my tongue another minute."

Another shift, and they were now nearly nose to nose. Dan felt the warmth of her breath on him. Neither of them looked away.

"Lucy, I—"

He saw Lucy's lips part slightly. Whether to steady her breathing or say something else, Dan didn't know. Before he'd gotten the chance to find out, he'd closed what little distance there was between them, pressing his mouth to hers.

Her kiss was warm and sweet…everything he'd thought it might be over the past two years when her eye would catch his for an extra second or two and his mind would wander more than it probably should've. He loved Jack like a brother, but that didn't make Dan feel any different about her.

Still, it felt like there were only a matter of seconds before the spell would be broken, and he knew it. Despite everything she'd said, she might pull away, shrink to the other side of the car, and ask him to leave. Or, much more likely given how well he knew her, she'd push him away, call him a low-life creep, and how dare he make a move like that, and he must have some nerve. Then, maybe haul off and smack him across the face for good measure.

If that's what it came to, it'd be well-deserved, and Dan would take whatever rebuttal, refusal, or punishment came. But as the seconds passed, it seemed like things wouldn't be going that way…

Instead, Lucy moved closer, softly pressing her body against his. She took his hand, then pressed it against her waist before slowly wrapping both arms around his neck, silencing the last of the alarm bells in his head for good.

Away in the distance, however, the sound of sirens started again.

Chapter Fifteen

"C'mon, keep it together," Eddie Prescott said, praying that Unit 2's worn-out suspension and bald tires would hold as he bounced along the rutted dirt back roads on the way to the Sherbrooke place. Dark had come on full, but he could see red flashing lights just ahead on a small rise…two sets of them. One set was his boys, the other from that big, white Cadillac out of Price Memorial Hospital in Harlan Heights.

After hearing that telephone call from Crawford and starting to move his chess pieces around, he'd hoped that Dorothy Sherbrooke might have just had a bad fright and gone into hysterics over nothing. But before he'd taken two steps toward the station door with that comforting idea, there was a buzz and crackle from the radio, then Alan's voice.

"Boss? It's Alan, come back."

"You got me, hun," Martha said. "Go ahead."

"We got a stiff up here."

Eddie slowed Unit 2, swinging it into the gravel drive. His headlights picked up Perry Wilcox, a rookie in the truest sense of the word, leaning against the dairy's mailbox, and looking like he wasn't quite sure where he was. He brought Unit 2 to a stop, then cranked the window down. Perry stepped closer, shoving nervous hands into his pocket.

"How's it lookin' up there, kid?"

"Not, not good, s-sir. There's a Ford Victoria up there in one of the sheds; the victim is still inside, last I saw. Boys driving the meat wagon are waitin' on you before they move him. The man, he's…"

Perry trailed off, averting his eyes, his mouth looking like he'd just taken a bite out of a lemon.

"Is it Dick Sherbrooke?"

Eddie knew him, and thanks to a few calls down to the Broken Wheel on account of the man's behavior, he didn't have a high opinion. Dick was a mean bastard on a good day, and booze only made it worse. God only knew what went on behind his and his missus' closed doors, but Eddie thought he could guess well enough. And if Dorothy Sherbrooke had stopped that man's clock for good, well, after they got her into a cell, he'd see that she had a fine steak dinner.

"No, it ain't him," Perry said. "I'd say the man looks familiar, but his face…it's hard to tell."

"Probably have to move him around to find a wallet," Eddie said. "Either of you boys call Martha with the plate number, try to raise the Sheriff?"

"Not while I was up there, but I heard Alan get on the radio just before you pulled in, could be he's doin' that now."

"Could be you're right," Eddie said, then stepped out of the car, leaving the door open and the engine running. "Here, Perry, hop in. And park this thing across the lane. If anyone shows up that ain't one of us, Doc Horton, or Sheriff Buck, radio up or blast the horn, got it? Hand me that flashlight of yours, too, so I don't trip and break my neck…last thing we need is another stiff."

Perry did, relief spreading over his young, round face. Eddie clicked on the flashlight and continued on foot. There were voices and pops of static, and Eddie guessed that Alan was indeed making all the necessary call-ins.

He liked Alan. True, he was only a kid, just a few years older than Perry, but he was sharp and confident. Not like a cocky little twerp too big for his britches…for the most part. But more possessed of the assuredness that comes from a man doing the thing he knows deep down he's built to do. Eddie thought it'd only be a matter of time before Alan rose through the ranks and started eying his spot.

Eh, let him have it.

Eddie only had the job because he'd been nominated against his will…sort of an everyone stepping back and pushing him forward situation after his predecessor had decided to pull the pin. Sure, the pay was decent, and he liked the respect he got around town, but the being in charge part of it could go take a walk. He could do that part well, but that didn't mean he much liked it. Or maybe it just all felt that way because it's hard to be excited about what you do when no one is around to hear about it at the end of the day.

A minute, maybe two, passed before he crested the hill and started on level ground. He saw the ambulance off to the left parked next to the house, arms out the rolled down front windows, flicking cigarette ash. Its headlights were on and pointing at a steel blue Ford Victoria, a shadow man just visible inside.

Off to the right, he saw Alan sitting in Unit 3, leaning over to rack the mic. Eddie showed his light in and held it there.

"You been drinkin' tonight, sir?" Eddie said, desperate for a little humor.

"Wish I had been," Alan said, sitting up and shielding his eyes. "But you can just blind me with that thing, that'd be fine too."

Eddie clicked off the light and leaned against Unit 3, staring at the Ford. Alan stepped out and stood beside him.

"Where's Doc Horton?", Eddie said.

"Out of town visiting his wife's folks. The hospital put us in touch with him. He should be here before too long. Said he wouldn't bother with the county wagon, he'd just take his personal straight here."

"Anyone raise Buck yet?"

"Yeah, thought he'd be passed out at The Wheel, but I guess he's stuck sick at home. His wife won't even let him use the telephone, let alone get out of bed. I said we had a body, she said she didn't care if we had ten…it's all you, boss."

"Alright, guess let's have a look."

And what a look it turned out to be.

The face was reddish brown with blood that'd already started to dry, same as the formerly white shirt. Shards of glass were embedded in the eyes, nose, and left cheek. Bent gold wire that'd been eyeglasses not long ago hung down the sides of the face. And, angling his flashlight to get a better look at a sight he'd rather not be seeing, Eddie noticed the long, dark slash under the jawline, pulled slightly open by the tilted back head, and looking like a second mouth.

Fighting his gorge, Eddie looked on as Alan moved to the passenger door and pulled it open. The dome light clicked on, shedding more light on the scene, and, wait…he knew this face, he guessed he could be wrong, only…no.

"Over here, boss," Alan said. "There's somethin' else, something I found after Perry headed back down. Not the wallet, but—"

"It's Jack Lawrence."

He looked up, meeting Alan's questioning look.

"I saw his girl," Eddie said, trying to keep himself calm. "Lucy. And that bookstore clerk he goes around with, Parker, is out at the fairgrounds. They said he was out on a work call in Harlan Heights, fixin' some old lady's sink."

"Just a guess here, but I think he was more interested in takin' care of Mrs. Sherbrooke's pipes tonight," Alan said. "I can call Sullivan's Hardware, see when they sent him out, and try to see when he might've made it here, but there's somethin' else."

Alan was bent down, hands on knees, staring at the floorboard. Feeling light-headed and like he still might lose that hamburger dinner he'd grabbed while doing his rounds earlier, Eddie walked over to the passenger side, happy to have some distance between himself and the awful sight in the front seat.

He bent down next to Alan, training his flashlight on where the kid had been looking. On the floorboard, he saw two books, both of which looked like murder mysteries by that Christie woman. Sticking out of one, he saw a receipt from Walker's Fine Books for the order, signed by a Mr. Dan Parker. Next to those, he saw a straight razor caked in blood.

Beep! Beep-beep, beep!

Chapter Sixteen

"Ma'am? M-ma'am, you aren't supposed to go up there."

"It's alright, Perry, won't be a minute."

Penny stepped around the black and white blocking her way, then began the walk up the gravel drive of Sherbrooke Dairy, slowly, and wishing she'd thought to pull on better shoes before heading out the door. Whatever she thought might've come from turning on that old radio of Eddie's, not long after getting back from the fairgrounds, this certainly wasn't it.

Back when they'd been together, he'd tinkered with the thing to pick up the police chatter so she could listen in and maybe not worry about him so much. She couldn't say just what possessed her to turn the thing on tonight except that she'd been tired of the radio but didn't feel like only hearing the clack-clack of her typewriter as she worked either.

Snippets of conversation had come through the static, mostly in one ear and out the other, as she'd sat typing away. There'd been something about Sherbrooke Dairy, but she hadn't thought much about it until the static broke again and another voice…Alan's, but she couldn't be sure, said "we got a stiff", and that'd gotten her attention.

She'd stood then, leaving her lead sentence about how Ruthie Crispin stunned the judges by abandoning her award-winning rhubarb pie and going for blueberry this year, unfinished. Then, pulling back on her shoes and slipping her notebook, pen, and press badge back into her handbag, she'd set off.

Now halfway up the small rise, Penny heard a few small blasts on a car horn but didn't turn around.

All around, she could hear the wind rustling through the fields, crickets chirping in the tall grass, and the sounds of men's voices and radio static up ahead. That last unnerved her a little…a perversion of the otherwise sweet stillness around her, but she steeled herself all the same.

New Chapel wasn't the sort of place where ambulances and police were out at the same time of night, which meant that something big had happened. And for the moment at least, she was the only reporter around. The fact that she'd stumbled onto the chance to do something besides puff-piece editorials thrilled her, and a mixture of dread and excitement washed over her as she crested the hill and got her first good look at the scene.

The boys driving the ambulance out of Harlan Heights tonight were leaning up against that imposing white thing, smoking and talking amongst themselves. They paused when she passed, giving her a look before going back to their talk. Just up ahead, two men were walking toward her. One was Alan, and her guess about him being who she'd heard over the radio seemed to be right on the money, and the other was Eddie.

She and Eddie locked eyes, and Penny remembered the last time they'd been together in the same place…at the courthouse downtown, signing the paperwork that'd made their divorce final.

"Evening, boys," she said, pushing that thought out of her mind, and trying to sound like they were doing nothing more than passing the time of day on the street instead of meeting at a crime scene.

"Ah, geez," Alan said. "I oughta skin that kid down there; what're you doing here, Penny?"

"Seems like there's a commotion goin' on tonight, came to see what it is, get a few statements, things like that."

Her gaze found Eddie again and held. A slight tilt of the head and a cocked eyebrow was as good as if he'd asked the question out loud, and Penny nodded.

"Well, I don't—"

"Relax, Alan, let the scoop hound through," Eddie said. "Probably better to have someone here to get the story straight from the start."

What a change in attitude, Eddie…don't I remember you sayin' something months back about how my job was just a cute little hobby?

That night…the last night, had been bad, and Penny didn't like to think too much about it if she could help it. It was the sort of thing where two people get to fighting so that they don't hear each other anymore, and they start saying whatever pops into their mind, whether they mean it or not.

They'd fought like that off and on for some years. They'd rushed into getting married before he'd deployed to England back in '43, and in '45 when he'd come back, it hadn't taken long to realize that maybe they weren't the best fit for one another, though she'd certainly tried.

But after he'd said what he did, and her meaning to give a slap that instead had turned into something like a right hook, well, it was obvious that'd been it for both of them. What was worse, Penny thought the whole thing had started because she'd asked him to take out the garbage and he didn't empty the bathroom can on his way out…ain't life funny.

It'd certainly thrown her off tonight, getting support from Eddie instead of indifference or outright hostility, but she found her stride again quick. Penny reached into her handbag, then pulled out her press badge, showing it to Alan.

"All official and everything, officer," she said, tipping him a wink before slipping it back in her bag, and out of the corner of her eye, she saw Eddie look away, smirking.

"I thought you only did women's bake club sales, kittens getting pulled out of trees, that sort of thing," Alan said.

"I'm branching out. So, what's the story up here? Someone go for a ride in the milk bottling machinery?"

"I wish it were that simple," Eddie said, and Penny noticed for the first time what looked like a blue Ford spotlighted in the headlights of the ambulance, a figure she couldn't quite see slumped behind the wheel.

"Alan, go radio in and see how they're making out at the Crawford place."

"Boss?"

"See if they need that white car to take Mrs. Sherbrooke over to Price after all, or if she can ride in Bart's car."

Alan looked between the two of them, wanting to say something, perhaps a little more direct, by the set of that brow, but didn't.

"Yessir, I'll also see where—"

The three of them turned, seeing another pair of headlights come up the drive. Penny thought the kid down there might've found his nerve and decided to try to take her back down in style, but instead, she saw a dark green Chevrolet emerge from the darkness, coming to a stop next to one of the barns further away.

"That was fast," Alan said, then walked over toward the newcomer. A tall, sandy-haired man in his shirt sleeves got out carrying a large, black bag and a camera around his neck. He waved over at them, then stood talking to Alan.

"Forgot about that old radio," Eddie said, his voice low. "Picked a hell of a night to mess with it."

"I'll say. I'm surprised you didn't turn me away at the door."

"Can't say I exactly like the thought of you bein' here, but you're the first writer to come sniffin' around, so I guess that's your right."

Penny turned toward the shadow figure behind the wheel of the Ford again…the stiff.

"Who is it, Eddie?"

"Geez," he said, letting the word out in one long sigh. "We haven't moved him to get at his wallet yet, but that's just a formality. I know the face. It's Jack Lawrence, that fella who works up at Sullivan's Hardware in town."

Penny turned again at the sound of footsteps, then watched Perry and the newcomer walk over to the ambulance and exchange a word or two with those boys before heading their way.

"What happened?"

"Let's wait, I don't wanna explain myself twice…once is gonna be hard enough as it is," Eddie said, then took a few steps forward, hand outstretched. "Evenin' doc, sorry to pull you away like this." The other man reached out and shook.

Penny had only met Dr. Adam Horton a few times before, but generally found him to be a very pleasant sort of man. Despite the nature of his work, or maybe because of it, there was always an ease and humor with him.

"It's what they pay me the big bucks for," Dr. Horton said, putting a cigarette in his mouth and striking a match. "Besides, my assistant Art is stuck in some hospital up in Maine. Damn fool climbed up on some rocks to get a picture, slipped, and went right into the drink…broke both his legs on the way down."

"Oh my word!" Penny said, and Dr. Horton turned his attention to her.

"Not to worry, oh…Penny, isn't it? I'm sorry, I didn't realize…though workin' for the paper, I guess it makes sense, nice to see you again."

Penny extended her own hand, and Dr. Horton gave a few firm pumps before letting go.

"You too. Is your assistant okay?"

"He's fine. That girl of his can swim and got him out. He's laid up with that crisp ocean breeze, havin' fresh seafood brought to him; I'd still call that a vacation."

They all had a laugh at that, Penny included, before Dr. Horton spoke again.

"Well, I suppose we'd better get to it. I'd like to have the man on ice and a good night's sleep under my belt before I give my full report, but since that car didn't get wrapped around a pole, a preliminary should be enough to get everyone started."

Dr. Horton led the way, and she, Eddie, and Alan followed.

"You sure about this, Penny?" Eddie said.

No.

"Yes."

"Alright then," he said. "Just hang back outta the doc's way."

Penny took out her notebook and pen, then flipped past her notes from earlier in the night to a fresh page. Alan opened the driver's side door, and Dr. Horton bent inside. She'd been about to head over to where she could get a look through the windshield when she felt a hand in the crook of her arm, pulling her back.

"Eddie, what're you—"

"There's one thing," he said, pitching his voice low. "Somethin' on the floorboard that don't sit right with me…I don't want it written up in the papers."

"Then why are you lettin' me see it at all?"

He seemed to consider this for a moment, taking turns looking between her and the Ford.

"Because…depending on how things turn out tomorrow, I might need your help."

As if the night couldn't get any stranger.

Penny nodded, filing that information away for the time being. Breathing deep, she tried to steady her nerves for whatever was over there. Alan might've been a jerk putting it the way he did, but he was right: she did normally cover those light, fluffy things…but with any luck, those unfinished pages about a surprise blueberry pie would be the last of them.

Chapter Seventeen

Lucy walked down the stairs of the neat little Sears kit home, the boards creaking slightly under her feet. She reached the bottom, turned into the kitchen, and started opening cabinets, wondering where Danny kept the coffee.

In the bright morning sun, Lucy could almost picture her aunt, sitting in the corner of this place in that old rocker of hers, squat and judgmental with her needlework in her lap and her endlessly scowling face looking up at her.

"It's been some time since you've been to church, Lucille," she'd say. "You'll be sure to join us next time."

But that'd be just the polite, civilized version of what she'd really mean: that she, Lucy, was a brazen, sinning hussy who needed to repent and ask for forgiveness for the sake of her soul for what she'd done, spending the night like she had. Then, settle down and "stop all this foolishness" …said foolishness being working and living on her own when she had, in her aunt's opinion, a perfectly good man.

Lucy found the coffee on a high shelf and grabbed it. In another cabinet, she found a percolator.

My soul is just fine, thank you very much.

And it was. Better than it'd felt in a long time, if the absolute truth of the thing was told. Last night, she'd finally quit beating around the bush, waiting for things to get better, and accepted the decision she'd known deep down she'd already made: to let Jack go. It wasn't easy, things like that never are, but if you know in your heart that something's right, you've gotta do it even if it scares you to death. Though she hadn't expected to begin down that path in such a fashion as she had.

Danny.

Ever since they'd first met, there'd been something that had drawn her to him. Something about the way he talked and carried himself…he wasn't like anyone she'd ever met before, though she couldn't point to exactly why that was. But what she did know was that his company had always felt right somehow in a way Jack's never had, even at their best, and it was a relief to not pretend about it anymore.

Setting the percolator on the stove, Lucy turned on the gas, then watched as little blue jets of flame started to lick up the sides. She thought about stepping outside to check for the paper, but thought better of it. The least she could do was wait a little longer before popping out the front door and giving the neighbors something to talk about…as if they hadn't likely done a good bit of that already at the fairgrounds last night.

Shaking that thought from her mind for the time being, she walked out of the kitchen, through the small entryway, and into the living room. There was a record cabinet over in the corner, and thinking that a little fresh morning air and music might be just the thing, she cracked a nearby window, then bending down, opened the cabinet.

She'd spotted an Artie Shaw record and had reached for it when she all of a sudden stopped. Sitting on top was what looked like an electrical cord. Lucy picked it up.

It was strange-looking, with a bulky white plug that had to have been made of Bakelite. The cord was braided but looked like it'd either broken clean off or had been cut at the tip. Running a nail across it, she wondered what it might be for. She knew Danny did like to tinker from time to time…whatever he'd done to make her Buick's radio sound clear as a bell a while back was proof enough of that, and she thought that this was just another little curio… a new kind of experimental replacement cord for lamps or radios maybe.

"Smart fella," she said, smiling, then put the cord back. She'd ask him about it later.

Off in the kitchen, she fancied she'd heard the coffee start to boil on the stove, then stepped back in to check. It was boiling, but the liquid in the little glass topper was light amber like fresh motor oil…not ready yet. Lucy opened a few more windows to let the morning air in and took a seat at one of the kitchen chairs, looking around, enjoying the breeze.

Sitting there, thinking about how odd a thing it was to see this particular kitchen in the bright, early morning hours, her mind turned to last night.

It'd been wonderful. And as luck would have it, Lucy happened to have on one of the silk slips that she'd thought always did great things for her figure. And by his, well…enthusiasm, she supposed there was a consensus.

They'd gone on for a while…a long while, and after they'd finished, they'd lain there in bed talking for some time before drifting off to sleep.

"There's something I need to get off my chest, Luce. I've had something of a thing for you for a while, too. You're fun, you're a great conversationalist, you're smart…"

"You know, Danny, that's the sort of sweet talking you should say to a gal before, well…you know," she'd said, giving him a wink.

"I really did mean to before I leaned in, but," Danny said, chuckling a little, "but I guess I didn't make it that far. I just wanted you to know out loud that you weren't the only one holding onto feelings like that. And I don't want you thinking that I'd just used the opportunity to take advantage of—"

"Hush," she'd said, curling her head into his chest. "I know you're not that kind of man."

There was quiet for a while, just listening to the crickets outside while he ran a gentle hand across her bare shoulders. It was nice, but she knew that under the circumstances, it couldn't last. Finally, Danny broke the silence.

"What do we do now?"

Lucy could tell by the unevenness in his voice when he asked the question and what little she could see of his face that, despite all the fun they'd had, he was still bothered, and it didn't take a scientist to work out where his mind likely was. She took a moment, gathering her thoughts; it'd be the first time she'd tell all this to another person and not just her diary.

"Danny?" she said, sitting up a bit and moving to face him. "There's something you oughta know too, and I'm telling you the God's honest truth. If you're thinkin' that you're some awful person who came between Jack and me and ruined something special, you can quit on it, because you didn't ruin anything."

He looked at her, puzzled. "What're you talking about?"

Lucy told him everything about how things between her and Jack weren't as rosy as they might've seemed by looking in. How he'd come to feel like a stranger to her lately, and nothing she'd tried seemed to help. How he'd been a stone around her heart even before the distance, and she couldn't take being hurt one more day.

All the lies, the fights, the tearful promises to change, only to have everything go back to the way it was as soon as they'd kissed and made up. How that she'd come to consider the fair as the last chance she'd been willing to give Jack, and how, after he'd pulled his little disappearing act, that'd been it for her.

By the time she'd finished, tears stood in her eyes, but she felt all the better for really getting it off her chest. The whole time she'd talked, Danny looked like someone had just come along and told him that down was up, and once she'd said just about all she could, he pulled her close, and she settled herself back into his chest.

"I'd started to wonder here lately…actually earlier today, if something might be wrong, but just, wow…I'm so very sorry," Dan said, and she thanked him.

"Please don't think that tonight was about gettin' back at him or anything like that," she said, looking up. "Like I said in the car before, you know… I like you, and since I'm tellin' the truth here, I've liked you for a long while. Tonight, things just sort of came together, and I can't say I regret it."

He'd paused long enough for her to wonder if maybe she'd said too much or misjudged, but when he spoke, relief washed over her.

"I can't either," he said. "Can't say it might not be complicated later, and what all this means—"

"Is something that can surely wait until after we've had some sleep, don't you think?"

"I guess you're right," he said, a half-grin spreading across his face.

They'd talked for a little while after that. Lucy couldn't remember exactly what, but thought it must've been about pleasant things since she'd fallen asleep soon after and had woken up feeling peaceful and refreshed.

Lucy stood, then walked back over to the stove, watching the percolator now bubbling up perfectly dark coffee. Just as she killed the heat on the stove, she heard footsteps coming down the stairs. Turning, she saw Danny standing in the archway, working at the last button of his shirt before looking up. He smiled as she met his eye, then walked over to her. Holding her around the waist, he pulled her in close, and she planted a long, deep kiss on him.

"Here I was thinking that a good night's sleep changed your mind, and you'd left," he said.

"Sorry, mister, you're not getting rid of me that easy," she said, then kissed him again.

After a lingering moment, Dan moved off, took a couple of mugs from a cabinet, and began pouring them each coffee. He thanked her for going to the trouble, then pulled out cream and sugar, setting everything out on a tray. As he walked over, it occurred to her to ask about that odd-looking electrical cord, but she thought there'd be time enough later.

"No angry Jack at the door, screaming for our blood? After I woke up, I realized I'd parked your car on the street for anyone to see."

"Can we please leave him alone for a little while? I'd like some peace with my coffee."

"Sorry," he said. "Do you maybe want breakfast too? I need to go shopping, but I've got enough to throw together—"

Knock-knock-knock!

Chapter Eighteen

"Be there in a sec!"

On feet that didn't feel quite steady, Dan stepped out of the kitchen and looked left toward the front door, Lucy hanging a few paces behind, and started to walk.

Could be a salesman trying to pawn off some encyclopedias or a new sweeper.

Possible, but he didn't think his luck was that good. The balance of probability said that there was a pissed-off Jack on the other side of that door waiting for him. He was willing to take it. Everything Lucy had said last night aside, there was part of him that still felt like he had at least something coming. All the same, he looked around, wishing there was something more substantial nearby than the umbrella hanging off the coat rack, just in case Jack had a mind to do more than split his lip and give him a shiner.

With a last, steadying breath, Dan opened the door.

It wasn't Jack on the other side, but the sight of the two cops standing on his front porch filled him with more dread than if it had been. One was a younger guy Dan couldn't place, but the other one was a different story.

"Eddie?"

Lucy slipped past, corralling Dan out onto the porch where she stood next to him, arms crossed. Both men took off their hats, and Eddie stepped forward.

"You're both here," he said. "Well, guess that saves me a trip up the road."

"What's this about?" Dan said, a sinking feeling starting up in his stomach.

"It's best discussed in private, I think," the other man said, and Dan cleared his throat.

"Am I in some sort of trouble?"

There was a look between the two men that Dan didn't like at all, and he felt fear begin to surge.

Aside from blowing through an intersection out on County 12 when he'd been seventeen, unmindful of the cop hiding on the other side of an outbuilding, he'd never been in trouble before. And since taking up residence here, thinking that the key to being a successful time traveler had to be flying under the radar, he'd taken to following every rule, law, ordinance, and well-meaning suggestion like he was following instructions on how to diffuse an atomic bomb…until last night when he'd "stolen" a car and went on a little joyride through the center of town…

Could that really be what this is about? I didn't hit anything or…hang on, what'd he say? Something about both of us being here? What—

"There are a few questions," Eddie said. "Things you, in particular, might be able to shed some light on. Can we come in?"

That wasn't quite the "no, sir, not at all" he'd been hoping for, but thought it was as good as he was likely to get. Also, he wasn't thrilled about the idea of letting these guys inside. The power of boners last night meant he'd not done the usual sweep for things that didn't belong yet before having company. Lucy obviously hadn't found anything, but he didn't want to press his luck with these two.

"S-sure, is out on the back porch all right? We were just about to have coffee, be happy to throw on some more."

"A coffee would be just the thing, thank you," Eddie said, and Dan led the two men through the house and onto the back porch. Lucy said she'd take care of the coffee, and so Dan sat with Eddie and a man he now knew as Officer Alan Riley. They sat, chatting idly, dancing around the edge of what'd brought them out for the time being, when Lucy appeared with a tray of mugs, the percolator, cream, and sugar.

"Thank you, ma'am," Alan said, taking his offered cup. Eddie did likewise, and soon they were all sitting with their coffee. Lucy settled down on the bench next to Dan and began to sip, but he found he'd lost his taste for coffee…and just about everything else right now.

"I won't drag this out any more'n I have to," Eddie said, setting his cup down on the porch railing. "When I saw you both last night at the fairgrounds, you said that Jack had been called out on a job. Did you see him later that night? Talk to him on the telephone, maybe?"

He and Lucy looked at each other.

"No," she said. "We waited for a little while after, and when he didn't show, we left."

"And what time was that?"

"I don't remember. Danny?"

"Maybe seven thirty, eight o'clock?"

Alan had set his coffee aside, too, swapping it out for a small notebook that he'd pulled out and started to jot notes on. Eddie looked over at the page, then nodded. Dan watched this, nervous to the point that he felt like he might puke.

"Does the name Dorothy Sherbrooke mean anything to either of you?" Alan said.

Oh great, they're tag-teaming us.

"Not offhand," Dan said. "Sounds familiar, maybe she'd come into the bookstore. But no one, I think, that I can place off the top of my head, no."

"And what about you?" Alan said, turning his gaze toward Lucy.

"Only that she's married to the man who runs the big dairy farm out that way. Why? Did she and Jack run away together? Stick a big sign out by the road saying Bon Voyage?"

There was a smile on Lucy's face as she spoke, but there was a hardness in her voice, and her normally bright eyes seemed to go stormy. Alan jotted a few last notes, then leaned back as Eddie leaned forward, looking between the two of them.

"Where's Jack?" Dan said, his voice small, unable to ignore the feeling of dread that seemed to fall over him with each passing second.

Eddie sighed, then looked between the two of them.

"This is hard, and know that I'm sorry, but—"

As Eddie spoke, a high-pitched whistling started up in Dan's ears, sort of like when a room is very quiet and still. He watched the man's mouth move, but there was a disconnect…the words weren't making any sense. Eddie sat there, elbows on knees, fingers laced and looking him dead in the eye. Lucy was in his arms in an instant. Dan held her tight, warm tears running down his face as the words finally gained meaning; Jack was dead.

There was no wailing, no drawn-out screams. Just two people choking back wet sobs as they held onto one another for what felt like dear life.

Sometime later, Dan couldn't have put an exact number of minutes to it, the world started to come into focus again. He could hear the breeze rustling through the trees, birds chirping not too far away, and the sound of the two occupied rockers on the porch in front of him slowly creaking back and forth. Lucy pulled away, wiping at her face as she sat back in her seat, and Dan ran an arm across his eyes.

Once he and Lucy had managed to pull themselves just about as together as either of them was likely to get under the circumstances, Eddie explained how things were. About Dorothy Sherbrooke turning up at the farm next door like something out of a horror movie. How they'd gone to the dairy and found the Vic, Jack sitting behind the wheel, a gash across his throat, shards of his broken glasses sticking out of his eyes. At that, Lucy buried her face in his shoulder and started crying again. Dan put an arm around her, stunned.

There'd been no call from Sullivan about sending Jack out to Harlan Heights. Dorothy Sherbrooke was non-responsive, so they could only speculate, but it wasn't hard to put together exactly why he'd gone over there.

That phone call…Jack, why in the hell did—

"The sirens," Lucy said, once again getting herself under control and wiping at her face.

"Yes ma'am," Alan said, sipping at his coffee again, and Dan wondered how he had the stomach for it.

"This is a nightmare," Dan said, and he truly hoped it was. Just guilt playing a few sick games with him before he woke up for real. But no matter how hard he tried to apply it to the situation, the idea wouldn't stick. Unbelievable as it was, this was actually happening.

"We do have one or two more things, but" Eddie paused, looking between Dan and Lucy, then landing on Lucy, "you mind givin' us a minute?"

"I certainly do," she said, steel in her voice that Dan himself wouldn't have dared to mess with if it'd been aimed in his direction. "You told me Jack was steppin' out on me, then, found himself with a slashed throat…what more could you possibly have to say that's worse than what I've already heard?"

"It's not a matter of worse, it's—"

"She stays," Dan said, trying to borrow some of the vibes Lucy was putting out. God knew he didn't want to be here alone with these two, staring him down.

"Alright," Eddie said, in a tone that sounded like it was anything but, only he was too tired to dick around. He looked Dan straight in the eye. "What do you use to shave?"

Whatever Dan had expected in that moment before Eddie spoke, a question about his toiletries certainly wasn't it.

"I, uh, a safety…no, sorry, a straight razor."

"You care to describe it?"

Faint alarm bells started to ring in the back of Dan's head as he struggled to flip through his mind for what his usual razor looked like. But at the moment, the only thing he could think of was the new one still in the front pocket of the pants he'd been wearing yesterday.

"It's, oh hell, um, light brown. Gold trim too…I think? No, wait, sorry that's not right. I just bought a new one last night because I left the other one in Jack's car so he could sharpen it and I…hang on, was that how…"

He looked over at Lucy, whose eyes were wide. Eddie and Alan were busy whispering, taking turns reading over whatever it was Alan had been writing on his little notepad.

There were other questions after that, about the books they'd found in the Vic with Dan's name written on the receipt, about how Jack had seemed in the days before, and about a dozen other things. But Dan thought they'd already found out the thing they were most interested in; it was his straight razor they'd found in the Vic… the murder weapon. That itself was bad enough, but here he was, nervously fumbling over answers like a guy who wasn't sure how to keep his story straight.

Panic built up fast, and Dan wondered when they'd drop the facade, haul him to his feet, and take him out the front door in handcuffs. But that didn't seem to be in the cards. Once Alan had snapped that little notebook shut, the men stood, thanking Lucy for the coffee and Dan for his hospitality, reminding them both to please reach out if they remembered anything at all, no matter how insignificant it might seem.

As the two men left the back porch, disappearing around the corner between the garage and the house, Dan felt around for Lucy's hand, found it, and squeezed hard.

I have to get out of here.

Chapter Nineteen

"Well," Alan said, leaning against the fender of the street-parked Unit 2, arms folded as Eddie lit a smoke, "I guess that coulda gone worse."

"Wasn't counting on gettin' both of them at the same time," Eddie said. "That knocked me off stride a bit."

"Me too. You figure they got together early this mornin' trying to figure out what'd happened to our boy?"

Eddie thought about it for a long moment, dragging on the Chesterfield, letting the smoke fill his lungs.

"Doubt it," he said. "They might've been wonderin' about him, I'm not rulin' that out yet. But it's awfully early, and that little getup Lucy was wearin' was the same as I saw her in yesterday. Nah, she spent the night here."

"Lucky guy," Alan said, and Eddie agreed, though he didn't much care for the situation.

It could be that they'd been waiting up late for Jack, she'd fallen asleep on the couch, and he'd tossed a blanket over her, and that'd been it. But with a dame like that? Eddie seriously doubted it. And all on the night Jack Lawrence just happened to turn up dead?

"Parker seem nervous to you?"

"He did," Alan said, "but that makes sense. We knock on his door first thing in the morning, all but catch him foolin' around with his buddy's girl, break the news that Jack's gettin' measured for a pine box, then ask him questions about a blade he owns being found at the scene? Shit boss, I'd be terrified if it were me…my hats off to the guy for stringin' more'n two words together."

"Suppose you're right," Eddie said, looking out at the street as people started to open their doors, reaching for their paper, the milk, and to take in the morning air. A boy made his way down the street, but when Eddie waved hello, the kid turned tail and headed back the other way.

He thought Alan made a decent enough point, and Eddie was willing to let it be just as he said for the time being. The receipt and the books seemed innocent enough, and easy to check with the old man who ran the bookstore. The razor he had a little tougher time dismissing, and he'd be lying if he said that the two things together didn't irk him.

"We'll give Parker a few days," Eddie said. "Let him get his head around the situation, then we talk to him again when he's clearer; see if he doesn't have somethin' more useful for us after all. Meantime, we've got plenty to do."

Eddie continued to smoke, tossing an occasional glance over his shoulder at the house behind him, and talking about the only other lead they really had at the moment, Dorothy Sherbrooke.

They'd tried getting in to see her last night and earlier this morning, but she'd fainted dead away when the ambulance came for her at the Crawford place and hadn't woken up since; over-stress, the doctors said. Even rougher luck was that, unconsciousness notwithstanding, she was being moved from the psych ward at Price Memorial to Alcomb Sanatorium right about now.

"Dick Sherbrooke is going to have our asses when he gets here," Alan said. "Then again, he's got at least a day's train ride ahead of him to get back from that trade show in Nebraska…plenty of time to cool off."

Truthfully, Eddie doubted the delay would do anything except make the man even more like an angry bull than he usually was…but kept that to himself. That, plus how he wished the son-of-a-bitch had been anywhere near New Chapel last night so he could've gotten the man in a cell and kept him there just on general damned principle.

"He'll be here soon enough, like as not, but let's not focus on him just now," Eddie said. "It's gonna be a lot harder to get to Dorothy Sherbrooke now that she's in the nuthatch, so when you get back, get on the phone with the admin at Alcomb, see about getting in to talk to her as soon as she's awake and with the world again."

"Yes, boss."

Eddie took another look at the house behind him, wondering why a fella who lives all alone needs a whole house to himself. Could be the guy just likes the space, God knows he'd trade the shithole he'd been hanging his hat at for the past few months for a house in the blink of an eye, even if he did need to take care of it himself.

He flicked his eye to the garage, just as neatly kept as the house itself, staring at the line of dark windows when—

"Eddie?"

Static came from the open window of Unit 2, then Martha's voice, and he turned, leaning in to grab the mic.

"I'm here, Martha."

"You on your way back? 'Cus—"

A dull, garbled voice in the background cut her off, and Eddie thought he could hear what sounded like muted shouting. He waved a hand at Alan, who moved to the other side of the car and slipped in behind the wheel. Eddie got in, mic still in hand.

"Sorry," Martha said, clearer now. "Got a concerned citizen here who wants a word about all the commotion last night."

"On our way," he said, racking the mic, then told Alan to step on it.

Chapter Twenty

Penny sat in the office of Harv Ellison, editor-in-chief of the New Chapel Gazette. A rinky-dink little paper from a rinky-dink downtown office with a surprisingly large readership throughout the county. She'd stayed up late last night working, the clacking of her typewriter no longer much of a concern, and had come in early in hopes of catching Harv before the day really started for him. No dice, though. She'd knocked on the door and cracked it open to find him already on the telephone, waving her in and pointing her toward an empty chair in front of his desk.

"Yes, yes, I understand that, but you've gotta understand that if you want to change your mind and go for a full-page ad, there's gonna be an additional fee, Harry."

Harv looked over at her, miming a pistol at his temple, then slumping over in his seat, and Penny stifled a giggle.

Smoothing out her skirt, she then reached down into her bag, pulled out a folder, and set it on her lap. In it was her coverage of the pie bakeoff, and a first draft pass on what had happened last night. She wished she'd been able to take it through at least another draft, but the excitement of the night had left her tired, and sleep had eventually won out.

A bad first draft is better than no draft at all.

"Fine," Harv said, leaning forward over his desk. "Fine. Drop off the first part of the fee tomorrow, then the second part next week, then…yes, yes, we'll take a look at it then, yes. Goodbye, Harry."

"Cheap bastard," he said, not-so-gently hanging up the telephone. "Runs that big old Pontiac dealership and then complains to me about a few more bucks for ad space…sorry Penny, what can I do for you? Your fair coverage isn't due til tomorrow."

Penny took a deep breath, looked briefly around the office with its fit-to-bust filing cabinets, the large fan in the corner, and the architect's board where Harv had started to lay out the newest issue of the Gazette, then spoke.

"I do have that, yes, but there's somethin' else. Late last night, something fell into my lap. It's different than what I usually hand in, and I'd like you to have a look at it."

Harv just sat there, one eyebrow cocked above his eyeglasses. A moment passed, and she'd begun to wonder if she'd maybe made a mistake approaching him so boldly like this. The idea of being laughed out of the office and told to either stay in her place or worse…pack her things…came clear as a bell and—

"Well, you gonna show me what you've got in that folder or do you like keepin' me in suspense?"

Oh, you ditz!

"Oh, yes, sorry about that," Penny said, opening the folder, then handing over the pages. "Didn't get much sleep."

Harv took the pages and started to read, and she laid out what'd happened last night, him taking turns looking at her, asking a few questions, then going back to the pages. After she'd finished, Harv grabbed a red pen from the cup on his desk and started marking her copy, a very good sign. If it were trash, he'd have said so and handed it back. She'd seen him do it before.

"I know anything like this should probably go to Tony," she said, watching him work. "It's more his area."

"You got there first, kid, not him."

Harv spent another few minutes making his notes before sitting up, then handing the pages back over the desk. Penny took them, her eyes flicking across the pages.

"Do I need to explain any of that?"

She shook her head, smiling.

"Good. Let's aim for a second draft by this afternoon, huh? And leave your pie story…can't say if anyone will be excited to read it except Ruthie Crispin herself, but hey, it's what we do."

"Absolutely," Penny said, sliding those papers across his desk. "And thanks, Harv."

"Don't thank me just yet," he said, leaning back in his chair. "You've just stumbled into murder most foul in small town nowhere…more's gonna come of this, you mark my words. And when it does, it's yours. You think you can handle that?"

I think so.

"Yes, I can."

"Tell you what, then, you've got more grit than I do. I'd have turned tail or at least stayed far back if I were in your shoes last night, story or no story, and I'm not ashamed to say so."

Harv made a small cough, then shifted his eyes to the red pen still in his hand.

"Speaking of last night, and I hope you'll forgive me for talkin' like this about it, but seein' as you and Eddie are, well, you know…no longer married, do you think that'll be a problem if we need him further down the line? Things like this have a habit of gettin' bigger, Penny, not smaller…take that Elizabeth Short business out in California some months back as a for instance. Eddie's a good source, and I wanna know if you think he'll continue to be as helpful as he was last night."

Well, how about that for a question? And all before she'd had her coffee too. But truthfully, she should've expected it. Not many folks around here get divorced, and she'd be willing to bet even fewer have a professional, working relationship with the person they used to share a bed with.

"I don't think our history will be a problem, no," Penny said, considering as she spoke. "He seemed real eager that his office be involved from the start with how things came out, and I have every reason to think he'll want to continue to do that."

Sounds like I may have to play spy for the police department in return, but I think I'll just keep that to myself.

"Well, that's just fine," Harv said, looking as relieved as she felt. "Alright, second draft by this afternoon. Haven't had anything this big in about ten years, and I'd like to try and beat the gossips on this one…out with ya, kid."

Smiling, Penny said she'd get to work right away, then grabbed up her things and headed out.

Out in the small open office, abandoned at this hour, Penny headed over to her desk and took a seat. She'd just opened her folder to the page of edited copy and loaded a sheet of fresh paper into the typewriter when she noticed a small envelope sitting at the corner of her desk. It only took a second to recognize the handwriting.

Geez, were your ears burning?

Penny picked it up, slit the top with her letter opener, pulled out a small sheet of paper, and read. She'd expected a letter, maybe something more personal that'd make what she'd just told Harv back there about hers and Eddie's history being no problem at all a big lie. But instead, there was only a single line.

"Gotta talk."

Chapter Twenty-One

Dan leaned back in one of the porch rockers, his feet resting on an old RC Cola crate. Next to him on the bench, Lucy lay asleep, an empty bottle of what he'd been pretty sure was Coors next to her, her fingers gently grazing the edge. He sipped at his own bottle, Jack Daniels, and watched her for a moment before turning his attention to the backyard again. He spotted the clothesline Jack had helped him put in earlier that spring, then raised his bottle.

"Here's to you...some Jack, in honor of Jack."

He didn't know how long they'd been out on the porch, but the light was much different than when the two men had left. He and Lucy lingered there for a while, Lucy trying to listen in on Eddie and Alan's conversation before the radio went off, putting an end to her eavesdropping. Dan, leaning against the railing and wondering if the pounding in his chest might just hit a fever pitch, leaving him dead.

But no, here he was, sound-ish of mind and body, somewhere between buzzed and shitfaced, trying to process the last twenty-four hours as actual fact.

This time yesterday, he'd been at work. Later on, Jack had come by, and they'd gone to see Lucy. Jack ditched them, claiming it was for work, but he was actually going to screw some bored housewife. He and Lucy spent the rest of the day...and night, together, only to wake up and have cops banging on his door to tell them Jack had been killed late last night.

Oh, don't forget, they found your straight razor in the Vic, too. Nope, can't forget that.

"This is awful," Lucy had said when she'd still been mostly with the program, another long cry on the porch behind them. "I don't like what they're implying with your razor and all that. I mean, if anything, they should be less inclined to that way of thinkin' now."

"How? I feel like I stumbled over my answers like an idiot…a *guilty* idiot."

She'd given him a ghost of a smile that made him *feel* like an idiot, but he was still happy to see it.

"*I'm* here," she said. "And it doesn't take Sherlock Holmes to figure out that I've likely been here all night. I'm your…oh, what do they call it in those crime pictures…your alibi."

That'd made him feel better, a little, but only about that particular part of the dumpster fire; there was still plenty eating at him.

Even though he didn't exactly have the moral high ground and knew it, he was pissed at Jack. Pissed at the side of him he'd learned about last night. Pissed that Jack made that phone call before they left, and lied about it, leaving the world to come crashing down on all of them.

But at the same time, Dan was trying to square that with all the fond memories, times when Jack had been the sort of stand-up guy that'd made him consider the man his best friend, and the knowledge that all that was now memory. That much at least he could talk to Lucy about, and they had at some length right around the time the liquid breakfast had started, each of them coming to the uninspired conclusion that people are often both good and bad. But there was something else.

Out of the corner of his eye, Lucy shifted, and Dan heard the *clank-tinkle* of the Coors bottle first falling over, then starting to roll across the porch. He watched it til it hit one of the porch railings, then stopped. Dan stared at it for a moment before his thoughts turned again to the thing bothering him the most…the thing he couldn't share.

I don't remember this. Any of it. People still talk about the semi-truck overturning and taking out the original Kent County Fairgrounds sign back in the seventies. And about that shootout at The Wheel back in the thirties…how in the hell have I never heard about a slasher-style murder out at the dairy farm?

But of course, he knew the answer even if he didn't understand the mechanics of it…ripples, waves…a butterfly beats its wings, causing the winds to shift and so on and so forth…changes in the timeline. The fact of the matter was, he wasn't supposed to be here…

I did this. Just by being here, I killed Jack.

And as the thought came, Dan knew it was true beyond a shadow of a doubt. It somehow made the cops finding his razor in the Vic just about right…karma making sure that the books were balanced off. When he'd made that first trip to '39 for the comics…the only real test run, he'd come back home, and everything seemed just as it had been. Or at least, the world hadn't descended into some dystopian nightmare. Sure, there might've been differences, had to be differences, but they must've been so small that they didn't matter in the grand scheme of things, right?

But that'd been just one trip…he'd been here for years now. Had he really been so goddamned stupid to think that if he didn't do anything showy like "predicting" where the Titanic was or writing *Psycho* or something, he'd be in the clear?

The answer was a resounding *yes*. And why wouldn't it be? The thing didn't come with any instructions he could find unless they were buried in with those moldy old boxes…meaning that the only real guideposts he had for time travel came from TV and movies.

And it's just cost someone their life.

No, not someone. Likely more than one someone. Who's to say that in the ordinary course of things, Jack didn't have kids that went on to lead rich, full lives who, in turn, had kids of their own and so on? What if the future he knew was only ever possible…directly or indirectly, because of Jack being around? What had been changed? Who else might've once existed that now doesn't? Just what in the hell had he done?

Tears began to well up, blurring his vision. Dan wiped them away, then grabbed up the whisky again, meaning to finish it off and drown the idea while he had the chance. But he could only bring the bottle to his lips, letting the liquor dance on the edge. After a moment, he took it away, fighting the urge to smash it against the porch floor, and instead set it back down.

He could drink all he wanted, but it wouldn't change anything, and he knew it. Nothing would be better. When he came back to himself…in misery and with a headache bad enough to make blinking hurt, it'd all still be there waiting for him. All the guilt, the visions of what Eddie had told him likely happened, brought to horrible horror-movie life in his imagination, and who knew what else.

So what now?

Dan looked over at Lucy, watching her sleep as the answer came to him. As soon as she was gone, he'd head down to the basement and get things ready. Once they were, and once he was packed, he'd…say goodbye.

He had to know what sort of things he'd changed, even though he was likely to be the only one to remember what'd been before. And then…*and then, once I'm back home, I'll destroy it. Destroy it before I cause any more damage.*

Chapter Twenty-Two

Carly walked through the aisles of Howard's Market, a shopping basket on her arm. Work had been exhausting, and all she wanted was something nice to eat before she called it a night…day, whatever. A frozen pizza with stuffed crust would be just about the best thing in the world right now, but unfortunately, those and a ton of other things she loved were now permanently out of reach.

After a few minutes of perusing, Carly found herself in something of a usual spot; waiting in line at the deli counter. There wasn't much these days in the way of easy prepared foods, but she'd found that grabbing some sliced roast beef, cheese, bread, and maybe some nice mustard wasn't too bad, all things considered.

Part of her wanted to go out for something hot…always more satisfying, but these night shifts were exhausting, and it was enough of an effort just to come here, without changing out of her nurse's whites and coming back out again, especially without a car. Her muscles ached, and she stank of blood and sweat. Though not all of it had been from work.

Carly looked down at her left hand…the one that'd been dripping crimson and holding a razor not twelve hours ago, remembering how the blood ran down in little threads towards the drain in that farmhouse kitchen as she'd washed.

It'd been a long walk back to Harrington House, but a good one; she thought she'd never seen the stars so bright or heard the crickets and the breeze flowing through the fields quite so clearly. She'd gotten back to her room later than she'd meant to, leaving just enough time to change her clothes before her ride to work came. Showering would've been nice, but something about the smell of her sweat…knowing why and still feeling that pulsing awareness through her body in response to it…she'd been almost glad she hadn't fully cleaned up.

Stop it, she thought, patiently waiting her turn, watching the guy behind the counter grab a big chunk of pastrami and begin to slice. Just stop it.

That awareness…that high, had left her not but a few hours ago, as she'd known it would eventually. It wasn't a great feeling. No, tell the truth, it was awful. She'd had comedowns off things a little more recreational in the past that left her wondering…usually in the middle of the night when all she wanted to do was sleep and seemed to do anything but, if she'd ever feel normal again. But this was so much worse.

More than once, Carly had thought about seeing what she might be able to lift from the hospital pharmacy to take some of the edge off, only to realize that while seriously low-tech, this version of the place was ironically very secure. There were heavy doors and legit keys, which only, like, three people had, instead of everybody and their brother being able to tap their badge and get in.

Still, with how shitty she felt, she'd almost risked it anyway…the thought of not wanting to lose her job being the only thing that'd held her back.

"Next!"

Carly took a few steps forward, then stopped, waiting, feeling dull and tired and slow…trying to put last night out of her mind.

She stood there looking at the meat counter, making herself focus on it and think if she wanted to mix it up and get something else when she heard footsteps coming at her from behind.

Turning, Carly saw two women about her age…relatively speaking, chatting to one another as they joined the back of the line. She gave them a small nod before turning back. And just as she was wrangling all her brain power towards dinner…or breakfast, or whatever this was, the women started talking again.

"I'd just been about to drop off to sleep when I heard the sirens go past. Henry didn't hear anything; that one'll sleep through anything."

"Michael's just the same, but when I shoved him after hearing it too, he was up like a shot. Couldn't see much by the time we got to the window, and it was a while before I fell asleep again. Something about that just about scared me to death; it's not right."

"Well, I felt about the same, so when I woke up this morning, I started calling around. Apparently, there was a big to-do up at Sherbrooke Dairy. The Crawfords' place too, but the dairy, I guess, is where most things were happening…policemen and ambulances…"

"My word! Where on earth did you hear that from?"

"My cousin Mabel lives just down the way from them, you see, and her husband…poor man hardly sleeps, was already awake and decided to go over there and have a look. The boys in charge shooed him away, I guess, but he told her, and Mabel told me, that he thought there was a body up there."

"No!"

"That's right. I'm gonna call her again to see if she's heard anything else, but I expect we'll know more soon. But until I know for sure that it was just an accident, I've told Henry I want our doors kept locked for a while. He's not big on the idea, says my imagination is gettin' the better of me, but I—"

Carly tuned the chattering housewives out, wishing they could've had their conversation anywhere else. These two, probably moms with nice little kids, were standing next to the very person…killer, who'd been the cause of all their gossip, and they had no idea. The thought didn't fill her with a sense of pride or cunning at seeming to have gotten away with it for the moment. All she wanted to do was put both hands over her head, drop to the floor, and start screaming…she felt insane and stupid, and so, so tired.

All at once, she thought of the phone sitting in her dresser drawer. It disgusted her knowing what she'd done, but the fact that she'd just sat there like a creep, filming the aftermath? It was wrong. Worse than that, it was sick…but at the same time, she…

You have to delete it.

Yes. Yes, she would…but maybe, she could watch it just once. Maybe some of that sharpness and clarity from last night would come back, help her think.

Probably that was wishful thinking, but she at least owed it to the universe to make sure she never forgot every single detail of what she'd done…what he'd made her do…all with that smarmy, smug, patronizing smile…probably seeing her from across the road just like she'd seen him, rubbing it in her face that he was doing fine in their shared exile to the dark ages while she was struggling just to keep her head above water…now more than ever.

"Next!"

Picturing that smile in her mind, feeling heat begin to creep up around her neck and cheeks, Carly moved forward.

Chapter Twenty-Three

Dan burst through the basement door, slamming it hard behind him. He stumbled in the near-dark to the kitchen, meaning to grab for the nearest chair, but missed. Instead, his knees gave out, and he collapsed onto all fours, head down and breathing hard.

"No…no-no-no-no…"

His jaws tightened to the point that he wondered in a far-off way whether or not his molars would break. The sound of blood pulsing in his ears drove out all other sounds of the night in the dark kitchen.

Lucy had woken up earlier that afternoon, and by then, Dan had sobered up somewhat. When she said that she wanted to head back to Harrington House to bathe and sleep, and that she'd call him later on, he'd been sad to see her go. But on the other hand, he understood and thought it was for the best. With the way he'd felt, the realizations of the damage he'd caused being held at bay by sheer force of will, he didn't think he'd be good company. Besides, it wouldn't be long now before they'd have to say goodbye.

Once the Buick had disappeared up the street and around the corner, he'd headed back inside, then upstairs, hoping to sleep off the rest of the drunk. He knew what he had to do, and being even a little blitzed wouldn't do him any favors.

He'd come to again around mid-evening, just as the light had started to fade from the sky. He'd known he should eat something…his stomach had been pretty clear on that, but somehow, he just couldn't. Instead, he'd gone to the kitchen junk drawer, grabbed the keys to the padlock, and made for the basement. Once he got things moving down there, he'd head back up and start packing a bag. And when Lucy called, he'd ask to meet up. Telling her the truth was out of the question, but he still wanted to see her one last time.

Dan reached for the chair again, managing to get hold of it this time, and pulled himself up. He sat at the table, head down on his arms like it was an elementary school time-out, wondering for the second time today if this was all just some sort of horrible dream.

No chance, his mind said, sounding like a heckler in a crowd. *This is real, too. You wanted to stay, right? Well, guess what? Now you can! Because that thing doesn't work anymore. Whatever powered it seems to have died out…congrats, the universe made the decision for you. What's wrong? Aren't you happy? You wanted to keep your simple little life. Only, it isn't so simple anymore, is it?*

You screwed around with Lucy on the very night some psycho slashed Jack's throat…actually, your fault by the way, and now it'll only be a matter of time before the cops want your ass. And the best part? You can't run away! Not back home, where it's safe, and you have all that money to try and console yourself with. Nope, you shit this particular bed, and now you have to lie in it…enjoy your immersion.

Snapping his hands into fists so fast he heard knuckles pop, Dan screamed. In it was fear, rage, and loss that his mind could only begin to accept as a real thing and not a nightmare. The scream finally came to an end in a fit of coughing that nearly took his breath away.

The idea of staying was so easy when you knew you could always just change your mind and leave, huh?

Throat now raw from screaming, Dan could only groan from deep in his chest and sweep his arm across the table, sending a nearly empty bottle of Coke to shatter on the tile floor.

He raised his head, looking down at the shining little shards of glass reflected in the dim light, wondering if he should grab one of the larger pieces and drag it from elbow to wrist; make an end to all the problems right here and now. But the thought wouldn't take, and so he looked away.

Probably just make things worse somehow.

Sometime later, he was never sure how long, Dan managed to stand. He thought about cleaning up the broken Coke bottle, but decided to leave it at least for now. If all the screaming he'd done had concerned one of the neighbors enough to check in on him, he could probably use the mess to work up some sort of believable excuse.

In the near darkness, Dan left the kitchen. He saw clearly enough to pull the phone off the hook before heading back upstairs.

Chapter Twenty-Four

Lucy closed the book she'd been reading and set it aside, the scrap of paper that'd been intended as a bookmark still in her hand. Life was too short to read bad books, and this one had been truly awful. A murder-mystery where, after a quick flip to the back to confirm, it showed that she had guessed who the murderer was sometime around chapter three, leaving her to wonder why the author had even bothered with the rest.

"It's a wonder how these things get published," she said, then looked around.

Harrington House was a sprawling Tudor manor, and the small library where she now sat was by far her favorite room in the whole place. Dark oak paneling with matching bookcases, red leather chairs, and fine antique rugs. A place where you could curl up with a good book and happily disappear for hours…not that she could afford to do such a thing today, even if the story she'd grabbed had been a real page turner.

Thunder began to roll just outside, and she looked through one of the nearby diamond lattice windows. Last time she'd noticed, the sky had still been bright blue without a cloud to be seen, just like the paper said it'd be. Now it'd gone a steely gray and storm clouds had begun to stack off in the distance, and she wondered who had a better record of true predictions…Midwestern weathermen, or carnival fortune tellers.

From behind there came a soft knock and a soft voice, and Lucy turned.

"Lucy? I'm sorry to bother you."

"Don't be silly, Caroline, come on in."

Caroline Wells stood just inside the library door, peering inside, looking a little timid as she always did. They hadn't gotten the chance to talk much since Caroline had taken a room about a month or so back, but Lucy found herself liking the girl just the same. She was sweet, if a little shy; mainly keeping to herself because of the odd hours she worked at the hospital, Lucy supposed. But that last part wasn't much of an issue. Being a good waitress means you can talk up just about anyone; it'd only be a matter of time before she got to know Caroline better, she was sure of it.

"I was, I was just wanting to know if you wanted to come to the kitchen and have some tea before you headed off to the funeral."

"Oh, you're such a sweetheart, and thank you, but I think I'll have to take a raincheck if that's alright. Danny Parker, he's," Lucy looked at the clock over the mantlepiece, "he should be here any time. Have you met him yet? He works just down at the bookstore in town."

She hadn't seen Danny since they'd both gotten the news, a few days ago now. They'd talked on the telephone, and she thought that he didn't seem quite himself. A little quieter and more apt to get lost in conversation than normal. Lucy thought that being alone, the news must've really settled on him, same as it'd done for her. Truth be told, she didn't feel quite like herself either.

"I'll try to stop in sometime to say hi. Are you still heading to…where was it? Your aunt's place, for a few days?"

"Um-hmm," Lucy said.

Well, now, that part wasn't true. The woman who raised her after Mother and Daddy died was now miles away in upstate Michigan. Lucy supposed that she ought to make it a point to visit…sometime, but Danny wouldn't be taking her much further than his place over on Eastbridge. Not that she'd have anyone else knowing much about that, even though it was her idea.

"I've thought about things on my own plenty," she'd said last night over the telephone, Danny having just asked if she'd needed more time to, how did he put it? Process? "And after everything is said and done tomorrow, I don't wanna be around well-wishers, and I certainly don't wanna be alone. Do you?"

"No, I really don't," he said, after a pause long enough to make her wonder if she'd lost the connection. "Eddie called earlier, too busy to spare some time to talk in person, thank God for small favors."

"And?"

"Well, I'm not calling from the sheriff's office, so that's at least going my way. They're working on fingerprints right now, mine are already on record from that break-in at the bookstore last year, but that's about all I know. It wasn't a long conversation, just telling me about that, and asking me if there's anything else I can think of that I didn't tell them the other day, but I'm still scared to death. So, yeah, I guess that's a long way of saying that I could do with a friendly face."

The memory slid away, and Lucy found herself brought back to the present, sitting in the same chair where she'd had that telephone call, only in a black dress this time instead of her nightgown, looking at Caroline framed in the doorway.

"Why don't you come have tea?" Carly said, with an odd, pained expression on her face. "It'll probably rain later, and you'll be glad for it. The water should already be boiling."

"Oh, thank you, but I couldn't. I like to take my time and enjoy. Next time, we'll make an afternoon of it."

"Well, if you change your mind, I'll be waiting," Caroline said. "I'm so sorry for your loss."

Lucy smiled and thanked Caroline as the door clicked shut once more. Picking at a small bit of lint on her dress, Lucy wondered how many more times she'd hear some of version of Caroline's parting words before the dust settled.

Word about what'd happened up at the dairy spread quickly, as news always did in New Chapel; a lot of people seemed to know at least part of the story before the story in the Gazette filled in the rest of the missing pieces. Since then, she'd been enduring kindly meant words and offered prayers for the past few days.

Though it was tiring, she accepted them all with what she hoped was grace; smiling, saying thank you, welcoming hugs and offered hands, and listening to one person after another tell her what a tragedy it was for something like this to happen to such a fine young man. Folks either wanted to forget or chose to ignore the reason Jack had been out at the dairy in the first place, not to mention that he'd been playing her for a fool. Lucy couldn't decide if she wanted to slap Penny Prescott for how candid she was in her story and adding to the attention, or hug her because at least she wasn't one of the ones trying to paint Jack as a saint.

You're hardly a saint yourself, sweetie. What was it you were doing that night? And what's that small traveling bag next to your feet all about?

Lucy bent down to look at the bag as if it'd been the one to speak up, then sat back in the chair again.

Going to the funeral with Danny was going to cause some talk; she wouldn't kid herself about that. But if word got out on the New Chapel Rumor Exchange – main offices located in the beauty salon, barbershop, and corner market – about what she'd been up to that night and what she was planning to do today, well, folks might just hold her down and sew a scarlet letter to her dress. Okay, maybe not in the literal sense, but in the ways that mattered in a person's community life.

The thought should've been enough to make her grab the bag, run it back upstairs before Danny got here, and just forget the whole business; it'd happened once before already as she'd been packing. But Lucy only sat, watching the clouds get darker out the window.

No, I won't advertise, it's not proper. But if it gets out, that's where I'm goin', and everyone starts to whisper that I'm a floozy or a harlot or a hussy, what of it? People have been sayin' that behind my back for years ever since Bobby Richards, and I snuck away during youth fellowship camp and did a little more than kiss before Pastor David found us. I didn't feel bad then, no matter how much Aunt Trudy wanted me to, and I don't feel bad now, funeral or not. And if that's a sin, may God forgive me. People are gonna say what they're gonna say and think what they're gonna think.

And it was true. It wouldn't matter that even after realizing she'd wanted nothing more than to see the back end of Jack, a part of her still truly loved him. Same for the fact that she'd spent the whole rest of the day after leaving Danny's, crying and looking through old photographs of her and Jack, remembering, and trying to get her head around what it's like to be angry at the person you're also mourning for. No one would care that the idea of being alone after the funeral felt like poison in her veins, and she needed to be around the one other person who understood, and not just as a voice on the other end of the telephone. Then maybe, just maybe, she wouldn't feel like things were so bad.

No. Lucy thought she could explain it all, tearfully and in detail, but most people would only shake their heads and say something that started with, "poor boy wasn't even cold in the ground…" before dismissing her.

What I wouldn't give to just leave this place behind, she thought, then, standing, grabbed up her handbag and traveling bag before walking out of the library.

Stepping out into the checkered tile foyer, with its walls paneled in dark oak and dressed in fine old furniture, Lucy looked around. It was quite something, and on those rare times when she really stopped to see the place, it nearly took her breath away. When that happened, she thought about what sort of parties the place must've seen in its heyday – back in those long-ago times when men wore starched collars and sat around in smoking rooms, talking about the newest marvel of the day, the electric light.

Lucy turned, meaning to head to the kitchen to say goodbye to Caroline again, and maybe set aside a time to sit and have that tea, when she caught sight of her wristwatch and decided against it. She walked toward the large set of front doors, her heels making a click-click that echoed in the silence.

A shiver ran up her spine at the sound. Had it ever been this quiet in here before? Usually, there were sounds of muffled conversation coming from the rooms upstairs, as well as at least two girls playing their records. But at the moment, the only thing Lucy could hear was her own footsteps.

Click-click, click-click.

The light coming through the foyer windows showed even darker skies than what she'd seen in the library. Overhead, the crystal chandelier, usually cheerful and opulent, hung there dark and menacing. Shadows were beginning to creep in from the far corners. Thunder rumbled, sending more chills and shivers.

Almost to the door now, Lucy stopped, looking over to her left at another set of doors, cracked just slightly open. They led into a ballroom, Lucy knew, but she'd only been inside it once after moving in and getting the tour. Usually, those doors stayed locked. Her heart beat hard in her chest as she looked through that dark gap.

She didn't like the look of it, that darkness. Didn't like that the doors she and all the other girls had been told so many times should stay locked, weren't. A thought came, and try as she might, Lucy couldn't push it away.

Jack hadn't been alone in the car. Someone had been there in the shadows, waiting.

At that, she tore her gaze from the void and stepped back. Her breath came and went in shallow gasps. Lucy turned, looking around the darkening foyer. Every shadow was a hiding place, and from every hiding place, she imagined she could see eyes watching her.

Thunder clapped again, louder than before, and Lucy made for the door fast, not daring to look back. She pulled the door open with a hard jerk and almost fell out onto the front steps. Before she backed into the door, slamming it behind her, Lucy thought she could hear the faint sound of the tea kettle beginning to whistle.

Chapter Twenty-Five

Carly stood just out of sight, her breathing not quite steady as she watched Lucy first jump at the sound of thunder, then go bolting out the front door. Behind her, the kettle began to whistle, but she barely heard it.

What were you going to do with that?

She looked down at her hand, a kitchen knife gripped hard in one shaking fist, then looked back toward the front door again.

So he was *Danny*, huh? Something about the way Lucy had said his name…the ease, and that smile on her face a person would have to be blind to miss, had caused that feeling to start creeping up. The one where it felt like her world had narrowed to a pinprick and everything was red…it was still on her now, and what was worse, it wasn't fading. It wasn't because she wanted him, God no, that ship had long passed them by, but just the fact that in addition to everything else, he seemed to have managed to get ahold of a little side piece too.

The idea came to her then to follow Lucy or maybe start screaming for help. No one else was around, not even the old woman who ran the place. Or maybe, she could just run up to the door, rip it open, grab Lucy by the hair, and yank her back inside. She'd fall, then before realizing what was happening, Carly would plunge the knife into the nape of her neck…yeah, that'd be the perfect spot. Then she'd sit there waiting til Danny got here.

But it wasn't right…the moment had gone.

That's what crazy people say.

Carly ignored the thought. It'd been getting easier and easier to do that just lately…obviously, or else she'd have never gotten as far toward…well, what it was she'd been thinking about doing just now.

She wasn't insane. She was desperate and alone and exhausted…and there seemed to be no end in sight.

But really, how could there be? With all this shit piling on her…all those people…first Dan, then Lucy with those knowing, jeering smiles…those two women in the grocery store. It'd been those two that'd made her think of that video again, and when she'd gotten back to her room later that morning, she'd watched it. Then she'd watched it again, then again.

The first time might've been punishment or penance or whatever someone on the outside looking in might want to call it. Still, after a while, she didn't see the point in lying to herself about why she kept watching…when she watched, her memories of the night sharpened, everything rosy…it was almost as if she were right back there, not feeling lost or tired anymore. Holding the phone close to her face, she'd watched Jack's…it was nice to finally have a name for the lifeless body just sitting there. Remembering all the while that underneath the shock and horror, she'd felt powerful and alive.

But the high never lasted long. Not like it had before. And each comedown seemed to hit that much harder for it. Like today, when it was all Carly could do to not lose her shit. She turned back into the kitchen, slipped the knife into her pocket, and turned off the burner. The whistle of the kettle began to slow.

Despite that knowing, shitty smile, part of her did like Lucy just a little bit. And honestly, Carly would've loved some tea with her before making some excuse to get behind Lucy, the knife sliding slowly out of her pocket as she did.

Leaving the kitchen and making her way into the foyer, Carly looked around, her gaze lingering on the stairs, remembering the reception she'd gone to here once upon a time. What'd started out as a good night quickly went to shit, and somehow, everything in her life started to go to shit from that point on. All because he couldn't just be a man and apologize without comment and move on. No, he had to backpedal and bring up all sorts of shit in public to make himself look better. To pass off his responsibility and make his bad behavior somehow all about her.

Carly could remember him, lying there at her feet, feeling a red flush creep up her cheeks as everyone's eyes were on them…on her. Judging her. Mocking her without saying a word. Feeling that, knowing that it was his fault, she remembered instead of just kicking him in the ribs, instead feeling like she could just

From outside, thunder rumbled, pulling Carly out of memory lane and back to the present, leaving her feeling more enraged…her breathing harsh, the sound of blood rushing through her ears joining the thunder.

I wonder if Lucy's getting rained on yet.

Turning away from the stairs and that awful night, Carly moved on tiptoe toward the front doors to peek through the thin stained-glass windows running along either side. It was sort of like looking through a kaleidoscope, but her eyes adjusted in just enough time to watch a car first pull up, then park as a man stepped out.

It was him.

"Sorry," Dan said, getting out and only just remembering to shut the door. "I got caught up."

"Everything okay?" Lucy said. Carly couldn't see her but guessed she had herself pressed up against the doors.

"Yeah, had to swing by the store. The new girl, Elise, is closing tonight, and I forgot to leave her a few extra notes. Ollie'll be there, but he'll be pretty busy with the ledgers, and I guess he's got a bunch of vendor calls to make. What're you doing waiting out here?"

"Thought I'd get a little fresh air before the rain comes."

"Makes sense. Are you ready?"

"No. No, I'm not. But shall we?"

Carly's eyes never left Dan. She watched as he smiled…that same goddamn smile…how could he have anything to smile about today? Wasn't this killing him inside? If so, he definitely didn't look it. The way he held his arm out to Lucy, and she came into view to take it, she still didn't look all that broken up. Then something occurred to her.

He'd been all wrong…Jack had been all wrong…of course. There'd been no way to know before, but now it all made sense. These two were screwing behind Jack's back…absolutely had to be, and she, Carly, had just done Dan the biggest favor in the world by removing the middleman…after all the risk and the anguish of that night, the only thing she'd done was make his life that much better…

As they walked, Carly wrestled with the urge to run out after them, hand on the knife still in her pocket, something began to ping in the back of her mind. And like the first time she'd seen him again, Carly found herself pinned to the spot. It was something she'd seen as Dan got out of the car, she was pretty sure, only she couldn't quite place it.

As another threatening rumble of thunder sounded overhead, she heard Lucy's car start up…then that thing she couldn't quite place clicked. And what's more, an idea started to form.

"Oh, come on," she said, crossing her fingers. "Keep going, come on, just keep going."

And they did. Carly watched the big, red car roll down to the end of the drive, turn left, and disappear. She waited, expecting them to turn around and come back any second once Dan realized what he'd done, but they didn't. Two minutes passed, then three, then four. After five minutes, she stood, then walked outside.

She hurried over to where his car sat parked and opened it. Then, looking inside, she saw it…turned into the Off position, but still stuck in the ignition, was the key.

Carly smiled.

Chapter Twenty-Six

Local VFW Post 473 opened its doors today as mourners with umbrellas in hand filled the spacious hall before winding through the corridors and out into the parking area itself to pay their final respects to Johnathan Edwin Lawrence, better known as Jack to those closest to him.

When asked about why today's events, a viewing of the body with graveside services to follow, were changed from their original venue, Alfred Cole of Cole & Sons Funeral Home told this reporter—

Whunk!

"Oh, for goodness sake!"

It'd been about five minutes or so since Penny had ducked into this little room…a lounge complete with sprung armchairs, photographs on the wall, and the smell of stale cigars…trying to get a decent start on her coverage while the lead was still fresh in her mind.

Penny looked at the door some oaf had just bumped into before turning back to her notebook, pen at the ready. But no words came. Between that little scare and the dull murmur of voices on the other side only getting louder, her concentration had broken for the time being.

"Probably just as well," she thought, capping the pen and tossing it into her bag. She'd been about to shut the notebook and toss it in too, when something clipped to another page caught her attention, and she turned to it: Eddie's note.

"I just can't shake Parker from my mind," Eddie had said later that same afternoon after dropping off the note. They'd taken a booth at Bill's, for the moment, no one in there besides them and an older gentleman reading his paper at the counter. "I can understand how those things happened to find themselves in Jack Lawrence's car, but something about it still rubs me the wrong way."

"You don't think it's just, well, a coincidence?"

"It's possible, but I'm not entirely convinced of it."

"Not meanin' to tell you how to do your job, Eddie, but why not just bring him in? Sounds like you've got plenty of cause to question him in one of your little rooms."

"Because I need to gather some more information and think on it before I really go after the man. I've still got my hands full with the rest of the Sherbrooke mess. The big one wants my ass, and the pretty one might as well be deaf-mute from what I hear, but I've gotta try and talk to her anyway. Not to mention a bunch of other people, and there are only so many hours in a day…Buck picked a hell of a time to come down with somethin' that left him bed bound."

Penny had sipped her coffee, thought about reaching for Eddie's hand if only for a moment, tried not to, and did it anyway. It wasn't for long, surely not long enough to give the wrong impression, but he'd been hers once, and old habits die hard.

"So, just where do I come into this?" Penny said, pitching her voice even lower and looking around before returning to Eddie, who sighed.

"Just watch him at the service. Lucy Rodgers, too, if she's there with him, which I expect she might be. See if anything about him strikes you as, well, odd. I've noticed a few things, others have too… But I won't say just what now because I don't wanna taint your observations, but keep an eye on him…talk to him if you think it'll help. More'n anything, I'm curious how they act when they see Jack laid out. If it was one of the boys or me out there lookin', I think he'd put on an act. But I don't think that'd be the case for you, which is why I'm askin'."

She didn't really know what to say other than, of course, she'd help…play spy just like she'd thought it might come to and let Eddie know how things went after. Something didn't feel right about spying on folks during mourning; maybe there was something in the Bible about it, but Penny thought she could work past that. It was the price she had to pay for Eddie not turning her away when he'd first seen her walking up to the scene the night before, giving her the chance at something serious. And, if she meant to get away from frilly journalism, that meant getting used to talking to people when the situation was uncomfortable.

Sighing, Penny checked her watch and then closed the notebook. She tossed it into her bag and stood. Squeezing her way out the lounge door, she pushed past folks giving her "I'm so sorry, excuse me," and "If I could just get past, oh thanks so much" over and over again until she finally slipped through the nearest doors leading outside.

Chapter Twenty-Seven

"Oh, my goodness."

"I thought this was gonna be a lot smaller, Luce. We maybe should've driven ourselves."

"Too late for that now."

Lucy rested her hand on the crook of Dan's arm as they began to walk toward the back of the line, not terribly far away from where he'd parked the Buick. Dan thought about maybe asking her to take her hand back before anyone saw…touching him just felt like a red flag or something, but under the circumstances, it'd probably be weirder if he wasn't escorting her like this, so he let it go.

The drive over had been mostly silent, which didn't much surprise him. Driving to a funeral doesn't, as a rule, put people in a chatty mood. That'd come later, after the show was over and everyone who stayed filed into a church basement to eat casseroles and pies, while trying to pick up the pieces of day-to-day life again. Not that he thought that last part would happen for him any time soon.

The last few days had been a special type of hell. Ollie had strongly insisted…bullied him into taking some time off, which honestly felt like the last thing in the world he needed. What he'd needed was distraction. Anything to avoid being alone with his thoughts and with what'd happened.

But of course, he ought to have known better. Because no matter where he went…a football game over at the high school, to the movies, he seemed to run into someone who wanted to take the time to apologize and say what a tragedy it all was.

It really is! And you wanna hear the ironic thing? It was a total accident. The moment I moved here, using a machine I only understood enough to pick a destination and hit Go, I knocked over the first domino that ended up in Jack being killed! Because this didn't happen originally, oh no. No, I'm a history teacher and a goddamn nerd who's read all about the town's scandals and secrets…and I can tell you, this is entirely new. But don't worry, everyone, the thing doesn't work anymore, so I'll be stuck here, changing all sorts of shit from now on!

Dan made a swipe at his eyes, then tried playing it off as adjusting his hat in case Lucy had noticed. No dice there.

"Are you alright?"

He looked at her, her wet but curious eyes fixed on his, and not for the first time wished he could just tell her everything. There was no way of knowing what she might think of him after, either as a murderer or a lunatic, but it might be worth it just to not hold on to this secret anymore.

"Oh, don't worry about me," Dan said. "What about you? Are you okay?"

Lucy didn't say anything, only smiled in a way that didn't touch her eyes and shook her head. He put a hand over the one she still held onto him with, rubbing gently for a moment before letting it drop and continuing on.

They joined the end of the line, the two men standing in front of them giving a look and a tip of the hat with a brief "Afternoon", before turning back to their conversation, and Dan did likewise, then looked up at the sky.

It was an inky blue-gray, and the clouds were moving fast, thunder sounding off and on. Dan thought it might start pouring on them any minute, and here he was with his umbrella still sitting in the Model A's front se—"

"Oh no."

"What's wrong Danny?"

"I just realized, I left my damn key sitting in the A's ignition."

"Well, that's alright, you were in a hurry. You didn't have your house keys attached to it, did you?"

"No, I walk more often than I drive, so I keep 'em separate, but do you think the A is okay over there?"

"Of course, why wouldn't it be?"

Dan opened his mouth to say what if there's a new social media challenge and some little shits break in and steal it, but stopped himself. First off, if the key was still in the ignition, that meant the door was unlocked, so there'd be no need to break in. Second, no social media. But he still didn't like it.

"I think I may want to head back, just real quick, to grab my key. I know it'll be a little bit, but if you save my place, I'll—"

"Danny, do you remember when you and I and Jack and Patty Truitt went down to the lake, and you realized you'd left your kitchen door unlocked?"

"Yeah."

"What happened?"

Dan tried to think. Patty spent a lot of the time sunning herself or trying to sweet-talk him…an early attempt of Lucy's to set him up. Lucy got some sunbathing in while making it through at least one book, and he and Jack thought it'd be a riot to rent one of the motorboats and—

"What happened was nothing," Lucy said, leaving the memory of the lake behind. "You were all worried somethin' would be stolen, and not so much as a scrap of paper was out of place. Remember what I said the other day? This is a nice…place."

Lucy fell a little on that last word, and it didn't take Dan long to pick up on what might've just run through her head. New Chapel was a mostly nice place…or had been at least until a few days ago, when some unnamed psychopath hid out in the backseat of the Vic, waiting to slash Jack's throat.

"Please stay," she said. "Don't leave me here alone, not even for a minute."

Dan thought about the car sitting open at Harrington House and resigned himself to letting it sit there. Lucy was right about one thing; the A would be perfectly fine until he headed back over to get it. And for another thing, if some jackass kid did take it and wreck it in a ditch, well, so what? Now that staying here was no longer a hypothetical, it'd be just as good an excuse as any to buy a new car.

"I'm not goin' anywhere," he said.

They made idle chat as the line moved, mainly keeping to themselves, except for saying a quick hello and goodbye to the occasional passerby they recognized heading back to their car, having passed through the VFW already. One woman, though, who'd stepped out of the building, instead of passing them by, got in line right behind them.

"I don't like the looks of those clouds," the woman said, and Dan made a half-turn in her direction, looking up again.

"It'll hold off," he said. "At least for a little while longer."

"I sure hope so. I don't know about you folks, but I didn't bring an umbrella."

"Looks like you're in good company then," Lucy said, giving something approximating her usual winning smile. "What's your name, dear?"

"Oh, my manners," the woman said, extending a hand. "I'm Penny Prescott."

Dan took the hand and shook, that name circling around and around in his head. He knew it, but for the life of him, couldn't think of from where. After a moment, it clicked, and he found himself tightening up just a bit.

"You write for the Gazette, don't you?" Lucy said, also taking the hand, her tone slightly icier than it'd been only a moment ago.

"That's right," Penny said, smiling, gloved hands clasped in front of her. "You're Dan Parker and Lucy Rodgers, yes?"

Dan nodded. Of all the people they could possibly get stuck in line with…

"I'd love to ask a few questions if I may. I'm covering today and—"

"No, thank you," Lucy said, her voice seeming to all but scramble for something like patience and calm. "We're here to mourn Miss—"

"You can just call me Penny."

"Penny then," Lucy said, nodding. "We're here to mourn, Penny. Jack meant a great deal to both of us, and I think I can speak for both of us when I say we'd rather be left in peace."

"Oh, of course! I'll put my press badge away with you two. Please don't think me rude, I'm just—"

"Just doing your job," Dan said. "I get it."

And it was the truth. Just happening to hop in line behind the widowed girlfriend and the best friend of the deceased? She'd be a fool not to try to get something out of them. He would if their positions had been swapped.

But Penny was as good as her word, and as the minutes passed, slowly but steadily shuffling toward the open entrance to the VFW hall, when they spoke, it was about anything but what they were all here for. After a while, Lucy had thawed a bit, and Dan himself even got close to forgetting that Penny could end up putting a blurb in her story about being in line with them.

"Oh, all that stuff is a bunch of baloney," Lucy said, now so close to the building they could see inside the propped-open doors. "A spaceship crash? Sounds like someone's been havin' too much fun with their funny books. Whoever wrote that story should've checked their sources before printing that."

"Maybe they did," Penny said. "Who's to say for sure? Could be they got the real story out before the military boys sent down the word to keep quiet, just tryin' to sweep the whole thing away."

Dan's attention had been wandering around as the two women talked, but snapped back.

They're talking about Roswell. Holy shit, that was just a few months ago. Man, if I'd thought more about it, I'd have taken a little camping trip out to New Mexico, just me and my iPhone. Although all that stuff did end up getting taken to Wright Field, only like fifteen minutes away and—

"What do you think about all this nonsense?" Lucy said, and Dan looked between the two of them.

A few things occurred…something about there being more in heaven and earth than Horacio dreamt of in his philosophies. Or maybe how reality was stranger than fiction…he was living proof of that one. But instead, he settled on something else. Definitely too early, but what the hell.

"The truth is out there."

The subject of Roswell gave way to more ordinary things, and before long, they'd wound through the halls and were standing in the open lobby of the VFW hall. Dan was pretty sure that he'd been here before, probably for a grad party or something like that, but there wasn't time to be bothered by either that or the slight headache that'd started up from the past and present doubling over on itself again.

Through the open doors just ahead, Dan could see the line of mourners disappearing into a decent-sized hall. The lights inside were dim, and there were no windows; it looked like they were heading into a cave. The murmur of voices coming from it was low and deep and sounded almost like a part of the thunder that'd started up again.

Lucy's grip on his arm tightened as they approached the doorway to the cave. She eased up to sign her name in the visitor's book before handing the pen to Dan. His eye lingered on the heading "Friends" for a moment before signing his name under Lucy's and passing the pen on so Penny could sign.

As they moved closer, eyes adjusting to the dimness and the thinning crowd up ahead, Jack's coffin slid into view. Though they were still a way back, Dan could see pale hands clasped, nostrils that would never again breathe air, and a golden tinkle from the edge of Jack's glasses.

Dan tried to take a deep breath, but between the lump in his throat and the slight hitching in his chest, the best he could manage was a shallow gasp.

I'm so sorry, man.

The line moved again. Dan stepped forward but felt himself being anchored to the spot. He turned toward Lucy.

"I can't do this," she said, her voice so soft he almost couldn't hear.

"Wh-huh?" Dan said, forcing the word out around the sob, just waiting to come out.

"I…I can't do this," she said again, louder this time, then let go of his arm.

Without another word, Lucy turned and made her way, weaving in and out back through the crowd. People let her pass, looking after her as she did. A moment later, she passed through the doors and disappeared back into the lobby.

Penny, who hadn't spoken a word since they'd set foot in the cave, turned, an expression of sad concern written all over her face. Dan shook his head, not really sure why or what he'd meant to communicate. Reaching out, Penny grabbed his hand, for the moment not a reporter, just one person being kind to another.

"I'm so sorry," she said, giving his hand a brief squeeze before letting go.

Dan nodded, looking up at the box…at Jack, for what he knew would be the final time. The folded hands, the glasses. A flood of memories came…a distillation of all the good times. All the reasons he'd come to call this man a friend. There was bad too, but in his heart, it didn't cancel out the good, not even close. And it only took noticing the crowd here today to know he maybe wasn't the only one who felt that way; he could be at peace, feeling both angry and sad. The guilt of his part in this would remain until the day he died, he was sure, but at least there was some easing of his heart.

He wanted to say something more, one last word to Jack, but everything that came to mind felt cheap. In the end, he could only smile and give a shaky nod before turning and following Lucy's path back out into the lobby.

Chapter Twenty-Eight

"Have a good night, Mr. Walker!"

"You too, cookie, great job today. See ya tomorrow."

While Dan Parker was in a crowded hall considering pale, clasped hands, Elise Crawford stepped out of Walker's Fine Books with a dress box under her arm, taking a look up at the sky as the door locked behind her. It was a deep, dark blue, and thunder rumbled in the distance like a tractor engine. Letting Momma and Daddy drop her off instead of taking the Farmall truck like she'd planned on was maybe not such a good idea after all. They were probably at that Jack fella's funeral by now, and who knew when they'd be back.

Thunder rumbled again, deeper this time. Elise stood still, frozen underneath the scallop-edged canopy as it began to flap a little in the wind. She thought of her umbrella…pale blue with pink roses, sitting propped in a corner of her bedroom where it was no good to her at all. And a quick rummage through her handbag, hoping for a scarf, turned up nothing but her pocketbook and a pack of gum.

"Isn't that just dandy."

Elise looked up and down her little part of the street, watching people pass by and cars doing likewise. So far as she could see, though, no one she knew seemed to be out and about. No one she felt comfortable enough asking for a ride from, that was. She supposed she could ask Mr. Walker for a ride home, but he'd mentioned something about needing to stop in the market on his way home, and she didn't want to put him out. Sighing, she began to walk.

As she strolled along, every so often catching glances at the sky, Elise thought about ducking into the hardware store. They sometimes had a few spare umbrellas for sale in a forgotten corner, Lord knew why.

No, Daddy'd never let you hear the end of it…spending money to buy somethin' you've already got. Treats me like I'm nine instead of nineteen half the time.

Instead, she thought about the white box in her hand with the cellophane window. The box she'd picked up special on her break with the pale purple dress she'd bought for church tomorrow inside.

Momma and Daddy didn't know about that one, yet, but she just had to have it. A few days ago, when Bobby called, his usually smooth voice almost squeaky, asking if he could talk to her after church but before they went out for lunch with Andrew and Wendy…well, she thought it might just be an occasion where she'd want to look her best.

Elise had left the center of town and made it as far as some of those fine old houses when the first tiny drops started to fall from the sky, darkening the pavement in a series of tiny polka dots. With a sigh and a silent prayer that the cellophane covering and the box itself were as sturdy as they looked, she grabbed it a little tighter and started to hurry.

The light sprinkling held for most of the walk back to her family's farm, and Elise couldn't have been more grateful. She prayed as each block passed, all the while the wind picked up, occasionally blowing misty rain into her face, forcing her to squint.

"Please lord," she said, blinking and wiping the drops away as best she could. "Just a little bit longer, I'm almost there."

She could feel the waxed cardboard getting a little softer. A few times, she'd stopped to check the dress. There might be a wet corner; it was hard to tell in such little light, but she thought it wasn't much worse for the experience. And if it was, there was plenty of time for it to dry before she wore it.

The last of what she called the "townhouses," even though she knew full well none of them were townhouses, fell behind, giving way to fields. Corn and beans are about a month away from harvest. The nice cement-paved road became dirt and gravel, now mud and gravel. Well, mostly mud.

Oh, I'm glad I didn't wear my nice shoes today, Elise thought, taking her first step into the muck.

Ahead in the distance, she saw home. A two-story, old brick farmhouse with a small handful of barns and sheds surrounding it. The house sat on a small hill, and from her bedroom window, she felt like the queen of all she surveyed. Not that there was much to survey besides fields, the tractor barn, and the lane that ran up to Sherbrooke Dairy. Passing by that lane now, Elise saw the police sawhorses and couldn't help but stop and stare.

The place was quiet without all the trucks coming in and out of the place. The cows had still been getting fed and milked, she knew that. Daddy'd been lending a hand with that when he could. Where the folks who normally did those things hadn't been mentioned, and Elise hadn't asked. The day before yesterday, Daddy asked if she'd like to come and help, and she'd turned him down flat.

"If it's all right, I'd just like to stay and clean out the chicken house," she'd said, before complimenting Momma on the biscuits and sending the conversation in another direction.

Cleaning out the chicken house was about the last thing on earth she wanted to do. The place stank no matter how clean it was, and for whatever reason, those foul fowl ignored every other person in God's creation except her. It'd gotten to where she wouldn't step inside without wearing the boots from when she'd shown horses; they went up all the way to her knees and kept the pecking injuries mostly at bay. Still, it beat the pants off going to the Sherbrooke farm.

Her gaze followed the lane up to the house, sitting alone and dark on the hill, looking somehow both abandoned and like it was full of spooks just watching her…or maybe just one. Elise shuddered thinking about that. Wondering if the soul of the man murdered not far from her own home was looking at her now.

She knew what Pastor Brian would say, that those two were up there, sinning in the eyes of the Lord, and that the wages of sin is death. And that if Jack's spirit still roamed, he was doing penance for his ways, hoping God would be merciful in His judgment and allow his soul into heaven. Maybe that was so, and maybe that was just, but her heart still ached for both of them just the same, Mrs. Sherbrooke most of all.

Coming down the stairs that night, listening to the sound of banging on the front door, watching Momma peek through the window, and Daddy come up, a shotgun in hand, Elise had struggled to make sense of it.

"Daddy?"

"Get back upstairs, Elise, you mind me now," Momma had said, and she did, making it halfway back up the steps before the door opened and Mrs. Sherbrooke ran inside, screaming. Her clothes were torn and dirty, and her normally beautiful hair was a mess, and Elise guessed she'd been running through the fields to get to the house. Her eyes were wide and staring, and she looked like a thing half-crazy, like in some of those horror pictures Bobby had taken her to.

One look had been enough for her heart to swell with pity, but at the same time, she didn't want to stay downstairs a second longer. Something about that spooky look made her want to start screaming, too.

Elise had turned and headed the rest of the way back upstairs, closing her bedroom door behind her, and lay with her pillow covering both ears for the better part of an hour. First listening to Momma and Daddy trying to get the screaming woman to stop, then listening in when the men came and finally took the poor soul away, leaving silence in the house again.

Thunder rumbled, and Elise tore her attention away from that haunted house. Her eyes snapped to the fields, looking less like corn almost ready for harvest as the light faded, and more like a giant shadow about to shoot out its shadow arms at any second and grab her. Elise turned and ran.

As she splashed through the small puddles toward home...still in the distance, but oh so close now, the heavens opened up. And what she'd been walking through before might as well have been a clear, sunny day. The rain fell hard, forcing her to look down at the ground. Breath caught in her chest as the cold water soaked her from head to toe in a matter of moments, setting her teeth to chatter.

Elise raised the dress box over her head, feeling her fingers sink through the cardboard and touch the fine fabric underneath.

Be upset later, she thought, her shoes making a faint squelching sound and threatening to come off at any moment. *Once you're nice and dry in front of the wood stove, you can be upset all you like.*

Her right shoe stuck in the mud, and Elise only just managed to catch herself before flying face down in the mess when the shoe and foot parted company. That didn't matter, though; she'd come back for the thing later.

Squinting through the rain and feeling like home might as well be a million miles away, Elise pressed on, her one bare foot already muddy up to the heel. She'd only managed another few yards when she noticed her shadow appear as the world grew bright around her. Unable to help it, she stopped and turned.

Car!

Sure enough, two headlights were headed her way, and from the looks of things, she thought they might be slowing down. Elise lowered the sunken, soaking mess of her box to her chest as the car came to a stop. It was hard to say, between the lights, the rain, and the soaked curtains of her own hair, but something about that car looked familiar.

"Mr. Parker?" she said, calling over the rain. "Is that you?"

Beep-beep!

"Oh, thank God!"

Elise hurried over, feeling awful about the sort of mess she was going to leave in that nice man's car, and already working out how much she should probably offer to help put it right.

The thank you card in my purse I'd written for him trainin' me should be a nice start, she thought, opening the passenger door just as another set of headlights began to crest over the small rise in the distance in front of her.

Chapter Twenty-Nine

The Buick jumped as it transitioned from County 12, a dirt, now mud, road back onto pavement for the time being. It skidded a little from side to side as the radial tires, caked in mud, tried to get purchase on the wet pavement. After a heart-stopping moment when Dan thought he might lose control and drive them into the nearest ditch, the Buick righted itself, and the ride smoothed as much as it could.

He'd no sooner seen Lucy waiting by the car outside the VFW hall when the skies finally gave way, and it'd only gotten worse since. It came down in sheets, and the wipers weren't doing much to help. The headlights cut through the deluge and the dark as best they could, leaving Dan just able to make out things like street signs, fences, other cars…the sort of thing most drivers would generally like to avoid hitting.

"Sorry, Luce," he said, leaning back in the seat to catch his breath.

"It's alright," she said.

Out of the corner of his eye, Dan sensed movement and, sparing a glance, saw her still looking out the window, but reaching a hand toward him across the seat. He slowed, taking one hand off the wheel and met her halfway, lacing his fingers in between hers.

She hadn't said anything about what'd happened in the hall, except for a shaking of the head and a tear-choked "I'm sorry, I…I just couldn't" after they'd gotten back in the car; Dan didn't need any more explanation than that.

Some people need funerals as part of their coping and for closure when a person dies. Others, himself included…Lucy, too, maybe, found the idea of seeing the person they'd once known and cared for stuck in a box and looking like a wax dummy…having that be the last image of them, no matter how hard someone might try to shake it, to be just too much. And honestly, it'd been no small measure of relief when he'd turned to see her heading out the door.

Sitting in all this silence, with not much besides his own thoughts and the squeak-squeak of the wiper blades for company, something did finally surface and break the silence that'd held since then. Rubbing the back of her hand with his thumb, Dan took a breath.

"Are you absolutely sure that you don't want me to drop you back at Harrington House, or anywhere else? This has been, well, *hard* doesn't quite come close, but—"

He'd prepared for her to pull her hand away from his, saying something about how it'd probably be best given everything. But instead of pulling away, her grip tightened, and she slid over next to him. A glance over to the right, and he saw she was staring down the side of his face.

"Please, please, Danny, don't," she said, her voice barely audible over the rain and the wipers. "I don't wanna be alone, and I don't wanna be with anyone else right now. Don't leave me at that place."

Dan spared a quick look at her again, and her eyes, while still shiny with tears, were set. The intensity unnerved him a bit, so, checking to make sure he wouldn't need a tow truck after, he pulled over near the edge of a field and brought them to a stop.

"Are you mad because I had to leave?" she said, as he put the Buick in park and turned his attention to her. "Is that why you want to take me back?"

"Oh…no, nothing like that, I swear. I just, after everything, I wanted to check if anything had changed, that's all. Don't get the wrong idea, I'm perfectly fine having you."

Lucy looked at him for a moment, a half-grin crossing her face.

"You really are, aren't you? Not concerned with what folks might say or anything like that?"

"I mean, maybe a little. But I guess nothing I can do or say is going to stop them or change anything, so what's the point, right? People minding their own business is always an option."

"Anyone ever tell you you're a bit odd?"

"Loudly and often, yes."

That got a choked half-laugh, and Dan was glad to hear it. Lucy took a handkerchief out of her bag, then rubbed at the bottoms and corners of her eyes where the makeup had long since started to run. Some of the tension had eased in the car, and that was good, but something else about what she'd said had sort of snagged in his mind.

"Luce, is there something, well," he said, pausing to gather his thoughts, "*wrong* at your place? You said, *don't leave me at that place* and earlier, when I came to pick you up, you were waiting outside. Are, I don't know, are people being jerks about all this?"

Lucy sat, looking at the handkerchief in her hands, smiling and shaking her head.

"No, nothing like that," she said. "They've all been dears. It's just…it's a pretty old house, but spooky when you're alone and sad, that's all. It was silly, it got dark while I was waitin' and I felt like all the shadows were creepin' up on me and, well, that's why you found me outside."

"There wasn't anyone there to, you know, sit with?"

"The new girl, Caroline Wells, her name is, was there. She'd even offered me some tea, but you were due any time, so I'd passed on the company."

Dan felt a small jolt when he heard that name. He knew a Caroline Wells, only she'd been going by Carly since middle school. Most likely not family since Carly's from Michigan, but he thought he'd still check out Caroline Wells in the archives on his MacBook, just out of curiosity.

It'd been a while since he'd thought of Carly. She'd never shown up that day for her card, never texted him back either. Even his amazing discovery hadn't been enough to drive that completely from his mind. He'd tried calling, but it kept going to voicemail. After a day or so, he assumed that she'd just taken the easy route, cancelling the card and blocking his number so they wouldn't have to interact with each other again.

That was probably for the best, all things considered.

"Danny?"

Dan blinked, looking at the rain sheeting down the windshield, the wipers almost for show at this point, then over to Lucy.

"Are you okay?" she said. "Do we need to swap seats?"

"No, no, I'm fine. Long day. I'm ready to be done, is all."

Lucy nodded and squeezed his hand. Dan looked at their interlaced fingers, and another thought came up. He knew he should probably just keep it to himself, but he didn't think that sort of thing would be happening much today. He raised their still clasped hands.

"Wonder what he'd think of this," he said, and Lucy gave a brief, humorless laugh.

"All things considered, Danny, I don't know if I'm the best judge of what Jack would or wouldn't have thought about things. But what I *like* to think is that since he isn't around, he'd feel better knowing you are. I know I do."

Dan nodded. Right or wrong, he felt about the same. And it could be wishful thinking…probably was, but he thought that if there was such a thing as communicating with the dead…maybe a plane of existence where he and Jack could sit together in some crisp, clean diner wearing white and having burgers, Jack might have more to say than just that.

"Question for ya," he'd say, leaning back in his seat, hands behind his neck, and a cigarette poked out the corner of his mouth. "Were you the one who hid in my backseat?"

"Well, no. But—"

"Did you hand over that razor with the plan to pay some seedy lowlife to do me in so you could take my girl?"

"No! No, of course not, I—"

"Well then, would ya quit on it? You've got plenty of other things to worry about, Tomorrow Boy. Startin' with a busted time machine, and the fact that I really did end up gettin' you into trouble after all. If anything, I should be apologizing to you. Might've been if I'd gotten your razor back to you, we wouldn't be in this mess."

He knew the little scene was just his subconscious telling him what he wanted to hear, but it hit pretty hard for all that. Was it so crazy to think that's how such a conversation would've gone down?

Dan raised Lucy's hand, pressing his lips to the back of it before letting go and settling his hand on the shifter.

"Let's get outta here."

"Please. Being near all these dark fields is giving me the creeps. Just, if you still wanna go and grab your car key, can we be quick about it? My clothes are wet, and I've been thinkin' about that fireplace of yours for a while now."

"We can leave the A til tomorrow. If some kid goes joyriding and wrecks it, then I'll just have to head over to the Ford dealership and grab the '46 Coupe that keeps staring at me every time I drive by."

"The red one, or the black one?"

"The black one."

Putting the Buick into drive and moving carefully, Dan got them back out on the road and moving once more. A few minutes and another turn later found them on another mud-bogged back road running past the Starlight Drive-In, then past Sherbrooke Dairy…though he did his best not to look at that last one as they passed.

The dark had come on even stronger, and Dan started to feel around on the dash for the lights, remembering that the Buick was new enough to have high beams. His fingers happened on it, and he shot his eyes to the side to try and see what he needed to do to flip them on when Lucy yelled out.

"Danny!"

Jerking up, he saw they'd drifted onto what passed for the shoulder and toward what looked like a parked car off on the side of the road.

"Shit!"

Dan pulled the wheel hard left. The Buick started to drift, but it righted itself, and the other car passed by in a flash. He flicked on the brights, then put both hands back on the wheel, chancing glances behind through the rear-view mirror.

"Ah, I probably should've stopped…they might've been stuck."

"I don't think so," Lucy said, a hand on her chest. "Probably just pulled over, waitin' for the rain to let up some. I guess if we had any sense, we'd still be parked by the field doin' the same thing. And listen, buster, if you're not more careful with my car, I'll make you buy me a new one."

"Yes, ma'am," Dan said, and continued on, slowly.

Chapter Thirty

Flipping his notebook shut, Eddie straightened his back, stretching. Outside the nearby window, it was almost full dark, but he thought he could just make out drops moving from side to side across the pane instead of straight down. They hit the glass like handfuls of thrown pebbles, but it was a welcome sound…it helped to tamp down the laughing and crying and screaming that seemed to come from all around him.

He sat in a small, empty waiting room on the fourth floor of Alcomb Sanatorium, the great stone fortress out in the woods between New Chapel and Springdale, keeping the local lunatics separate from the normal folks. It'd been built just after the Civil War, but with its great stone bricks, its turrets and towers, and the high windows covered in wrought iron bars, Eddie thought it looked more like a medieval prison than anything else.

It was the first time he'd ever driven through the gate with its stone gargoyles flanking either side, and if there was any good luck to his name, tonight would be the last time.

Wwwuuuurrrrzzzz…wwwwuuuurrrrzzzz…wwwwwrrrr…

Eddie looked up, watching the chandelier above his head start to brighten and dim in time with the electrical whirring sound going on around him. The lights went low, leaving him in near-darkness. The muffled screams were louder and more manic than before. Laughter that sounded neither amused nor sane. And after a long moment of wondering if the loonies would burst in on him, it was over. The whirring stopped, and the lights shone bright again.

"Jesus."

"Not to worry!" a voice called. Eddie looked over and saw the nurse who'd directed him to this little room when he'd arrived sitting behind her desk.

"Oh?"

"Only the generators kicking in, you see. They must've had a strong one in Suite #2," she said, checking a clipboard before adding, "My apologies, Suite #3."

She said it with a calm smile. As if they were in her sitting room having tea, explaining that the knocking sound was just that old radiator acting up; that bothered him. And it bothered him the more he thought about it. That was damned loony stuff. Was that what happened when a person worked in a place like this? Or were the folks who wanted a job here already touched in the head to begin with?

"Ah...thank you, ma'am," he said, turning and opening his notebook again, grateful that he had something to pull his attention away from that woman and the sound of those screams.

Flipping through, he combed back over his notes from the last few days, his eyes catching on the few things he'd written before bringing Buck up to speed.

"Let's have it," Buck said earlier that day, his wife finally deciding he was well enough to see folks, and after Doc Staunton had checked the sheriff out and said that he didn't have anything catchy.

And Eddie had laid it out. The scene at the dairy in all its detail, complete with photographs. Doc Horton's postmortem findings. About the meeting at Dan Parker's place the morning after, and finding Lucy Rodgers with him. And his chance encounter with Elmer Robertson, the head fry cook at Bill's, raised his suspicions and went a long way toward explaining the car Martha saw joyriding up Main the night of the murder.

"Parker's a peculiar fella," Buck said, pushing himself against the backboard and wheezing like an old engine. "Though I can't say just why. Where'd you say he's from again?"

"Upstate Indiana. Fairvale, I believe it was," Eddie had said, and Buck grunted, saying maybe that was it.

"The books and the receipt alone don't mean nothin'. But you put that razor in there, and I agree that we've got a different story. Talk to him again, son. This time in person, and don't be so nice about it. Let him see a little of what you're thinkin' and see what he does. And if you think you can stick someone on him after without him noticing, do it. Guilty men have a bad habit of breaking their routine when they feel like a target has just been painted on their back. Watch him."

Eddie had nodded, saying he'd do just that, not mentioning that he'd already put a tail on Parker; using a skirt to help out with a murder case, he'd never hear the end of it. Still, he wanted to hear what Penny had to say before doing as Buck asked.

If they ever allowed women on the cops, Eddie thought she'd be a damn good one. She had a way of making people feel comfortable, and when they were comfortable, they started to talk; he'd seen it enough times when they were together. As things were, the best she could do with that talent was to go work for the local rag, which still had its uses. And if part of the news that Penny came back with was that she and Parker had got on well, he might just call on her to follow him again after they have their little conversation…

In the waiting room, a shrill laugh that made the witch's cackle in *The Wizard of Oz* sound like the innocent titter of a schoolgirl broke Eddie's thoughts clean off, and a shiver ran down his spine.

Outside the waiting room, Eddie heard a door open and what sounded like footsteps heading in his direction. Flipping the notebook closed once more, he stood and settled his hat under his arm. No sooner than he'd righted himself, a slight, haunted-looking woman appeared in the doorway, her hands placed primly behind her back.

"Deputy Prescott?"

"Yes, ma'am."

"Dr. Hart will see you now. Please follow me."

Eddie followed the woman through dark corridors and past rooms with little windows set in the doors where he guessed it'd probably be best not to look, making sure to stay close. The place might as well have been a maze, and the last thing he wanted to do was get caught looking at something, only to turn back and find he'd lost his way. But he kept pace…and his wits, and finally, he found himself ushered inside the office of Dr. Roderick Hart.

In his mind, Eddie thought he'd be meeting with a dumpy, older gentleman with thick glasses, a worn tweed suit, and a face as inviting as a dead animal on the side of the road. But the man who rose and walked around the desk, hand outstretched, was much younger. Slicked back brown hair and an even slicker suit, complete with two-tone wing-tipped shoes. There was a pipe clenched in his teeth, and the smile around it was jovial. Though something about the man's eyes unsettled him. They were somehow both dead and blazing, like those funhouse portraits that look like they're following you as you walk by.

"Deputy Prescott! How good it is to meet you! I'm Dr. Roderick Hart."

"Sir," Eddie said, taking the offered hand. "I appreciate you makin' the time to see me. I promise I won't use too much of it."

"Not at all! My apologies, I wasn't able to accommodate you sooner, what with Mrs. Sherbrooke's state and all. Also, when a new patient comes in, I like to see that they're properly settled and run through my…I guess you could call it my *housewarming party*, first."

Eddie didn't like the sound of that or the smile it brought to Dr. Hart's face when he said it, but pressed on.

"Like I said over the telephone, I'm following up, dotting some T's and crossing some I's on the Jack Lawrence murder, and—"

"Gruesome stuff," Dr. Hart said, shaking his head. "Nasty business. Won't you have a seat?"

He didn't much want to, but thought it'd be rude to refuse, and so settled into a chair in front of the desk. Dr. Hart perched himself on the corner facing him, arms crossed over his chest. Eddie took a breath, knowing that the sooner he could get down to business, the sooner he could leave.

"Mostly what I'm interested in is whether or not Mrs. Sherbrooke has enough wits to answer a few questions I've got here," Eddie said, tapping a finger at his notebook. "Just between us, she's about the only hope I've got of findin' out who else was out there that night."

Dr. Hart nodded and pulled out a match. He struck it on the heel of his shoe and lit his pipe, shaking out the match as he puffed.

"I'm only too happy to assist, of course. However, I'd also like to caution you if I may. Your…intent is to speak to her directly, correct?"

"If that's possible, yes."

"All well and proper. Yes, it is possible; however, don't expect much in the way of conversation. The fine folks at Price Memorial saw that the few cuts and bruises she'd sustained were patched up fine, but the mind…well," he took another few puffs on his pipe. "Whatever Mrs. Sherbrooke saw that night gave her quite a shock. She's back to being able to answer "Yes" or "No" when questions are put to her, and she no longer screams in her sleep, but aside from the fact that she's now awake, she's not much the better than when your colleagues first brought her in for care. I'm afraid that if there isn't some more pronounced improvement, we'll have to resort to something, well…stronger."

As if to emphasize the last word, the electrical whirring started again. The desk lamp went dim, and the sound of screams grew louder for a few seconds before everything went bright and silent again…mostly silent.

"In my line of work, you can get pretty far with yes or no questions, Doc. If you ask the right ones."

"I've no doubt. Well, Deputy Prescott, if you're ready to proceed with your questions, please follow me."

Dorothy Sherbrooke's room was at the end of a long corridor, just off to the left. As they approached, Dr. Hart motioned for him to look inside the small, barred window set into the door. Eddie did, and looking around, felt his hand go to his mouth, wondering if this was some kind of trick.

The vibrant, bubbly dish he'd seen walking around town less than a week ago was gone. The woman before him sat hunched forward at the end of the small bed, long, greasy reddish-brown hair hanging down over her face. Her fingers were hard at work, apparently determined to turn the sheet of paper she was holding into confetti. Eddie jumped a little as Dr. Hart appeared at his side, clearing his throat.

"Dorothy?"

She didn't look up.

"Dorothy, I have a man here. He wants to ask you one or two things about the night you took ill. He assures me it won't take long. May we come in?"

Moments passed as the pile of confetti on her feet grew, piece by piece.

"Yes."

Dr. Hart leaned around the corner and waved. An orderly that Eddie hadn't noticed until just now stepped forward, pulling a ring of keys from his belt. He found the right one, slipped it into the lock, and opened the big, steel door. Dr. Hart gestured toward the open doorway, and taking a deep breath, Eddie stepped inside.

He jumped a little when he heard the metallic snick of the door being shut and locked behind him, but was assured it was just policy. A little fear ran through him, wondering if he'd be allowed out again, but Eddie shrugged it off and took a seat at the foot of the small bed. Dorothy looked up, and for a moment, their eyes met. Not long, but enough that he was convinced she was here in the world and seeing him.

"Evening, ma'am," he said, trying to keep his tone light and friendly. "Like the doc said, I have a few questions I'd like to ask."

Dorothy nodded, not looking at him, and Eddie flipped open his notepad. He went to reach for the pen in his breast pocket when another one of those electrical whirs dimmed the caged overhead bulb, followed by distant screams. Her eyes flicked up to the light, and the look of fear in them was unmistakable.

Oh, please, darlin', please talk to me. I don't wanna learn down the line that they made their little light show on account of you.

He scanned the list of questions he'd jotted down before coming out here, then looked back at Dorothy for a moment before flipping the notepad shut again. He'd be lucky to get clear answers to all that he had here from someone who wasn't soft upstairs, but her? No. Sighing, Eddie threw his plan out the window. Either this woman was going to talk to him, or she wasn't. So, he might as well throw away the yes or no questions and try for the big prize.

"Ma'am, I need to know who else was out there that night, other than Jack and yourself. Anyone you saw, anything you saw, anything you might've heard. No one knows what happened that night, but I think you might, so anything at all you can tell me, no matter what it is, I'm happy to listen."

There was silence after he finished, broken only by the sound of the rain outside the barred window and the *rip-rip* of the paper still being torn. Before he could think much about it, other than knowing it might be the sort of thing Penny might do, Eddie reached forward and took one of her hands. To his surprise, she didn't pull back. Instead, she dropped the paper and squeezed his hand hard.

"A woman…she came. She…she was by the car. I'd packed my bag. Wanted Jack to drop me off at the train station. But…when I came outside, she…I saw blood on her hands."

Off to his side, Eddie heard Dr. Hart take in a sharp breath, but thankfully, that was all. He had a feeling that if the man chose that moment to speak up, whatever spell was going on would break, and the poor thing would be back to "Yes" and "No".

"Go on," Eddie said, still holding her hand.

"She said she was a nurse and heard commotion. Saw a man running away, he dropped a knife or…" the brow furrowed, and Eddie thought he might lose her after all, but it cleared, and she continued in her low, raspy voice. "She said she knew him, but he ran away. She tried to help, but Jack was already g-gone…I fainted. Came to when it was dark and I got scared. I ran."

Dorothy went quiet again, and Eddie had to remind himself to breathe…and to write this down when he had both hands free again.

He couldn't believe his luck, and before he talked himself out of it, decided to press it just a little bit more.

"Thank you, Dorothy. You've done me and this town one hell of a favor. There's just one more question, and I'll leave you to rest. No one will bother you about this again til you're feelin' better and ready to talk, you've got my word. That man, the one the nurse said she knew and that she'd seen running away, did she tell you his name?"

Dorothy closed her eyes, leaning forward. At first, Eddie thought she'd decided she'd had enough and decided to climb back into her shell shock, not that she didn't have a good reason. He'd gotten more than he'd dared hope for before coming out here, and if what she'd given him was all he was gonna get for the time being, then he could count his lucky sta—

"Dan…Parker."

Eddie thanked her one last time, then turned to Dr. Hart and did likewise. The door was unlocked, and Eddie stepped out into the corridor again like a man in a dream. He shook hands once more before Hart directed the orderly to show him out. And after what felt like an eternity of turning corners and heading down long flights of stairs, Eddie found himself back in the main lobby of the building and heading out the front doors double quick.

Unit 2 was parked nearby, and he just managed to avoid bumping into a few secretaries on the outside steps before splashing his way down through the puddles toward Unit 2. It occurred to him to wonder why secretaries would keep such hours, even at a place like this, but he was content to think more about it another time. Right now, he had other fish to fry. Eddie reached Unit 2 and got himself inside.

He made to reach for the mic, but it crackled, and Martha's voice came through. But unlike her usual silky smooth voice, she sounded panicked.

"Eddie? Come back?"

"I'm here," he said, surprised at the evenness in his voice. "Just finished up business at the nuthouse. On my way back to town now, I—"

"We've got another body, Eddie; this time in the Crawfords' front field. The rest of the boys are already there, or nearly there, so you'd better hurry back fast."

Chapter Thirty-One

Dan lay watching the dying embers glow in the fireplace, listening to the occasional *pop!* from the hearth, and Lucy's soft, steady breathing as she lay beside him, arm draped over his middle and her head leaning against his bare chest. Feeling the soft silk of her slip under his fingers, he supposed it wasn't a huge shock that the night had turned out like this.

After slipping into dry clothes, he'd set about fixing dinner. Nothing special, just some ham steaks, mashed potatoes, and biscuits. They'd passed on the small dining room just off the kitchen, instead going for the coffee table in front of the fire Lucy had gotten going, talking, and listening to the radio. Once the plates had been cleared away, they'd had dessert…and after that, the blueberry cobbler he'd grabbed from the bakery.

There was only so much emotional relief laughing, crying, or commiserating could possibly get two people in their situation before it was obvious that the situation might need something stronger. Booze probably could've done a close enough job, but after the other night, he'd been in no mood to get shitfaced. He'd tried offering a nightcap just as a matter of etiquette, but Lucy had turned him down flat; probably she was thinking the same thing he'd been, and since his guilt hadn't chimed in, maybe it'd been the right call?

Whether he was right or justifying, he honestly couldn't have said. Aside from that, though, he could say that for the moment, his mind felt clearer than it had in days. And with the sound of the rain outside the window and the still lively remains of the fire coming together to create a peaceful vibe, Dan felt like he could actually think.

His thoughts turned to Jack, obviously. But for the first time, he felt as if he could remove himself and the whole butterfly effect part of the equation long enough to wonder who it was that'd hidden out there in the Vic that night. Was it a crime of opportunity? A random act of violence? Or had Jack been passing himself around to more women than just Dorothy Sherbrooke, and some jealous husband had gotten wise and decided that fists just weren't enough to settle up...

The cops would work it out, one way or another, and sooner rather than later. And now that it seemed he was off their radar, the pool had gotten that much smaller.

If I were still able to travel, the least I could do is jump ahead to figure out who'd done it, then jump back to tip off the cops before leaving for good. I feel like I owe the universe that much.

But even if he could, there's no guarantee having the full power of the internet back at his fingertips would yield anything; how many dozens of shows had he watched over the years about unsolved murder cases? Then there's also the temptation. Could he trust himself to go back to after the murder, and not before?

Doesn't matter; the machine is essentially a doorstop now anyway.

Letting the thought dissolve and settling back into the couch pillow again, Dan closed his eyes only to open them a second later, jerking a little. Lucy barely stirred as he settled down again.

Wait, wait-wait-wait...that thing may not work, but maybe it doesn't have to...

Among the things he'd decided were necessary for his extended stay in the post-war era, Dan had brought his laptop. Loaded with other less informational things were all sorts of archives and reference materials. He thought he'd be referring to them constantly, like a sort of Hitchhiker's Guide to the Past, but it must've been six months since he last touched the thing. He was smart and observant, and by now, felt like he'd just about gone native. But those archives...

Would they still be the same ones? Or did they start to change when other things started to change?

He couldn't imagine opening a PDF on his computer and watching the words shift and change like magic…a newspaper ad for a casino turn into one for an auto detailing place or something. But at the same time, reality probably didn't give much of a shit what he could or couldn't imagine; it had its own way of doing things.

Every part of his tired body screamed to just be left alone. To stay where he was, Lucy curled up next to him and sleep til morning. But his brain wasn't having it. Now that he'd started to wonder about the state of those records, there'd be no rest or peace, no matter how tired he was. He absolutely had to know.

No, you don't. You're tired, and your anxiety is through the freaking roof, freshly laid or not. Nothing's going to change. There's no hurry. Anyway, it'd be better to look when you know you'll be completely alone.

It was good advice. Sound, full of concern and possessed of a certain logic – it was just a shame he knew he wasn't going to listen to it.

The idea was there, and it was just going to keep squirming in his mind, keeping him awake and turning things over and over again; getting even thin little licks of sleep was out of the question. It wasn't the first time that nagging questions had kept him awake, and it wouldn't be the last. He knew that it was an issue and that he should work to unplug his mind and get some rest, but…

"Lucy," he said, making a point to keep his voice low, shifting himself a little as he did. She sniffed and let out a small cough, but that was it.

Good enough.

Moving slowly, with all the care of someone handling high explosives, Dan started to extract himself from her and the couch. He moved his right arm from her waist, then with his left, lifted her arm draped across him while sliding out and supporting her. What he was about to do aside, he really did want her to get some rest.

Lucy stirred when he settled her head onto the pillow, her body moving and stretching before lying still again, but that'd been the final hurdle, and he stood. Dan bent down to pick up his shirt before moving around the couch and out into the entryway. Moving around the squeakier floorboards, he ducked into the hall closet just under the stairs and clicked on the light, then shut the door behind him.

There wasn't much to see. Just a narrow sliver of storage space with a rickety stool off to the left that'd been here when Dan bought the place, and sketchy shelves to the right where he'd been stashing newspapers for the last two years. On top of those was a wooden box. It was larger, with a dark wood exterior and a blue velvet interior, and he guessed it might've held fancy silverware once upon a time.

Dan picked up the box, considering whether or not he *really* wanted to do this right here. By all rights, the box should've been downstairs. But he'd been running behind earlier in the day, then he'd forgotten for a while where he'd stashed the keys, and so the thing had made it as far as the closet before he'd needed to head out.

After another pause where he turned over the idea of just trying to forget the whole thing and going back to the couch after all, Dan eventually decided that he might as well have a look; Lucy was dead to the world, and he *was* already settled in here…

Dan waited a few beats just to make sure. When he heard nothing but the house's usual night sounds…creaking, rain, that sort of thing, he opened the silverware box.

Inside were the few things from life before all this. His *original* wallet, his phone, Kindle, MacBook, and associated charging cables. Dan reached for the laptop, sliding everything else off to the side before closing the lid and setting the Mac on top.

Makes a neat lap desk, he thought, and opened the Mac.

The screen stayed blank just long enough for him to wonder if the battery had gone dead when the logo appeared, followed by an entirely forgotten about, full volume *Whhhuummmmmmmm.*

"Shit!"

He tried to block the speakers before remembering that they were part of the vent and hinge. Half-rising from the stool, Dan put an ear to the door as the power-up chime died away. There was what sounded like a knot popping in the fireplace, but that was all, and he sat down again, heart racing. After a few tries, he finally managed to type in the password and began looking around at folders on the desktop.

No, no…no…

It hadn't taken long to throw most of this together. He'd been volunteering at the Kent County Historical Society for years and had a habit of plugging in an external hard drive to dump copies of the stuff he'd worked to scan and categorize. It'd started just as a pure interest thing, but took on a whole new life when he realized that the director was too old school to fully understand how much better it'd be to have backup copies of the backup copies.

Opening folders, Dan scrolled through old document scans, notes, spreadsheets he'd thrown together, all of it broken out by subject. Civil Rights Movement…way too early, well, more like too late. Urban Development, not helpful. Pre-War Years, also not helpful.

With all the information, he thought he'd be clicking and scrolling til morning. But a glance at the top right corner of the window showed him a little magnifying glass…

Duh, he thought, rolling his eyes, before clicking on the icon and typing "Crime" into the search bar.

"A Brief History of Crime," he said, reading the first result out loud, half-smiling and unable to decide if riffing on the title of Stephen Hawking's famous book was clever or just stupid. Either way, it only took opening the PDF to show this is what he'd been looking for: tidbits and highlights about crime in New Chapel going all the way back to the town's founding in 1806.

Arrests for break-ins and traffic stops. Public drunkenness, public indecency. Possession of alcohol during those dark days of the Temperance Movement. Assault. Assault with a deadly weapon. Assault on a woman…a very averted-eyes term for rape. Domestic issues.

So much for "this is a nice town", he thought, and continued to scroll through the section headings until he found the one he'd been looking for.

"There you are," he said, his eyes locking onto the heading Violent Crimes before dropping down to the first and biggest story.

Out at the Broken Wheel Tavern on Route 4, Herb Walker and Alvin Winscott got drunk and started fighting over Eloise Preston the day before Thanksgiving, 1933. After the talking turned to yelling, and after yelling had turned to fists, Alvin reached behind the bar for the barkeep Noah Randall's shotgun.

Noah went to call the police, and just as Alvin got the gun pointed at Herb, Herb broke a beer bottle over the bar, and with one slash, tore Alvin's throat to shreds. With his dying convulsions, Alvin squeezed off a shot that took half of Herb's face, spraying chunks of it all throughout the bar, and sending them both to the floor, twitching and bleeding out more or less in each other's arms.

A good story for anyone who's into gruesome love triangles, and it's been a local legend ever since. Dan had grown up hearing it told over and over, seen the bullet hole behind the bar with a frame around it, and around the time he'd turned twenty-one, done his local rite of passage by having the morbid, but delicious, mixed drink served during the anniversary of the killings called Eloise's Lament.

According to everything he knew, everything he saw in front of him at the moment, this was the most gruesome crime on New Chapel's books.

It used to be.

He looked at the screen for what felt like a long time, hoping that maybe it would pixelate or go swimmy, then when it cleared, there'd be a story about what'd happened to Jack with a complete timeline, ending in the person found to be responsible. But there was nothing. The document stayed as it'd been when he'd knocked it together another life ago.

Tears *did* blur his vision, and he wiped them away, nearly sending the Mac crashing to the floor. And after managing to avoid what would've been a noisy crisis, he then sat, trying to clear the lump that'd started to creep up in his throat.

Maybe there's a lag.

It sure sounded good. Changes in the timeline are akin to changing a profile picture or renewing a Costco membership online, where everything just needed a little more time to refresh before settling into place. He doubted it, but again, what the hell did he know?

I could check the obituaries.

True, maybe the refresh…if there was such a thing, could've started there first, but all at once, the walls of the closet felt too close, and even behind a closed door, he felt way too exposed. If Lucy just happened to barge in on him when he was scrolling through lists of people who'd died…and were going to die soon…

That's a "you" problem. Lucy'd be a hell of a lot more concerned with the Mac.

Resigning himself to spending some time down in the basement tonight, Dan closed the computer and slipped it back into the silverware box. It slipped from his grip as he stood and popped open slightly, spilling out some of the contents just as a rumble of thunder broke outside. Thankful for the audio cover despite his racing heart, Dan grabbed for the phone cord and the Kindle and shoved them both back into the box. He settled the thing under his arm and stepped back out, shutting the door behind him.

He turned and made his way toward the door leading to the basement. Resting with his hand on the knob, he turned, seeing the faint outline of Lucy's head in the dying firelight.

So far, so good, he thought, then slowly opened the door.

He took a single step down before pulling the door not quite shut behind him; in the near silence, he was afraid the latch clicking would sound like cocking a shotgun. Dan felt for the switch off to his left and flicked it, squinting against the light. After a few blinks, the basement steps came into focus, and he began to head down.

At the bottom of the steps, Dan flicked another switch, turning on more lights and revealing the basement in all its glory.

A little on the larger side, maybe, considering the size of the place. Brightly lit and mostly empty except for some old boxes and broken furniture from the previous owners, it would've been entirely unremarkable if not for the room off in the corner. According to the agent who'd sold him the place, it'd been set up by those same owners as a darkroom for developing pictures. But Dan had taken one look at the ample space, boarded-up windows, sturdy door, and thought that with a padlock, it'd be perfect.

Dan ran a hand along one of the beams just above his head, feeling around until his fingers touched the padlock keys. With company over, keeping them in the kitchen junk drawer felt like he'd be pressing his luck a little too hard.

Walking over to the unassuming room, Dan shifted the silverware box more securely under his arm, reached up with the key, and popped the lock, leaving the door to swing open on its hinges. He reached in and pulled the cord to the single overhead bulb.

The room wasn't much larger than a decent-sized walk-in closet. Along the left side was a rough, wooden worktable spanning the length, and not much else. Dan set the silverware box down on the worktable, then, turning, looked toward the far end of the table at the only other thing in here…the machine.

Chapter Thirty-Two

Lucy poked her head over the sofa, blinking and hazy as Danny disappeared through a closet door, shutting it behind him and cutting off the light. It sounded like he was moving something around in there. As the moments passed, she contented herself with thinking that maybe a fuse had blown or some such thing, when she heard the oddest sound coming from the closet.

What in the world?

It was a strange, gong-like sound, and she only had time to look over at the record player, wondering if it'd started up on its own when the noise stopped. In the silence that followed, she began to wonder if she'd heard anything after all. It had been something of a long day, and she had only just come to.

Lucy settled back down, her head leaning against the armrest. She began fingering the small purple gemstone she'd been wearing around her neck since the night of the fair, its facets catching what was left of the fire, the light seeming to dance and fork inside. She thought about that night and how much things had changed between then and now.

Jack is in the ground, and I'm playin' house.

The brief feeling of guilt was enough to make her wonder if she should've gone to her aunt's house after all. Or if she should gather her things now and head back to her lonely room at Harrington House. But Aunt Trudy would only preach, and she couldn't shake the feeling that her room wasn't the place to be. And then there was Danny; she couldn't bear to leave him. Not because of what they'd been up to earlier, trying to keep the sadness away, but because the house felt safe…he felt safe.

At least I had the sense to have Danny park in the garage. Oughta keep some of those tongues from wagging too much.

Moving the stone between her fingers, she sighed, knowing that those tongues were likely already wagging by now with news of the scene she'd made at the service.

Jack's hands had been the thing that'd just about done it. Hands she'd known so well, crossed in a way that wasn't natural to him, knowing they'd never move again. And if she looked at those hands for long, she'd have to look at the rest of him, including that great gash she'd heard was slashed across his throat. Alfred Cole and his boys had probably done as fine a job as they could, but what if she could still see it? And if she could, knowing that it hadn't been put there by accident, she might've just broken down screaming.

So, she'd left. Hurrying past those folks on her way out the door, she'd managed a small prayer.

Lord, forgive me that I can't bear to stay. Receive Jack into your arms, if that's Your will. He's sinned, but there was…is…plenty of good in his soul. Jack? I'm so, so very sorry. Please know, even though I was ready to walk away, part of me still loves you and always will. Amen.

Lying on the couch, she thought over that prayer again, and wiping at her eyes, felt it was good. It was—

Lucy's thoughts broke off as thunder rumbled loud enough to rattle the glass in the window frames, and sounds came from the closet again, like something falling. And unlike that humming gong sound, she was sure she hadn't imagined this one.

"What are you doing in there, Danny?"

Peeking over the top of the sofa again, she watched the closet door first open, then watched Danny step out of it with something under his arm.

She took a breath, not to call out exactly, but just to make herself known when he headed back her way…only, he didn't. In the dim light, she watched him turn and head toward another door; the basement, if she had the layout of the place right in her head.

No longer interested in cozying back into the sofa, Lucy got up, walking on tiptoe and bending to peek around the corner to get a better look. Not that there was much to see besides a few doors: one to the basement, one to the bathroom, and one to the hall closet under the stairs. Taking a few steps toward the basement door, she paused, seeing a thin band of light creep up over her feet. Turning, she saw that he'd left the closet light on, and she found herself stepping toward the door. Her mind, now fully awake, began to work.

It could be that there was some tool he needed from downstairs, and he'd be back up any second, but somehow, she didn't think so. Even though she couldn't put a finger on why, Lucy felt sure that whatever he was up to, it had nothing to do with a little late-night electrical work.

He slipped away when I was asleep, now he's sneakin' around.

Could it be there were reefer cigarettes in the little closet, and he'd headed down to the basement to smoke one? Were there dirty picture books in there, hidden away in some old box under bank papers, so no one would chance to look? She supposed, being a bachelor and all, that the last one was possible. But no, a man with a home library like his wouldn't have those filthy little things in the house.

Are you so sure? You've been wrong before about what the men in your life get up to when you aren't around, she thought, but stopped, reminding herself that Danny wasn't Jack.

Now able to see more or less fine in the dim light, Lucy caught her reflection in the hall mirror and smiled, giving herself an appraising look.

So what if he does have those little books in there? I've got any ink and paint hussy beat by a mile. Still…

Beneath her feet, she heard movement coming from the basement. The jingling of keys, a door being opened. Now what on earth would he need with keys down—

Oh, stop it! You're thinking about snooping around, and you shouldn't be. Whatever he's up to down there, it's none of your business.

That much was true. It wasn't any of her business. But it was also true that, dirty books or no, reefer cigarettes or no, she was curious. And once she got really curious about a thing, there wasn't much stopping the feeling until that itch was scratched. Over the years, she'd ruined Santa Claus, birthday surprises, and a lot of other things with that curiosity. It's why sometimes she tried not to look too closely at some things…if she didn't look, she wouldn't get curious, and if she didn't get curious, nothing could come around to bite her as it had a nasty habit of doing from time to time.

Maybe if you'd looked a little closer at Jack, then—

She cut the thought off clean; it wasn't as if her mind hadn't already been made up. Lucy stepped forward and opened the door, shielding her eyes against the brightness.

There wasn't much to the place. Just a small, dusty closet with stacks of newspapers and an old stool. For the life of her, she couldn't see what Danny had been so involved with in here. Lucy stepped down hard, testing to see if one of the boards might be loose. Off to her left, she spotted a small electrical box, then stopped pushing on the boards.

Guess he must've been messin' with that thing after all. I think the past few days have made you a little daffy. You need some rest.

Lucy turned, feeling relief. Probably that thing under his arm was just a toolbox, and whatever the problem was, it wasn't in this little electrical box after all. She'd head downstairs, see what's wrong, maybe ask if there was any way she could help, and—

No sooner had she taken a step, her foot seemingly unable to help itself from testing the board under the stool, when her toes pressed on something soft and she jumped back. Lucy moved the small stool aside, looking down.

It was a wallet. Nothing fancy, no stacks of cash spilling out or anything like that, just a brown leather wallet like any other she saw men pull out on a daily basis at the diner. Adjusting her slip, Lucy squatted down to grab it, but instead of getting back up, she only stared at it…curious.

Just what do you think you're doing now? What if he comes back and sees you looking through that?

That was a good question with an easy answer. Lucy could lean against one of the shelves to ditch the wallet behind herself between the newspapers, letting a strap of the slip slide down her shoulder. Then she'd walk toward Danny, slowly, whispering something about looking all over for him before leading him back to the sofa…if it turned out that she shouldn't have been in here, she'd have him forgetting all about that in no time. Danny was a kind, well-mannered, learned man. But recently, she'd come to understand…to her delight, that there were one or two areas where he was certainly no gentleman.

Ready to give her sauciest, "I've been lookin' all over for you, tiger," at the slightest hint of footsteps, Lucy opened the wallet.

There was cash in the bill pocket, and large ones too, twenties, fifties, and even a few hundreds. But they were strange. They were smaller for one thing, and they were greener. And on some of the bills, there was a bluish stripe running along the side that she'd certainly never seen before. Sliding them out and shuffling through, things only got queerer when her eyes caught the years…2018, 2016, 2021…

"They're phonies," she said, though she couldn't think of what use they'd be if anyone tried to pass them off. Even the slowest, sleepiest clerk would know in a second that this was funny money. Could it be that maybe he read something in one of those science fiction stories full of ray guns and flying cars, and thought to make these as a gag? Thinking that must be it, Lucy slipped the bills back and had been ready to leave the thing where she'd found it, when she noticed something else that didn't strike her as quite right.

On the inside fold, there were slots, each of them holding strange, thick cards. A blue one caught her eye, and she pulled it out. The name running across the top, Ashland Savings and Loan, was one she knew well. It was where she did her banking, too, though she'd never been given anything like this. Raised silver letters spelled out DANIEL PARKER, and under that, a string of numbers she didn't understand.

Frowning, she put the card back and pulled out another, then another…then another.

A punch card from a sandwich shop she'd never heard of, with "Family Owned Since 1978!" printed on it. A "Gift Card" to Howard's Market that she was certain would get her laughed out of the place if she tried using it to buy groceries, even if she knew how to use such a thing. A AAA card with a line under Danny's name that read "Member Since 2017". The phony bills she could understand, but all this?

Lucy continued to look through the cards, her confusion only getting worse, while at the same time, an idea had started to form in the back of her mind. It was silly…crazy even, but—

"That's…that's just nonsense," she said, pushing the thought away as she reached for the last card. As she looked at it, Lucy felt her eyes go wide.

It was a *Driver's* License…not an *Operator's* License, issued by the State of Ohio to Daniel Martin Parker. Out of everything, this card, with its colors and reflective pictures, was by far the strangest of the bunch; the thing that truly did not belong. But try as she might, she couldn't dismiss it. Like the other cards, the corners of the license were boxed, scratched, and peeling a little. The wallet itself was worn, those little silver letters on the Ashland card pressing through the leather of the wallet like a stamp, as if it'd spent years in a back pocket…

Feeling her heart race, she looked at the license, her gaze drawn to a single line: Date of Birth: 11/5/1996.

Lucy stood, letting the wallet, which had been nestled between her knees, fall to the ground with a flat smack, as the idea she'd been trying to push away finally hit. If it'd just been the cash, or maybe that punch card too, she could've written the whole thing off as a joke. Maybe not one that made much sense, but…

Still holding the license and feeling like she'd just been struck dumb, Lucy could only stand there, her eyes closed. What felt like a thousand questions had just elbowed their way into her mind, and it was all she could do to not start shouting for Danny to get up here right now and explain this.

Okay, okay, okay…if it's not a joke, could I be dreaming?

The thought was certainly appealing, but the pain she felt in her feet from all that squatting down was enough to put that notion to bed as quickly as it'd come. Unfortunately, that left only two possibilities in her mind. Either she'd gone completely crackers, and a car from Alcomb Sanatorium would be here any second to wrap her in the madman's dinner jacket and take her away. Or…

"Or…the man I've been sharing the night with won't have been born for another…fifty-one years."

That was the truth, and as soon as Lucy heard it out of her own mouth, she knew it. What's more, she felt it. A lot of the things about Danny that she'd always thought of as being a bit odd…the unusual way he talks sometimes, how sometimes she'd catch him looking around as if he were a tourist…those things and more now started to make some sense. If their places were swapped, she could see herself being unable to help herself from doing the same thing.

What's someone to do in a situation like this? she thought, giving an unsteady sigh.

Well, like anything else, she supposed it depended on the person. The only question that mattered to her right now was, what was *she* going to do about it? She'd come across something that –

You didn't come across anything! You went snooping where it wasn't your business to snoop and found something you weren't prepared to find!

That might be so, but at the moment, standing here in this little closet with something that not only didn't belong to *her*, it didn't belong at *all*…at least not yet. Talking like that wasn't what she'd call terribly helpful.

"Alright," Lucy said, opening her eyes. She bent down, grabbed the wallet, and slipped the card back where she'd found it. "We're just gonna have a little chat."

And with that, Lucy stepped out from the closet, turned, and headed toward the basement.

Chapter Thirty-Three

Dan looked at the machine, sitting there under its tarp like some harmless thing, for he didn't know how long, somehow too afraid to get too close, like all of a sudden it'd gone radioactive.

How do I know it hasn't? Not like I know what powers...powered, it in the first place. When the rock or whatever it is down in the guts of the thing is glowing purple and sparking like a scene in a Frankenstein movie, it works. When it isn't...

The thing wasn't much bigger than a decent-sized Amazon box, and yet, it'd managed to do all this. Part of him wanted to grab the hammer near the stairs, smash the goddamn thing to pieces, and be done with it. If it was useless now, what was the point of having it around except for something someone would at some point accidentally stumble on, leaving him struggling to explain? It'd already been a small but constant source of stress as it was, sitting down here in this little room.

What if it wakes up again?

Dan thought it was possible, but when would that be? Another day? A week? A month? There was no way to know for sure, but a feeling deep down told him if it did decide to wake back up again, it'd probably be years, maybe even decades down the line. Too late for him to step back into his old life like nothing had happened, making it useless all over again.

An image came then. It was him, an old man, sitting in the basement of this house or another, listening to President Reagan on TV while clearing out some of the crap from the past four decades. He'd bend down to move some old trash bags of things he'd long since meant to donate to the Salvation Army, and his eyes would fall on the box…a soft purple glow coming from beneath the dusty tarp…

Rage, confusion, and hurt welled up inside him at the thought, and before he gave himself another chance to think about it for fear he'd lose his nerve, Dan turned and left the darkroom. Near the bottom of the stairs was a toolbox, its lid open, and a hammer sitting right on top.

Don't do this, he thought, his gaze down to a pinhole, the hammer its sole focus. *It could start working again tomorrow!*

Fat chance. The thing was done. Dan grabbed for the hammer.

When he stood straight again, testing the weight of the thing and wondering just how many whacks it'd take to turn the thing from a figurative pile of junk to a literal one, there came the sound of footsteps. He looked up, and before he could do more than take a breath, he found Lucy silhouetted in the doorway, hands on her hips. Dan let the hammer fall to his side.

"S-sorry, I didn't mean to, uh," he said, aware of the open door behind him and the steady, racing pulse in his ears. "I just…"

He didn't really have a good way to finish that one. With how deeply she'd at least appeared to be sleeping, his money had been on needing to shake her awake well after sunrise. Making up some sort of excuse as to why he was up and about tonight hadn't crossed his mind.

"Did the storm blow out a fuse, Danny?"

"Something like that," he said, throwing a glance over his shoulder. "Should be a quick thing, I'll be back up in a few."

"Don't be silly, why don't I just come down and keep you company?"

"Oh no, no that's okay," he said, taking a step back toward the open door behind him. "It's dusty down here…it'll drive your allergies crazy."

"I don't mind a little dust."

Lucy began to walk down the stairs, and Dan took another few steps back.

Just what in the hell had he been thinking? All this could've easily waited until Lucy was back at Harrington House and he had the place to himself again. Shit, two or three shots of whiskey would've probably put him clean out no matter what'd been going through his mind, and he could've been back on the couch, asleep.

"Hey," Dan said, taking another step back and feeling the padlock hanging by its hasp poke him square in the back. "I've got an idea. How about we…go out? There's a diner in Harlan Heights that's one of those twenty-four-hour joints, and I hear they've got a chocolate malt that'll knock your socks off…my treat."

The last thing on earth he wanted to do right now was get dressed, get back in the car, and drive all the way to Harlan Heights for a malt, but if it knocked her off course long enough that he could get everything squared away down here and make up a more believable thing to be up to this time of night, so be it. His research…and the hammer, would have to wait for another day.

"That does sound tasty," she said.

"Right? And by the time you're dressed, I'll have everything buttoned up down here. Trust me, it'll be a great time."

Lucy stopped halfway down the stairs, looking at him, and Dan felt a chill work its way up his spine. The stairs were mostly dark, but between what he could see of that dark hair, pale skin, red silk slip, and piercing blue eyes, she looked more than a little like a vampire. One that he was pretty sure wasn't buying a single bit of what he was trying to sell…

"And it's your treat?"

"Yes, ma'am, anything you want."

"Well, that's aces. And ain't it a funny thing, but I just happened to find your wallet on the floor upstairs."

Without warning, she tossed it down to him, and Dan caught it against his chest.

"But maybe don't try usin' the cash in there or else we'll be washin' dishes to pay the bill."

"What're you talking about? Most of it's the change you gave me the other—"

Dan had only just opened the wallet to see what the hell she was talking about when he caught sight of his driver's license…the one with the Real ID so he could fly, his debit card, and an Amazon gift card he somehow remembered still had about six bucks left on it…

Pulse now pounding hard enough to send sparks flashing in and out of his vision, Dan looked up.

Chapter Thirty-Four

"You all right, doc?"

"I'm fine, ma'am. Just got a little bug, is all."

Penny watched Dr. Horton walk away from the open door of the car, looking like it was all he could do not to double over and start giving up his dinner. Not that she'd have anything but sympathy for the man if he did. Professional though he was, decent people weren't meant to see things like this.

A few uniformed men were roaming the fields, their flashlights making them look like lightning bugs moving through the stalks of corn. When she'd gotten here, parking her jalopy half in the ditch, she watched them for a time before turning her attention to the Crawford house. Seeing its lights on, she'd said a little prayer. Tonight, those poor people were going through what surely must be every parent's worst nightmare.

When he'd called and tipped her off, Eddie said he'd meet her on the edge of the road and walk her into the scene himself this time. He'd given her a heads-up about what she'd find here, but seeing it all for herself, Penny thought it wasn't close to being enough.

A black Ford Model A, maybe a '29 or '30 she'd been told later, had been driven a far way into a field, muddy tire ruts and broken stalks in its wake. A few men were standing around it with flashlights pointed inside, though it seemed like they were doing their best to look anywhere else. Much like at the dairy, she didn't want to look inside but knew she had to…she was in the fold now, and she wasn't about to back down. And when she finally forced herself to look inside, it was all she could do not to drop to her knees in hysterics.

Elise Crawford sat on the Ford's front passenger side, the front of her dress ripped clean open, including her underthings, leaving her bare chest exposed down to the naval in the steady beams of light. Her head lay over on one shoulder, and at the nape of her neck, Penny saw the handle of what could only be a chef's knife…the rest of the blade presumably pinning her to the seat like a bug in a display case. Dark blood ran from the handle, down the curve of her breasts, the flow ending in a puddle in her lap, staining a soggy cardboard box and its contents…what must've been a very fine dress.

"My god," she'd said, and backed into Eddie, hand over her mouth and not minding the arm he'd put around her like it was old times.

Same as before, Dr. Horton arrived not long after she had, a black bag in hand and a camera around his neck. And even in the dim light, she could see that the man had already started to look green.

"You sure you're alright, Dr. Horton?" Penny said, stepping forward and putting a hand on his shoulder.

"I'll be all right," he said, putting on something like a smile and patting the top of her hand briefly before she took it away. "A gust of wind blew through the car, past that poor girl, and, well…"

Penny nodded, understanding. She'd smelled a little of that, too, before she'd backed away. Eddie walked over to join them, and Dr. Horton cleared his throat.

"My best guess right now is she's been dead three, maybe four hours. Cause of death at the moment appears to be blood loss; that blade probably sliced through the carotid artery like a hot knife through butter. She would've only had minutes."

And I pray she was long gone before that, that monster, ripped her clothes to do God only knows what.

Dr. Horton set his black bag down by one of the front tires, then reached for the camera around his neck.

"Give him some space," Eddie said to her, then to the few men still gathered nearby. "Actually, Perry, set your flashlight on the hood, facing inside. Glenn, do likewise, then go up to the house, see how Alan's doing up there. You boys, check and see if they've turned up anything in the fields yet. The bastard couldn't have just disappeared without leaving something behind."

The rest of the boys moved away, leaving just Eddie, Dr. Horton, and herself. Seemingly unable to help it, Penny took a few steps forward to watch as Dr. Horton began to snap pictures. The base of the knife handle in the throat, the blood splatter on the seats and windows, the poor, sweet face, the stained dress box. Every shot clicked like rifle fire in the night, momentarily flooding the scene with bright light before going back to near dark. Again and again the camera flashed, and Penny felt a cold chill work its way up her spine.

"C'mon, Penny," Eddie said. "Let's talk back here, huh?"

"Sure."

Penny followed him a few steps back, and they turned, watching. She knew she ought to have her notebook out, but somehow, even if there'd been enough light, she didn't think she could hold a pen steady, much less scribble out anything that'd make much sense. At the moment, it was hard to think of any questions Eddie hadn't already answered for her.

"Eddie," she said, pitching her voice low, "what in God's name is going on here? What happened out at the dairy was bad enough, but somethin' like that again so soon? It's like lightning striking the same place twice."

"More like just across the road. Looks like we've got ourselves a Jack the Ripper-type."

They watched Dr. Horton settle the camera back around his neck, reach into his black bag for an instrument Penny couldn't see, grab one of the flashlights, then lean back inside as Eddie spoke.

"What'd you find out at the service?"

Penny turned, a little shaken. The sight of the girl seemed to have driven everything else clean out of her mind, and she'd all but forgotten about her assignment.

"Oh, well," Penny paused, thinking of just how to put it that she'd ended up spending time with some very sad, but very nice people. Deciding not to complicate it, she put it to him just that way. "Those good people are just as shocked as any of us are, is my feelin'. Whatever happened that night, and maybe tonight if that's where your mind is goin', that man isn't involved."

Eddie nodded, ran a hand through his hair, then settled his hat back on his head.

"You sure about that?"

She blinked.

"Why, of course I'm sure."

"What if I told you we looked up the plates, and that's Parker's car. Or what if I told you that the dead girl in the front was someone he worked with in town?"

Penny took a small step back, feeling like she'd just been slapped. She looked at the car again, as if she was only seeing it for the first time. Eddie wasn't the type to make a mistake like that when it came to his work. If he said that's who the car belonged to, that's who it belonged to. And if he said Dan Parker knew that little girl, well, she had no choice but to believe him. But it didn't change the fact that it didn't change her opinion one bit.

"Alright, well, be that as it may, I still don't agree with what you're implyin'. I spent a good deal of time with him today. He's such a nice man. A little head in the clouds, maybe, but—"

"But that makes sense, don't it? How many times have you heard about these sickos and monsters finally getting caught, and all anyone has to say after the truth comes out about what they'd been up to is *but he was such a nice man*?"

Off the top of her head, Penny couldn't say just what those figures would be, but knew enough from reading papers and magazines that it happened often enough for Eddie to have a good point. In stories, it's always the shifty loner types who turn out to be the villains. In real life, it was more likely to be a neighbor, a friend, or someone in the family.

She'd have to have been born foolish to think someone couldn't pull the wool over her eyes. Plenty of people in the world were a lot smarter and more devious than she could ever dream of being. And for all she knew, that nice bookstore clerk could be one of them…*could* be.

Only, she'd seen the hurt in the man's eyes when he saw his friend laid out like that. She'd held his hand, felt him, and watched as he'd turned away. It was hard for a man, especially a man like Eddie, to understand that what she felt meeting both of them wasn't something she could really put into words. It was just a thing she knew, just like sunrise comes after sunset.

Part of her wanted to try and explain it anyway; Eddie was full of surprises these days, who knows, he might just be able to find his way there. But after looking at him, seeing how he stared at the car, how his jaw was set, Penny knew it'd do no good. There was something in that gaze that reminded her of a big, mean dog about to pounce on a rabbit.

"So, what now?" she said. "Do you have him locked away?"

"That'd been my plan after my little visit to the nuthouse to talk to Dorothy Sherbrooke…she named him, too, by the way. But then this call came in." He nodded at the Ford where Dr. Horton was still doing his work. "There's still a lot to do here. Still gotta go up and talk to the family too; Bill Crawford is a friend of my old man's, and I'll ask you to steer clear of their place for the time being. Also, I'd really like these boys to find something that'll stack the odds a little more in my favor…a dropped watch, wallet, something like that. But even if they don't, once we're all buttoned up here, I'm headed back over to Eastbridge myself, and by the end of the night, Dan Parker is gonna find himself in a cell."

Chapter Thirty-Five

Over the years, there'd been more than a few daydreams about being found out—the iPhone always felt like the thing most likely to give him away somehow, even though it rarely left the house.

Maybe at work, bending down to move a box…maybe at Bill's as he was taking a seat, it'd fall out of a pocket. And before he could toss his keys or something as a diversion…complete with a comment to at least try and cover his ass, someone helpful would grab the phone, and it'd be game over.

This, however, wasn't a scenario he'd even remotely considered… Or maybe he had.

That day, when he'd woken up from his nap, sitting on the couch and thinking about how he should've taken all that stuff that didn't belong and dropped it back off at home. He'd written it off as being fine, but he knew damn well none of that stuff should've been there once he'd slipped into the groove of things. Or better yet, it should've never been brought along in the first place.

How about, oh I don't know…you could've put the box behind literally any locked door when you couldn't find the key to the darkroom earlier, you could've let it keep collecting dust under your bed, or easiest of all, you could've just stayed on the damn couch like you knew you should've in the first place and done absolutely nothing!

Dan snapped the wallet closed, shutting off the stream of thoughts—they were all too little, too late anyway. Trying to shake off this newest blindside hit to his life, he forced himself to look at Lucy. She only stood there, arms crossed, one step above him.

"Where'd you find this?"

"That little hall closet. I heard you moving around, saw the light on, and wondered what you were up to this time of night. When I turned to leave, I stepped on it."

He wondered for a moment just how that could be when he remembered the crash of thunder and how the goodie box had slipped from his grip, dumping a few things out onto the floor.

At least she didn't find the Kindle.

But would it really have mattered? The wallet, the Kindle, his phone, the Mac…they would've all come to the same no matter what she'd found. That's why all that stuff had been put away in the first place.

"And you just couldn't resist a look, huh?" Dan said, vaguely aware of his shock giving way to anger. He took a step up so they were on the same level. "Couldn't have just left it where it was, called for me and said, hey, by the way, I was looking for you and found this?"

"I just, it was there, so I—"

"So you see me moving around, and decide to fake being asleep til I'm out of the room so you can follow after me? Go snooping through my stuff?"

"Danny, I—"

"You what, have a reasonable explanation?"

He'd had enough. As if the truly jacked-up turns his life had taken recently hadn't been enough, he wasn't about to sit and listen to whatever pathetic excuse, justification, or whatever for snooping around where she had no business going. And faking being asleep to do it too…watch, she'd probably find a way to turn it around on him, to –

Stop! For the love of…just stop! It's over. She knows.

"I was just…I'm sorry," Lucy said, taking a step back as Dan took another forward.

Dan clenched his fists, making damn sure to keep his mouth shut. All he wanted to do was yell. Not because it was her fault, even now, he saw that…it's hard to blame a person for literally stepping on a wallet and deciding to take a look inside. But because everything he'd been feeling was still festering, and thanks to this, all of it was now desperately searching for any way it could to get out. No, if he did nothing…said nothing, and let the initial moments of pure anger pass, it'd die a quick death. And whatever passed for his rational thinking these days would reassert itself.

He raised his arms, meaning to go in for a hug. "Lucy, I—"

"Hey! Hey, get back!"

"What the?" Dan said, confused, feeling the weight still in his grip, it hit him…he was still holding the hammer.

In about half a second, Lucy had moved nearly back to the top of the steps, her wide eyes on him. He saw fear there, and a wave of shame hit him so hard it made him want to double over. Dan slid the wallet into his pocket and raised his free hand. He set the hammer down at Lucy's feet, and she grabbed it up quick.

"Listen, I'm sorry," he said, backing away. "This isn't…that wasn't what it looked like, I swear. I wasn't trying to threaten or whatever else it looked like I was doing just now."

She didn't say anything, only continued to look at him from above, her face a study in confusion, the hammer tight in her grip. He couldn't blame her. Walking up the stairs toward her with a hammer in his hand, her knowing something she by all rights shouldn't know? What the hell else was she supposed to think?

"We can talk," Dan said, putting his hands up around his middle like she had a gun on him instead of a home improvement basic. "Until dawn if you want. Look, you know me, okay? Strange as that sounds, you do. Please, you're in no danger of anything from me. Never have been, never will be."

"You know," Lucy said, her voice unsteady, "I was hoping, when I came down here and showed you that, you'd just laugh in my face and call me a big dummy."

"Sorry to disappoint you."

"What was in that box I saw you with?"

"That's, well, complicated. And it's more than one thing, actually. It's in that little room just behind me on the worktable. If you want, you can go look and…

Lucy took a step forward, not exactly raising the hammer, but it wasn't resting at her side anymore either; now it was Dan's turn to take a step back.

"Walk right into some little basement room with a lock on the door in a house no one knows I'm at? Do you think I'm foolish?"

"Okay, fair, and no, I don't."

Dan looked around at the junk left behind down here, he'd never bothered to clear out, and spotted two worn, but sturdy-looking camp chairs. With his face to Lucy and his hands still up, he backed toward the chairs. He unfolded them and set them facing each other, a good-ish distance apart. If she wanted to leave, that was fine, but he couldn't have her leaving the way she was now. Not until he'd at least had the chance to explain.

"Please," Dan said, gesturing to one of the chairs. "I'll explain everything. And if I try anything funny, anything you don't like, then take that hammer, bash my brains in, and run. I won't stop you."

But he really hoped it wouldn't come to that. Despite everything that'd gone wrong because of his little extended study abroad, he wasn't ready to do the soft shoe off the mortal coil just yet. It was uplifting, really.

Lucy didn't say anything. Didn't so much as move a muscle for what felt like at least half an eternity. He could see her just chucking the hammer at him, running upstairs, bolting out through the kitchen door, and screaming for help. Dan wasn't sure exactly what his next move would be in that situation, but luckily, the hammer came to rest at Lucy's side, and he didn't have to think about it…not right now, anyway. She walked the rest of the way back downstairs and toward one of the chairs.

Oh, thank God.

"Can I get you a drink, or…?"

"I'm fine," she said, taking a seat. Dan did likewise in the opposite chair, not exactly sure where to begin.

His eyes flitted to the hammer now lying across her lap. He wondered in a detached, academic way if she was planning to use it. Would she kill him? Put him in the hospital? Or leave him with disabilities bad enough to earn him a room at Alcomb for the rest of his life…a prisoner in an H.P. Lovecraft haunted house if the things he'd heard about the place were true.

Only until the '80s, when they'll abandon the place and rebrand as the Alcomb Home for New Beginnings.

"Danny?" Lucy said, breaking the silence…the image of two dudes dressed in white, wresting his limp, rubbery arms into a straitjacket dissipating like smoke.

He looked at her, hopeful. It was still Danny. Not Dan, or Daniel…that was a good sign, right?

"Yeah?"

"I'm sorry I snooped. You were movin' around, then I saw you come out. I thought you'd see me too, and I was about to speak up, but then you disappeared. I got curious. And when I passed the closet, I got more curious because I thought I'd heard things in there. That's not an excuse, and I was certainly raised better, but…" As she spoke, Lucy set the hammer down near her feet, another good sign. "Oh gosh, I just, I thought I'd find a stack of dirty books in that closet, and then I'd, well, I don't exactly know what."

Lucy crossed her arms; her eyes cast down toward the floor.

"Porn is in the top drawer of the upstairs dresser…all you had to do was ask."

Dan's heart lightened as he watched her face first pucker, then the corners of her lips pull up into a smile before letting loose with that laugh of hers. Dan laughed too, feeling what was left of any anger he had dry up.

"All joking aside, I get it. And I'm sorry. Freaked out or not, I did not mean to scare you like that. No matter what you know, the last thing in the world I'd do is hurt you."

"I know," she said, and reached briefly for his hand. "And thank you."

"It's all my fault anyway. That box you saw me with spilled, and I didn't notice the wallet fell out. I'd meant to move all this down here earlier today before I left to pick you up, but…"

He let the words die out and leaned forward, looking down at his feet. Before long, he heard the sound of something scraping across the floor and looked up to see Lucy scooting her chair closer.

"So," she said, sitting back down, "there's no chance at all…not in the whole wide world, that you're just having me on for a joke?"

"I wish," he said, and Lucy nodded, sighing.

"No, I didn't think so," she said, arms resting in her lap and leaning forward, giving him a view that, everything else aside, was making it hard to concentrate. "But I had to ask again; probably won't be the last time. You did say we could talk, right?"

"I did."

"Til dawn, if that's what I wanted?"

"That's…certainly what I said."

Lucy fixed him with a piercing stare, one eyebrow cocked up as if expecting him to back out. Tired as he was, he wouldn't, and he met her gaze full on. This wasn't how he imagined getting found out, but now that he had, he wasn't about to beg off. Keeping so much of himself a secret for so long had been a lot, even before things went to shit. And sorry or not, this woman was going to ask her questions come hell or high water. Honestly, his only regret right now was that he didn't have a glass of iced tea and a more comfortable chair.

"And you're not gonna sit here and feed me a bunch of baloney, are you? Because I've had about enough of that just lately, thanks."

"The truth, the whole truth, and nothing but, scouts honor… Though I was never a Boy Scout."

"That's some big talk."

"Not for me. You've already seen so much, I can't see any reason to lie now. I'm not creative enough or quick enough to feed you anything that'd believably explain away anything you've already seen, and I'd never insult your intelligence by trying. Also, I'm not a big fan of lying as a rule. Seriously, the truth is weird enough without me trying to mess around with it."

"You don't say," she said, nodding over at the small room with its open door and single bulb shining. Dan followed her gaze, staring at what he could see of his secret boxes.

"You wanna hear something funny?" Dan said, looking back at her. "Once or twice, I'd actually thought about telling you."

"Now, now…you promised me no lies." Her tone was serious, but she was smiling in that way of hers, and he knew she was only kidding around. "I imagine it's a lot to keep to yourself."

"You've no idea."

Lucy reached out and grabbed his hand again, but this time held it and said, "Why me, though? Why not, well, you know…"

Dan considered the question.

"I guess it was just that it was always your face that came to mind," he said. "You're smart, you're kind, you're trustworthy. Not that Jack wasn't too in his way, but you're open-minded too, and maybe that's the biggest thing. In my head, I figured you'd at least give me the benefit of the doubt and not immediately call to have me carted off to the loony bin."

"The night is young, Mr. Parker," she said, giving him a wink and a squeeze of the hand. "Thank you."

Silence hung in the air for a little bit after that. Not uncomfortable, at least not for him. Just basking in the relief that'd begun to creep in underneath the anxious beating of his heart at the thought that, right or wrong, a weight was about to come off his shoulders.

"So," Dan said.

"So," Lucy said, crossing her legs and adjusting her slip. In other words, settling in.

"I guess I can do this one of two ways. Story time, or you can start asking me stuff, and we'll start going down rabbit holes."

She leaned back in her chair, head cocked and looking up toward the ceiling. A second later, she met his eyes again.

"You choose. It'll be you doin' most of the talking anyhow. Do it how it feels best."

"In that case, it'll probably end up being both."

Dan closed his eyes, drawing in a slow, deep breath. He held it for a four-count, then let it back out.

Alright, here we go.

Chapter Thirty-Six

Penny turned the corner, hurrying along Eastbridge Road, looking around as if she expected to be caught at any moment. But there were no cars out, and so far as she could tell, no one was peeking out their windows. That was good. Driving here would've been swell, but even if her old Lincoln didn't cough and sputter, she still wouldn't have chanced it; Eddie would've picked it out in an instant.

When the ambulance arrived in the field, she'd whipped out her little notebook and started to jot things down, finally able to see well enough to do so, thanks to the Cadillac's headlights. Though the story she'd have to write had been the last thing on her mind. As she scribbled, her mind had gone back to earlier in the evening, to Dan Parker and the deep sadness on his face. Then she'd thought of Eddie, remembering that look like a hunter about to spring a trap. She'd kept up the act as long as she could.

Eddie had been busy talking to the boys driving the big, white thing when she'd walked over and laid a hand on his shoulder.

"I'm going home," she said, then held up her notebook. "I'd like to try and get some of this roughed out before I go to bed…if I can sleep, that is."

He said he understood, and before she could stop him, he bent, planting a kiss on her cheek. It tingled pleasantly, just like it used to, but still, she didn't much care for it. They'd have to talk more about that later, but for the moment, she'd been willing to leave it be. Eddie still had his hands full down in the fields, and he hadn't gotten up to the house to make his manners to the Crawfords. There was plenty of time to do the thing that'd started to form in her mind, but only if she could leave right then.

She'd turned and left the scene, waiting until she was well out of sight and safely back in her car before pulling out the slip of paper where she'd copied Dan Parker's address out of the phonebook some days ago, just in case she needed it.

Coming on the house now, its windows dark like most others on the block this time of night, it occurred to her that she didn't know just what to say. "You need to pack your things and leave, now, while there's still time" was about the best she could come up with. And after a moment, she thought that was just fine. No sense dressing the thing up.

Stepping off the sidewalk and up the driveway, her heels clicking and echoing in the night's stillness, Penny made toward what looked to be a side door between the garage and the house, more privacy than the front. She mounted the small set of steps leading up to the door, her hand raised to knock, when she heard what sounded like muffled voices coming from inside.

Penny took a step back down, looking around, wondering if she'd maybe missed the lights being on after all; she had. Running along the foundations of the house, there were a few small windows that she supposed looked into the cellar, casting little squares of light on the ground nearby. It was a wonder how she'd missed them.

She knew she ought to go back and knock at the door. At least she wouldn't be waking anyone, intruding like she was at this hour. But those small squares of light seemed to call to her, and before she knew it, Penny found herself moving away from the door. Crouching down at the nearest window on the other side of a bush, she looked inside.

Dan Parker and Lucy Rodgers were both in their night things, sitting on chairs, facing one another. She couldn't make out just what they were saying, but she'd bet every cent to her name that it was serious. There was what looked to be a hammer lying across Lucy's lap, and she wondered what the story was there.

If she knocked on the door now, whatever spell down there would be broken, and it'd only taken a moment's look at the two of them to realize that she had to know just what it was they were talking about.

Maybe a closer window will let me hear 'em better. Yeah, that's the ticket. And if it doesn't, well, I'll go back and knock on the door like a polite member of society.

Either way, it'd only be delaying what she'd come here to do by a minute or two. There was still plenty of time.

Throwing glances back over her shoulder every few seconds, Penny moved around to the next window, and the next, trying to see what she could make out. Each window let her hear that much better, but only so the odd word came through; not helpful.

Finally, she found a window that let her hear just enough to make out their words. The thing was boarded over, but the glass had been broken, and for whatever reason, this arrangement seemed to be just the thing she needed.

"I guess I can do this one of two ways. Story time, or you can start asking me stuff, and we'll start going down rabbit holes."

Story time? What in the world?

The words clanged in her head, and Penny thought about the hammer. Had she been wrong all this time? Had Dan Parker been up to something nasty after all, and Lucy Rodgers had caught him out on it? Could it be Eddie was right? The idea didn't sit right in her heart, but that didn't mean it wasn't possible all the same.

"You choose. It'll be you doin' most of the talkin' anyhow. Do it how it feels best."

There was a pause, and Penny began to panic. What was she doing just sitting here listening? That woman could be in danger. She needed to get to a telephone. At least be ready to move toward one, even if it meant breaking into the house itself, and—

Through the darkened window, Dan Parker began to speak. Once he did, thoughts of calling the police, of the scene out at the Crawford field, of Eddie…all of it fell away, and it'd have taken a team of big, strong men to pry her away from this spot.

Chapter Thirty-Seven

When he finally took a breath and checked his watch, Dan saw that he'd been talking for about forty minutes. He'd expected to stumble around for a while, starting and stopping, trying to find the right place to start. But it hadn't gone that way.

Once he'd started, it was like opening flood gates, and he just let the words come as they wanted. This wasn't an interrogation; it was a confession. Every word coming out of his mouth was a weight coming off his mind, chest, shoulders…hell, pick a body part.

Dan laid out his story, really just hitting the broad strokes. He'd been born at Price Memorial Hospital. Mom and Dad moved them from Osborne to New Chapel not long after he was born, both for the schools and so Mom could be closer to work. Grew up in town, went away to Ohio State before coming back home with credentials to teach American History, as well as a job offer from New Chapel High School. He hadn't made it to the elephant in the darkroom yet.

Most of the time he'd been talking, Lucy barely said a word. She'd sat on the edge of her seat, seeming to listen with every fiber of her being, her blue eyes never leaving him. Here in the last few minutes, she'd started asking questions, running them off into rabbit holes just like Dan had expected. He'd brought out the silverware box and pulled out his iPhone, feeling like he needed a few visual aids courtesy of Photos, and they'd lost a good chunk of time right there, the idea of fitting a camera and a photo album in a pocket blowing Lucy's mind most of all.

"How long have you been a teacher?" she asked, still holding the phone, a picture of his classroom on its screen.

"About six years, not including the, well, I guess you'd call it the leave of absence I've been on for the past two."

Dan leaned back in his chair, stretching his legs, thinking about the career he now had no choice but to leave behind. He'd miss the kids. Most of them anyway. A handful were really excited about history in the way he'd been at their age, and it'd been fun to encourage and engage them. The rest were decent enough. Although there were a few where he wanted to toss their precious phones out the second-story window and let them know that there was a real world outside that portable idiot box.

"Why history?" Lucy said, bringing his attention away from his students and back to the basement. Dan smiled; it was hardly the first time he'd been asked that question.

"Because history repeats itself. Always," he said. "Studying the past is the best way to understand the present and prepare for the future."

"Until what you've got in that room came along, I'm sure," Lucy said, nodding at the darkroom. "What a thing for a man like you to have. I mean, to see history…"

Lucy fell silent, her brow furrowing.

"Hey, what's wrong?" he said, leaning to place a hand over hers. He'd long since quit worrying about taking a hammer to the head.

Moments passed, and Dan only just became aware of the ticking of his watch echoing in the basement, when Lucy spoke up.

"Danny? Am I a ghost?"

"Huh?"

"Not actually, but I mean, where you're from, I'm dead…aren't I? That or shut up in some rest home close to it?"

Dan hesitated, thinking about the obituary spreadsheet where he planned to go looking for Jack's name, and wondering where *her* name fell on that list. If in the ordinary course of things, she'd have stuck around here at all, that was. Either way, that was one thing he'd damn sure keep from both of them.

"I mean, this," she waved an arm around her, "this is all history come to life for you. But for me, this is just my life. Maybe ghost is the wrong word…maybe museum exhibit might be closer to what I mean? Is that what we are to you? All I am?"

Dan thought that on paper, her words might've come off accusatory or even a little hostile. But the look on her face and the tone of her voice gave the truth away; it was curiosity. Maybe spiked with a little reminder, not of mortality…there'd been enough going on to remind everyone of that, but of the passage of time. Nothing lasts. Everything new becomes old. The future becomes history. Hardly hot takes, but in his experience, a perspective still not many people seem to consider. Lucy, however, was being forced to consider all that now in what had to be the weirdest way possible, and he felt for her.

"Not even close," he said, then took a moment; she'd put his experience into a context he'd not thought about before. "I guess, it's like visiting a foreign country in a way. That's not exactly right, but close enough. Things look different, people act differently, but none of it so much that you can't blend in if you pay attention and observe the customs, ya know? It's not as hard as it sounds."

"I'll keep that in mind if I ever go traveling like you one day," she said, giving him a playful tap with her foot. "Speaking of traveling, how did you find yourself here?"

"Honestly? This is an incredibly fascinating time in history. A lot of the things that'll come to define America were born in these years. There are amazing changes in society, technology, the arts, everything, all just around the corner. I wanted to see some of it. More than that, I wanted to live it."

"That's…quite something to hear. And here I was thinking things looked brighter just because rationing was finally over. But, and I hope you'll forgive me for pushing, you still haven't said just how on earth you came by a device that allowed you to do such an amazing thing."

Dan took a few deep breaths, buying himself time to think on how to ease into this one, before just deciding to wing it.

"I didn't invent the machine that got me here like a mad scientist in a story or something. I found it, volunteering to clean up and catalogue some stuff down in the depths of Harrington House. The place closed to boarders sometime in the fifties, and opened as a museum in the nineties, and even in the twenty-twenties, there were still things that hadn't been touched yet. I don't know if you've ever been under the place, but it's like catacombs down there.

Anyway, there was some construction work going on down there, and they found this hidden-away room, right? Behind some boards and loose bricks, behind what I guess was a wine rack. They knew I volunteered at the historical society, and called me in to have a look at all the boxes and stuff they'd found to see if we'd want any of it.

"And it, the machine, was just sitting in there?" Lucy said, her eyes wide.

"It was under an old, busted bed, covered in a canvas tarp. And when I got it out and pulled the tarp off…

Dan thought that every day for the rest of his life, he could close his eyes and find himself in that cellar again. Pulling the tarp away, feeling the brass housings, the knobs, the lever, completely hypnotized. The purple light that came from deep within it, pulsating outward when he'd first fiddled with the dials, and the strange feeling in his stomach he'd come to associate later with using it.

"I didn't know what it was at the time. Just some sort of strange clock," Dan said. "But when I pulled the lever on the side, there was this weird feeling, and when I looked up, I was still in the room, but the wall was bricked over again. And when I looked at the dials, I saw the date…just a few months ago, actually.

Anyway, when I got back, I knew this was too special to tell anyone about. Not the museum director, not my friends at the historical society, no one. And, since at the moment, no one but me knew it was there, I just…" Dan looked away, feeling ashamed. Though not a willing liar, at least once, he'd only been too happy to steal. "I took it."

All at once, he wanted to beat his own ass for how he'd started to go off on Lucy earlier, blindsided or not; she'd found and grabbed a wallet…he'd found and stolen a time machine. He wanted to apologize all over again, at length, trying to restore what he felt was probably a major hit to his character in her eyes. Something of what he was feeling must've shown on his face because she scooted close enough that their knees nearly touched and, leaning forward to plant a finger under his chin, turned his face to hers.

"I don't know if this'll make you feel any better, but if it were me, I'd have done the same thing."

It didn't make him feel any better. And that guilt was one of the reasons he'd ended up donating a large chunk of money to the Kickstarter Harrington House had going for renovations once he'd liquidated the comic books. But he patted her hand and thanked her anyway.

They sat talking for a while longer, Dan's watch ticking away the minutes as she asked more questions, and as he pointed out some more about the phone; each new feature he explained added to her awe. At one point, she said it made everything she'd seen at the World's Fair in 1939 look like a cheap dime store toy. He could hardly disagree. It was fun there for a while, but the smile eventually slid off her face, and she set the phone aside on a box.

"Can I ask you something?" Lucy said.

"Isn't that what we've been doing here all this time?"

"Cool it with the jokes, mister, I'm serious."

And she looked it, serious as a heart attack. Dan nodded, apologized, and told her to go right ahead, feeling his neck and back begin to tense.

"What got you up and about tonight after I'd fallen asleep? Because what I think is you were comin' down to fool with your little pieces of science fiction to see if there's something you could do to help Jack…to save him."

Dan felt a sort of half-smile cross his face.

"See? You do know me," he said, then sighed. "You're close; I was thinking about him. In that silverware box, I've got almost all the town's history. Records, newspaper scans, tons of stuff like that on something more impressive than the phone. I'd thought maybe there was something in there that'd changed, something that'd tell me how this all shakes out, so I could give the police a heads up and help the process along before anyone else got hurt. And I can't go back to have a look myself. The machine, its…"

Dan couldn't finish the sentence. A lump had started to work in his throat, and his vision had gone a little misty. He made a swipe at his eyes with the back of his hand and gave a single wet cough. Lucy stood then and sat in his lap, wrapping her arms around him, and he held her back hard, letting the tears come. After a while, he straightened up, wiping at his eyes again.

He told her about the crystal that seemed to power the machine, and how, after she'd left the day they'd learned about Jack, he'd gone down to check on it. To get it ready to go. To get himself ready to go, only to find that its charge seemed to be gone, and as of now, he was a permanent resident. He left out the part about considering suicide by pop bottle.

"Oh, Danny," she said. "For the life of me, I can't think of a single thing to say except that I'm so very sorry."

Dan could only nod. Her words hung in the silence for some time as they sat, and he thought he saw tears in her eyes, too. But just as he opened his mouth to say something, maybe suggest that they continue this somewhere a little more comfortable, Lucy straightened and turned to him. There was something in her face that made him sit up a bit, his brow furrowed.

"What is it?"

"You didn't know, did you?"

"Huh?"

"Before, you said that you were looking at your records, wondering if anything had changed; that means something *has* changed. This…this all didn't happen before, did it?"

It still took a second for his tired brain to catch up with what she was getting at, and when he did, Dan could swear he heard the realization audibly click into place. He sighed, then shook his head.

"What's changed?" Lucy said, then hesitating, added, "Is it you?"

He opened his mouth, then closed it, thinking hard on just how to put this. The thought of risking Lucy seeing him as a pariah, or even worse, a villain, wasn't something he thought he could take. But he'd gone too far to start holding out now, and he knew it.

"Probably," Dan said. "Maybe? But I swear, I don't know how or why for sure. The thing didn't come with instructions, so the best I can do is guess. Please, you have to believe me. I'd never intentionally do anything to hurt anyone.

"I wasn't accusing you of anything," Lucy said, and he saw the faintest suggestion of a smile. "Don't get that idea. And I do believe you. I just, I had to know. Seems like you must know a lot of the town's history, and if you'd known about Jack and what was gonna happen and still didn't help, then we'd be having a different conversation."

Lucy settled back against him, and Dan felt relief, sliding his arms around her waist.

"If that gadget ever starts working again, could you help him? I'm not askin' for myself mind, but what happened was wrong."

No argument there.

Dan thought for what felt like a long time before answering.

"I don't know," he said, finally. "I'm sorry, I wish I had a better answer. Or if there is something more than pop culture hypotheticals, I knew what they were. But my gut feeling is that it isn't as clean as the books and TV…television, and movies make it out to be, where the heroes just hop back, tackle the gunman before he gets off a shot, and save the day. If I tried to go back and change a change that'd never happened in the first place, who the hell knows? It could be fine, it could destroy everything, or something else entirely could happen."

Shrugging, Dan fell silent, unsure of how to continue or even if he should. What more was there to say, really?

In this post-war world where men strove to be heroes like the guys returning from the front, Dan wondered if she would start calling him out as a coward for not even chancing a rescue if he could. Maybe she'd be right to, but it wouldn't do much to change his mind. What was it that one of his favorite pop culture thinkers said? The needs of the many outweigh the needs of the few?

He'd loved Jack like a brother, but there wasn't anything on earth to convince him to risk potentially breaking reality to save him, or anyone else, even if he could. No, assuming he didn't end up taking a hammer to the thing at some point, if the box ever kicked back on, the only thing he'd do to help is leave before he did any more damage.

"How've you managed to keep your wits with all this going around in your head, Danny?"

He gave a short laugh, "I've no freaking idea. I keep waiting to go crazy, but it hasn't happened yet, unfortunately."

Lucy gave a small laugh, then sat up, turning in his lap to face the open darkroom again. He was pretty sure what she was about to ask, and was content to wait, grinning. They had all night for show and tell.

"Can I see them? The rest of what's in the silverware box, and you know, that gadget? And just what's so funny?"

"Nothing. But yeah, if you're up for it, I'll show you. I'll even bring it upstairs, just in case that darkroom is still giving you the creeps. But I'm gonna need some coffee if —"

Knock, knock, knock!

Lucy slid off his lap onto her feet, and Dan stood, reaching for the light switch near the bottom of the stairs, leaving the darkroom as their only real source of light.

"Expecting company?" she said, sounding more than a little uneasy, her voice soft.

Knock, knock, knock!

Dan swallowed, feeling a dry click in his throat and the sour taste of adrenaline in his mouth. Each knock could've been his own heart pounding in his chest…he knew that last phone call from Eddie, where everything seemed okay, was too good to be true. Carefully, he began to move toward the stairs when he felt a hand grab his arm and jerk him around.

"Just what do you think you're doing?" Lucy said, her blue eyes blazing. "Your car isn't outside, and neither is mine. There are almost no lights on down here now; just pretend you're not home."

Dan checked his watch, then angled it toward her.

"Whoever's knocking on my door this time of night isn't gonna just go away."

There was a thin coating of hope that someone's dog had gotten out or something, but Dan knew better. The cops were finally done playing around with him about what they'd found in the Vic that night. And as an added bonus, now that they'd had a reason to look closer at his background, maybe they noticed that things didn't look quite right. Like how there was no Dan Parker that fit his description from upstate Indiana, and that's just for starters. He told all this to Lucy, who only stood there, shaking her head.

"All the more reason to act like you're out of town. Wait til they go, then pack a bag and leave. I could…I could come with you."

More knocking.

"Listen, if it's the cops, then I'd damn sure rather go quietly than give them any reason to force their way in here and start looking around," he said, his eyes flitting to the phone still sitting out in the open. An idea came to him then. He couldn't say whether or not it was a good one, but if Lucy agreed to go along, it might just fly.

Talking fast and keeping his voice low, Dan laid out what he was thinking. Lucy wasn't thrilled, but in the end, she'd agreed.

"Danny," she said, pulling on his arm again, and he put a gentle hand over hers, squeezing it for a moment before pulling free.

"I'm sorry. I'll be right back," he said, and turned, beginning the slow walk back upstairs, hoping like hell that turned out to be the truth.

He heard Lucy moving around as he shut the basement door behind him. The hallway was dimly lit by the still-open hall closet door. Walking past, he reached in and turned off the light, then shut that door as well. Less attention, just in case he'd dropped something else he and Lucy both missed. Staring at what little he could see of the front door, feeling like he was about to step into hell, Dan forced his legs to move.

About halfway there, the knocking became more frantic, and Dan stopped. It wasn't coming from the front door; it was coming from the side door in the kitchen.

Huh, looks like they're doing me the courtesy of not making a scene at the front door where anyone could see. That's nice.

He turned into the kitchen, making for that door instead.

The short walk across the tile felt like it took forever, and Dan did his best to get into the headspace of acting like he'd just been woken up; exhausted as he was, he didn't think that'd be a hard sell. Flipping the switch on the porch light, the outlines of two men appeared through the curtain, and he could swear his stomach dropped clear down to his feet.

Dan took a deep breath, squared his shoulders, and with a shaking hand, reached for the knob.

Chapter Thirty-Eight

"How've you managed to keep your wits with all this going around in your head, Danny?"

Well, I don't know about him, but I'm certainly going to have a hard time.

Penny stood, wondering just how long it'd been since she'd squatted down in front of that broken window, meaning to listen for a moment or two, wondering if everything was all right. Lucy Rodgers didn't seem to be in any danger, but she'd certainly learned much more than just that.

Mostly about how there was a busted time travel gadget mere feet away, a treasure chest of technological marvels which she'd hurried around to see before heading back for fear of missing something…all of it belonging to a gentleman who wouldn't be born til she was herself an old woman. Not to mention everything that'd happened in town during the last week or so, shouldn't have, which in itself was a struggle to think about. What she did find herself thinking about, however, was that if these two weren't having her on for a joke because they knew she was listening, then that man down there was in far more trouble than she'd thought.

It was easy to kick herself about the time she'd spent listening in when she could've warned him, and he could've been at least across the county line by now, but part of her was glad she'd heard the full story and seen it with her own eyes. It made her that much more motivated to see him go and stay gone. Rubbing at her legs, brushing bits of dirt from her stockings, Penny moved to the side door once more and mounted the steps.

She raised her hand to knock, wondering just what she should say now that there were so many questions running through her mind, when she glanced over her shoulder. Her gaze fell on the nearby intersection, red lights flashing in the distance. Briefly, she thought it was probably the ambulance heading out with Elise Crawford's body in tow, but that was wishful thinking, and she knew it; she knew those lights.

"No," she said, breath catching in her chest, panic building. She'd run out of time.

There was no making it back to her car without risking being seen, and there was no knocking on the door to warn anyone now; Eddie was too close. Sure, if pressed, she could come up with some reason to be here. But there'd been that look of his, and she felt it'd be an awfully bad idea. Being here now, especially since she'd made no secret that she didn't share his opinions, would get his dander up, and any excuse she came up with to explain herself would sound just like that, an excuse.

The red light continued to move closer.

Get behind something or into the trees, fast! You've made enough of a mess tonight without adding to it! Now move!

Seeing what she knew to be Unit 2 turn onto Eastbridge seemed to break the spell holding her to the spot, and with a last woeful glance at the door, she made for the back of the house, just managing to tuck herself in the crawl space under the back porch as headlights splashed up the driveway. Penny held her breath for a beat before chancing a look around the corner.

Eddie stepped out first, then Alan, undoing the catch on his service pistol. She watched the man who'd been her husband mount the steps and give a few sharp knocks. He turned, and Penny pulled her head back, praying she hadn't been seen.

Long moments passed, broken only by more sharp knocks and bursts of static from the radio. Penny heard the sound of a doorknob being turned, then footsteps moving away. She heard another knock, further away this time, and there was silence.

"Let's check the back," she heard Eddie say. Penny did her best to make herself small, pushing up against the foundations of the house like she was trying to melt right into it, her heart beating in her throat.

Holding her breath, Penny watched shoes moving from off to her right, then heard them go up the porch steps before coming to rest right on top of her, knocking down dust, forcing her eyes closed. She heard the storm door open, followed by more knocking, even louder this time.

"Son-of-a-bitch skipped town," she heard Alan say. "You just see if I'm not right."

"That or he's hiding," Eddie said. "Waitin' til we give up and leave before he makes a break for it."

"You want me to break it open, boss?"

There was nothing for a moment aside from the sound of footsteps shuffling just above her. Penny, alone in the darkness, afraid that some noise would escape and give her away, put both hands over her mouth.

"Not yet," Eddie said. "He still might've jumped town long before now, and I don't wanna deal with the paperwork for forcing our way in if we don't have to. Get on the radio to Perry. He should be up at Harrington by now. See if he's gotten in touch with Lucy Rodgers yet."

One set of footsteps moved away, then came close to her right side again before disappearing behind her, back toward the car. Several pounding heartbeats later, Penny heard the faint sound of men talking over the radio.

"She's not here," Perry said, his voice tinny. "I spoke to one of the young women by the name of Caroline Wells, and she said Lucy Rodgers had taken off for her aunt's place in upstate Michigan. Likely left right after the funeral, I guess."

"Not surprised considering the scene I heard she'd made when I talked to Bill Crawford," Eddie said, now leaving the porch and moving toward Alan. "If I were her, I'd be miles away looking for a nice place to bury my head in the sand for a while. Tell Perry to come on back."

Alan did, and the radio went back to static.

"Waited til the girl left town before getting another sick thrill," Alan said.

"That's what I'm thinkin'. Either that or she's in on all this too somehow."

Penny slowly took her hands from her mouth, blinked her eyes open, and chanced another look around the corner.

This had gone from bad to worse. It'd only be a matter of minutes before those two buffoons decided to break down the door anyway, paperwork be damned. And it was all her fault. She could've gotten them both away if she'd just knocked on the damn door when she'd gotten here, she could've—

"Ready?" Eddie said, cutting off her thoughts.

Whatever they'd been talking about, she'd missed. But seeing Alan nod and draw his pistol, Penny could fill in the blanks on her own; they were going through the door, and God only knew what'd happen then. And here, hidden in the darkness, Penny could only watch.

There was another one of those sharp, rapping knocks at the side door. No answer. She watched Eddie bring up one black shoe, ready to bust the latch clean out when the porch light clicked on, and the door opened.

"Evening, Eddie," she heard Dan say, his voice surely a lot calmer than hers would've been if they'd swapped places. "You mind telling me what the big idea is with all the noise? And why the kid has a gun in his hand?"

"Took you long enough to answer the door; we've been knocking for some time."

"And I've been trying to sleep. It's been a hell of a long day, and it's late, in case you hadn't noticed."

"I'll cut to the chase then," Eddie said, stepping forward, every drop of kindness in his voice gone. "Your car was found in the Crawfords' east field a few hours ago. Elise Crawford's body was in your front seat, clothes ripped open, and a knife sticking out of her neck. You care to explain that to me?"

"She…wait, what? No, that's not…my car, it's just up at Harrington House and I…tell me you're joking. She can't be, she…"

Penny's heart ached as she heard the man struggle for words, seeming to struggle with shock and tears. How she wished she'd have pulled herself away to warn him in time.

"We're not, and she is," Eddie said. "Headed out to Price just now, her grieving parents not far behind. And you, well, I suppose you're headed out with us."

"You can't…can't be serious, Eddie, come on, you don't seriously believe that I—"

"Cut the shit, Parker, you're under arrest."

From her corner view, Penny watched as Eddie pulled cuffs from his belt and locked them onto Dan Parker's wrists before yanking him down the steps, then shoving him into the back of Unit 2, Alan with his gun trained on the man the entire time. In what felt no more than the blink of an eye later, the car had backed out of the driveway and headed off into the night.

It was a long time before Penny found the strength to move again.

Chapter Thirty-Nine

It was quiet in this little corner of Price Memorial Hospital tonight. Carly had already done several rounds, checking in on a few patients, taking care of a few messes. Between the light workload and the general quiet of the place, it would've been enough to leave her struggling just to make it through her shift; somehow, the worn-down feeling from boredom was worse than when it came from being worked half to death.

Not tonight, though. Tonight, Carly felt like she could've walked through the entire hospital, taking care of every single room by herself. All in spite of the fact that she'd already made one hell of a trek all the way back to her room in the pouring rain before her shift had even started.

"I thought there was time for just a small walk before the storm really let go. I'm such a silly," she'd said when Mildred cornered her after having just stepped into the foyer, clothes too damp and the lights too dim for Mildred to notice the blood, apparently.

Carly scooted her chair closer to the small duty desk, continuing to flip through the magazine she'd been working on since coming back from her last round of check-ins. It'd become something of a game to see how many ads were targeting women, telling them if they bought this or that, they'd be sure to have dinner on the table just in time for when Mr. Hubby Man came home, and look fabulous while doing it. Sexist messaging aside, it was honestly a wonder that boardrooms full of advertising dudes couldn't come up with some more original angles.

Despite the boredom of tonight, Carly still felt fantastic. Her nerve endings seemed to pulse in time with her heart. Once more, sounds were crisper, smells were sharp. Right now, everything smelled like cleaning solvents and piss, so that wasn't exactly great.

But when she'd pulled the car – Dan's car – over, it'd been so much stronger…

Looking back on it, Carly thought she might've only been able to restrain herself for a few seconds, just long enough to hear that girl blather out "oh, thank you, thank you, sweet Jesus, thank you" before reaching under the seat for the knife and swinging it wide, burying it in the girl's throat.

She remembered the sweet, sharp coppery smell that'd filled the car once, frantic hands scrambled to the handle of the knife, trying to pull it out as the blood began to flow. A few large drops fell on her hand, and before she could stop to think what she was doing, Carly licked them off, thinking it was the sweetest-tasting thing she'd ever had in her life. The smell of copper, watching the blood spurt against the glass, the lingering taste on her lips, hearing the gurgling gasps as the girl's legs skittered at the end, was more than music to her ears. It was the high of highs; it was ecstasy.

Clearing her throat, a small and insignificant sound in the vast silence, Carly shifted her legs and pulled at the hem of her dress, all of a sudden comfortably uncomfortable.

You're a psycho.

She smiled, turning her thoughts away from the girl and the magazine, then picked up the clipboard nearby, looking at the room assignments. There was just too much going on inside her to sit here reading any more. Besides, it'd probably been long enough that she could stand to do another round of peeking in at the rooms. There was a sweet old man down at the end of the hall who sometimes woke up with nightmares. When she was on shift, Carly liked to check and make sure there were plenty of warm blankets because—

Bang!

Carly looked up, her body's heightened awareness getting her on her feet and around the front of the desk in a split second.

To the left, she saw one of the guys who drove the ambulance, pushing a gurney. There was a body, a white sheet covering that'd long since been stained red down the center…my God, what have you done. At the head was a cop and Dr. Horton, the county coroner. Despite the entrance, the guys seemed to be doing their best to keep quiet. But with not much else going on in the way of noise tonight, their whispers carried to her down the stretch of tiled hallway.

"You say they've got the bastard?" Dr. Horton said, taking peeks over his shoulder at the body.

"That's right," the cop said.

"Thank Christ. I've got a girl of my own, just a little younger than Miss Crawford was, and the whole drive back, I'd been planning to telephone and send her to my sister up in Toledo til this mess blew over. Who is it?"

"C'mon, doc, you know I can't say—"

"All you do is run your mouth, Glenn. Come on. At worst, you're only tellin' me a day or so early til the next issue of the Gazette comes out."

"Fine. But you didn't hear it from me, okay? Eddie said his name's Dan Parker…fella that works at the bookstore in town."

Carly closed her eyes, breathing deep and fighting with all her might, the smile threatening to break out. She knew this sort of thing would happen quick; the car hadn't exactly been hidden. But still, she hadn't expected it *this* quick.

At most, she'd expected the cops to run the plates or whatever they called it these days, find it was Dan's car, and haul him in for questioning or something. But no, it was better than that. It sounded like the cops had put tonight together with the dairy a few days before, and Dan was either in the back of a patrol car or already thrown in a cell, screaming and howling.

A small giggle escaped her pursed lips at the thought; this she'd have to see…she had to see that shit-eating grin finally wiped from his face.

She opened her eyes again. The men were nearly to the front of the desk, and Carly stepped out to meet them.

"Dr. Horton?" Carly said, sounding demure and pathetic to her own ears, but still having fun with her persona. "What's happened?"

The doctor stopped as the cop and the girl…*Elise Crawford, her name was Elise, and you*…what was left of her anyway, continued on down the hall.

"Looks like the monster who'd killed that man over in New Chapel hit again, this time with a poor young woman. But don't worry, Miss Wells, they've got him this time. He won't hurt anyone anymore, so you rest easy, okay?"

"Yessir. Thank you, sir. Can I be of any help?"

"Actually, if you've got the time and the stomach for it, I could use a hand getting the young lady prepped."

"I can do that. I just need to find Doreen and let her know, and I'd like to drop off a warm blanket to Mr. Bronson down the hall first if that's all right."

"Perfectly," Dr. Horton said, and caught up with the rest of the party.

Carly walked down the hall to the lounge, where she knew Doreen was working her way through a pack of cigarettes with one of the orderlies, to let her know that she'd be away from the desk assisting Dr. Horton. She walked back to where the warm blankets were kept, grabbed one, and stepped into Mr. Bronson's room. Draping it over Mr. Bronson's thin, sleeping form, she wished him a whispered "sweet dreams" before making her way toward the morgue.

Chapter Forty

The morning sun found its way inside, shining into Dan's face. Fighting to keep his eyes shut, for the moment not ready to look at anything, he turned away.

Pieces from the night before flashed in his mind: the outlines of two men, the painful tightness of the cuffs on his wrists, the pure venom in Eddie's stare when their eyes met, how Lucy had grabbed his arm…

Risking arrest to keep the cops away from both Lucy and everything that didn't belong had felt like the best choice he'd had at the time. And for once, Dan was glad he'd just rolled with the worst-case scenario in his mind, or else who knows what would've happened. After sleeping off the night before, what little sleep he'd managed on something that felt only a little comfier than bare concrete, Dan found himself feeling pretty much the same. Besides, even if it'd been the wrong move, there wasn't much he could do about it now.

Dan found his mind turning to Elise, and the guilt that'd been just off to the side in his mind took center stage. If Eddie was to be believed, someone took that sweet kid, did things to her that Dan couldn't bear to imagine, before leaving her in the front seat of the A like she was nothing.

If he'd only grabbed his goddamn keys or hadn't let Lucy talk him out of going back that first time, or if he'd stopped on their way back to the house like she'd suggested the second time. Or maybe -

Or maybe you could've done all that, and the maniac could've found another unlocked car with the keys in it and done the same thing. You probably wouldn't be on the hook, true, but she'd still be dead, and you know it...first Jack, then Elise, who's next?

He thought of Lucy, remembering that look of reproach on what little he could see of her face before leaving her in the basement. For the moment, he didn't give a shit about anything down there. Instead, he just hoped she was safe and far, far away from here.

Tears came up then, and he wiped at his face before finally gathering the courage to open his eyes. As he did, Dan's head gave a throb as he looked around, the past and present doubling over strong.

He'd been here once before during an elementary school D.A.R.E. field trip. Maybe this was even the cell he and his friend Levi had taken pictures in, each grabbing the bars and screaming to be let out, but not quite managing it since they'd both been laughing so hard. It wasn't quite as funny now.

The room wasn't huge. Not much more than a long rectangle with four cells along one wall, a desk, and a door to Dan's left and another door to the right...just about like he remembered it. Sitting up, he couldn't help but notice no drunks were sleeping one off, no nasty-looking dudes with shiners from some barroom brawl...

New Chapel is a nice town.

In spite of how horrified he was, Dan felt a sick grin cross his features. Running a hand down his face, he heard a loud click and thunk coming from the door to the right. He swung his legs out of bed and crossed to the bars. A moment later, the door opened, and Eddie stepped inside.

Dan watched him make toward the desk and grab the chair, then wheeling it in front of the cell, Eddie took a seat. They stared at each other through the bars for what felt like a long time. Dan tried with everything in him not to be the first one to talk. To let that bastard in front of him set the tone so he had an idea what direction this was going in. But he could only make it so long. And just as he felt himself start to crack, Eddie spoke.

"Quiet in here last night. Most times when men claim they've been falsely accused of something, they bang and scream and carry on til their throats just about bleed."

"I gave you all that and more last night on the ride, and it didn't make one bit of difference, so I thought I'd save it and get some sleep. Wasn't half bad either, all things considered. What about you, Eddie? Get some good sleep?"

"How about we make it Mr. Parker and Deputy Prescott?"

"Ah, so, probably not a good night then. Makes sense. You've got all the signs of still having your head planted firmly up your ass…Eddie."

The relaxed, easy expression that'd been on the other man's face fell away, and Dan was glad to see it. He knew the last thing in the world he should be doing right now was antagonizing this man. What he should be doing is getting down on his knees, kissing ass, and whatever else might get him out of here. But in the moment, Dan just couldn't help it. Now that the worst had finally happened, it was like all the nerves he'd had before just being in Eddie's presence had been burned right out. He'd pay for those words later, he was almost sure of it, but for the moment, the only thing he felt was relief.

"I don't much care for your disrespectful tone."

"You'll survive."

Dan noticed for the first time the clipboard and pen in Eddie's hand. Following his gaze, he raised them just a little.

"You 'n me need to talk, and I'd prefer to do it like men," Eddie said, looking stern, but not quite so venomous as last night. Maybe he'd been wrong, and the sleep had done the man some good. But Dan wasn't about to let himself confuse that with hope. "I've got questions, and I like to think now that you've been found out, there's enough decency in you to answer them."

Sitting down on the bunk, Dan felt another unhelpful, petulant, snarky comment come bubbling to the surface. He fought it back. But just as he'd found something more respectful knocking around in his head, snarky blitzed past at the last second and made it out.

"Why should I?"

Eddie blinked, then frowned. "Excuse me?"

Dan considered apologizing then, trying to walk the comment back. If there was even the slimmest chance that he could make it out of this, then every little outburst like this was costing him… If there was a chance.

And the more he thought about that, about the words "now that you've been found out", Dan didn't think he actually had much of a chance, not with Eddie, not later on when it finally came time to face a jury. He'd begged and pleaded last night, but there was still plenty he hadn't said. Now, though, he was going to have his say…every damn word of it.

"You've already got your conclusions," Dan said, doubling down on his attitude and feeling at peace with it. "All you want me to do is tick off a few of your boxes so you can go run to your boss or the press like a little kid showing his parents he got all A's on his report card, so they can all tell you what a good boy you are, catching New Chapel's own Jack the Ripper.

On my life, every single answer I'd give would be the absolute, honest truth, and because that would screw with the conclusion you've decided on, you'd dismiss me as nothing but a liar trying to save his own skin. Sitting here, answering your questions for hours on end would get me nothing, so I'll just say my part, clearly, and be done with it.

I did not kill Jack Lawrence. I did not kill Elise Crawford. If it's any of your business, yes, Lucy Rodgers and I slept together. It was easy enough to do without killing Jack, and believe me, he was the furthest thing from my mind that night for quite a while. Lucy dropped me off at home after the funeral yesterday, before starting the trip to her aunt's place.

I'd left my car at Harrington when I picked her up, but decided to leave it there because I didn't want to drive back home in the downpour; I was too tired, and we'd had a close call already. I'd planned to head there first thing this morning to get it, that is, until you showed up and broke the news to me that the A was in a field, with that poor sweet girl dead inside it. You're wasting your time with me, Eddie. But I guess you'll figure that out when another body turns up…or maybe you won't."

The whole time he spoke, Dan's eyes never left Eddie's. Sitting on the bunk, leaning forward, Dan had laced his fingers together, willing them not to shake or move despite the tears rolling freely down his face. Through the cell bars, the other man only stared blankly back at him; Dan couldn't be sure if Eddie had taken in a single word.

Part of him wanted to get up, rush the bars and scream for Eddie to move, to say something, but after that, he felt hollowed out, and so very tired. Dan lay back down on his bunk, turning toward the wall and closing his eyes. All of a sudden, the mattress didn't feel quite so bad, and sleep began to rush in on him from all sides.

He heard movement and the *click-thunk* of the door as if from somewhere far away. A moment later, he was fast asleep.

Chapter Forty-One

Lucy stood in the basement, watching dust float in the bright shafts of morning light coming through the small windows. Everything was buttoned up, looking just like the cellar of any other house on the block, she supposed, with its collection of dusty, half-forgotten things.

Sleep had come, but it hadn't been peaceful. Lucy dreamed of the services, of Jack bursting through the door instead of the police, a pale, bloodless mouth under his chin, looking like something mad. The Vic had been behind him, done up like a hearse, while she and Danny seemed chained to the spot, trying to find something on his telephone about changes in time creating Frankenstein-like monsters. Those bloodless, waxy hands had come toward them, then…Lucy had woken up in a cold sweat, the first light of dawn streaming through the window.

Knowing that getting back to sleep would be impossible, she pulled on some fresh clothes from her bag and began to dress.

"Good morning," she said to the emptiness, not really sure why except that the silence was a little too much to bear just now. She thought about going upstairs and putting on the radio, but decided against it. For the time being, she had to maintain the illusion of an empty house.

"If it is them," Danny had said, tossing his marvels into that silverware box and handing it to her, "I'll tell them you're heading to your aunt's, just like you've been telling everyone. At least we'll be consistent, and they shouldn't bother with you. Then if they take me, you can—"

"I'm not going anywhere," she'd said, wanting to slam the box down, but not daring to move. "And neither should you be. This is wrong; you didn't do a thing. I oughta know better than anyone, just like I'd said before. Let me talk to them, to Eddie, if he's the one out there knocking. He and I go back, he'll listen—"

"Luce—"

"Don't you interrupt me, mister! Aren't you even willing to hear me out? Why are you so determined to risk those men out there taking you away?"

Any illusion they'd had that the knocking at the door was only a neighbor in need of help had died fast. Through the windows, they'd seen headlights and identical pairs of black shoes walking back and forth, trying other doors.

"I can't chance them getting their hands on this stuff," he'd said, nodding at the box, "or you to get involved. Please, if they take me, you've gotta go."

Something in what little she could see of his face told him that wasn't the whole story, even if he didn't quite know the whole story himself. But after a moment, Lucy thought she could make a guess.

"You didn't kill anyone, Danny," she said, her voice soft. "Whatever you think you did, don't let those men punish you for it."

He didn't say anything, only stood there with the sound of muffled voices, radio static, and more knocking. She'd put a hand on his arm.

"Danny."

"I'm sorry. I'll be right back."

Standing in the morning light, Lucy let out a sigh, wiping at her eyes. Maybe he was right to do what he did. Maybe it was the only real choice they'd had. But part of her resented that they hadn't even tried to think of something else.

Stop it. It'll all come out all right.

Walking just a little way further into the cellar, she got up on her tiptoes, reached toward one of the beams, and pulled down the silverware box. Once, she'd heard someone say that if you wanted to hide something, put it up high, because people rarely look above their standing eye line. Even in a pinch, this seemed to fit the bill nicely. As for the other wonder down here…

After hiding the silverware box last night, she'd started to make for the darkroom door but stopped when she'd heard raised voices. Making her way toward one of the windows, still holding onto hope as thin as lace that they'd both gotten it very wrong and had just been jumping at shadows, Lucy heard the sound of car doors slamming shut, then the firing of an engine. Standing on a crate to look out, she'd made it just in time to see the headlights in the driveway disappearing.

"Danny?"

There was no answer, aside from the sounds of the empty house. She'd sat down hard on the crate and cried before simply shutting the darkroom door, throwing on the lock, and taking the keys up to bed with her. She didn't think anyone would be coming back that night, and no one had.

Lucy sat on the bottom step with the silverware box in her lap. Something Danny had said the night before came to her then. It was about how all the town's history was sitting in this box, inside another device more impressive than the portable telephone, a thing that seemed hard to imagine considering what she'd seen last night. Still, it'd be quite something…

You're thinking about doing some more snooping, aren't you?

Yes, that was so. And just what of it? There was plenty of time.

Danny had said there were a few loose floorboards in the bedroom closet where he thought these things could be stashed before suggesting that she leave town for a few days. But Lucy thought that was foolish. If she'd been in that hall closet wondering about loose floorboards, surely a couple of flatfoots would think the same, then last night would've all been for nothing.

No. Lucy would leave town come nighttime if it came to that to give the illusion of going to her aunt's, but if she did, these things would be coming with her for safekeeping. At least until all this foolishness gets straightened out. But if there was any good sense in the world, and she believed in her heart that there was, Danny would be walking back in that door by suppertime, and they could forget the whole business.

Until then, if I'm goin' to be keepin' an eye on these things, I oughta know just what it is I've got.

Lucy opened the old silverware box and looked inside.

Over the next several minutes, she looked over the wallet, the telephone…a misnomer in her opinion, considering everything she'd been told it could do. Inside was the cord she'd seen some days ago, stuck in the record cabinet, and had finally worked out that it belonged to the telephone. There were a few more cords, and particularly interesting, what looked to be an electric book that seemed to hold a lot more than just a single story. She'd wondered if this was the thing all those records were on, but when she glimpsed what looked to be pictures of book covers lined up in a neat little row, she supposed not.

"Hell House…The Life-Changing Magic of Tidying Up…Game of Thrones…Sharp Objects."

All those titles sounded terribly interesting, and the idea that she could spend the rest of the day upstairs reading books from the future was a temptation. Almost too much to bear. But it'd have to wait until later if things…*when* things were all right again, and she could allow herself to do something as nice as sitting down to enjoy a story. Besides, there was one more thing in the silverware box…

"And just what are you?"

Lucy pulled the gadget out, about the size of a thick magazine, only a good deal heftier, and set it carefully on her lap. Looking around it, afraid of touching it just the wrong way before she had an idea of what she was doing, Lucy spotted a groove running along the side and guessed it must open on a hinge. And sure enough, it did.

Inside was what looked to be a keyboard like on a typewriter, only not quite. The half facing her lit up, showing her all sorts of boxes on something that looked like the telephone screen, only bigger. Lucy lifted a finger, touching the screen to see what would happen. Nothing did. She instead let her fingers dance across the strange keys when out of the corner of her eye, a little arrow began to move. After repeating the gesture over and over again, she worked out that running her hand along the square under the keys moved the little arrow around.

"Ain't that somethin'?"

Minutes ticked by as Lucy amused herself by moving the arrow around, and found out that if you pushed on the square while moving, you could move things around. Studying the little pictures and words on the screen, she worked out that this must be some sort of electric filing cabinet. And after a little frustrated tapping on the square started to bear fruit, she figured out just how to go about opening the files.

Moving back into the living room with its sofa and drawn shades, Lucy spent some time reading, her mind positively reeling. Though she stayed clear of things like "Taxes" and "Mortgage" and "Bank Statements" ...anything that seemed too personal. Instead, she restricted herself to the sorts of things Danny had spoken about last night: many, many folders containing many, many documents about the history...past, present, and future...of her hometown.

After some time, realizing that she'd not relieved herself since waking up, Lucy stood, her legs tingling, and headed to the restroom before hurrying straight back. Her eyes stung with the strain of looking at the gadget, and she went to grab her specs from her purse before taking her seat and resuming her reading. It was all too fascinating to stop now, and she hadn't even made it past a folder called "Newspaper Archives" yet.

She'd jumped around, picking years at random just because she could. The shooting out at The Wheel back in '33. An article from 2004 about the grand opening of the brand-new New Chapel High School. An accident in 1973 involving a truck crashing through that sign over the Kent County Fairgrounds. A front-page story back in 2008, where it seemed the United States would elect its first colored president.

A fine thing in her opinion; she'd never taken up with the nonsense of treating people differently because of what color they happened to be. And for all the other sins of the woman who'd raised her, that hadn't been one of them.

Lucy looked at those things and dozens more. She steered clear of the Obituaries section of the papers...those were things she certainly didn't want to know. But when the folder marked "1947" caught her eye, she didn't hesitate…hadn't that been the real reason she'd kept on reading long after figuring out somewhat how the contraption worked? Hoping that there might be good news after all? That maybe she could take that same curiosity that'd made her peek at the end of that book, that'd gotten her into the hall closet, that'd gotten her flipping through the wallet, and put it to good use?

June, July, August…September.

Straightening herself against the sofa, Lucy took a deep breath and opened the "September" file.

Flipping through, seeing things she considered to be current events presented to her as faded news clippings was a surreal experience. The fundraiser for the high school, advertisements for the fair, and the police blotters. She remembered a lot of these articles, having only read them a few days ago. Lucy continued to look, not sure of just what she was looking for, only—

Lucy read the headline several times, using her finger just to make sure she was following along and not just seeing things; she wasn't.

It was coverage of the services yesterday. Words she guessed that right now were still sitting undone next to Penny Prescott's typewriter. The story was brief and made no mention of Lucy's own dramatic exit, like she'd been afraid of. Penny hadn't…won't, make any mention of them at all, except for a single line.

"Jack Lawrence is survived by dear, close friends Mr. Daniel Parker and Miss Lucy Rodgers."

A tear came to her eye as well as a smile.

I think I like her after all.

Looking down, she saw there was one other issue for September. She said a silent prayer that what she'd find would help or put her at ease and opened the file. Unfortunately, opening it did neither.

Local Clerk is New Chapel Ripper! By: Tony Frank

Local bookstore clerk, Mr. Daniel Parker of Eastbridge Rd, was arrested on September 23rd, 1947, in connection with the gruesome deaths of Jack Lawrence and Elise Crawford that had left New Chapel residents stunned and locking their doors.

Sheriff Robert Buck told this reporter, "If you've got the need to thank someone for getting this madman off the streets, thank my second-in-command, Deputy Edward Prescott."

Sheriff Buck went on to say how Deputy Prescott single-handedly put the case together to bring Mr. Parker to justice, and that due to health reasons, he'd be stepping down, putting Prescott in the top spot. When asked, now acting-Sheriff Prescott had this to say about the recent arrest and about Mr. Parker himself.

"Based on the conversations I've had with him, Daniel Parker is an ill man. That doesn't excuse his actions, and much as I'd like to see him answer for what he's done at Stonehill Penitentiary, I do believe he should be treated as best fits a man in his condition. We're in talks with the district attorney's office, seeking that Daniel Parker be moved to care at Alcomb Sanatorium within the next few days, under the care of Dr. Roderick Hart."

Making the visit out to Alcomb, located just on the outskirts between New Chapel and Springdale, this reporter—

Lucy closed the lid of the electric wonder filing cabinet, her shaking hands plastered over her mouth.

Chapter Forty-Two

Penny sat at her desk, fingers gently tapping on the keys of her typewriter. Across the top of the page, she read the title she hadn't chosen but had been told to use: "Local Clerk is New Chapel Ripper!"

After managing to sneak back to her car, once she'd gotten home, all she'd been able to do was take the telephone off the hook, undress, and crawl into bed as the sheer exhaustion of the day finally caught up with her. She'd expected to lie in bed a long time thinking on everything that'd happened, but no sooner than her head had hit the pillow, she'd fallen asleep. If there'd been dreams, Penny couldn't remember them and thought that was probably a mercy.

It'd been a thoughtful journey to the Gazette, and she'd only just begun to really get her head around the night before when she'd walked inside, Harv all but meeting her at the door, before being ushered away into his office. She'd gone willingly enough, but with a sense that something else had gone wrong. And just as she was about to explain why her coverage of the services was still so rough and what else had come about, Harv spared her the trouble.

"Seems your husband couldn't get hold of you last night, so he called me, and I got the story," Harv said, sitting on the edge of his desk, arms crossed, not exactly his usually pleasant self. "We've got another poor soul for Alfred Cole's boys to take care of, and we've got an arrest…where the hell were you last night?"

"I was tired," Penny said, bristling at Eddie being referred to as her husband, yet still looking down at her feet like she'd been called to the front of the class to be scolded by the teacher. "Took the telephone off the hook, and—"

"Took the telephone off the hook when you'd just come from the sight of another murder, and more information…like that arrest, for example, could've come in at any time?" Harv had said, but as soon as Penny opened her mouth to say something in her defense that wouldn't risk her accidentally spilling her guts about what she'd been up to last night, he pressed on. "When I gave you this, I told you in so many words that this would be a serious commitment, didn't I?"

"Yes, Harv."

"Serious commitment means that someone needs to be able to reach you at any hour when you're dealing with something like this. Am I in any way unclear?"

"No, Harv."

"Alright then," he'd said, and something in his manner shifted. "I'm sorry if I was sharp just now. You've got the stuff to do this, and I want you to do well. If I didn't, I'd have pulled you off and put Tony on without a second thought. Here, take this."

Harv handed over a piece of paper. "When Eddie called, the title came to me, so there's your start. I'd like to get coverage of the arrest and Miss Crawford's death in the same go for the sake of time, but if it won't shake out that way, let me know, and we'll hash out something else. In the meantime, the cops nailed the bastard, now let's tell the people."

They got it wrong. There's something else going on here.

All around her, telephones were ringing, chatter was lively, and people were clacking away at their typewriters. Figuring she ought to get something started before Harv came out to check on her and found nothing but a blank page, Penny started to type.

> Local clerk, Daniel Parker, was arrested in connection with the murder of Elise Crawford, after the young girl's body was found in the driver's seat of his 1929 Ford Model A. Sources tell this reporter that he's also wanted for questioning in connection with the recent murder of Jack Lawrence, in which...

She stopped, grabbed a pencil, and made a cross out on the page. She started again.

   Lawrence, who was also found murdered under similar circumstances at Sherbrooke Dairy. Deputy Eddie Prescott, lead investigator on the case, feels that he's already got everything buttoned up and that he's got everything he needs to send a likely innocent man to the electric chair, and doesn't give a damn that he might've gotten it wrong and won't listen.

Penny ripped the sheet of paper from the typewriter, jaw clenched as she re-read over her words. It infuriated her to have to write this. Eddie might be in the right as far as the law was concerned, every box ticked, but deep in her gut, which rarely steered her wrong, this wasn't right. And it just plain didn't make sense. The receipt, the razor, the Model A…just what sort of fool would a person have to be to commit back-to-back murders, leaving their own personal things all over both crime scenes, with not even an effort to hide it? Could Eddie honestly not see that?

Crumpling the page into a ball, Penny made to toss it in the wastebasket, but instead, tossed it into her open purse. She loaded a fresh sheet of paper into the typewriter and just sat, her fingers once more drumming on the keys, waiting for the words to come. At the very least, she could get out a rough draft regarding the death of Miss Crawford, telling Harv that coverage of the two things isn't working in a single story, and drop it in his inbox for now.

The words were dull and lifeless, but eventually they came. But that was just as well. Families read the paper, and it wouldn't do to give the gruesome details of everything she'd seen last night, even if her now jittering fingers could've written them out.

Strangely enough, as she typed, looking back and forth between her hurried notes from the night before, Penny found herself thinking of Lucy Rodgers. Was that poor woman still in the house, all alone?

Or had she split just after she herself had gone, heading God only knew where?

You could've gotten them both away before Eddie got there.

That was true. And telling herself that the best she could've done is send them on the run with the state police eventually on their tails, didn't do much for her guilt. On the road, there would've at least been a chance. She dearly hoped that the house was empty, but couldn't shake the feeling that it wasn't. That was just no good. It'd only be a matter of time before that story about heading to her auntie's place fell apart. Or who knows, it might've already.

Penny ripped the paper from the typewriter, decided it sounded good enough for a start, and scratched out a quick note to Harv before dropping it in the inbox just outside his office. That done, Penny grabbed up her purse and started to make for the front door.

"Leaving already?" someone called from behind.

She didn't stop to turn, only waved a hand over her shoulder and left. Penny got into her coughing, sputtering Lincoln and headed toward the maybe empty house on Eastbridge Road.

Chapter Forty-Three

"Mr. Parker?"

Dan heard both the sound of the open door and the voice, but had been too involved with his current project to bother to turn around. Said project being, seeing how many layers of paint he could work his thumbnail through before it got to the brick underneath. There were no books, no radio…nothing really to do besides pace, sleep, and shit, until he'd happened on this.

He was on either what had to be the second or third layer of paint before he heard a clearing of the throat, and good manners forced him to turn.

A woman stood just outside the bars of his cell, holding a tray. She was nice looking, with a pleasant smile and a blonde bob-style haircut that gave him the odd impression that Marilyn Monroe was standing in front of him.

And why not? Things are so screwed up now, I don't know how much that'd surprise me at this point.

But she wasn't, and Dan knew it. He turned, swinging his socked feet onto the floor and stood up.

"Good morning," he said, then added, "Is it morning? My watch stopped."

"Still bright and early," the woman said, stepping closer to the bars with the tray, delicious smells coming off it. "I thought you might like a little breakfast. Sheriff managed to get hold of some C-Rations after the war, but they're the pits."

Dan walked a little closer, seeing scrambled eggs, home fries, bacon, and what he guessed was a thermos of coffee.

"Thank you," he said, feeling a knot starting up in his throat. "Thanks so much, um—"

"I'm Martha."

"Nice to meet you," Dan said, taking the tray as she slid it through the small space in the bars.

It occurred to him to ask why she'd presumably walked over to Bill's when she could've just tossed him an army ration from a supply closet or something, after all, he was…to use his own modern terminology, a suspected serial killer. But he thought maybe it was best left alone. Any kindness from others seemed like a thing he'd be experiencing less and less from now on; best to not poke too hard at it and just let it be what it was. When she was gone, he sat down to the solitary breakfast, making himself savor it. He was pretty sure the food wasn't going to be any better where he was going.

Thoughts like that had been intruding in on him since he'd woken up again and his feelings about it had run the gambit between tentative resignation…maybe he could get put in charge of the prison library, all the way to despair that left him wanting to rush whoever was unfortunate enough to open his cell, hoping for either escape or to be killed trying.

Last night, Lucy had told him that he hadn't killed anyone and that whatever he thought he'd done, to not let those men punish him for it. And he'd come to with the sickening realization that by not at least trying to run or fight his way out, that might've been just what he'd done.

There was still half a plate of breakfast and a goodish amount of coffee, but Dan, thinking once more about how he'd left her in that basement, found that he'd lost his appetite. He set the tray on the floor, then, lying back down, turned to the wall and his scratch mark. He lay that way for some time, thinking of guilt, thinking of Lucy, and remembering the day before, standing in line at the viewing, asking him to not leave her all alone.

I'm sorry.

He drifted off again.

Sometime later, Dan didn't know just how long, the door clanged open again. He sat up, rubbing at his eyes, wondering if Martha had come back for the tray. Swinging his legs out of bed, he caught the thermos with his foot and knocked it over.

"Sorry, I didn't finish all of—"

Eyes cleared of sleep, Dan had taken his fists away. But when his vision cleared, the words turned to dust in his throat.

Standing in front of him was Eddie, and next to Eddie…

"Carly?"

Chapter Forty-Four

Carly stood there, fighting the smile threatening to break out across her face as she looked down at Dan behind those cell bars—like when he'd been at her feet at the bottom of the staircase, but infinitely more satisfying. She'd paid him back. She'd taken that sweet, happy life from him and left him all alone, just like he'd done to her not once, but twice. Now he was alone, and joy of joys, she could see the loneliness and suffering for herself.

Seeing the look of pure confusion on his face, Carly couldn't help but remember the last time they'd both been together at Harrington House. Not their confrontation at the foot of the stairs, no. But after.

"I need my card, Dan," she'd said, walking across the way from her new apartment, tossing a trash bag in the dumpster. "And if I check my statement and find you've been using it—"

"I haven't been using it. Honestly, I'd forgotten it was there until you called and asked about it. You'd had me hold onto it when we went to the reception so you wouldn't have to carry a clutch, and it's been there ever since."

Carly's hand had tightened on the phone, and it was all she could do not to crack the case.

Liar. It's been over three months, and you didn't know it was there? I call bullshit.

"It better be. Where are you?"

"Harrington House. Doing a little volunteer work. If you can swing by, I'm at the back of the house. There's an open set of cellar doors where I'm working in the basement and—"

"Fine. My car's acting up, but I guess I'll come all the way over there and get it myself."

"Listen, I can—"

Carly tapped the End Call button, opened Uber, and ten or so minutes later, she was in the back of a Subaru headed toward Harrington House.

Because of course, on top of everything else, her Mazda had decided on the way back from her last interview that it wanted to dick around with her life and blow out part of the rear suspension, which is what'd prompted the whole credit card thing in the first place. Maybe she should've remembered that a few days after he broke up with her, but whatever, she didn't.

Not like I haven't been through enough shit since then.

After the embarrassment that'd been the scene at the wedding reception, where thanks to him, everyone thought she was crazy—and that'd stuck with her, playing in her head over and over again.

In the days and weeks after she'd gone back to work, it was hard to think about anything else: the deceit, the lies, the excuses, the unforgivable violation of her trust in him from someone who said he loved her…the stares of everyone else, judging her. Finding out after getting one-word text responses from people who'd been there that night…people who she'd thought were friends, or just being outright ghosted, that they'd abandoned her, too. Daydreaming about what it would've been like to put the spiked heel of her shoe through something vital that night.

The cycle just played on and on in her head. She'd taken the wrong meds to the wrong rooms several times. True, probably should've made more of a concentrated effort, but all that electronic reporting software and scanning guns were supposed to prevent something like that from happening in the first place. Then there'd just been a run of days where the patients and their families were so goddamned awful about literally everything. After all she'd been through lately, she wasn't about to put up with anyone else treating her like shit.

It'd been maybe a week or so when the head nurse had called her in and talked to her, asking if everything was going okay. Carly had said things were fine. She just had to let this pass and get everything under control again. Put it all behind her. And for a while, she did…mostly.

She'd only just started to feel like she'd gotten ahead and things were maybe not looking so bad when something else, just forgetting to chart a few things a few days in a row…an innocent mistake anyone could make, got her brought into one of the admin offices for "a chat".

"We're giving you a week to shape up," the admin said, the head nurse standing off to the side and behind, both of them staring her down. "All your work will need to be logged and verified with an immediate supervisor every shift. If there isn't one available, you'll choose someone else with you who will log and verify your work."

Carly could only sit there, stunned. It was insulting. She'd been to school the same as any of them and consistently got higher performance marks than anyone else, but all that seemed to go out the goddamn window. It sucked that she'd made those mistakes, and she'd felt terrible both at the time and when everything was being rehashed in front of her, sitting and being berated like a kid in the principal's office instead of a professional. But it didn't seem to matter to them how bad she felt.

And in the middle of it, all she could think about was Dan. How he'd berated her…given her an unfair, bad-faith ultimatum, showing how little he cared about her after all, and something in her started to stir. She knew she should've bit her tongue and said nothing except, "yes, okay", but she couldn't. She was done taking shit from the world when all she did was give…

"I'm not doing any of that," Carly had said, hands drawn into claws, digging at the arms of the shitty office chair. "I'm not some first-year moron. I'm more qualified than most of the people out there…and that includes you!"

Anger flowed through her in waves, and before she realized it, Carly was on her feet, one hand planted on the admin's desk, while the other pointed at the moron this hospital had the nerve to call a head nurse.

"I'm sorry for my mistakes; no one is sorrier than me. But I've had a lot of shit going on in my life lately! My boyfriend is turning into the world's largest asshole and dumping me in front of a room of strangers, making me look like I'm some sort of psycho! Forgive me if I'm not perfect, and I can't just leave all that at home and come here, whistle, and pretend like everything is okay! This is the one place that I need to just be on my side until I can get shit sorted out again! Til I can feel like a normal person again!"

Carly hadn't been aware right away, but slowly realized that she was talking at the top of her lungs. Not yelling, but not far from it either.

"So if you want to give me a write-up or whatever, that's fine. I'll sign it, and we can all move on with our lives. But I'm not running every single thing I do past someone else; I'm a professional, and that's insulting as hell. So think some more and come find me when you come up with something more respectful and fair."

Carly had left then, heart racing, but feeling good at having gotten some of that stuff off her chest—walking off the field a victor. Pretty soon, the truth of what she'd said would sink in, and they'd realize they were all adults here and that a write-up and feeling bad about what'd happened was more than enough punishment for any decent person.

As it turned out, they did come back with something. Not a write-up, but a dismissal form.

"Unprofessional attitude", "not a team player", and "actively hostile to others" were among some of the shiniest examples of bullshit they'd included. She hadn't even been given the chance to defend herself. It was all final. No one wanted to take the time and really understand what she'd been going through. Just like Dan, the hospital also decided they were done with her and kicked her to the curb.

Finding a new place with what little she had in savings sucked, and the job searching had been even worse. But a while later, she finally got a lead with a home care place; it was hardly a first, second, or third choice, but beggars couldn't be choosers. And despite her Mazda choosing right then to act up…not great since she'd been DoorDashing to make ends meet…it seemed like the home care job would at least be going in her favor since she'd had a first and second interview.

Doing her best to hold onto the hope that the third interview she'd scheduled for would be the charm, the Uber had pulled into the parking lot of Harrington House Museum. Carly had gotten out and watched as the car drove away. She grabbed her phone to text Dan, but slipped it back in her pocket instead. If she texted, who knew how long she'd be sitting here waiting for him to come out. No, her card was that last reason in the world that she needed to talk to that piece of shit, and the sooner she could get it done, the better.

A moment later, she found herself walking around the back of the old museum, running her hands along the latticework running up the sides of the place, looking for the alleged cellar door, alone and feeling like some stupid bitch in a horror movie before the knife comes down. But she did find it, and it was open.

"Dan."

No answer.

"Dan! If you're in there, come out. I'm not walking down there!" she said, louder this time, but still no answer.

She'd heard noise like something heavy being moved around, and Carly bent down to look inside. It was brighter than she'd expected, courtesy of a few of those LED painter's work lights. Resigning herself to the idea that the idiot probably had his earbuds in or something, Carly made her way down the stairs.

The carved stone foundations of the place rose up, making her feel like she was in a cave instead of a basement. Carly turned, looking around, ready to call out again when she saw him: Dan, squatting down in a room that looked like it'd been broken open, his back to her. She'd opened her mouth to call out, but…

But seeing him like that brought on anger, hot and acidic, and her vision began to tunnel. She felt her hands tighten into fists, the nails beginning to dig into her palms, a sort of high-pitched humming starting up in her ears. He didn't turn. Instead, he seemed intent on the tablet, or whatever it was he had that was making that purple light. At the base of a nearby work light, Carly saw an open toolbox. And sticking out of it, a short crowbar.

Bending down, Carly grabbed the crowbar.

Feeling her heart beat fast, she'd taken slow steps toward his back, her eyes focused on a spot just at the back of his head.

I'm just gonna scare him, she thought, moving closer, hand tightening on the cold steel in her hand. *Just going to scare him, that's all. He deserves that much, he—*

Carly had been no more than three feet from Dan, the bar in her hand starting to rise, when a bright purple pulse, faint but electric, knocked her on her ass and the crowbar from her hand—a feeling in her stomach like she'd just been on a sketchy fair ride with the stomach flu. It'd only been seconds, and she'd just gotten to her feet again, ready to scream, when she noticed that things had changed.

Those LED work lights were gone, the only light now coming from a string of dim Edison bulbs. Dan was gone. The doorway where she'd seen him just moments before looked like it'd never been there at all. A big, dusty wine rack sits in its place.

She'd turned then, not really sure what was going on, but desperate to get out. But turning, stumbling as she made her way back toward the steps she'd just come down, Carly saw the door was shut...a shiny padlock staring her right in the face.

Panic had settled over her, quick, driving her away from the cellar door and down the dimly lit halls. After pulling on one door handle after another, one at the top of a set of stairs finally gave way, spilling her out into a dusty, forgotten...and familiar, ballroom.

She'd run toward the windows, feet making tracks in the thick dust, when she stopped dead. Trees that'd been red, brown, gold, and thinning were lush and green. Outside, the cars she'd seen parked were gone. In their place was something out of the old black-and-white movies. Carly stared at the noses of the two facing her…mostly at the year printed on the short, stubby license plates…1947.

Deep, uncut confusion eventually gave way to horrible understanding and grief like she'd never known before. The bright purple pulse had left her just where she was, yet at the same time, further away from home than she'd guessed anyone had ever been before. Also, she was alone. This time, well and truly alone.

Carly slid down the wall, too horrified to weep, staring off in the distance until the sky had grown dark. Once it had, and the sound of voices coming from inside the mansion died away, Carly crept out, making her way through the empty rooms, finding money, clothes…the beginnings of her new life.

All things considered, Carly thought, looking down at Dan, behind bars…now just as isolated and alone as he'd ever made her feel, *I'd have to say it was worth it.*

Chapter Forty-Five

Dan could only sit there, mouth slightly open, looking up at the two of them. It was all too easy to imagine he was still asleep or that this was a relative or something. But that lasted only about a second; there was no mistaking her. He tried to speak, tried to make some noise, but couldn't.

"Someone to see you," Eddie said, then turned to Carly. "You sure about this, Miss Wells?"

"I am."

"Well, I can't say I like the idea, but I'll have someone just on the other side of the door. Just knock when you're through. Holler if there's trouble."

Throat still dry as a dead Christmas tree, Dan watched as Eddie gave him a lingering "You'd best behave yourself" look before crossing to the room and disappearing out the door. Carly, who'd been following along as well, stood watching the closed door for a beat before turning to look at him, an easy expression on her face.

"Nice cell."

There was still a downed connection between his mouth and brain, and Dan continued to stare. It was jarring to see her hair done up like this. Ditto the dress and the handbag. Focusing on it too long made his head start to twinge, and so he made himself speak.

"How the hell did you get here?"

"Actually, I'd like you to fill me in about that. Because the last thing I knew, an Uber dropped me off at that museum, and I went down those creepy steps to find you and get my credit card back; the shocks in the Mazda finally went out. I found you bent down in a room or cave or something, and a purple flash later, everyone's wearing dresses and fedoras and I'm hearing Boogie Woogie Bugle Boy on the radio."

Dan stood, running a hand over his face; a lot of things had just started to make sense. Her never showing up to get her card, the unreturned texts and calls, and him just thinking that she'd decided to cancel the card and have done with it. But no, she'd disappeared right in front of, or rather, right behind him. How had he not known? No one had ever come to ask him about her. He supposed that if he'd still been on social media, he might've noticed something then, but…

"I…I didn't even know you were there. Jesus, Carly, I'm so sorry, I just saw it and I…."

Carly's eyebrows shot up; the weird, detached expression that'd been on her face was gone.

"What do you mean, *it*?"

Taking a deep breath, making sure to keep his voice pitched low, Dan explained all he could about the machine and how he'd found it. What'd happened when he ran his fingers across the dials then pulled the lever, and what'd happened since. But he brought it all the way to the end quick, not to leave her hanging with false hope.

"It's broken. Whatever powered it is dead, and I don't think there's any getting it to work again."

Carly, who'd started to look hopeful as he went through his story, sank into the nearby chair. She didn't speak for a long time, and Dan didn't rush her.

"So, when I was sent back, you were there too…just on the other side of that wall."

"I was. But only for like, a minute before I ran back to the machine. But everything's so screwed up, Carly. That murder at the dairy a few days back…another one last night, which, thanks to some psychopath stealing my car, is the reason I'm in here right now. All that and God only knows what else…none of it happened before. And all of it because we're here and shouldn't be. It's my fault for laying eyes on the damn thing. And I'm so, so sorry that you got caught up in the mess. If I'd have known you were out there just on the other side of the wall, shit…I'd have gotten through the loose bricks and boards somehow. I'd have never left you behind."

She nodded, neither of them saying anything for a while. Not that Dan really knew what to say, honestly. But now that the initial shock of seeing her had worn off, other things started to creep in around the edges of their little situation. Something that should've gotten his attention…would've gotten his attention before, if…

Carly looked up at him then, a smile across her face that made him step back from the bars, dread dropping into his stomach like lead. She didn't say anything for a long moment, only got up to stand near the bars, her eyes boring into him.

"That's good," she said, almost laughing. "You almost had me believing that for a second."

"What are you…hang on," Dan struggled to think, alarm bells sounding in his mind. "How did you know I was here? What are you doing here?"

"I needed to know," she said. "Part of me thought I was going a little too psycho for not just coming to you when I first noticed you the other day. But you just would've fed me the same shit you did just now. Lying, pretending that you had no idea what you'd done, when of course you did…how could you not?"

Dan felt his still sluggish mind trying to process her words, struggling hard to understand and unpack them all. It wasn't helping that she was talking fast, twitching a little, and gesturing with her hands almost like she was conducting an orchestra. That night, she looked like she wanted to stomp him into the steps in Harrington House he'd been scared. But it was nothing compared to the fear he felt now.

"Carly, I—"

"But seriously, I want to thank you. If it hadn't been for you playing your sick game and leaving me stranded in this nightmare, I would've never known…never even dreamed that it'd feel so…"

Martha's coffee and that last nap had seemed to be doing him more and more good by the second. And it was only a matter of moments before the full picture came crashing in.

"You did this."

Carly winked.

"You humiliated me," she said, giggling, and Dan took another step back. "Made me look like a psycho, threw everything I'd trusted you with back in my face, and tossed me away like I was nothing. You got in my head…I started making mistakes at the hospital because of what you did, and those assholes fired me…kicked me to the curb just like you. And just when things were maybe…*maybe* starting to go sort of okay again, you stranded me here. All the while, you were walking around with a smile on your face, just loving your happy little life here without a care in the world for what you'd done, well…consider us even."

As Carly's words rang through his ears, Dan could feel something start to burn hot inside him. It wasn't tears or anger…he was well past those now; it was white-hot rage. Though through it, he was aware that something inside him had changed. Guilt about everything that'd happened over the past week had made a subtle, but important shift to responsibility. He'd own all of this for the rest of his life, as it should be, but the feelings like he might as well have been the one holding the blade finally died.

Lucy and his mental version of Jack were right…he hadn't killed anyone…*she* had.

He continued to stare straight ahead, aware that his vision was shrinking to a pinhole, red bursts flashing around the edges in time to his own triphammer heartbeat.

"Wow," Carly said, slipping a hand into the pocket of her dress. "I really thought you'd have something to say about that."

Dan said nothing.

"Oh, I get it," Carly said. "You don't believe me; figure I'm just as big a liar as you are, huh? Well, I think I can fix that."

Pulling the hand back out of her pocket, Dan saw her holding her phone, and his eyes went wide.

"Don't."

Carly ignored him, tapping at her phone before turning it toward him.

"Look."

And for the same reason that people peck through their fingers at the scariest part of a horror movie or click on those blurred pictures online that have the graphic content warnings over them…he did.

He saw shaky night mode video from inside the Vic. Jack bathed in blood all down his front, head leaned back, pulling the gash open like a second mouth. Little shards of glass pushed into his eyes, reflecting back into the camera…all of it realized in horribly crisp 4K.

"A little boring, I know," Carly said, "but this one's better." She swiped at the screen.

Another video started. Dan saw the inside of his own car, watching as the knife handle sticking out of Elise's neck bobbed and jittered, blood spewing from it like a fountain onto the dress box she'd been so excited to…

Dan stood silent, fists clenched so hard that his nails began to dig into the palms of his hands, drawing blood. He felt tears in some faraway place and wished he could go back and look away, all the while knowing that it would be a very, very long time before he could close his eyes without those images coming to him.

"If I could do that one over again, I'd stick the phone on the dash and get the whole thing," Carly said, turning the phone back to look at herself. "You should've seen it when she could still kinda talk, choking on her own blood, begging for Jesus to come save her. Pathetic, right? Man, I really wish Lucy Rodgers had come back for some tea with me yesterday before you came to get her, then I'd have three. But I guess there's always next time."

Before he realized he was going to do so much as twitch a muscle, Dan crossed the distance between them, and in one swift move, shot his arms out through the bars, reaching for Carly's neck. But with a scary sort of speed, she jumped back, that insane grin never leaving her face.

Dan opened his mouth to scream, preferably about how he was going to rip her goddamn throat out with his bare hands, when Carly spoke again.

"Careful," she said, raising a finger and slipping the phone back into her pocket. "You scream, then I scream. I'll rip my dress, bang my head against the bars, and say you got hold of me and tried to rape me like you did with that poor little thing in your car before you killed her. Then, a few goons will come in here, knock you against a wall, and beat you senseless with a club or something til you don't even remember your own name. Not something either one of us wants to deal with, right? Besides, your shit's already about to get worse as it is after the statement I give to that hunky deputy out there."

Rasps came from his throat as he watched Carly first turn, then walk back toward the door, giving him the finger as she did. She made it as far as raising a hand to knock to be let out when Dan found his voice, weak and old.

"Don't hurt her…please. I'm sorry for everything. Just, please don't hurt her."

Carly didn't say a word, only giggled, gave the door a sharp knock, then disappeared through it, leaving him alone once more.

Chapter Forty-Six

Lucy paced the empty house, her footsteps falling hard in the echoing stillness, the article continuing to run through her mind. All she wanted to do right now was take a stroll outside and let the fresh air work on her thinking, but she supposed this would have to do.

Things had changed. Danny turning himself in last night meant he'd be sure to take the fall for everything. She supposed that she could look ahead to learn more about what'll happen to him, surely that information was in there if the rest of it was, but she couldn't bring herself to do it. If she had happened on a picture of a confused old man along with some article about how the New Chapel Ripper had finally passed away, she might just go loony…if being cooped up in the house knowing what she did didn't do that first.

"Okay, okay, okay," she said, talking out loud just to do something about the silence. "What can I do?"

The horrible thing was, she couldn't think of much.

Showing up at the station downtown with some baloney story about deciding to cancel her trip and only just hearing the news, all under the guise of trying to talk some sense into Eddie, was a bad idea. She wouldn't kid herself that it wasn't. The way her luck seemed to be going these days, she'd end up in a cell too, and then they'd be in a real fix.

Unless you have something to go on. Something that'd get the finger pointed away from him and in the right direction…

Lucy turned to the electric filing cabinet again and, pushing all thoughts of the bad news she might find aside, opened the lid. She'd only begun to look around at the next issue of the Gazette when another little box appeared telling her that the battery that powered the thing was going to run out. She continued to look, and a minute later, the screen went dark on her, taking its information with it.

"No!"

Tapping at the buttons did nothing. She remembered the cords sitting in the silverware box and wondered if one of them might do the job to power the thing up again. After a minute or two of fussing around, she managed to work out which cord went to the device and got it plugged in. She clapped when the screen lit back up and made that drawn-out gong sound, finally explaining what she'd heard coming from the hall closet earlier last night. But the excitement was short-lived when a different screen appeared, along with another little box asking for… a password?.

"Shoot! What are you, a speakeasy?!"

Fighting the urge to slam the lid, Lucy closed the electric filing cabinet again…her way to peek ahead at the story was closed off. If going to the police on terms she thought would make any difference at all was now out, what did that leave? Not much.

But she wanted to help…*needed* to help. Being told that parts of life happening around her hadn't happened before had been astounding, confusing, and had filled her with a vague sort of alarm. But she'd accepted it, because just what else could you do? Now, though, having spent all that time staring into the electric crystal ball, she knew a lot more.

She'd heard stories and whispers and rumors about that creepy place they called a mental hospital, and the thought of leaving Danny to rot in there, even if only half of them were true, was too much to just sit around and do nothing with. And she wouldn't.

But what would be the point? Even if she could get past the boys keeping an eye on him and somehow get Danny out, what then? He'd be a fugitive…and so would she.

Lucy stood, wandering into the kitchen and remembering how she'd sat here, watching him make dinner just the night before; the only man who'd ever done something like that for her…or made her feel like what she had to say mattered, or…

Forcing that thought away for the time being, Lucy turned in the direction of the cellar, thinking that she ought to finally have a look at the thing that'd caused all this trouble.

A short trip downstairs later, she stood, hands on her hips, down in that creepy room, looking down at something that didn't look all that much bigger than a bread box, covered in a canvas tarp. She grabbed the stool under the workbench, placed it in front of the thing, and took a seat.

She sat looking at it for what felt like a long time, almost too afraid to touch it. Like something might come up from under the tarp at any second and bite her.

"Oh, would you quit being silly?" she asked, pulling the tarp off and letting it fall to the ground behind her. As it fell, Lucy found herself involuntarily drawing in breath.

It was made of what she guessed was riveted brass. Dials and knobs were clustered around displays at the top, showing things like month, date, and year.

"My goodness," she said, letting her fingers dance over etched brass cylinders, spelling out 1-9-4-7.

Set in front of the box was what seemed to be thick glass. Inside it, among the wires and all sorts of other complicated-looking innards, a large piece of what looked like semi-clear quartz about the size of her own forearm sat suspended inside. Danny said it'd glowed bright with purple light once, but all she could see was darkness, aside from a few errant flashes that she guessed were coming from the lightbulb just above her head.

Lucy stared for some time, her eyes flicking from the readout dials to the inside workings, and back again. All at once, she felt fascinated, terrified, and so very curious about what it'd be like to use such a thing.

Her right hand found a single lever on the side. She guessed by the size and the fact that there was nothing else quite like it that this lever was what made the machine go when it had the power to do so.

Something about that struck her as a little familiar, but she couldn't think of just why and didn't press it further.

"Are there switches in the back?"

Lucy didn't think Danny would've forgotten or missed something like that, but a gal could hope. Standing, she bent over the workbench and looked behind the machine, not sure how much she wanted to go moving it around.

There were no switches to speak of, but when she bent over, feeling her necklace move and make a faint *tink* sound against the glass as she studied the back of the thing, Lucy started to become aware of a small upset in her stomach.

Probably because you haven't had a thing to eat since you woke up. And you know what being upset does to you sometimes.

Those things were certainly true, but they weren't exactly right somehow. And as Lucy continued to feel around the back, chancing to move the thing a bit so she could get a better look, the sick feeling only kept creeping up.

Thinking that maybe coffee would settle things a little bit, Lucy sat back on the stool. Her eyes danced along the dials and the numbers once more, wondering just who in the world had created such a miraculous thing. And how. And when. Danny said he'd found it under Harrington House, but how long had it really been there? Was it possible that—

Lucy bent closer; something had flickered purple just behind the glass like a slow lightning flash.

Without a second thought, she got on a level with the little window, breathing fast. She pressed her specs further up on her nose and stared inside.

It'd be terribly easy to dismiss what she saw as a trick of the light. Her mind was seeing things that she wanted to see, and she'd have been the first to admit it. But try as she might to poke holes in it, she wasn't imagining that flicker…something had changed. Only, the change seemed to be undoing itself before her very eyes. That brief glimpse of faintest purple had started to fade away.

Maybe I messed with something important back there after all.

Thinking that must be it, Lucy watched and waited to see what would happen. Moments passed, and the strange quartz stayed dark. She stood once more, leaning over and around, this time to see if she could get a better look at whatever it was she must've touched. But as soon as she did, her stomach twinged at her again, and she sat back down.

Is this thing radioactive?

She didn't think so. Anything that used the same power source as those atom bombs couldn't be so small, it just—

Lucy's thoughts cut clean off as she sat, bending her head down, meaning only to find a good place to rest her feet, when she caught a look at her necklace…it was glowing purple, little flecks of lightning dancing through it.

"It can't be."

But it was. Lucy unclasped the necklace, then, letting the stone hang by its chain, moved it toward the glass…the insides began to glow with a dim, purple light. She pulled the stone away, then after a few moments, the light would fade once more. Looping the fine chain over one of the knobs, letting the stone come to rest against the glass, the purple glow came again, and it stayed. She stared for what she'd find later on to be the better part of half an hour, and in all that time, the light remained.

And just before she left the small room on legs that didn't seem altogether there, her mind suddenly alive with possibilities, she thought the glow inside had grown just the tiniest bit brighter.

Chapter Forty-Seven

Eddie sat in the sheriff's office, listening to the mumbled talk from just outside the glass.

Buck had returned and was making his rounds. Eddie had been told after shaking the man's hand that he was to go have a seat and wait, and that he'd only be a few minutes. That'd been about ten minutes ago, according to his watch, but Eddie thought that was just as well. Let the old man talk; he needed to think about that nurse, Caroline Wells.

Miss Wells had come in to give her statement, telling him how she'd been passing by Sherbrooke Dairy on an evening walk when she'd heard screams and went to see what the matter was. Only to see Parker with a razor in his hand and making toward where the Victoria had been parked, and not moments after she'd hidden herself away in a barn, she'd heard screams and knew something awful must've happened. Once things were quiet again, she'd screwed up her courage to see just what it was she could do to help, and that's when Dorothy Sherbrooke came on the scene, and Miss Wells had given her the name.

"We'd heard something about a nurse on the scene from Mrs. Sherbrooke," Eddie had said, holding his pen. "Just how is it you're only coming to us now with this information, Miss Wells?"

"Because Dan and I used to date, and he always scared me to death. Now even more so. I only felt comfortable…felt *safe* to come forward when I learned he was safely behind bars where he couldn't hurt anyone anymore."

Eddie had continued to write his notes and ask his questions. Per her request, he'd taken her to see Parker and let them have a private word. Then, before he knew it, he'd been watching the girl walk out the front door. It wasn't until he'd excused himself to the men's room to take a leak that he realized something about their talk bothered him.

If it was just as she'd said, and she'd hung around til Parker was gone that night with the deed done, why did she leave Dorothy Sherbrooke passed out in the doorway once she'd realized it was too late for Jack Lawrence? Why didn't she telephone the police herself and wait for help? No doubt about it that fear makes people do crazy things, but that was certainly a stretch, especially for a nurse.

That didn't sit right with Eddie, and the feeling only got worse when he stepped into the cells to check on Parker, curious if he might be in a more cooperative mood. Maybe fill him in on some of what he and the nurse had been chatting about, too.

Parker was happy to talk. Practically salivating at the opportunity. The attitude from this morning had gone, but that fierceness and earnestness in the man's voice that'd set him back on his heels earlier was still there. Still there? Hell, it was even stronger than it'd been before, and Eddie had the distinct impression that he was seeing the man himself for the first time with all his walls down.

"Is she still here?" he'd said, gripping onto the bar so hard Eddie could see the whites of his knuckles.

"No, she's just left."

"You need to get her back in here, now!"

"Now, why would I do a thing like that?"

"Because she's the one you want, not me."

Eddie had wanted to laugh at that, but something in the man's eyes tamped it down to just a dry chuckle, and nothing more.

"I can prove it," Parker had said, his eyes hard and sober. "First Jack, then Elise Crawford, and now I think she's going after Lucy. Please Ed…Deputy Prescott, you have to believe me."

"And just how would you prove such a thing? You've been hiding your old girlfriend's secret diary, or did you find some incriminating photographs? If so, you should've said something earlier. Saved us all this trouble."

Parker opened his mouth to say something, then closed it, shaking his head and running a hand down his face. Eddie took a step forward toward the bars.

"There somethin' you wanna tell me?"

"I know she did it," he said. "She just told me. Flaunted it in my face before making a comment about Lucy, then disappearing. You have to get ahold of Lucy, wherever she is, and make sure she's safe."

"Now, why would she do a thing like that to you?"

There was a bray of laughter from just outside the office door, forcibly reminding Eddie where he was. Looking over, he saw the sheriff's huge, hulking outline come clearer and clearer before finally stepping through the door.

"Lively bunch," Eddie said.

"That they are," Buck said, lumbering over behind his desk and settling in, both the old man and the chair groaning. "Everyone's a little easier in their minds now that you've got that monster all shut up."

"Yessir."

"What's the matter, Ed?" Buck said, reaching for one of his nasty cigars and lighting one. "You look like someone just shat on your birthday cake."

"No, sir, just tired is all."

"Considering everything you've been up to since I've been on my back, I'd say you're entitled to it."

Eddie nodded, giving a small smile, but didn't say more. He could tell by the way Buck had settled into his chair, fingers laced over his wide expanse of belly, that the old man wasn't done.

"Somethin' I'd like to talk to you about, Ed. You did a hell of a job while I was gone, a hell of a job. And with my health being what it is, that's got me thinking that maybe it's time for me to step down. I'm gettin' pretty long in the tooth, and I'd like to be around to watch my grandkids grow as long as I can. So, you'll be takin' my place here soon."

He'd been prepared to get Buck all the way up to speed on their big break, and probably they'd get to it here soon, but Eddie hadn't expected anything like this.

"Sir, I don't…I don't know what to say."

"You'll say yes. It's a good step up. Just the thing you deserve for all your hard work. Help ya get back on the right foot after your personal troubles, too, I expect; skirts love a man in charge. Also, he's young, but I think maybe Alan would be the right man to take your place. Him or Glenn, but we'll talk more about that later, so be thinkin' on it."

Eddie nodded. He sat with his notes open, ready to start in with his own spiel, but Buck spoke again and took the ball from his hands.

"Now, about that rapin', killin' monster over in yonder cell," Buck cocked his head at a nearby wall. "What do you make of it after talkin' to him this morning?"

Now, which way should he answer that one? The way he felt last night after slamming the fool behind bars? How he felt walking to the cells first thing this morning? Or how he felt leaving the cells just a little while ago, hearing what he had in the man's voice, while all the time, playing over his conversation with the nurse, trying to make sense of the parts that didn't make sense.

"He denies everything, but the evidence we've got points to Dan Parker as being the one who killed those people. But if he's right, I'd say he's just about the unluckiest man in the world right now."

Eddie found his mind lingering on the words "if he's right", and thinking about how Parker looked when he'd said he could prove it.

"You collared the right man, don't you worry," Buck said, waving a meaty hand. "And don't worry because this is gonna be handled quick."

"Sir?"

Buck smiled, but Eddie couldn't quite match it.

"I got a call this morning," Buck said. "The doctor up at the bug house, Hart. Said he'd heard the news. Just how he'd heard, I don't know, but anyhow, I met with him and the district attorney, and we had a talk. And what it all boils down to is there'll be a trial, but until then, Parker's getting moved to Alcomb. Hart says he doesn't get many opportunities to study the criminal mind quite like this. Says he has a treatment that might even be able to set the man right, not to mention get Hart himself published in some big medical journal, but that's neither here nor there. Wants to use him as an experiment in the interest of science."

As if the words spoken had been a spell, Eddie found himself back walking the halls of Alcomb, hearing the laughter and the screams. Seeing Dorothy Sherbrooke through a window, looking like not much more than a living doll…except for when the lights began to flicker, and then there was only fear. She faded away, leaving Parker in her place, staring up.

He deserves it. Deserves everything that's comin'. A man who does a thing like that, he…well…

Only, Eddie couldn't finish the thought. Despite the facts of his case, everything he'd experienced today had left him feeling less and less sure of what he had. Penny didn't agree with him, he knew, but why? He'd never really bothered to ask her last night. Only told her why she was wrong. And hadn't the reason he'd had her along with him on this was because he wanted to know what she thought?

"It's a fair exchange if you ask me," Buck said. "Hart gets to do his little experiments, maybe save us all from the next lunatic that starts to run amok, and we're getting a madman out of our hair sooner instead of later. Personally, I'd rather just walk him down to Stonehill, have him ride the lightning, then be done with it, but this is modern times, I guess."

Oh, if you send him to Alcomb, he'll ride a whole different kind of lightning. One that'd make any man with even a scrap of sanity left to his name wish he were dead.

They talked for a little while longer, about Buck stepping down, what that'd look like, and how they'll handle it in the press, but Eddie was only half paying attention. He needed to talk to Penny.

Chapter Forty-Eight

It'd taken some doing, but Penny finally made it through that damned side door, feeling like it was true what they say…third time's the charm.

Like last time, she'd parked just up the road and around the corner, and walked the rest of the way. When she'd come to that small set of steps, sparing a glance toward the nearby cellar window, she knocked briskly.

There'd been some time waiting, and also like the night before, every passing second made her feel like she was more and more exposed, only there was no darkness to hide her this time. If it was as she thought and Lucy was still inside, the last thing she wanted to do was draw any attention to the house, but there was no helping it.

A car passed by on the street, and Penny followed it out of the corner of her eye, holding her breath. Once it'd passed, she turned back toward the door, only to see the twitch of a curtain and feel a drop in her stomach.

"Lucy?" she'd said, trying to find the balance between pitching her voice low and being loud enough to be heard through the glass.

There was no answer, just like she imagined might be the case. But instead of walking away, she pressed on.

"I need to talk to you. Please."

That brought another twitch of the curtain, but nothing more.

"Please. I really shouldn't be here, and I wouldn't be unless it was important."

Still no answer. Sighing and thinking about how she could plead her case another way, there was a small *click*, and a crack appeared, one familiar blue eye staring out at her.

"Can I come in?" she said, then the door shut.

Penny heard what sounded like a chain being undone and was about to start giving her thanks when the door opened wide and a hand wrapped around her upper arm, all but yanking her off her feet into a kitchen. Lucy Rodgers backed against the door, shutting it behind them, staring.

"Excuse my rudeness, but just what are you doing here?"

The good manners instilled in her since earliest childhood told her she should thank Lucy for letting her inside before commenting about what a lovely place it was…even though it appeared she was only a houseguest, before finally settling down to business. Penny did her best to push all that aside and get to the point. She had the feeling that time was pressing.

Might as well get the worst of it out in the open first. Then maybe the rest won't seem so bad.

"I came here last night to see you and Dan Parker both. Only, I saw you through the windows and, well, I heard…everything."

"Beg your pardon?"

Penny took a deep breath, knowing that this probably wouldn't go so well, and she was right. As she laid out her story, about being out at the Crawford farm the night before, then running here to warn them, only to be taken in by what she'd seen and heard through the windows, coming back to herself just in time to watch the police come, she watched Lucy's face grow steadily redder and redder.

"They're gonna pin both murders on him," Penny said, trying to look anywhere except those blazing blue eyes that seemed to be trying to burn holes right through her. "Eddie thinks you've skipped town for your aunt's place because that's what one of the girls you live with, Caroline Wells, told one of the others. I heard it. But listen, I don't think that's gonna hold water for much longer. They might've already telephoned your aunt by now, and unless she's the type to lie for you, you might already be in trouble. I'm sorry, I was too late last night, but please, you have to go now while you've still got the time, I…"

But the words died away from her just then; something about the look in the other woman's eyes. There was plenty of anger, and well-deserved anger at that, but there was something else, too.

"You aren't leaving, are you?"

"No, I'm not."

"Can I ask why?"

"Ask all you like."

It was plenty infuriating knowing she wouldn't get answers, but for once in her life, Penny didn't feel much like pushing the issue. The woman standing in front of her was a good deal taller and a good deal stronger, probably on account of the plates she'd seen her carry around before at the diner, and could probably put a serious hurt on her if she had a mind to.

"So, did you just come out to warn me to leave soon, or is there something else?" Lucy said. "Because if you're feeling guilty and looking to be forgiven, I can't say I'm in much of a forgiving mood…I'm a little busy here."

"No, nothing like that."

Actually, that wasn't true. Guilt had driven her here just as much as that hunk of junk Lincoln had. But spilling her guts so she could go forward with a clear conscience wasn't the only reason why she'd come. Just as she'd thought before coming here that chances were good Lucy Rodgers was still in the house, her choosing not to leave hadn't been all that great a shock either. You only had to spend time with her and Dan together to know there was something there. And since that was the case…

"I want to help," Penny said. "That man doesn't belong here, and from what I gather, the sooner he leaves, the better…even if he can't truly go home again. But aside from that, he's a nice man who I don't believe for a second did the things they're accusing him of. I'd rather see him on the run, living out the rest of his life on a beach somewhere in Mexico than have to be the one to write that he's been taken to Stonehill Penitentiary or some such place, knowing that I'd all but helped put him there."

For the first time since being dragged through the door, something in Lucy's face softened. Not much, but at least it didn't feel like the woman was eyeing daggers at her, and that was something.

Penny stood there for what felt like a long time in the silence that followed. Silence wasn't generally something she was all that comfortable with, and it was all she could do not to babble just to fill it. But somehow she managed, and when Lucy spoke again, things seemed to have cooled even more.

"You heard everything last night through that little broken window?"

"I did."

"So, you know there's something a little more special than that telephone down in the cellar."

"Yes, I do. A few things, by the sound of it."

And even under the circumstances, she'd be an awful liar to say that she didn't want to get a closer look. But she restrained that, too. Things seemed to be going well now, and she didn't want to lose any ground by overstepping.

Lucy took another one of those long, considering pauses before speaking again.

"Things are a little different this morning. For the better, I hope. There's a way to get him home, or at least, there will be soon." Penny opened her mouth to ask more, but Lucy raised a hand, cutting her off. "I think I'll keep that to myself for now. Hope you understand."

"I'd like to help," Penny said again.

"And I'd be grateful for any ideas you've got, if you're honest about what you've been sayin'. Because fluttering my eyelashes before knocking out some poor fool just doing his job is the best I can come up with right now, and that's not all that good."

Now it was Penny's turn to consider. The thing they had going in their favor was that the Kent County Police Department wasn't some impregnable fortress. It was an office building with a few cells put in as a matter of course because that's all that's ever been needed in New Chapel.

She'd been in enough times when she and Eddie had been married, and he'd shown her where the cracks in even that admittedly lousy facade were. Like how a nail file and a bobby pin in the hands of someone who really knew what they were doing would be enough to jimmy open those old cell locks. Or how the building, old as it was, suffered from electrical issues from time to time…and how more often than not, the alarm someone had rigged up over the second door in the cell block that led outside would short out.

Penny explained this, leaving out how she came by that last part in a single evening when Eddie had the watch of the place to himself for a little while, and they'd, well, snuck away for a little fun in one of the cell bunks.

"What're you suggesting?" Lucy said, moving closer, arms crossed over her chest.

"Well…"

Over the course of the next several minutes, Penny spoke, laying out her thoughts as they came. Lucy gave suggestions here and there, and finally, they agreed on something that, while not entirely foolproof, stood a decent chance of working while preventing anyone else besides Dan from getting in trouble.

It occurred to Penny to wonder why she was letting her guilt drive her this far into the thick of this mess. But the answer came quick. Aside from wanting to see an innocent man safely returned to where he came from, she couldn't stand to let Eddie and his boys rest on their laurels.

After all, Penny thought, taking an offered cup of coffee sometime later, waiting for dusk, *the real killer is still out there*.

Chapter Forty-Nine

Dan paced the cell, running unsteady hands through his now greasy hair. The light coming in through the small windows opposite the cells was fading to dark orange with bits of purple beginning to creep in around the edges.

Earlier, Eddie had asked why Carly would do this to him. Dan hadn't known how to answer, and so said nothing. Figuring out how to tell enough of the truth to be useful while still keeping the guy from knowing what he ought not to know felt like trying to walk through a minefield blindfolded. But it didn't matter. When a commotion started up outside, Eddie had excused himself and then left.

Since then, he'd been trying to sort out his thoughts, all the while, flashes of those videos intercut with each other went through his mind like an Instagram reel from hell. Some time later, just as he'd started to put something half-intelligent together, Eddie had walked back in. Apologizing for the interruption, he came to rest in front of the cell again, apparently as ready to pick up where they'd left off with their conversation as Dan was.

"She knows a lot more than she's telling you, and she told me plenty," Dan said. "Please, I'm not stupid…I know exactly how this has got to sound to you. Like some desperate guy grasping at straws, looking for a last-minute way to save his own ass. But listen, from the moment you took me in, I've played straight with you. I'm still playing straight with you; that woman is dangerous."

"That's not a new one, ya know. Even for me."

"Okay, fine, so my wording isn't original but—"

His brain shorted out on the words once again, and Dan sat down hard on the bunk, elbows on his knees, staring down at his feet.

"You say," Eddie said, causing Dan to look up again, "that Miss Rodgers is in trouble from Miss Wells. Jealous lover?"

"Hell no," Dan said, unsure if that was the case, but he seriously doubted it. He paused, considering how to skate close to the truth without going straight into what Eddie would obviously see as psychotic ramblings. "It's…complicated."

"Well, if it's like you say and a matter of people's lives, Parker, you'd best make it real simple, real fast."

Eddie was right, and Dan did his best to think before he spoke.

"She says that I ruined her life. She had to leave…Indiana, too, but not by choice; there's blame for me there for sure. But she can't go home, see, and when she happened to find me here, I guess it all became too much and she just…" Dan trailed off, waving a hand around like a real estate agent showing off a dining room. "All this is my punishment, I guess."

Eddie studied him, one eyebrow creeping up while the rest of his face fell, and Dan was reminded of what felt like a long time ago, when they'd just been two guys standing outside the Merchant's building, passing the time of day.

"That's not the whole truth," Eddie said, no trace of a question in his voice. "No, there's something else you aren't sayin'."

Dan thought about denying, but a vision hit him hard and clear…Lucy's glazed eyes and bloodless face were shown to him on a screen, and he knew he couldn't.

"You're right, I'm not telling you everything. But only because you'd never believe the rest of it if I did. Not like this anyway. Please, man, we're wasting time here. You've gotta find Lucy before Carly does."

Eddie didn't say anything, not right away. He stood there for a long time, feeling like the word "Liar" was tattooed on him somewhere, and if Eddie found it, all would be well.

"When I have some time to sit, I'll call her aunt," Eddie said finally. "And if Lucy took off yesterday evening like I keep hearing she did, there are a few motels I know between here and just over the state line…about as far as I figure she'd make it since yesterday, that I can call and give her description to. I'll leave word that they're to call me, and if they do, I'll be in touch with her. But I expect to get the whole story from her aunt soon enough. Best I can do."

Goddamn it, what I wouldn't give for just two functioning cell phones.

"Thank you."

Eddie nodded and began to move away, but only got to the next cell over before turning back.

"I'm sending a few men out to give your place a look over. Things being what they were last night, it seemed like that could wait a little while. Tell me, are we gonna find anything funny in there? And before you answer, think hard. Because if you say, no sir, everything's just aces, and I find out otherwise, I can promise you'll never see another day as a free man…and not in the way you probably think."

That last part sounded ominous as hell to Dan, but he couldn't dwell on that now. Instead, he saw Lucy's dead face again, took a deep breath, and started to step around the minefield once more.

"I think you might. Though I can guarantee that whatever you think you might find in there, you're wrong."

"Awful cryptic."

"For the moment, I've got my reasons. But if you find those things and trust me, they'll stick out like sore thumbs as not being right, I'll explain everything."

Eddie gave him a lingering look.

"Rest yourself," he said. "We'll talk later."

And with that, he left.

Chapter Fifty

Penny stepped into the Kent County Sheriff's Office, feeling her heart beginning to beat out a fast tune. She adjusted the press badge she'd pinned to her lapel, then held onto her notebook like it was a child's blanket…she hadn't told anyone she'd be coming.

At the time, she and Lucy agreed it was for the best; get them off their guard. But now she wasn't so sure. Unexpected visits did sometimes knock folks off their toes, but they also had a way of making people edgy.

Surely, though, they would have to have known I'd be here sooner or later.

Martha was on the telephone as she approached the desk. Penny pointed at her press badge when their eyes met, and Martha waved her in, smiling. Smiling back, Penny moved into the bullpen. She knew a lot of the faces and waved as she passed. But no sooner had the inner office with its frosted glass walls come into view, Alan appeared from a short stub of hallway, and she about ran into him.

"Penny? What're you doing here?"

"Looking for Eddie," she said, trying to act as though she didn't have a care in the world when the exact opposite was true. "I hear one of those cells is occupied."

"Probably that funny radio of yours," Alan said. "I suppose you're wantin' to talk to our guest?"

"It is my job."

Penny was determined to hold her ground on this one. The first time they'd had an exchange like this, she'd been a snoopy reporter, poking around where she hadn't been invited. This time, she was the voice of this thing, and she wasn't about to take a single drop of this man's nonsense about how she didn't belong, if that's what he had a mind to do.

"Figured you'd be around. Though I'd expected you sooner. He's in the office. I expect he'll be out soon."

Alan slipped a flashlight into his belt, then went about tapping parts of it like he was checking to make sure everything was there.

"Going out on patrol?" Penny asked, needing to fill the silence creeping up once more, even though she thought herself too nervous for her small talk to be much good.

"Unfinished business from last night."

Penny didn't quite like the sound of that; it made her wonder if there was something else they needed to worry about, but she did her best to put it out of her mind as the door with "Sheriff" painted on the glass opened and Eddie stepped out, followed by a couple of fellas. There was a murmur of conversation, but it died out quick once Eddie and the rest of the men noticed her standing there.

"Radio in if you see something funny," Eddie said. "Got a feeling you'll know it when you see it."

Once the area had cleared, Alan led the two men to another room. The urge came over her to grab Eddie, haul him into the office, and spill her guts, hoping that she might be able to convince him instead of doing what she'd come to do.

She thought about the thermos in her bag, the antihistamines she'd bought from the drug store earlier in the day, crushed up and mixed along with the coffee. Penny didn't much care for the idea of drugging Eddie, no matter how checkered their history, but it was certainly preferable to hiding a brick in her purse and knocking him over the head with it.

Once he's nice and dozy, you know that shouldn't take long with him, you just reach on his belt to grab the keys and—

"Penny," he said, walking toward her. "I'd been meanin' to talk to ya, but I couldn't get away. I guess I thought you'd be here before now. Listen, I didn't get you into trouble at the paper callin' Harv like I did, did I?"

"Everything's fine."

"I expect you're here to talk to Parker," Eddie said, nodding over at the door leading to the cells. "Get the exclusive before he's hauled away to some place with more guards and thicker walls?"

"That's about the size of it," she said, putting on a smile. "You mind?"

"Be pointless to say no now, wouldn't it?"

"Yes, I suppose it would."

Penny shifted her handbag, hearing the coffee slosh inside the small thermos. Knowing that she couldn't put this off much longer if she had a mind to go through with it, she reached into her purse, careful to make sure he couldn't see what else was now in there.

"A little congratulations for you," she said, then, hesitating only for a moment, handed it to him. "Just the way you like it…coffee-flavored sugar."

Eddie smiled in that way of his, thanked her, and took it.

"Thought you had reservations about all this," he said. "That you didn't agree."

"I don't," Penny said. "But I'm not the law, you are. I just report and let people make up their own minds."

Something about the smile on Eddie's face flashed when she said this, and it made her very curious. But it'd have to wait for another time.

"I'll show you in," Eddie said, then led her toward the cells.

Once he'd done his piece, securely locking the door and telling her to call out if there was trouble, Eddie left them. And after she was sure she'd heard the office door beyond them close, Penny started to walk to the cell.

He'd sat up when she'd walked in, only saying hello and looking politely curious. He looked like he had something to say…something about how he wasn't interested in talking would be her best guess, but Penny didn't give him the chance and started talking herself.

What came out was something like the explanation and apology she'd first given to Lucy earlier in the day. They had to wait just long enough for Eddie's special coffee to kick in, and despite doing what she was planning to do to help make amends, she knew she still ought to apologize first and foremost.

After she'd finished with that part, Dan sat staring at her, looking like he couldn't decide if he wanted to cry or scream.

"You've got every right to be upset with me, and I—"

"Forget it," he said. "It's done."

And looking at the man's face, she believed that might just be the case. He ran a hand through his hair, then spoke again.

"But there's a bigger problem. I'm not the only one who isn't supposed to be here. Caroline Wells, a housemate of Lucy's, is from when I'm from. I never knew she'd been sent back. But she's stuck here now, taking people out to get back at me for what I'd accidentally done to her. Carly is the one the cops want. And she has a phone here too…showed me a film of both Jack and Elise that she'd taken right after she did what she did to them. Lucy would've been next the day of the services, but I guess something changed, and Carly decided not to…"

Dan sighed and shook his head. "Eddie said he'd call around, but I don't know where she is now. Penny, you have to find out, you've gotta warn her."

Shoving the name of the alleged killer aside for the moment, Penny put up a hand, quieting Dan. She explained everything. And as she did, Dan's eyes grew so wide that Penny thought she might just fall right into them. He stood, then came to the bars.

"Please tell me you're not joking," he said, but Penny shook her head.

"I wouldn't dare. Lucy never left your place. She didn't hide your things away either, and it's a good thing she didn't. From what she explained to me, she got it so that contraption might have enough juice to send you home later on tonight or tomorrow morning. But first, we need to get you out of here."

A shaky smile crossed his face, and Penny could see his eyes go shiny as they flicked off to the side, but a moment later, the smile disappeared.

"You've gotta get Lucy out of there. Eddie said he's sending guys to check out my house. He knows something might be there, but not what. If I don't have to explain it to him, so much the better. Please, call her."

"I can't," Penny said, nodding over at the telephone on the desk. "I don't know if anyone would be listening in. Besides, I think it's too late. I saw Alan and two others looking like they were just about ready to head out."

"Shit, shit, shit…shit!" Dan said, slamming a fist against the bars, making Penny jump just slightly. "Sorry…okay, so, what now?"

Penny explained, faster now, about the special coffee and how she'd planned to get Eddie's keys away from him once he was good and groggy.

"That's insane. You'll get caught for sure by someone, if not Eddie."

"Oh, I don't think so. You'd be surprised what a few well-timed giggles or a few tears can hide."

"Now, is that so?"

Penny felt her blood go cold as she turned toward the door she'd come in, only to find that it wasn't open. Instead, she turned to find Eddie standing in the now open doorway leading outside…to where her Lincoln sat parked in the alley, ready.

"You know," Eddie said, stepping in and closing the door behind him, "you can hear a lot more at this back door than at that main door over there, funny but true."

His voice didn't seem the least bit sleepy, and Penny found herself scooting back toward the bars…for all the good it'd do her.

"That thing with the coffee was pretty clever. Can't say anyone's tried that one on me before."

"Listen, Eddie…" she said, but stopped. What would she say? It wasn't how it looked? That he'd misunderstood or that they'd only been having him on for a joke? Ridiculous.

He started to walk toward them, seeming to focus on Dan in particular.

"You know, Penny's a good one for getting people to fess up and tell the truth. Better than most of the men I've got out there, if I'm bein' honest. And sending her in here, I had a feeling that you'd give her a little more than what you'd given me, but this? Gotta say, that is a doozy, even for you, Penny. You expect me to just swallow that?"

Penny shifted once more, her back now pressed hard up against the bars. Her handbag slid down to the crook of her arm, and as it did, something else clinked inside.

Before heading to the station, Lucy had insisted that they split up Dan's things—that it'd be better for everything to not be in one place in case things went south in a hurry. Penny thought it was silly, not to mention risky, but took what'd been offered to her without argument. But now, looking over at Dan, she was delighted that she'd taken that particular moment to keep her mouth shut.

"Here, I believe these are yours."

Reaching into her bag, she pulled out both a wallet and the strange telephone, then handed them over to Dan. Eddie jumped back a step, his right hand flying to the butt of his service pistol.

"Just what in the hell are those?"

Dan fiddled with the telephone, then held it up to Eddie. There was a small flash and a clicking sound.

"Proof I'm not from here," Dan said, turning to face the telephone toward them both. On it, she saw an image of Eddie, hand on his pistol, looking terrified. He flipped out the wallet and pulled out a card. "Oh, and here's my license officer, my *real* one."

"My god," Eddie said, moving forward to look first at the license, then at the image of himself.

"Carly Wells has a device just like this. The psychopath took pictures and vid…film, of what she'd done to Jack and Elise. She didn't just tell me earlier, Eddie; she fucking showed me."

"I'll get her back in here," Eddie said, wide-eyed and trying to find his bearings again. "Search her good, and—"

"No," Dan said. "If she even thinks someone's onto her, I'm afraid she'll ditch the thing or delete the film. But if I can get to her first, I think I stand a good chance of being able to get the phone away from her. You deserve real proof for everything that's been going on."

Eddie stood, looking between both of them, each second ticking out on her watch, making Penny more and more anxious.

"Please," she said. "You have an innocent man who doesn't belong here, and a dangerous woman on the loose. We're running out of time."

He appeared to consider this, then reached forward and grabbed her arm, moving her away from the cell door and toward another. There was a moment where she thought she'd be getting to know this time traveler fella a lot better, but then Eddie let go. He reached for the keys on his belt, slid one in the lock, and ran the door back, reaching in and pulling Dan out, staggering.

"Here's the story," Eddie said. "I walked too close to the bars, you grabbed me and knocked my head against 'em, got my keys and made a break for it. That's what I'm gonna tell people, and if you're caught, I expect you to do the same. Even with that gadget, this is some pretty thin paper I'm trusting you on here, and it could cost me my job or worse."

"Understood."

"I'll wait as long as I think I can; twenty minutes at most. She lives at Harrington House and works over at Price Memorial in Harlan Heights. I'd start with the house, then hit the hospital if you don't find what you're looking for there. Best chance of keeping my men out of your hair, especially if you take the backroads. I will want to see those photographs and that film."

"I've got an idea for that."

"Good. Then handle your business, take the rest of your things, find Lucy Rodgers and leave…fast."

Penny watched the two men reach out to shake hands, but once clasped, Eddie pulled Dan forward.

"One more thing," Eddie said in a tone that made Penny feel as if an ice cube had just slid down her throat. "If it's like you say and the Wells bitch is to blame for what's happening in my town, you leave her behind, you hear? Let us handle it. I don't give a damn that she doesn't belong here…that'll never leave this room, but she's not getting away with this."

Dan hesitated for what felt like a long time, or maybe it only felt that way because she really wanted to have been gone by now.

"Deal," Dan said, then Eddie turned to her.

"Are you going along?"

"I've gotta see it through," Penny said. "Besides, if it turns out there's trouble, I want the story."

That brought a sad look to his face, and Penny took a step forward, closing the distance between them. She wrapped her arms around his neck and kissed him briefly, just like they'd done once upon a time.

"Be safe," he said when they broke. "Stay out of trouble. Telephone once he's gone, then we'll see about Caroline Wells." He turned to Dan. "I hope you don't take offense when I say, after this is over, I hope to never see you again."

"Likewise."

Dan started to make for the door, and Penny followed. They'd gotten as far as the edge of the nearby desk when she heard a throat-clearing sound, then turned.

"Forgetting something?" Eddie said.

"Oh," Dan said. "That, well…"

"Just hurry up and really put your weight behind it. If you knock me out cold, you'll buy yourself a little more time, and you'll be doing me a favor…I really haven't been getting much shuteye."

Penny looked between the two men, confused by the small laugh that'd passed between them. Then she watched, not without some reservation, as Dan first wound back and then let his fist fly, knocking Eddie to the ground near the bars.

"C'mon," she said, grabbing Dan's arm and making her way toward the back door.

Chapter Fifty-One

Being more careful than she thought she'd been with anything else in her entire life, Lucy first set the silverware box, then the machine itself, into the Buick's trunk, its tarp back in place, but doing almost nothing to hide the light now coming from it.

Her necklace had continued to lie against the glass. And as she went about the house, throwing some of Danny's things into a suitcase just in case, trying to eat, and just waiting for the sun to go down, she'd step downstairs every so often to check in. Each time she did, the purple glow coming from inside had only gotten stronger.

Lucy shut the trunk, feeling a little relief at cutting off that unearthly light for a bit, and peeked around the garage. There was nothing here but a workbench, a few tools hung from the walls, and a canvas tarp that looked to be for a car; nothing she thought that would be missed.

Penny called only a few minutes ago, letting her know that she and Danny were on their way. Not in those exact words…she didn't know if Danny was on a party line or not…instead, using a phrase they'd agreed on, even if someone was listening in, no one would think twice about.

"Oh, excuse me, dear, I do believe I've called the wrong number."

That'd sent waves of relief so strong flowing through her that it made her knees go a little weak. Was that when she'd made the decision?

Lucy didn't think so and didn't think it much mattered. What mattered was that she meant to go along. Even in those moments before the police came and she thought Danny might take her idea and make a run for it, she'd meant to go along. Strangely enough, that last one bothered her more than the notion of leaving her own time did now.

There would be changes if she went, she understood that. Who knows what sort of things might be different if she weren't around? She'd miss her job, her few friends, and maybe Aunt Trudy, too. But after everything she and Danny had been through in such a short time, Lucy wasn't about to drive him out of town to some hidden spot, only to see him off before he disappeared if she could help it.

And all that aside, who wouldn't try for the opportunity to see beyond their own lifetime if it was just sitting there?

Besides, now that I've got an idea how the thing works, I could go home if I had a mind to.

Lucy walked to the front of the car, then leaned up against the hood, thinking. If she really meant to try and do this crazy thing, then she might want to stop by her room and do a quick bit of packing of her own. That bag she'd brought before leaving for the weekend was all fine and well for a few days, but maybe not for however long she might be gone.

Pulling a pencil and a piece of paper out of her pocket, Lucy began to make a list. She'd gotten as far as: "savings billfold", "picture box", "books" when she heard the sound of an engine and looked up to see what she thought was a sweep of headlights coming through the thin crack of the garage door. Lucy stood, slipped the pencil and paper back into her pocket, and walked over to the door, getting up on tiptoe to peek through one of the small windows running across the top.

There was a red flashing light and a group of men. They'd parked on the street, and Lucy watched doors open.

"Oh no," she said, her voice barely a whisper.

Penny only called a few minutes ago. Surely things couldn't have gone so wrong so fast, could they?

Lucy didn't know but thought it must be so. She also didn't know what to do. From the other side of the door, the voices of the men were coming clearer and clearer.

"Light wasn't on last night, I'm sure of it," a voice said, and the garage door began to shake.

Backing away from the door, her breath tearing in and out of her chest, Lucy looked down, just managing to avoid barking her shin on the Buick's front bumper. She made for the side door leading into the garage. No sooner had she locked the door, now starting to back away, than the doorknob began to twist, and the door started to shake.

"The hell? It's locked."

"Here, lemme try."

"Quit messin' around. He's probably got a lamp timer in there; we'll get in later. C'mon, Eddie told us to search the house."

Pulling the thick shade over the window back just a smidge, Lucy chanced a glance outside. Three men stood clustered around the side door leading into the kitchen. She drew back, but stayed nearby, waiting. Long moments passed before she heard the sound of the door being opened, then shut. Saying a prayer that there wasn't anything else in that house that shouldn't be, Lucy moved toward the garage, undid the lock, and lifted up the garage door.

It was full dark, and not a car in sight, unfortunately. Staying to wait for Danny and Penny had been the plan, but that wasn't an option now. The best she could do now was leave and hope to spot them on the way. Lucy wished she and Penny had considered something like this happening and come up with a different place to meet, but you just can't think of everything on short notice. Some things are bound to fall through the cracks.

Lucy considered flipping off the garage lights, decided against it, and instead slipped behind the wheel of the Buick. She reached for the ignition but stopped just short. Instead, she shifted into Neutral and, getting half out, began to push. It was hard work, and she could feel sweat breaking out everywhere, but it thankfully didn't take long. She pushed the Buick six or eight feet before the slope of the driveway took over, and it began to roll on its own. Lucy jumped in, easing the brake so that she came to a silent stop just as the Buick's nose was about even with the tail of the black and white.

Shifting into Park, she got out, then tiptoed up to the garage, pulling the door back down as quietly as she could. She was back down the driveway with one foot back inside the Buick when a door opened behind her.

"Hey! Hey, just a minute there!"

Lucy didn't stop to look back. She got in, slammed the door, and turned the ignition. The V8 roared into life. Lucy flipped on her headlights, shifted into Drive, and put her foot down, tires squealing as she left the house behind her.

Chapter Fifty-Two

"Wait, look, the garage door is open…Lucy's gone."

They were stopped at the intersection, and from here, Dan could see the first-floor lights of his house on as well as those in the garage. Men were milling around, pointing, and talking with raised hands. One was heading toward the car parked on the street.

"We've gotta go," Dan said, turning to Penny, who was hunched over the steering wheel. "Did you guys happen to pick a backup place to meet?" She turned to him.

"Sorry, no, this is my first time helping a man from the future break out of jail and escape with a time machine," she said, and Dan couldn't help but laugh a little.

Penny got them rolling again, leaving the house behind. Honestly, all things considered, he'd have liked to take one last look at the place. He'd grown quite attached to it after the past two years living there, and up until yesterday, depending on how long he lived, it could've been his forever home.

He settled back in the seat, crunched low, and thought. Eyes shut, Lucy's face swam in front of him. Not the happy, smiling one he knew. Not the dead and mutilated he'd been imagining. But that look she'd given him just before he'd gone up to face the cops. And it killed him to know that, if everything Penny told him was right, he'd have to face that look again tonight.

Only you're going a lot further away this time.

He tried not to think about that for the time being, instead focusing on the steps between here and there. There was still Eddie's request to be considered, too, proof of Carly's guilt in exchange for his freedom. Dan thought he had an idea, but…

"Where would she have gone?" Penny said, and Dan opened his eyes. "Harrington House, maybe?"

"Maybe," Dan said. "If she got out before the cops noticed, unlikely but possible, that'd be one place she could park her car, and no one would think twice about it, at least for a while. If they had noticed, she might be in the wind or driving around the back roads or something."

"Oh, I hope it's the second one, and if it's the first one, that Caroline is working a night shift."

Dan agreed, but didn't say more, instead thinking once again how many problems with their little operation would be solved by just two phones with cell service. Hell, even a set of walkie-talkies would help.

A few minutes later, most of them, Dan spent wondering if the shuddering old heap they were riding in would actually make it up the hill, Penny finally brought them to a stop in the gravel drive of Harrington House. He looked up at it through the window, the place suddenly seeming like a house in a horror movie.   They got out; Lucy's car was nowhere to be found. Sighing, he and Penny moved closer, coming to a rest at the corner near what he knew to be the ballroom windows.

"Ready?" she said.

"As I'll ever be," Dan said.

"How in the world do you plan on getting in?"

"There's lattice running up the sides of the wall, see?" Dan leaned around the side and pointed. "Those bigger windows are the bedrooms; the third one in is Lucy's, I think. Should be able to climb right up and slip through. Then, if I remember what Lucy's told me before about her roommates, Carly's room is just two doors down from hers."

Penny turned to look at him, a questioning eyebrow raised and a crooked smile on her face.

"No, nothing like that," he said, grinning and shaking his head. "Jack got in this way a few times before. Even managed to reinforce things after getting back down the first time left him nearly on his ass."

"Why not just go straight up to Carly's room?"

"Lucy's room feels like a safer place to slip in, just in case."

"I guess I see the sense in that, alright…you head back. I'll head around front and ring the bell, say I'm lookin' for either her or Lucy. Guess I'll figure out why in the moment."

After wishing one another good luck, Dan left, creeping around the side of Harrington House, trying to keep clear of any low windows. The moon was full, and it felt like too much light to be doing something like this. Someone could have a little peek out their window, see him, call the cops, then they'd be back where they started. But there were no hushed voices or quick whipping of curtains that he could see, and finally, he stood facing a piece of latticework that went all the way up, coming to an end under a third-floor window.

Reaching out with one hand, Dan gave the would-be ladder a little shake. It moved more than he'd have liked, but between whatever reinforcements were under the ivy and the fact that Jack had outweighed him by at least fifty pounds, Dan thought it'd hold him. He reached above his head, found a firm grip, then settled his left foot into a slot, and pushing off with his right, he began to climb.

About halfway there, a cool breeze kicked up, and the lattice swayed a little under his weight. Dan came to a dead stop, wanting to shut his eyes and wait for the wind to pass, but there just wasn't time. Heart pounding from somewhere around his molars, he continued on. And in no time, he was sliding the window up and lifting himself inside just as, faintly, the doorbell began to ring.

The room inside was dark, but there was just enough moonlight coming in so Dan could see where to step to avoid knocking anything over. Once fully inside and back steady on his own two feet, Dan began to walk, first moving around the foot of the bed, then walking past a small desk and a dresser on his way toward the door. Putting his ear to it, Dan thought he heard movement going down the hall.

Someone heading to the front to talk to Penny…I hope.

Waiting for the sound of steps to die completely away, Dan turned and looked around the room. He'd never been in here before, true, but something caught his eye, and he realized that he'd been too keyed up before to count the windows before he started to climb.

"Steady as a stone now," Jack had said once upon a time, sitting on the porch, telling him all about the fasteners he'd gotten in place on that lattice to support him. "You could send a platoon up that now, and it'd barely move."

I got the wrong one…or the right one, depending on how you look at it.

On the small desk, sitting amongst a scatter of makeup was a clutch. It was deep plum, and the moonlight was shining off what he knew was a silver buckle. And he ought to know…he'd bought it as an anniversary present at the Coach outlet about three years ago. Feeling around in his pockets, Dan got hold of his phone, pulled it out, and clicked on the flashlight.

"Where are you?" he said under his breath, his vision entirely focused on the circle of light he was putting around the room.

Dan heard movement from one of the nearby rooms, and he froze; his light trained on the dresser. There was the sound of a door being shut, then more footsteps, but that's about all he could pick out before it faded away again. Breathing in shallow little gasps now, trying not to make noise, he made for the dresser and started opening drawers.

In the second drawer from the bottom, Dan saw it. That hateful phone with its robin's egg blue case, its charms hanging down the side, and the horrors on its camera roll. He killed the light on his phone and put it back in his pocket, and had only reached in to grab Carly's when he heard another door open, this one much closer. Dan stood, turned, and had just enough time to register a shadowy figure only about a foot away, something raised in its hand.

There was a *crack* sound, and pain exploded in his head before shooting down his spine like lightning. His head swam, the world went full dark, and he dropped.

Chapter Fifty-Three

Carly stood, the lamp still clutched in her hand, as she looked down at the man crumpled on the floor. But of course, she knew who it was.

She'd only just pulled on her yoga clothes…the clothes she'd come in that'd become her pajamas, and passing by the window, caught sight of him making his way up the wall like a freaking demon. Grabbing the first heavy thing she could find, Carly had ducked into the closet. How he'd not heard her in there, she didn't know, but chalked it up to luck.

Carly let the lamp fall on the bed, then, squatting down, turned Dan around.

Dan blinked drunkenly at her, but it was obvious he wasn't seeing her, or anything else. She felt the side of his neck, counting to herself. Probably a concussion, but if so, not a serious one since the heart rate was only slightly elevated as far as she could tell. Still, she grabbed him by the shirt, pulling him up so they were nose to nose.

"What are you doing here?!"

Her voice was a whisper, no more than that, but in the silence of the room, it felt much louder. He continued to breathe, but said nothing, eyes slipping closed.

Just how in the hell had he even gotten out? And why come here? Last thing she knew, he'd been behind bars. Had the cops found something that'd made them let him go? That had to be it. But what did they find? Did they decide everything was circumstantial bullshit, or did they find something else that maybe pointed to her? She really hoped not.

The idea of Lucy being the one who got away had been eating at her ever since the night before. And leaving Dan with the idea that she wanted Lucy for the "canonical third" hadn't all been bullshit. But after walking out of the police station, knowing that she'd just sat in front of the man investigating all this and got away with it? Why stop with three?

This is insane.

Carly barely heard the thought. The sharpness, the high, the aliveness started to come on her again strong, blocking out almost everything else. She looked at the helpless man now in her hands, and an idea started to form.

Maybe sitting back, watching him rot in a cell before reading one day about how he'd taken a seat in the electric chair, wasn't the best way. Who's to say this wasn't better? The two before had just fallen into her lap, and now here was another one…unconscious, alone, and sent to her like a gift from God.

Smiling, Carly moved Dan aside just slightly, getting him away from the dresser. She opened the bottom drawer and saw light glinting off steel. Reaching inside, she took one of the long-bladed knives, feeling comfort once more at its weight, then looked down.

The how of his getting out might be something of a mystery, but all at once, that seemed unimportant, because another thought had come to her; she now knew exactly why he'd come here…and she could kick herself for not thinking of it before now.

Dan's version of the machine might've been broken, but he had found it here, hidden away in that secret little room that'd disappeared when she'd come into this world. Right behind that wine rack…

That's why he'd come here…he was trying for the machine. And if it was there, he was going to escape and leave her behind…again.

Carly pinched the knife handle between two fingers, then began to swing the blade, watching the tip dance back and forth, reminding her of that Poe story she'd read in school. It scratched the tip of his Adam's apple, and when she felt it, she grabbed the handle once more. She pressed the tip to the nape of his neck, not rushing, not in a hurry. Just taking her time, watching the knife bounce up and down a little on the springy bit of flesh, thinking.

If she was quick, Carly thought she could slip right out and make her way to the ballroom before anyone knew anything, and after that, back through the little door. It'd probably take some time to find the place where she'd come through…the place was a freaking maze…but she'd find it. According to Dan's story, all she had to do was throw down a bookshelf and bust her way through some rotted boards. The way she felt right now, Carly thought she could do that one-handed. And by the time someone finally discovered Dan's body, she'd be long gone.

As she sat there trying to tease out the details, Carly heard footsteps. She got to her feet and had only just turned toward the door when there was a sharp knock, a "You awake, sweetie?", and watched as the door opened. Mildred stood, framed in the doorway, tugging her powder blue bathrobe closed a bit more.

"Caroline, sweetie, I'm sorry to bother you, but there's a woman at the door asking for y—"

Mildred's words died away, and her eyes went wide, going from her in a black sports bra and leggings, to the knife, to the unconscious man by her feet.

"Oh!" Mildred said and started to back away.

Grinning, her body one pleasant tingle, Carly stepped forward.

Chapter Fifty-Four

Penny paced inside the foyer of Harrington House. She'd grown up hearing stories about the lavish parties that had happened up here around the turn of the century and always wondered if it was as lovely inside as it looked from the outside. Turns out it was. Between the Edwardian decor, ornate woodwork, and gorgeous furniture, she wondered if this was what it would've been like to stand inside the Titanic.

But as she neared the staircase, a commotion of some sort began to pierce her fantasies of elegant dresses and men in white dinner jackets serving glasses of champagne. There were what sounded like many footsteps, hurrying. Muffled voices and the slamming of a door. There was knocking or pounding…there were what sounded like screams.

"Hello?" she said in a hushed, creaking voice as she placed a shaking hand on the banister, taking first one step and then another.

Every part of her mind and body begged her to stay right where she was, but she ignored the feelings and pressed on. Someone, maybe Dan, maybe someone else, was clearly in a fix up there, and she didn't need a second lesson on what comes from sitting there doing nothing, just hoping everything's all right. Meanwhile, the voices were getting louder and clearer.

"Caroline! Caroline, what's going on in there?!"

"Open the door!"

"Damn it, girl, let us in!"

All at once, it was hard to breathe, and Penny stopped one stair short of the landing, for the moment, her fear winning out, and her hand might as well have been welded to the banister. But another muffled scream got her moving again. She turned left and ran down the corridor.

A group of young women in their night things was clustered around a single door, along with an older woman that Penny knew in passing, Ruth Harrington. The girls were beating their fists at the door, shouting to be let in, while Ruth fumbled with a set of keys.

More screams from behind the door…piercing, horrible… followed by noises that sounded sickeningly like cutting into a watermelon. One of the group heard her approach and turned.

"Go downstairs! Call the police!"

"What—yes, I—" Penny tried to say, but got no further.

Turning to see if there was maybe a telephone nearby, she saw an open door across the way. Just out of sight and beyond anyone's notice at the moment was what looked like a man lying on the floor in the dark room…what little light there was in the hall spotlighted a single hand.

No!

Penny drew in breath to scream herself when the door behind her finally burst open, and she turned again. In an instant, the women who'd been trying with all their might to get through the door rushed past Penny in a flash, their screams and footsteps trailing down the stairs behind her.

Standing, frozen with fear, she looked in the open bedroom door.

A young woman…the one who'd answered the door, lay on a bed, the blue robe she wore turning a steadily darker color as what could only be blood began to soak it. There was time to take in that, and the hand hanging off the side of the bed, blood dripping down the fingers, the collecting at the fingertips before making a soft drip-drip sound on the floor. Penny tore her gaze away and toward the room's other occupant.

A woman…Carly, it could be no one else, stood on the far side of the bed, wearing what looked like some sort of too-revealing ballet outfit. Blood stood out in sharp contrast against her pale skin, long blonde hair was caked crimson. She ran a red, dripping hand through her hair, pushing it away from her face, revealing mad eyes.

Penny wanted to shout, to run, but for the moment could do neither. Instead, she watched this horror begin to move around the bed toward her, swinging the knife she held in one hand like a pendulum before grabbing something off the bed…what had to be another one of those futuristic telephones, and slipped it in a pocket.

"Sorry about this," Carly said, so pleasant under the circumstances that it left Penny even more terrified. Her eyes snapped to the dying or dead woman on the bed before going back to Carly. "Hope you weren't waiting too long. You said you wanted to talk to me, right?"

The paralysis broke.

Penny let out a scream that pierced the night like lightning, then ran, sparing a glance at the hand…Dan's hand, illuminated by the hall light, before bolting down the stairs and out the now wide-open front doors. Only, she'd forgotten about the front steps and went sprawling in the gravel, her hands running with fresh blood before scrambling to her feet again, making for her car. She threw open the door, fell inside, and turned the key still in the ignition.

Click-click…click-click…click…

"No!" Penny said, her voice almost a scream. She tried again, then again, then again. Each time, the engine only clicked.

"Want me to call AAA?"

Penny jumped, turning, the blood pulsing in her ears so hard she hadn't noticed someone standing next to her open door.

The mad woman came quick as a flash, grabbed the front of her blouse, and started to haul her out. Screaming, Penny stuck out one leg to stop herself before putting the other into Carly's stomach, knocking her away from the car and onto the ground.

Penny turned to the ignition again, voice already hoarse from screaming, tears running down her face.

"Please, oh God, please!"

Meaning to get locked doors between her and this woman, Penny went to pull her left leg fully inside. But when she looked up, Carly was there again, both hands on the door and a smile on her face. Before she'd gotten so much as a chance to twitch, Carly slammed the door. Pain exploded in her exposed leg, and Penny screamed as Carly pushed, drew back, and slammed the door again, then again, then again. On the last swing, through the haze of pain, she was aware that bones had begun to crack inside her leg.

The driver's side door opened all the way. Penny went to hold her leg when rough hands grabbed the front of her blouse once more, this time, hauling her out of the car and onto her feet so she was roughly face to face with the lunatic before being spun away from the open car door. But as soon as the weight settled on her left leg, something inside snapped, and Penny cried, falling to the ground.

"A broken tibia would be my guess," Carly said. "Physical therapy will be a pain in the ass, trust me. But I think I've got something that'll help."

Through her agony and tears, Penny watched Carly bend down to pick up the knife that'd been dropped by the rear tire. Gritting her teeth and fighting the pain with everything she had, Penny got shakily up onto her feet and rushed the psychopath. Carly had only gotten the chance to look up when Penny grabbed her by the throat, and putting her whole weight behind it, slammed the other woman's head into the Lincoln's rear door, leaving a sizable dent.

Carly went down like a sack of potatoes. Penny wanted more than anything to do the same, but shock or providence seemed determined to keep her on her feet. Her voice was too hoarse, too raw to call through the still open door of Harrington House…to Dan, or Lucy, or whoever was still alive in there to run while they had the chance. Instead, she said a silent prayer, made the sign of the cross, and started to shamble down the gravel drive toward the road, blood flowing freely from her maimed leg.

Chapter Fifty-Five

There was a ringing, garbled voices, screaming. Dan tried to edge back toward consciousness, seeing little and understanding even less. All around him, the world was a fog of alternating darkness and light. Through it, he saw what looked to be his own hand, reaching, pulling himself along…wherever he was. But the effort was too much, and there was blackness once more.

An unknown length of time later, he felt himself begin to sway. The voices were back, louder, but the words didn't make sense…it was all so murky like—

"Danny! Oh, Danny, please, wake up!"

Pain exploded across his face, and the thick fog in his mind began to clear. Darkness started to resolve itself into familiar shapes…the corner of a bed, a dresser…

"Lucy!"

He sat up, unmindful of the dizziness that'd hit him or the pulsing sore spot that was his entire head, and grabbed onto her. The grip she'd had on his shirt released, and her arms wrapped tight around him like a vice. She was crying.

"I thought you were dead! What in God's name is going on here?!"

Over her shoulder, still blinking clarity back into the world, he saw the open door leading out into a hallway. He knew he was in a bedroom, but connections were still down in his head, and he couldn't remember where the bedroom was or how he'd gotten here. A few seconds later, it came to him, and Dan managed to extract himself from Lucy's death grip to look at her.

"You were already gone…cops at the house. Had to get Carly's phone. Eddie, he let me go. But I have to show him proof."

"What are you talking about?"

Dan closed his eyes, breathing hard, waiting for his brain to reboot a bit more.

"It's Caroline…she did all of this… she's my, we used to be…she was there when I found the machine, only I didn't know. Something happened, and she got sent back. I never knew. Jack, Elise Crawford…this is her getting even…that monster recorded all of it on her phone…where is she? Did they get her? Did Eddie get her?! Where's Penny?"

Dan tried getting to his feet, lost balance, and sat down hard on the bed.

"I've only just got here," Lucy said, pulling him to his feet, and for a wonder, he stayed on them. "I drove around the back roads til I thought it was safe, took a service road that leads right up to the back of this place, then climbed up the trellis to my room—all the doors are shut, and the place is dead silent…but *she* did this? Caroline?"

"Yes. Showed up at my cell to gloat…showed me the videos she took on her phone. You were next."

Lucy let out something between a scream and a sob, then said in a small voice, "…she wanted to make me tea."

"We've gotta find Penny," Dan said, holding onto the dresser for balance, before Lucy grabbed an arm and looped it around her shoulder. "Let's…wait, shit, hang on…"

Moving slowly but finding more and more as the moments passed that he was able to do so under his own power, Dan went to the vanity and grabbed the clutch wallet. He tried bending down to the drawer he'd gotten a peek into before the world went dark on him, but bending down, he felt like he might pass out again. Dan asked Lucy to grab the phone, explaining that his promising to show Eddie those videos as proof was part of why he wasn't still in a cell.

"There's nothing in there."

"What?"

"There's no phone, Danny."

He went to the drawer, fighting the urge to faint, hoping against hope that Lucy was wrong; she wasn't. The phone wasn't in any of the drawers, under the bed, or seemingly anywhere else. Luckily, there was nothing else in here that didn't belong, which made sense. She hadn't planned on coming here.

"She took it," Dan said through gritted teeth.

"Here," Lucy said, producing a bag he'd seen but hadn't really paid much attention to. "Put whatever you've got in here. Then let's go before the police show up."

"What's with the bag?" he said, doing as she asked, but Lucy only shook her head and led them out.

Once back outside, standing in front of Harrington House, Dan looked closer at the getaway car that'd brought him here, its open driver's side door somehow seeming even more ominous than those thrown open on the house just behind him. The moon was bright and the sky cloudless, and by its light, it was obvious to see by the large skid marks in the gravel that something had gone down. There was a sour smell nearby that he thought was puke, and for a moment, Dan fought a battle with his own gorge. He got control of himself just in time to hear Lucy gasp.

"What's wrong?"

Other than everything.

"There's blood," she said.

"Huh?"

"Look."

Dan followed where Lucy was pointing, and sure enough, she was right. One larger spot by the car, then moving away in little drips. He hadn't been hunting since college, but there was no forgetting what a blood trail looked like. Following it down to the road, he saw that it turned right. Off to the left, a way in the distance but still perfectly clear, he heard sirens. Lucy spoke.

"They know you're gone."

"We need the phone, and we need to find Penny. If she's still alive, I'm not leaving her."

"I wouldn't dream of it. Not after everything she's done…but we need to shake a leg. That machine of yours is in the trunk, glowing like a lighthouse. You get it ready the rest of the way, and I'll drive. Which way did they go?"

"Right. Away from town."

They ran to the Buick, footsteps crunching over gravel as the sound of sirens grew louder. Around the back of Harrington, just inside the tree line next to a reflective sign that read "Service Road…County Vehicles Only," was a familiar chrome grill, twinkling in the moonlight.

Lucy got in the driver's seat and fired the engine. Dan hurried around the back and popped the trunk. Under the tarp, which was doing almost nothing to hide it at this point, was an ethereal purple glow that he'd been all but certain he'd never see again. And even as low-grade nausea started to settle in, the sight still lifted his heart. Dan reached in, picked it up, and carried it around to the now open passenger side door.

The light pulsing from the machine was more than enough to see by, and Dan went about setting the dials to the destination before he noticed a new addition.

"Is this your necklace?"

"It is. My guess is that the shard and the gemstone of my necklace are part of the same type of strange rock. Maybe even the same rock for all I know."

"Penny told me you'd got it to start cycling on again somehow, but that was all."

"I didn't think she needed *all* the details. Let me know when I can start moving."

"Two seconds."

His mind was reeling from the knowledge that whatever powered this magnificent machine, Lucy had managed to buy what amounted to a jump starter for it at a county fair jewelry booth. Thinking that he'd really like to circle back on that one if there was a later in his future, Dan continued to work, careful not to move the necklace. But as the final adjustments were made for the destination, his heart sank.

Off to the left side, there was a small gauge. It ran from 0 - 100…somethings…there were no units listed. The 90 - 100 range was written in green, which he'd always taken to mean that the thing was ready to use. But now, he saw that the indicator needle stood at 78.

"Everything okay?" Lucy said.

God, I hope so.

Chapter Fifty-Six

Carly walked at a calm and steady pace up the middle of the empty road, dark trees on either side, moon shining. Not far ahead, where the road curved, a hill sloped steadily down, dead-ending right into Sugar Creek. Behind her was the faint sound of sirens, and not far in front of her, there was the sound of shuffling steps and sobs.

Whoever this girl was, she'd given her one hell of a good hit; the fact that it was done on what had to be at least a fractured leg made it even more so. The blackness had been sudden as Carly's head was slammed against the side of the car, but thankfully, it wasn't for long because when the world reasserted itself, the girl had only just made it to the end of the driveway, and Carly watched her turn right. Getting to her feet, the world had swum, and Carly had doubled over to puke. Then, groaning, she plucked her knife from inside the stinking, sour mess and followed after her.

Every so often, the girl would throw glances over her shoulder as she hobbled along. She did it again, and Carly waved.

It was fine. The girl wasn't getting far. It would only be a matter of time before the adrenaline-fueled panic would wear off, or that leg would finally give, or both.

You should go help her.

Carly's hand ran to the knife she'd stashed behind her, the elastic of her sports bra holding it flush against her back. Occasionally, the tip would dig in a little, drawing her own blood to mingle with others', but she no longer much cared.

Before, she'd hoped to go on for a while. Flying under the radar, seeing what opportunities came her way. Even get Lucy in for that tea. But after tonight, it was hard to kid herself that there was any chance of that left. Mildred had seen her and the…was blood lust the right word? Carly supposed that it was. The blood lust came on her, sight and sound and smell, all of it sharp as cut glass, driving everything else clean out of her mind. And the poor, sweet thing had made it so easy…*made a horrible mistake*, and backed right into the open door of her own room and…

It'd been wonderful, their screams and the blood making her breath shudder, senses alive, each stroke of the knife making her want to cry out as if in the throes of an orgasm. She'd just brought out her phone, opened the camera, then the door burst open and, boom, the party was over…almost…

Her steady pace began to falter, and Carly stopped, bending down and spewing more puke. Her vision went dark, and her head went woozy, but little by little, the world righted itself again. She stood, leaning her head back, sucking down the fresh night air.

Definitely a concussion…forget her and go find a doctor. Better yet, go back to the house and down to the basement. Remember? Before you saw red and attacked like a bull? There could be a way out down there.

Could be, but probably there wasn't. With the way her luck was going, she'd get down there, only to find nothing at all. There was no way to know when that thing got stuck down there, and she couldn't risk it now that the place was probably crawling with cops.

When Carly opened her eyes and looked straight ahead once more, she watched the girl get one leg up over the guardrail running along the curve of the road, then another, then disappear from view. There wasn't a scream, so Carly didn't think she'd fallen…good for her.

Feeling like she could chance to take what little remained of the distance at something more than a leisurely stroll, Carly jogged a little before coming to the rail itself. Leaning to look over the edge, she pulled out her phone and started to record.

"Hey, what's your name?" Carly said, looking at the girl now standing several feet down and away, just at the edge of the rocky creek bed.

"You'd better run! Don't you hear the sirens? They'll find you! Leave!"

"No, sweetie, you see, I'm having too much fun."

You should take the knife and cut your throat. Right now.

And why not? After all, it'd been what she'd planned on doing ever since she walked away from that blue Ford and the woman in the doorway, Jack's blood staining the inside pocket of the dress now shoved in the back of her closet. For a while, it felt like there might be another way after all, but now it had to be done. And now that the time was here, honestly, the only thing she felt was relief.

Her life had been taken straight to hell over the past several months, but she'd seen that the unkindness he'd done to her was repaid in double. And she'd gotten to experience what it felt like to truly be alive…awake and aware and in control of herself, a euphoria that no drug could ever match. If there was a high note for life, this surely had to be it. Better that it should happen now when she felt on top of the world instead of later on, depressed and miserable and alone when the comedown finally came.

Phone trained on the girl who still wouldn't give up her name…*please, tell me your name, tell me your whole life story…if I see you as a real person, maybe I'll stop*, Carly got one leg over the guardrail, then stopped to make sure she wasn't about to drop the knife. Convinced it'd stay where it was on the way down, Carly made to swing the other leg over but stopped and froze as headlights crested above the hill.

Chapter Fifty-Seven

"There!"

Lucy slammed on the brakes, bringing the Buick to a screeching halt. Dan jerked forward, one foot bracing himself against the dashboard while his arms held the machine, keeping it from crashing into the floorboard.

It was a near thing, and the momentum slammed him back into his seat. Wishing there were seatbelts in this damn car, Dan looked down at the machine, fighting a fresh wave of nausea from the machine's cycling. Nothing seemed to have been broken off, so that was good, and the light was as bright as ever. He looked at the gauge…the needle now stood at 82.

"Lucy, what—"

But as he saw Lucy staring straight out the windshield and followed her gaze, the words died away. Carly stood, one leg on either side of the guardrail, looking like she'd only been about to hop over and slide down into Sugar Creek.

In the headlights, she looked utterly deranged. Her long, blonde hair caked auburn in places, blood running in rivulets down her pale skin, shining eyes turned toward them…like Carrie White coming back from a bad yoga class.

They both watched as Carly pulled her leg back over the guardrail and started to walk toward them, drifting side to side like a drunk trying to walk a straight line. Lucy grabbed hold of the steering wheel and revved the engine. Carly seemed to stumble a little, but after a second, continued her bar crawl pace toward the Buick.

"Jesus, she's messed up," Dan said, no sympathy whatsoever in his voice. He thought of the puke near the rear tire and the dent in Penny's car. "Concussion. How is she still up and moving?"

"She's a nightmare," Lucy said, one fist clenched around the steering wheel, beginning to shake. "Do you think that's Penny's blood?"

"No, Penny probably escaped into the creek," Dan said, hoping like hell he was right. "But that does mean there was someone else in the house when we ran out of there."

A sound escaped Lucy's mouth then…something between a cry and a growl. Outside, Carly was close now.

"What is she doing?"

Dan thought, then looked down at his lap.

"She sees the light."

Sirens pierced the still night outside. Whether because the secret of his escape was out, or whether someone had gotten away from Carly and made it to a phone to report what'd happened, he couldn't say. Now that she was closer, Dan saw the phone clutched in her left hand.

She was going to record it. Penny was down there, and that monster was going to record it all.

He didn't know just what it was he meant to do, but time was up. Dan set the machine aside, leaving it to glow on the seat between them.

"Stay here," Dan said, reaching for the door.

"No," Lucy said, throwing the Buick into park and reaching for her own door.

"Lucy, I need—", he said, putting a hand on her arm, but she tore it away.

"No!"

Before he could grab her, Lucy opened the door and hopped out, rushing toward Carly. He followed, coming to a stop just in front of the Buick.

The three of them stood in the middle of the road, headlights spotlighting them like players on a stage: Lucy and Dan on one side, Carly on the other. No one said anything for what felt like a long time. In that moment, staring into that face, he realized they weren't players on a stage…they were outlaws, meeting in the middle of the town at high noon.

"You said it was broken," Carly said, her voice as hoarse and deranged as the rest of her. "You lied to me. Again."

"I didn't lie. Until an hour ago, I had no idea that things had changed. I never lied to you," he said, and added because this would be the last chance, "about anything. The night of the reception, I never wanted you to leave. I meant every word I'd said, that I'd be there for you work to get you the help I couldn't give you. The only thing I wanted was for you to finally get the peace you more than deserved. Despite all our shit, I loved you. That night, you said something about how you wouldn't have bothered saying anything if you didn't give a shit—that's how I felt too. And I'm sorry I didn't try and make that clearer at the time. Maybe that would've changed things."

Unmindful of the danger for the moment, unmindful of the knot forming on his head because of her and even the phone in her hand, Dan moved forward, feeling his voice catch and choke a little.

"With everything in me, I'm sorry you got caught up in this. If I'd had any idea you were behind me that day, I'd have never… But, Carly, why didn't you come to me when you first found me here? We could've talked, tried to figure out what came next. Avoided all of this. I still would've done anything I could to help you."

For a few moments, no more…sirens sounding a little louder now, something in Carly's face changed. The lunatic was gone, leaving only Carly. Fun, quick with a kind word, sassy in a good-natured way, and more than occasionally sweet, Carly.

"I want to go home."

And for an instant, Dan thought he might take her. In spite of everything, he'd invite her into the car and take her home. Not because he wanted her back, but because the idea of leaving her stranded once again…this time by choice like she'd thought he had all this time was almost too much to bear. Carly might've been the aggressor, but there was still plenty of blame for himself about everything that'd happened. Did he really want to add this to the emotional luggage he'd be carrying around for the rest of his life?

But then he saw the blood on her, wondering just whose it was. He remembered Jack lying in his coffin with his waxen hands, people ahead and behind in line, gripping hard to handkerchiefs. He thought about Elise Crawford, who, it seemed, the only wrong thing she'd done in her life was be in the wrong place at the worst time. He saw Carly, earlier that same day, bars between them…the smile creeping onto her face as she turned the phone toward him…that same smile still in place as he begged her to leave Lucy alone…

What's one more change in the timeline?

"No."

There was another shift. Carly, the real Carly, was gone. There was only the psychopath in front of them now, breathing hard and looking more unsteady on her feet.

"Shocker," she said, an odd grin playing on her features, as she reached behind her back. "Probably don't wanna offend your new little pet bitch. Makes sense." Dan took a step forward, pushing Lucy behind him…tried to anyway. Lucy shrugged past, and Dan only just managed to get a hand around her upper arm.

"You worthless, murdering piece of trash! I hope you burn in hell for everything you've done!" Lucy said, taking a step forward, her whole body seeming to vibrate under Dan's grip, but Carly only laughed.

"Oh, shit, something I forgot to tell you that day in the library, Lucy baby," Carly said, reaching behind her back, pulling out a nasty-looking knife. "I was in the car for a while before Jack came back. When I came up, wanting him to take me to this asshole," she nodded at Dan, "they had the windows open, and I heard everything…all the slapping and moaning and gagging. So, when I noticed the car, I thought I'd hang out there til it stopped so I could talk to him, but it just went on and on and on. So, you—"

Knife in hand, she took a step forward before bending down, hands on knees, spewing a fine jet of puke between her feet. Dan's eyes locked onto the phone.

He'd been about to pull Lucy behind him, throw her behind if that's what it took to keep her away, then rush Carly, when out from behind the guardrail a shadow appeared, creeping along. It moved out from the cover of a nearby tree and into the bright night…it was Penny. Her clothes were ripped and muddy, her leg was gashed and bruised wasn't moving right, but she was alive.

Their eyes met, but only for a moment. In her hands, Penny held a smooth, round stone about the size of a grapefruit. Lucy's pull against his grip let up. Hands that'd been raised, ready to punch or choke, only moments before, started to fall.

"Sorry about that," Carly said, standing straight again, turning her eyes to the sky before meeting their gaze again. "My head's a little—"

But Carly didn't get to finish that thought.

Penny came up from behind then, brought the stone back like a golfer about to tee off, then, with a scream, brought it down.

The stone was connected with Carly's kneecap, which first cracked, then bent in a way that knees were never intended to. She screamed, Penny screamed, and the knife dropped from Carly's hand. Raising the stone again, Penny did likewise with the other knee, dropping Carly to the ground. She tried to army crawl toward the knife, but Lucy stepped forward, kicking it away.

"Don't you move."

Past her, Penny started to wobble on her bad leg, and Dan rushed forward, catching her around the waist before she hit the ground.

"Hang on, I've got ya," he said, leading Penny away and back into the grass. As gently as he could, Dan got her down and leaned against the guardrail. She looked up at him, a pained smile on her face.

"Thank you."

"Let's get her in the car, Danny," Lucy said, taking a few steps toward them. "We'll take her to Price ourselves."

The sirens were a little louder now, and Dan thought he saw faint red lights being caught by nearby trees, but maybe not.

"Ow, ow, ow…no!" Penny said, sitting up a little straighter. "The police are just around the corner. We'll be hard to miss. They'll send for an ambulance."

"Oh, sweetie, I don't like leaving you like this," Lucy said, grabbing for her hand.

"I'll be all right," she said. "You did the hard part, keeping her distracted so I could get up here with my little rock. Just…", Penny breathed in through her teeth as she adjusted again. "Just leave me with the knife. I still don't trust her."

"I…can…hear…you," Carly said, her head jerking and twitching a little as she turned to face them.

Without a word, Lucy stood, walked over to where Carly lay, grabbed the knife and the phone, put a foot on one of the shattered kneecaps, and stomped down. Carly wailed, her cries like something barely human.

"Hear *that*, you bitch," Lucy said, her voice pure ice, and walked back over.

"Let me see that," Dan said, gesturing toward the phone, and Lucy handed it to him.

He turned toward Penny, tapping away at the screen, the password still in his mind after all this time, just as Carly probably still remembered his; neither of them had ever much cared for the other trying to use the phone while driving. Dan then popped the case, got the SIM card out, and put everything back together. Standing, he threw the SIM card over the railing and into the creek. Finally, he turned the screen so Penny could see.

"The password to get into this is now 1-9-4-7…seemed appropriate. Here's where the videos Eddie asked about are – if he still wants to see them. Tell him I said thanks again. Once you show him, if you show him, hold this down," Dan pointed at the side button. "That'll turn it off. Never turn it back on."

"I'll get a safety deposit box," Penny said, taking the phone. "Return it to you the long way around."

The sirens were louder now, and off in the distance, Dan saw two tiny white pinpricks of light with a red one above.

"You've gotta go," Penny said, all but pushing them away.

He and Lucy both got to their feet, making their way back toward the still-running Buick with its spooky purple light inside. Dan stopped with his hand on the top of the passenger door.

"Penny, I—"

"You're welcome, Mr. Tomorrow. Maybe we'll talk again sometime. Go!"

Dan slid back in the passenger seat, shut the door, and set the machine on his lap, once more careful not to disturb the necklace.

Through the windshield, Penny gave them one solitary wave, which they both returned. He spared a glance for Carly, then Lucy got the Buick pointed toward the backroads leading away from the scene and from Harrington House, and they were off.

"She's safe," Dan said, turning to look out the back windshield where a police car had now stopped. "Where're we going?"

"I know a little spot," she said. "Maybe you do too. That grain supply place with all those big silos next to the baseball field. There's a little dirt road running between the two that I don't think hardly gets used…no one will see us go."

Dan looked over, hit with strong Deja vu from…last night? Could that really be from last night? It was, though he couldn't say it felt like it: Lucy looking over at him, their places in the Buick swapped, asking him not to leave her alone. He thought of the bag she'd brought along, now sitting on the floorboard behind him, and Lucy's words clicked.

He thought about his own journey. He thought about asking why, after everything they'd been through. He wondered what would happen if the day came that she decided she wanted to go home, and for some reason, couldn't. The machine had failed once; there was no reason it couldn't fail again. This needed to be a long conversation. If nothing else, to warn about just what it was she was getting into. But it didn't seem like they were going to have that conversation. At least not now. Despite everything, he could see Lucy's mind was made up. Dan put a hand over hers.

"No one will see us go."

They drove on for a few minutes, the feeling of peace very close now. But just as something long tensed up began to ease, Dan's stomach dropped.

A car had been making its way toward them from the opposite side of the road, going fast, and they'd passed it in the blink of an eye. He'd only just been ready to open his mouth to comment on it when he heard squealing tires from behind. Dan turned in his seat to look…

"No," Lucy said, as they heard the wail of sirens.

The needle stood at 85.

Chapter Fifty-Eight

"Hold tight!"

Lucy dropped the accelerator all the way to the floor, the Buick's big V8 forcing Dan back in the seat. He turned, watching the lights grow a little smaller behind them. There was a one-lane unpaved road off to the left, and Lucy turned hard, throwing him into the door as rooster tails of dust and dirt flew out from behind. Soon they were barreling through the blackness at what looked like better than seventy. He turned to stare again out the back.

"Why the hell are they following us?"

"I'll bet it's me," Lucy said, taking another fast curve onto another road. "I got spotted leaving your place. Someone probably put out the word to look out for a big, red Buick. That's why I'd hidden myself in the trees."

"Damn it."

"I'm gonna hop onto County 12, then loop back around by the fairgrounds," Lucy said, and Dan was shocked to see a half-smile on her face. Was she enjoying this? "Think I can lose them around there, then head back into town, crisscross a few intersections, kill the headlights, and make for the park."

"Go back into town? Right where the police station is?"

"Do you have a better idea, Danny?"

"Not right now, no."

"How long til that gadget is ready?"

Dan looked down at the gauge. It'd only climbed to 86. He was too keyed up at the moment to be sure, but he thought the crawl up to the green part was starting to slow down.

"Soon."

County 12 was coming up fast. Lucy slowed down to take the hairpin turn, but she'd only just made it when they saw a set of lights closing in on them from another stretch of road off to the right. There was a stop sign up ahead where the two sections of road met, but Lucy blew past before the car coming to the right could head them off. Through the rearview mirror, Dan now saw two sets of lights.

"Jesus! Eddie let you out, can't he call these off?"

"Not without it looking suspicious," Dan said, continuing to brace himself, painfully aware for the first time that there were no airbags in this thing. "Official story is I attacked Eddie and escaped out the back. And if people saw you take off like a bat out of hell, they probably think that—"

Bang!

Lucy swerved, and Dan flinched away from the window, but not before he'd caught sight of a momentary spark as what could only be a bullet skidded across the top of the Buick's side mirror.

"Danny!"

"We're at 87!"

Another shot rang out, this one skidding off the left corner of the hood. Lucy screamed out and jerked the wheel again. Dan cursed, a sour taste in his mouth as adrenaline dumped into his system.

They came around the big loop of County 12, and off to the left, looming dark and empty were the Kent County Fairgrounds. Even in this moment, it was impossible not to think about just how much had changed since he'd walked through those gates less than a week before…

"Turn here!" Dan said, pointing at the entrance to the fairgrounds. "They'll cut us off for sure if we head into town at this point…kill the lights and make for the trees…should be just enough time."

Lucy did, flicking the headlights off as she turned hard into the open field that served as the parking lot, moving like a shadow in the darkness. But it was no good. Those bastards behind them were persistent and had closed the distance fast. Dan looked down at the gauge, the needle hanging at…86.

"We need to find a place to ditch," Dan said. "Quick! We're losing the charge!"

Bang-bang!

"I can't," Lucy said, ducking in her seat. "If we stop now, they'll be on us in a second! Even if not, that thing'll give us away!"

"Okay," he said, checking the gauge once more before resting his hand on the lever. "Okay, I guess we're doing this. I don't know if it'll…"

There was a sound like rubbing fabric, and he looked to his left. Just like the night they'd sat parked out in front of his house, Lucy had slid one hand across the seat…he slid his to meet it. Whatever future he and Lucy were going back to, it seemed it was now or never…they'd officially run out of time.

Their fingers now laced tightly together, Dan pushed the lever forward.

The machine cycled in his lap and began to glow even brighter. An ethereal humming came from inside, and the air around them began to flicker and spark. What looked like static electricity started to dance over everything, chasing and flicking out, then flicking back in again.

Lucy turned away from the ticket booth to avoid crashing into it, but all around, things started to change. The night was gone, replaced by morning. Then night, then morning again. Faster and faster it cycled until the sky resembled that dark, yet oddly bright quality it sometimes had before a really nasty summer storm. All the while, Lucy weaved in and out of people and cars that seemed to be no more than ghosts. Dan looked down at the brass wheels now spinning freely, showing the year.

1948, 1949, 1950.

As Lucy made for the entrance and back onto County 12, the speed picked up.

1967, 1973.

Coming and going in a blink-and-you'll-miss-it instant, a semi-truck took out the sign over the entrance, and a blink later, the cheap plastic sign Dan had known all his life appeared in its place, and his heart soared.

1983, 1994, 2001.

Lucy drove them into New Chapel, weaving in and out of the phantom traffic of bygone days.

"Head toward Mulberry," Dan said, and Lucy did, making for the center of town.

Stores appeared and disappeared in flashes. Signs flickered in and out of the windows and colors changed, giving everything a sort of jaunty look as if they were watching an animated Van Gogh painting.

2004, 2007, 2011.

Seeing home materialize in front of him like this brought tears to Dan's eyes that he couldn't bring himself to wipe away. The strange machine in his lap gave a shudder, and Dan looked down. The purple light that'd been so strong only an instant before had started to cycle and fade. A little at first, then more and more. Flicking his eyes up to the gauges, he saw the brass dials beginning to slow.

"No!"

"Danny? What's happening?" Lucy said, her face and voice perfect pictures of panic.

2016, 2018…2020…

"C'mon! Don't you dare die on me here!"

Dan put his hands on either side of it, feeling a growing cold in the brass housing.

"2023, 2024…"

All at once, the machine failed, dropping the Buick back into the normal flow of time and right into the path of an oncoming Honda, its horn blaring. Screaming, Lucy swerved to avoid the head-on collision. But just as they were now about to take out a mailbox, the machine cycled up again, and Dan's stomach took an uneasy lurch.

"How much longer?!"

"Almost there!"

Six months away…four months…two months…one month…

Day and night became two separate things again, the sky now looking like a strobe light being slowly turned down. They came onto the intersection of Mulberry, but Lucy wasn't slowing down.

"Which way? I don't want to stop and risk—"

"Left. Eight-sixteen…green house all the way down. Two more weeks."

Two weeks away…he could work with two weeks if the thing died again right now. His Amex was still in his wallet; they could rent a cabin or hotel room or something, and Past Dan wouldn't be any wiser. Not like he'd do more than dispute the charges if he even bothered to open his statement emails anyway. Especially not at this point.

"One day."

Eight-sixteen Mulberry came into view, and Dan was treated to an odd sight. He watched a sped-up version of himself grab a few bags out of the back of his Subaru, then disappear inside.

"Oh, my goodness, that's you."

Night came, then the morning…Past Dan was gone now, officially off on his little study abroad trip. He waited for night to come around once more, then brought the handle back to its neutral position. As he did, the machine gave a little rumble. The chasing sparks that'd surrounded them for the last two, maybe three minutes, faded away. And the purple glow that'd been like a searchlight coming from inside the machine faded to an almost imagined twinkle.

Lucy brought the Buick to a stop behind the Subaru and had only just put it into Park when she and Dan both reached for each other.

He looked over her shoulder, staring at his house out the front windshield. Dan opened his mouth as if to speak, even though he hadn't the slightest idea what he meant to say, when a flurry of noises erupted from his pocket. He jumped, then laughed as he pulled out his phone…it'd reconnected. The first thing Dan saw was a text from his brother that started out "Hey asshole…" and there were fresh tears of joy.

Dan slipped the phone back into his pocket, and Lucy straightened up, looking around.

"Well," she said.

"Well…would you like to come in?"

Epilogue

Lucy leaned up against the back counter, arms folded across her chest, looking out at an empty dining room, save for a couple of teenagers sitting in one of the corner booths. It was slow business for a Tuesday afternoon, but that was all right. Bill's Diner was plenty busy most other times these days, so any moment to be able to stop and breathe was nice.

Turning to grab a rag, she caught sight of her reflection in the mirror finish of the Coke machine and stopped. Even though it'd been nearly a year since she'd arrived here, it still occasionally took her a second to recognize the woman reflected back.

Her hair was shorter and a little less wavy than it'd been back in '47. Lucy hadn't been too keen on the look she'd chosen at first, thinking that it looked better in the magazine, but that feeling hadn't lasted long. Between that and her new uniform…blue jeans, red Converse sneakers, and a black t-shirt with "Bill's Diner" splashed across the chest in familiar letters, getting ready these days was a snap compared to what she'd been used to before, and she welcomed the change.

"You sure you don't want the yellow dresses back?" Danny had said, laughing as they'd sat, getting their last few ducks in a row before the grand re-opening of Bill's, and she'd flatly refused, laughing too.

It seemed that there'd been one last secret Danny had been holding onto; the fact that during his first *test run*, as he'd put it, he'd grabbed a stack of funny books for less than a dollar and sold them all at auction for millions before they'd even met. Hearing that, she'd about forgotten how to breathe.

Maybe a day or so after arriving, they'd decided to get out of the house and go for a walk around New Chapel, Danny showing her the sites, both familiar and not. It wasn't long before they both found themselves stopped, staring at a weed-choked, abandoned lot with a rusty silver building whose windows sat boarded up. Lucy found that if she focused on it hard, she could see both versions of the place, one on top of the other, and it gave her an awful headache.

"This wasn't here before," he'd said. "There was a little shopping center with a cell phone store, a tanning place, and a restaurant. They tore Bill's down in, like, the eighties."

"Seems things have changed," Lucy had said, patting his arm.

It wasn't the first thing they'd run across that was different from what Danny remembered, but it was one of the bigger ones. Her eyes danced all around the old place before landing on a white sign with faded red letters.

"It's for sale."

That was all it took. Pretty soon, there were contractors, and Lucy was down there often with the interior decorator, historical society photographs in hand for reference…though she didn't really need them. And today, while certain things had to be brought up to modern building codes and some modern conveniences were added, Bill's Diner was just about the way it'd been before…except for the yellow dresses.

A low hum started up from her rear, bringing her back to the now. Lucy reached into her back pocket and pulled out her phone. On the screen, there was a text from Danny:

Danny
The faculty meeting
ended early. Got a few
papers to grade, then I'm
heading home. You
wanna go out or make
something at home?

Lucy thought for a moment, unsure. Spending time in another restaurant after having just spent all day here might be a little too much, but then again, it might be nice to get out together and do something fun. Thinking that she still had a lot of lost time to make up for with Mexican food, Lucy began to peck away at the letters.

Almost a year on, she'd mostly gotten the hang of her phone. After all, little kids who still believe in Santa and haven't quite gotten the gist of reading yet seem to figure them out in a matter of minutes. True, it'd taken her longer…all of one afternoon and evening, but she thought that was pretty good for someone like her who felt like they were being handed something out of a Buck Rogers serial, even if her speed was still lacking.

After sending off her message, Lucy slipped her phone back into her pocket and pulled one of the nearby newspapers toward her.

This modern technological age, where news came faster than a speeding bullet, might all be very well, but after a few weeks of being constantly bombarded with news, Lucy felt like she was going nuts with what Danny called *information overload*, and she got rid of everything except her phone's bare basics. In that way, she'd decided that newspapers…with their simple printed pages and ease of being able to put down because there weren't all these things screaming for readers' attention…were better.

And so, she'd gotten a subscription to both the New Chapel Gazette and the Dayton Herald for both home…turned out Danny was just as excited as she was to have newspapers again, and the diner.

A lot of people thought the papers were retro…a word she learned meant old-fashioned but fun, which fit the rest of the place quite nicely. People raved about it on social media…another thing that lived exclusively on the home computer because she didn't like how it kept sucking her in on her phone; spending way too much time doing absolutely nothing at all except making her anxious.

A few stories caught her eye as she began to flip through the pages. An interview with a comic shop owner in nearby Weston City who'd been shot outside his store; by the sound of it, he was lucky to have survived. The bare beginnings of high school football coverage, it being mid-September already. It was going to be exciting to go and see the ad space she'd purchased at the stadium for the diner...right under the scoreboard where everyone would see it. One story caught her attention and held it for some time.

Two radio hosts...podcasters, were coming to New Chapel; a husband-and-wife duo who talked about crime and all sorts of things on their show. They were apparently going to interview some of the older folks in town and tour the famous, or infamous, sites of what was known as either the New Chapel Massacre or more often than that, the Jane the Ripper Murders.

Carly, she thought, sighing.

A few days after they'd arrived, it was time to face the Kent County Sheriff's Office for their part in the whole nasty business...though the context was certainly different than if they'd been caught back in 1947.

The official story was that Carly had left her Harlan Heights apartment for New Chapel, her phone's last ping putting her near The Harrington House Museum. But with the way she was dressed, the taxi...Uber driver guessed that she'd been headed for the hiking trails at another new addition to the timeline, nearby Prescott Park, which shares a parking lot with Harrington House.

Danny had been spoken to as a matter of course, but since he and Carly had broken up some months before...as far as the rest of the world was concerned anyway, there was no reason to suspect him. Game Wardens combed that section of the woods all the way back along Sugar Creek and found nothing.

But of course, that official story was all hogwash.

After the policemen had left and she'd felt safe enough to come back downstairs...Lucy hadn't had any legal identification at that point, Danny had immediately gone to his computer, and she'd sat down next to him. They looked for a long time, both in his own records and on the internet, and eventually had gotten the real story, courtesy of a series of articles…and later a book by one Penny Prescott which Lucy had managed to find a copy of, chronicling her investigation, including her life-or-death struggle with Caroline Wells who Penny went on to call Jane the Ripper.

A single picture stood out to Lucy most clearly, even now. A disheveled, crazed woman, her legs in bandages, strapped to a wheelchair, being taken in through the doors of Alcomb Sanatorium. The look on the face had been one of howling madness.

"Pictured: Miss Wells, following her transfer to Alcomb, insisting that she's a "time traveler"," Lucy had said, reading the caption at the bottom, before flicking her eye further down. "Miss Wells has been released to the direct care of Dr. Roderick Hart, head of patient care at Alcomb, due to the persistent nature of such statements. Dr. Hart insists that there are many new and exciting treatments for people suffering from such delusions."

After that, the article went on to list the victims from the night they'd left, and now Lucy had a name to go along with the blood running down Carly's body that night…Mildred.

"We did that to her," Danny had said, leaning away from the computer, looking sad and confused; she understood.

"We did," Lucy had said, wiping her eyes and wrapping an arm around his. "If we hadn't, there'd have been no justice for them, Danny. All the family, all the friends…they'd have all been left with not knowing what really happened. It'd have been an insult…an offense to all of them if we hadn't left her behind to answer for what she'd done."

That didn't immediately soothe either her or Danny, especially after learning how Carly's story came to an end in that place, and there were plenty of nightmares between the two of them about everything that'd happened for some time. But time keeps moving on, and eventually, so did they…almost.

There was one subject they'd not touched on until very recently. Frankly, there'd been a lot more pressing things going on back in '47 without sitting and having a gab about that too; it was just too much to talk about. But now that things had more or less settled down…as settled as life could be when there was a business to run, and your fella still taught school, Lucy had brought it up one evening not long ago while they sat out on the porch, having dinner and watching the sun go down.

"Danny?"

"Hmm?"

"Something's been on my mind," Lucy had said, "ever since that night down in the basement, really, but I guess other questions got in the way and I never got around to asking. Do you mind?"

"Never," he'd said. "What's bugging you?"

"That machine. Where on earth did it come from? I know you found it under Harrington House, but I mean, do you have any idea who put it there? Is it from here? Is it from outer space?"

Danny had sipped at his beer, then sat thinking. A minute passed before he spoke again.

"Good questions. Short answer is, I've no idea. The question had occasionally come up in my mind, but it was…I guess rhetorical isn't the right word, but…I guess I was too distracted by what I had and what I could do with it to care much about who actually put the thing down there, or where it might've come from before that. I don't think it's extraterrestrial…from outer space, at least not completely. And Harrington House has its own weird history…the whole damn town had some weird history even before I started messing around with things, but maybe it's time we do some digging. Try and find out just what it is we've got."

"Count me in, mister; I'm curious."

"Me too. And if that thing ever cycles back up again, then, well…maybe we could use it. Take the research a little further, ya know?"

"I don't think so," Lucy had said, almost at once, surprising herself. "After everything we've been through, I'd be content to fill it with cement and dump it in a river, marvelous technological wonder or not. No, I think if what you say about the town is true, then we can learn plenty without ever needing to touch that thing again. It's more trouble than it's worth."

"I guess you're probably right," Danny had said, sipping at his beer again before the conversation moved on to other things.

Coming back to herself, back to the now, where she stood in her diner, and that machine sat dark and stashed away in a basement wall safe, Lucy cleared her throat and continued reading the story on her phone.

"We're anxious to see New Chapel for ourselves, you know? To see the places we've all heard stories about and talk to the people lucky enough to still be around," Annie Stephens says. "To really get a feel for what it must've been like to live such a horrifying time in a small-town way back when and really bring that home to our subscribers in a way that I don't think has ever really been done before."

Lucy smiled faintly, fingering the purple stone hanging around her neck as she slipped her phone back into her jeans pocket. The little bell above the door tinkled as one of her regulars stepped inside, and she turned to grab the coffee pot.

Oh, Annie, I could give you the interview of your life, she thought, looking briefly at the counter, remembering how her two favorite men had come in toward the end of her shift in the late summer of 1947, all of them passing the time together in anticipation of a fine evening ahead. *And you'd never believe a word.*

ACKNOWLEDGEMENTS

This book would not exist if it weren't for the support of some amazing people. I'd like to start off by thanking my publisher, Mikeal Carlson, for giving me not one, but two chances at making a dream come true and helping me brainstorm ways to make that original one hundred and forty thousand-word submission bigger (smaller) and better.

Thanks also to my editor, Michael Waitz. I'll be forever grateful for your recommendation and all your advice. You were the first person not related to me to read my story, and your enthusiasm for it will always mean the world to me.

Next, I'd like to thank my friend and author of the *Godfrey* fantasy series, Mark Howard. At that long-ago chess club lunch, I introduced myself and mentioned that I like to write too. And instead of politely acknowledging that and moving on with your day, you talked to me well past when we both should've been back at our desks, and many days since. I'll never be able to fully express how grateful I am for your advice, support, and encouragement towards seeing this book become a reality, our chapter-sized text messages, and for just being a great friend.

A special thanks to my parents as well. Mom, for being one of the first test readers of this book and for making sure that I had a lifelong love of reading from the very start. Dad, for introducing me to horror and science fiction, and eventually to the world of Stephen King. And to both of you for always believing that my art could one day take me places.

Lastly, I'd like to thank my wife, Liz. For being the first reader of that long-ago draft and telling me that it was way better than you thought it was going to be, you gave me the confidence to keep going. For your patience during the nights when only a typewriter will do. And for your quiet support, never making me feel that all the time I spend pursuing my writing is wasted time. For all those things and many more, I love you.

ABOUT THE AUTHOR

Chris has been telling stories for as long as he can remember. He started drawing as a toddler, and his debut novel began as a few pages of brainstorming for what he originally planned to be a graphic novel. After writing a single chapter to explore the story further, one chapter quickly became two, then three, and before long he realized the story had grown into something much bigger than he had planned.

Along the way, he discovered something unexpected — every time he sat down to write, he felt a sense of fulfillment and excitement unlike anything else. Years later, after countless hours of writing and several stories completed, that feeling is still there.

Chris is an avid reader whose shelves are filled with horror, suspense, crime, fantasy, and science fiction. His biggest influences include Stephen King, Richard Matheson, Gillian Flynn, Agatha Christie, and Joe Hill, with King leaving a lasting impression after he discovered a worn copy of *Christine* in middle school and couldn't put it down.

By day, Chris works in finance, but in the evenings and on lunch breaks he writes stories about ordinary people who discover the world isn't quite as normal as they once believed.

Chris lives in Ohio with his wife, son, and their corgi. When he's not reading or writing, he enjoys classic movies, records, and spending time with his family.